Sherlock Holmes
and

The Jeweller of Florence

Christopher James

Paperback ISBN 978-1-78092-980-4
ePub ISBN 978-1-78092-981-1
PDF ISBN 978-1-78092-982-8

Published in the UK by MX Publishing
335 Princess Park Manor, Royal Drive,
London, N11 3GX
www.mxpublishing.co.uk
Cover design by Brian Belanger
Puzzle on page 143 by Anmol Rawat

For Winston and Hughie

ONE

The Underwater Cyclist

The truth is that many problems occupied the time and thoughts of Sherlock Holmes during the long summer of 1895. There was, for instance, the singular adventure of the Chelsea tenor, who believed that he had been poisoned by a rival with irreparable damage to his voice and career. Then there was the disturbing business of the smiling puppet, when a ventriloquist was not all he appeared. Inspector Gregson of Scotland Yard put himself further into Holmes' debt when my friend proved that the vaudevillian was in fact at the head of a notorious gang of counterfeiters.

But when I take down the cumbersome volume that records our exploits as spring turned to summer that year, I am reminded that nothing was quite as singular as The Jeweller of Florence. In fact, it is possible that you have heard something of this extraordinary and delicate affair. If you happened to be a regular at one of the public houses off Drury Lane in the mid 'nineties, you may recall such rumours, which Holmes and I always refused to corroborate. Only now, many years on and with the major players retired from the stage, do I feel I can present the facts.

Even with the distance of time, it feels indiscreet to reveal every detail and the reader will forgive my occasional divergence from the record where I have substituted a name here, or glossed over an incident there. In every other respect however, you may take this as a true and accurate account of a case that would not have left the papers for a year if even a tenth of the truth had been disclosed. I place the particulars into your hands and will allow you to consider the events for yourselves and judge the protagonists as you see fit.

It was late May, not three weeks after that diverting affair of the Three Students, which my friend Sherlock Holmes resolved with his usual efficiency. A thick mist had enveloped 221b Baker Street; so thick in fact, it felt as if the entire street had been lifted by some supernatural force and was now floating high above London. I felt nausea akin to sea-sickness and pitching over in bed, I nudged the clock so that I could glimpse its hideous face. It was barely half past five. I lay there, briefly considering my medical rounds and the inevitable difficulties of the day. I closed my eyes then opened them again almost immediately. Sleep was impossible. I tied up my gown, seized my rain damaged copy of Journey to Mars, the preposterous caper by Gustavus Pope, and trudged into the sitting room.

The grim fog of Holmes' tobacco smoke still hung suspended in the air. It was a mist no less dense that the one gathering outside and for a moment I considered the ruinous influence this smog must be having on both my own health and that of my fellow lodger. Yet while I was afflicted by insomnia, an unspecified aching of the frame and the constant dull throb from the bullet wound sustained in the nightmare of Maiwand, my friend Holmes seemed to enjoy the rudest of health. He could sit immobile for days on end, smoke until he disappeared into a cloud of his own fumes, live on a diet of nothing but obscure texts and still, when required, have the energy of an athlete. Despite my medical training, his physiology was a mystery to me.

I coaxed some embers back into life and warmed the small coffee pot Holmes kept for moments of self-sufficiency such as this when Mrs Hudson was either indisposed or not yet awake. It would not have surprised me to find my friend still sitting in his chair, with the stillness of a fakir, ruminating on some matter or the other, only the faint glow from his pipe indicating animation. The air was intolerable. While I waited for my coffee I clambered over his papers, stepped across his half completed monographs and pulled up the window. The morning mist curled into the room, meeting the ribbons of escaping smoke. The scent was cold; there was a slightly rotten smell and the street below was almost deserted. There was only one other living soul: a lone old man dressed in black, with a limp, a stick and a crumpled top hat, tottering like a wounded crow towards the Marylebone Road.

My life had reached a kind of stasis. Since Mary's death, I had fallen back on old ways – long nights with the bottle, introspection and wasted hours seeking solace in fripperies from billiards to science fiction. Only Holmes, with his unerring sense of purpose, could offer me stability. I had gravitated back into his mercurial orbit and before long, had found myself in my old rooms, embroiled once again in his work as if my marriage had been some strange dream or delusional interlude. Lulled by these memories and the early hour, my eyelids became heavy and I was only saved from tumbling from the window by the smell of hot coffee.

I took a final glance down the street and it was then that I saw her. She was a walking briskly through the mist on the opposite side of the road, a shawl pulled tightly around her shoulders. Her gait was unmistakable. I had seen it a thousand times, while waiting to meet her at the theatre or for dinner outside Simpson's on The Strand. There was the same thinness of the ankles, the same nimble step that a former dancer never loses. My heart thumped in my ears and my brow became damp with panic and fear for surely this was my own dear Mary Watson. I saw a strand of hair fall from beneath her bonnet and her dainty green gloves: the same pair I bought her on our first wedding anniversary. While I gaped, she looked up and for a moment, I peered into her mesmerising, blue eyes. She smiled a thin, sad smile then looked back towards the ground. I stared, gripped by a momentary paralysis, before resolving to go after her. Throwing on my moccasins I took the stairs two at a time and pulled open the front door.

Like a madman I dashed down the street in my gown, chasing the apparition. But there was no trace. I caught up with the old man, seizing him by the arm.
'You there!' I shouted. 'That woman who passed by just now; did you see which way she went?' A ghastly, yellow grin cracked across his face, his thin, pale skin barely papering over the bones. One of his eyes was clouded over completely with a cataract and the other was red and bloodshot.
'I wouldn't recognise my own mother in this,' he croaked. 'Never known a soup so thick.' He peered at me with his one seeing eye.
'You lost someone have you?' he taunted. 'A woman is it?' He broke into a cackle, his yellow tongue wagging against his broken teeth.

'Ran out on you, has she?' I lifted my arm, ready to strike the man for his insolence when I felt myself being restrained. I turned to find a beefy constable at my shoulder.

'Dr Watson, isn't it?' he quizzed, still holding back my arm. He had a grizzled, amiable face, one of those that seem almost constantly amused. 'Now what would a respectable gentleman such as you be doing at an ungodly hour such as this?'

'I... I...' I spluttered, quite unable to explain myself.

'If you ask me,' he ruminated, eyeing my dressing gown and slippers, 'you've been doing a spot of sleepwalking. Now I think the best course is for this fellow to go about his business and for you, doctor, to go back to bed. We shall say no more on the matter.'

When I awoke again, the fog had lifted. Bright sunshine spilled into my room and my mind was clear. The events of the morning felt as remote to me as those of another lifetime. I relocated to the sitting room and sat with my novel considering the strange occurrence with a cool and rational mind, as one might consider the account of a patient.

A pair of oval wooden boards flew through the air and clattered at my feet. These were swiftly followed by the person of Sherlock Holmes himself who strode into the sitting room dressed in a red striped bathing costume, accessorised only by a pipe, the stem of which was lodged firmly in his mouth.

'Watson,' he cried. 'Of all the inventions in all the world, I consider these among the finest. You have at your disposal the means to transform a man into a dolphin. They are what you might call flippers; the brain child of that splendid polymath, Benjamin Franklin, who first tested them in the waters of the Thames. I propose we proceed immediately to the more sanitary conditions of the Serpentine to put them through their paces.'

'Very well,' I sighed, throwing my book to the floor. 'But let us at least put some devilled kidneys inside us to sustain life and limb.'

It was not until his retirement that my friend Sherlock Holmes finally confessed to his love of swimming. I darted through the pages of The

Adventure of the Lion's Mane like any other of his acolytes, gripped by the exploits of this brilliant and infuriating man. For once I was able to enjoy the machinations of his quicksilver mind and the gallery of eccentrics like anyone else. For this story, in the company of only one other, was composed by the detective himself.

It is admirably written, I admit, making me wonder whether all along I have rather been surplus to requirements. Holmes pays me a compliment early in the adventure, suggesting how much more I would have made of it. However I believe this is merely a perfunctory remark to spare my feelings. It is as good a story as any I have committed to the page. Of course, there are purple patches. He describes how he strode 'the thyme-scented Downs,' a line an editor may have had the courage to strike-through if the name Sherlock Holmes had not adorned the frontispiece. There is melodrama too, what with the 'two seabirds circling and screaming overhead' shortly before the unfortunate McPherson meets his end. But these are minor aberrations. The story clips along at a pace and the characters are vividly drawn; they are as alive to me as if I was at Holmes' side. I have never met Inspector Bardle of Sussex Constabulary, but if I was to encounter the 'steady, solid bovine man with thoughtful eyes' I feel sure I would recognise him in an instant.

But if his public was unaware that Sherlock Holmes was a swimmer until that baffling affair, then the fact could hardly have eluded me. While lodging at 221b Baker Street, my friend would often summon me from my cot with a double knock on my door and announce that we would be heading off to the lake at ten minutes' notice. Barely with a spoonful of oats inside us, we would bowl down to Gloucester Place in a brougham, or even on foot, and enter Hyde Park occasionally pausing with our towels thrown across our shoulders to hear the latest ravings at Speakers' Corner. It was one such breezy morning in May 1895, after the necessary apparatus had been located, that Holmes and I embarked on such an expedition.

'Goodness, Holmes,' I said, my nose in the newspaper as we bowled through Cumberland Gate, 'don't you think they're being awfully hard on Mr Wilde? One minute he is the toast of London, the next he is a pariah. Not content with bankrupting the fellow and leaving him an outcast, it seems he's in for two years' hard labour.'

'It is the scandal of our age,' muttered Holmes peering up at the trees. 'Posterity will not look kindly on us. Future generations will judge us, not him. We are the bystanders while the greatest poet of our time is thrown to the lions. Every free thinking man in London should be ashamed of himself.'

'Not two months ago,' I mused, 'you could not move in polite society without someone quoting a line from The Importance of Being Earnest.'

'Quite,' agreed Holmes, 'and some of it was oddly prescient too, don't you think? How does it go again? "The good ended happily, and the bad unhappily, that is what fiction means." It is as if he knew his own fate.'

'Oh I don't know about that. As long as he has a pen and paper, the time will surely fly.'

'I think not,' Holmes broke in. 'His flame burns brightly, but it is only sustained by the gales of applause and the oxygen of publicity. Deprived of either of these and it will soon be snuffed.'

The park was a blaze of colour. The keepers had excelled themselves with the immaculate lawns and sprays of tulips, crocus and daffodils. It was as if a rainbow had collapsed upon London and had been carefully divided up. The Serpentine itself in the bright May sun was like a sheet of silver hammered into a thin brilliance. Cavalry officers rode three abreast on Rotten Row while the four-wheelers clattered their way along South Carriage Drive. The air was ripe with fresh manure, blossom and possibility. There was that indefinable exhilaration one feels in the air as May turns to summer. My friend surveyed the water like a hawk in repose.

'A splendid day for a dip, eh, Watson?' I shook my head and smiled despite myself.

'If you say so, Holmes.'

As a member of the Serpentine Swimming Club, Holmes had privileged access to the facilities; that is to say the shelter of an aged elm tree and a wooden bench upon which to lay out our clothes. Hanging our hats on the lower branches of the tree, we stripped

9

down to our bathing costumes, my own being a striped blue outfit received as a gift from Holmes on my last birthday.

Perhaps because there was something of a chill in the air, the swimmers were few in number. Come August and there would be whole schools of them, rivaled only by the multitudes on Brighton beach. I counted no more than twenty in total, each absorbed in their own private meditations as they glided silently across the water.

One such gentleman was within twenty yards of us and presently I heard the sound of singing: a clear strong baritone, entirely incongruous in the circumstances.

'Shall we meet beyond the river,
In the clime where angels dwell?'

My friend's face broke into a wry smile. He joined in with the next couplet, in his rather thin, reedy voice:

'Shall we meet where friendship never
Saddest tales of sorrow tell?'

'My dear Holmes!' the swimmer cried.
'Mr Perrin,' he returned, 'I see you are wasting no time preparing for the Christmas Day race. Only seven months to go now; the pressure is certainly mounting. You are planning to defend your title?'
'Why certainly,' the man confirmed, breast stroking towards us. 'But surely you are still not sore about being runner-up, Christmas last?'
'Allowing you priority was merely a courtesy,' explained Holmes. 'I could see that winning meant twice as much to you as me. Besides, I was obliged to return for Mrs Hudson's magnificent goose. One must never keep a goose waiting. Attending the prize giving ceremony would have fatally detained me.'
'Nonsense!' Perrin scoffed. 'I beat you fair and square and you jolly well know it.' He was a handsome man of thirty five, with a lustrous ebony moustache, intelligent, kindly eyes and a permanently inquisitive face. His outstanding feature was a pair of prominent ears.
'Watson,' said Holmes, 'may I introduce Mr Anthony Perrin, winner

of the 1894 Christmas Race and deputy choirmaster of St Paul's Cathedral'

'Delighted,' he said from the water.

'Now,' continued Holmes. 'How are you coping with the bishop's modernising influence? I see he has got his way with the new floor.'

The man's face crumpled into a frown.

'However could you know that, Holmes?' he enquired. 'I had no idea you followed ecclesiastical affairs?'

'I most certainly don't,' my friend acknowledged with a wry chuckle, 'and yet it is absurdly simple to deduce.'

'Please explain!' he demanded, treading water.

'You are rehearsing a rather modern hymn,' said Holmes. 'It is quite a departure for an institution such as St Paul's. Times are slow to change in the Church of England. I can tell you are not yet entirely certain of its melody.'

'Well as it happens,' the man laughed, 'you are perfectly correct. We have a rehearsal in an hour and I'm rather afraid to meet the choir without having entirely mastered the hymn myself. But that still does not explain the business about the floor. The details have not yet been released to the public.'

'Again, it is quite elementary,' smiled Holmes.

'I have just observed your shoes on the bench. No deduction was necessary beyond reading the name printed inside. However, I note that you are now wearing the type of shoe that cannot mark a polished floor. Your last pair would have left the most appalling stain on such a surface. The shoes, by their lack of wear, I can tell are no more than two weeks' old. I have simply married this observation with a recollection of reading about the appointment of the new bishop in The Illustrated London News.'

'Remarkable!' the man exclaimed, 'quite remarkable. Every word of it is true.'

I plunged into the icy waters with a gasp, followed swiftly by an expletive. Holmes, in contrast, slid in like a seal, his stoic features unaltered by the shocking drop in temperature. It made me wonder whether in fact my suspicion that he was a cold blooded creature was correct all along. After a minute or two when the pain had reduced to a tolerable level, I struck out for the centre of the lake, following in

11

Holmes' wake. Distantly, I could still hear Mr Perrin still rehearsing his hymn, one or two others in the Serpentine joining him as it gained in familiarity. A party of gentlemen in a passing vessel greeted him as cordially as if he was strolling down Regent Street, raising their hats and instructing him of their intention to attend matins.

'Who would believe,' asked Holmes, flipping over onto his back, 'that we are floating at the centre of the greatest city on Earth? In the midst of chaos, there is calm. One can almost feel oneself drifting through the universe.'
'Yes,' I said, feeling more cold than philosophical, 'but how much longer are you planning to spend in here?'
'Until my brain ices over,' my friend returned decadently. 'Swimming is one of the few activities that succeeds in slowing my thought process. Do you have any idea what it is like entertaining seven different notions at once?'
'I confess I do not,' I admitted through blue lips and chattering teeth.

'Now,' Holmes proposed. 'What would you say to a small wager?'
'Not a chance,' I said. 'You are twice the swimmer I am. If we raced every day for a year, you would win every time.'
'I'm flattered of course, Watson. But I had something rather different in mind. My proposition is as follows. We shall make the acquaintance of five different swimmers and I will tell you how they make their living without asking them a single question.'
'Impossible!' I cried. 'Without their clothes what would you possibly have to work with?'
'That is my problem, not yours,' he replied. 'If I succeed, you will extinguish the lamps at lights out and check the front door at 221b Baker Street for a month. If I fail, then these duties will fall to me.'
'Then I accept your absurd wager,' I laughed. 'But I fear you will come to regret it.'
'We shall see!' he returned, then struck off towards our first interviewee with his long, powerful stroke.

Our first candidate was so absorbed in his swimming it felt impolite to interrupt. He was a man of forty with jet black hair, a thin

12

moustache and a furrowed brow.

'Good morning!' I began. He nodded, but made no attempt to stop.

'Perhaps we will need to choose another subject' I suggested.

'Nonsense,' my friend laughed. 'I have plenty to go on. It is perfectly obvious to me that he is a barrister by profession.'

'A wild assertion,' I countered. 'On what grounds?'

'Numerous!' he replied. 'Firstly, there is his groomed appearance; the trimmed hair and clipped moustache, he is clearly a professional man. Now what would such a fellow be doing swimming during the working day outside of his lunch hour? Secondly, I happen to know that the morning hearing at the law courts concluded twenty minutes ago, ten minutes before he appeared at the lakeside. Thirdly, you will note from his furrowed brow and sceptical eyes, that he has a naturally probing nature, the perfect temperament for the legal profession. Shall we test my supposition against the fact?' We kicked after the man and soon drew alongside him.

'My dear sir,' Holmes, began. 'If I may be so bold, have you considered what he did with the poker after the blow was sustained?' The man stopped abruptly, clearly astonished.

'Who are you?' he demanded. 'Have you followed me from court?'

'Nothing of the kind,' explained Holmes. 'I merely wanted to prove to my friend here that you are in fact the prosecuting attorney.'

'I most certainly am and I don't mind who knows it. Now if you please, I have a complex case to unravel, and I would prefer to be left in peace.' Readying himself to set off again, he considered Holmes' words. 'The poker, you say,' he repeated. 'Yes, I think there may be something in that. Good day.'

He left us treading water, my mouth agape at my friend's extraordinary deduction.

'But how did you do it, Holmes?'

'Simplicity itself,' he laughed. 'But forgive me, Watson!' he begged, quite unable to conceal his delight. 'It is hardly a fair arrangement. The final detail, and on this count I would not blame you for crying foul, is that I read his lips while he swam. He was rehearsing his closing remarks, furnishing me with a full picture of the case. I believe, in the process, I may have identified the single most incriminating detail. What did the suspect do with the murder weapon after the fact?'

'Remarkable,' I whispered.

'Not at all,' he asserted. 'Merely a series of observations which taken together lead to irrefutable proof. A bird swooped low across the water leaving a series of ripples that quickly dissolved to nothing. To be properly observant, Watson, is to look beneath the skin of the world.' Not for the first time, I marvelled at my friend's powers.

'Now,' Holmes said, in a conciliatory tone. 'I would be prepared to release you from your obligations if you were to throw in the towel at this point. I shall not repeat my offer.'

'Never,' I laughed heartily. 'The same trick cannot work twice.'

Our next victim was of an altogether different kidney. In his late fifties, he had deep set eyes and thin, greasy hair. It was as if someone had tipped a cup of gruel across a perfectly smooth mound and allowed it to slide down the back and sides. He progressed across the lake with a terrible weariness, somewhat akin to an injured water beetle, employing a shallow, laboured stroke. He opened his mouth wide, gasping desperately at the air with each breath.

'Poor fellow,' remarked Holmes as we swam towards him. 'He looks like a beaten man.'

'I say,' I added. 'It seems we are on a collision course. Do you think perhaps we ought to adjust our trajectory?'

'Not at all,' said Holmes. We drew ever closer until we came to a halt.

'Good morning, sir,' greeted Holmes. The man grunted a reply. 'Now tell me, how is it that you lost your position as a dairyman?' The swimmer's mouth fell open; a poor choice in the middle of a lake.

'Why,' he began, expelling a plume of water. 'Only a month ago I was employed at the Welsh Dairy on the Euston Road. I was as happy as any Londoner with a pound in my pocket and mutton on the table. Now here I am reduced to filling my days with lengths of the Serpentine.'

'Perhaps you were caught stealing the cream?'

'And what if I was? We all did it!' the man protested. 'I swear it was Evans who shopped me. I'll give him a good slating next time I see him.' He peered at Holmes suspiciously. 'I suppose you were one of my customers. Funny, I don't remember you. You're a queer looking fellow too. I thought I knew all my customers.'

'Well,' said Holmes. 'You will think better of it next time.' We let the man go on his way.

'So you did know him!' I shouted. 'I'm afraid I cannot allow it.'

'My dear, Watson,' said Holmes, sounding a little hurt. 'I have never seen the man before in my life.' Once again I paused mid-stroke, baffled at this assertion.

'Then please explain!'

'His teeth, Watson,' reasoned Holmes. 'Did you not see his perfect teeth? No man of his class and vintage would have such a well preserved set of grinders without access to a free and plentiful supply of milk.'

'My dear, Holmes!' I shouted. 'It is nothing short of wizardry!'

'Nonsense,' he returned. 'It is merely the eye and the mind working together; observation and deduction, Watson, observation and deduction. You know my methods; I simply apply them.'

'Enough!' I cried. 'You have proved your point, Holmes. I accept my fate.'

The wind was gusting up now. My arms, I noticed, had turned an alarming shade of purple and every inch of my skin was goose-pimpled. I had no desire to spend the following ten days ingesting Dr Agnew's Catarrh Powder.

'If it's all the same to you, Holmes,' I admitted, as we drew near to the shore, 'I think I will call it a day.'

'Spoilsport!' he complained. 'One more, I beg and this will be the decider. Now perhaps we should take a different tack. Pick anyone you choose and he shall be our last catch of the day.'

'You are incorrigible,' I remarked, shaking my head. It was then that I noticed a gaunt, earnest looking man in owlish spectacles cycling along the edge of the lake. He was thirty, dressed head to toe in tweed and was clearly in an awful hurry. To my eyes he could equally have been a doctor, a teacher, an architect or archaeologist. He seemed as good a candidate as any. I pointed at the young man.

'There's our fellow,' I said decisively. 'Now what's his game?'

Holmes peered down the length of his hawk-like nose and scrutinised him.

'Well he's bookish, that's for certain. Do you see the three volumes in his pannier? Still, anyone could be a bookworm. The cap is distinctive, however. It was the height of fashion in Oxford ten years ago, possibly a relic from his university days. Unless of course,' he added, 'those days are not yet at an end. The owlish glasses certainly contribute to the air of academia. Are you sure you don't wish to change your mind, Watson?'

'I am quite sure, Holmes.' We watched the man work away at the pedals and as he drew closer we could make out the anguished expression on his face. Clearly some crisis was afoot.

'A troubled man,' said Holmes as he passed. 'I can tell you much about the fellow but I cannot look into his soul.' Presently, the cyclist changed course, veering wildly into the trees, before coming around and heading straight for the lake.

'Look out,' I cried. 'I do believe he's coming in!'

Sure enough, the cyclist ploughed directly and quite intentionally into the Serpentine. He was still pedalling furiously as they water rose up over his heels. Soon the front wheel was completely submerged but still he continued, as if he believed he could cross the bottom of the lake and come up the other side. Holmes was already ahead of me, crawling powerfully through the water to reach him. I flailed behind, watching aghast as the rest of bicycle sank and only the man's upper torso remained visible – still upright and oblivious to any obstacle the lake might represent. When Holmes reached him only the cyclist's head remained above water. However his expression remained unaltered, as if he had barely registered the change in environment. My friend seized him around the shoulders and hauled him back from his watery grave. The man thrashed about for a moment, but then fell slack, capitulating to Holmes' superior strength in the same way a man might resign himself to an alligator's jaws.

My friend hauled the unfortunate man up onto the bank and I swiftly joined them, believing some medical attention would be required. A red-faced park keeper, who had just reached us, stepped gingerly into the water in an effort to retrieve the bicycle. Several bystanders rushed up to gawp at the bespectacled man.

'Stand back!' I shouted, 'give us some room here.' I unbuttoned the man's collar and loosened his tie. He was pressing the base of his palms against his temples, his eyes squeezed tightly shut as if trying to contain some fearsome headache. He was babbling something unintelligible.

'Calm yourself man,' I instructed. 'I am a doctor.'

'A most inefficient way to end it all,' remarked a snake-like spiv in a bowler hat. 'He'll get a stretch inside for this, you see if he doesn't.'

'Whatever do you mean?' demanded Holmes, rising to his full height, seeing a policeman approach. 'This poor gentleman's bicycle slipped from the path and ended up in the water. There was nothing more to it than that.'

'That's not how it looked to me,' the man sneered. Holmes took a step towards him. 'That's an expensive pocket watch for a bit-faker like yourself. Would you care to explain to the constable how it came into your possession?' The man glanced around at the crowd, peered at the stern looking policemen, then took off at speed.

'Is everything in order, Mr Holmes?' asked the constable. He seemed possessed of a keener mind than your average bobby.

'Perfectly, Constable Webb,' smiled Holmes, 'merely a small traffic incident. This gentleman's bicycle left the pavement and finished up in the pond. Fortunately the good Dr Watson and I were on hand to fish him out. The doctor is examining him now and we will happily see him on his way.'

'That's not what I saw,' piped up another troublemaker.

'Nor me,' put in another, emboldened.

'Settle down now,' said the policeman. 'Mr Holmes' word is as good as his bond. There is no finer gentleman this side of Kathmandu.'

'But constable...'

'On your way!' he bustled and advanced on the crowd with raised arms as if he was shooing sheep from a country lane.

When the crowd had dispersed, he peered at the young man, still twitching in agitation and frowned. He leaned in towards Holmes.

'Are you quite sure there's nothing else you'd like to tell me?' he enquired under his breath. Holmes remained entirely unmoved.

'Nothing at all,' he said. 'Now do give my regards to Lestrade if you see him before I do.'

'I certainly will, Mr Holmes.' He glanced around a final time, fixed me with a piercing stare, then went on his way. 'Good day, gentlemen.'

We helped the man sit up and I draped my own jacket around his shoulders. Once more, we tried to prise some sense out of him, but succeeded in producing nothing but delirious ramblings.

'It's gone!' he shouted, staring into the far distance. 'It's no good. It's gone!'

'What?' Holmes demanded. 'What has gone?'

'Unless we all wish to catch our death,' I advised, 'I think it best if we continue this discussion in Baker Street.'

'The ever sensible Dr Watson,' my friend declared. He was still uttering these words when he marched into the middle of Rotten Row, directly into the path of an approaching brougham. The horses fairly reared up before him.

'My name is Sherlock Holmes,' he announced. 'We have a medical emergency: a matter of life and death. I would be grateful if you would surrender your conveyance and continue your journey to Holborn on foot.' Without waiting for an answer, he instructed the driver on his new fare while a flustered looking gentleman in grey whiskers stumbled out of the carriage. Holmes pressed his palm into his.

'Your generosity will not be forgotten,' he said. Once inside the carriage, the cyclist slumped against the door, utterly insensible. I saw a familiar gleam in my friend's eyes.

'Watson,' Holmes said, joining his fingers together like an oyster closing its shell around its pearl, 'I believe we have the beginnings of a new case.'

TWO

The Quarto

Sherlock Holmes was in bed. This in itself was quite normal, even mid morning at 221b Baker Street and it seemed perfectly reasonable that a mind as active as Holmes' should require more repose than others. In fact it was not unknown for my friend to retire to his bed for three days with the curtains drawn and then remerge without a word of explanation. My suspicion on these occasions was that Holmes was out of humour and simply wished to avoid any dealings with the outside world. It was even conceivable that he used such times to spiral deep into some devilish conundrum whose solution continued to evade him in the distracting light of day. Our unexpected guest was also still in bed (my bed to be precise). This was where we had left him the previous evening once we had contended ourselves that he was not about to expire while in our charge. I had administered a mild sedative then retired to the couch with some spare blankets.

That night I had found it impossible to sleep, not on account of the hard cushions, but because of the vision of Mary that still haunted my mind. Each hour, I opened my eyes to see her staring at me across the room. I blinked and she was gone. My mind swam with memories; how she had first walked into my life wearing that green turban at the beginning of the adventure I have recorded as The Sign of Four. Part of me began to doubt whether the nocturnal encounter had occurred at all. Suddenly, it seemed conceivable that the one-eyed man, the woman and even the subsequent discussion with Holmes were all part of some feverish dream.

I resolved to question my friend on the matter again in the morning. But for now, I needed to clear my head and resolved to descend the seventeen stairs of 221b Baker Street on the pretence of getting a little air. I had heard that Dickens himself walked miles in the hours of darkness, pacing the streets, formulating his labyrinthine plots. As a fellow author, perhaps a little night walking would deliver me a similar tonic. Silently, I collected my hat and coat, took up my stick and slipped out of the house. There was not a soul abroad. Lamplight spilt across the street and the only sound was the distant bark of an unseen dog. I had not gone five paces when a black cat slipped between my feet, causing me to stumble and cry out in alarm. I bit my lip, cursed the ill-omen and went on my way.

My copy of The Times was lit by the brilliant sunlight streaming through the lead glass and my tea was cooling at my side.
'What news, Watson? What news?' Holmes emerged from his cave, tying the band of his dressing gown in his customary sheep-bend, his first pipe of the day already smoking in his hand. His spirits, it seemed, were fully restored.
'A knighthood for Henry Irving!' I replied.
'For that old ham?' he scoffed. 'Well, he was bound to accept one sooner or later. "Light vanity insatiate cormorant!"'

At that moment, I heard the click of a latch and the pale, bespectacled face of our overnight guest appeared from behind the door. He was clean shaven with thin, fair hair, swept up on his high forehead, giving him a boyish look. His blinking, watery eyes were at the same time both nervous and inquisitive.
'He awakes!' cried Holmes.
'Do come in, sir,' I invited. Dressed in my spare dressing gown, he looked entirely confused as to his whereabouts.
'Aren't you...' the man began, staring at my friend. 'Aren't you Sherlock Holmes?'
'From the minute I was born,' returned the great detective. 'And you are?'
'My name,' he replied, in a soft, careful voice, 'is Professor Telemachus Spenning of Corpus Christi College, Oxford.' He moved to the couch and sat down, peering around our cramped sitting room. 'I must compliment you, Dr Watson,' he remarked. 'Your powers of description are remarkable. It is exactly as I envisaged.'
'Then you are a follower of my work,' exclaimed Holmes. 'How splendid.'
'However the question remains,' the professor added, 'how I come to be here?' I stared at him in astonishment.

20

'You don't remember the lake, or the journey to Baker Street?'

'The lake? Whatever do you mean?' I glanced over at Holmes, who nodded his consent.

'My dear Professor,' I explained. 'I am obliged to report that you suffered a misadventure in Hyde Park yesterday afternoon.'

'The particulars, quickly,' he demanded.

'Your rode your bicycle into the Serpentine and rather determined about it you were too.' Spenning clasped his hands together and bowed his head, deep in thought.

'Yes,' he said. 'Yes, I remember cycling through the park but not the lake. How did you come to be involved?'

'Holmes was the one who fished you out. Believe it or not, we were swimming at the time.'

'Ruined,' he whispered, clutching his head. 'The college will not stand for this.'

'I believe,' said Holmes, working at his pipe and fixing him with that piercing look, 'that you are in a certain degree of trouble. But there is always a way. Now the facts, if you please,' said Holmes, joining his fingers and peering intently at the man. 'As you have some knowledge of my achievements, you will know that I excel at extricating men from their predicaments. The extraction, I should add, is always quicker and less painful when I am furnished with a complete picture of the case.'

'Really,' the man faltered, his eyes beginning to well. 'There is nothing to be done.'

'Let me be the judge of that,' said Holmes, then lit his pipe and fell deeply into his chair.

'Very well,' the professor began. 'These last ten years I have acquired something of a reputation as the most daring, the most brilliant Shakespeare scholar of our day. It is not talk I have fought hard to suppress. I find myself at the vanguard of thinking on the Bard. My paper, Surrealism and Sorcery: the Supernatural in Shakespeare's Late Plays and Collaborations is considered definitive on the subject.' Holmes nodded in agreement.

'Go on,' he murmured.

'My career has achieved an unstoppable momentum. I am bombarded with invitations to speak at the finest universities of the world and corresponded with its most brilliant minds. My name has become a byword for original thinking on the subject. You may be aware that I am at the forefront of the defence of Shakespeare as the author of all 37 of his plays, 39 if we are to allow Cardenio and Love's Labour's Won. You will know there is a growing madness in America, denying him authorship of his own work. It is nothing but cheap sensationalism. Sir Francis Bacon no more wrote Macbeth than he built St Paul's Cathedral. My world is my college; the hills of Oxfordshire in which I roam for inspiration and the taverns of the town where I seek refreshment of another kind; where I debate with my students and toast the ghost of Sir Toby Belch.'

'I smell nothing but roses,' complained Holmes. 'Where is the turn in this tale?'

'The turn,' Spenning continued, the colour draining from his cheeks, 'came the day when William Somerville knocked on the door of my office.' Holmes and I exchanged a look. 'If you are acquainted with the London stage, you will know that Somerville is the most flamboyant actor manager in all of London. He is second only in reputation to Henry Irving himself and some would say surpasses the man in his gifts. Certainly he has the Midas touch. His last four productions have made him as wealthy as a Rothschild.'

'But the inkwells of academia and fripperies of the London stage are two different worlds,' challenged Holmes. 'What business did he have with you?'

'Business of the most monumental kind,' Spenning declared. 'Gentlemen, what I am about to tell you know will turn London on its head.'

'Then throw the spear!' laughed Holmes. 'You have something of a gift for the dramatic yourself.' The professor pressed his lips tightly together, breathed deeply through his nostrils then began.

'Somerville came bearing an unimaginable treasure. It was a moment I will not forget so long as I live. I was just putting the finishing touches to my new paper, Tempests of the Mind: Shakespeare's Use of Storm as a Transformative Psychological Agent, when I heard a thumping on the door. I had barely twisted the door knob when Somerville flew in and hurled himself into my easy chair.

'What day was this?' asked Holmes abruptly.

'What day?' asked Spenning, a little taken aback, 'Well, let me see. Today is Wednesday, so this must have been Monday.'

'What time?'

'Eleven in the morning. Why do you ask?'

'I like to be precise about the facts,' my friend stated. 'A fact has a beauty like a rock or a point of the compass. It is difficult to tamper with. Collect enough facts and you have a case. Put them in the right order and examine them in the correct light and you have a solution. Now please proceed.'

'"You are Professor Telemachus Spenning?"' Somerville demanded. "The same," I returned.

"Then prepare yourself," he said, "for a revelation beyond your wildest hopes." I warned him that my imaginative scope was perhaps larger than he might expect. This was before he handed me the play.'

'The play?' I queried. 'He had written a play?' Spenning shook his head and stared at me with a curious look of amusement and sorrow. 'The play was not his,' he explained. 'The play was a work by Mr William Shakespeare.'

'An odd sort of gift for a Shakespearian scholar,' I remarked, somewhat puzzled. 'I expect you are given the complete works every Christmas by unimaginative relatives.'

'My dear fellow,' said Spenning, his eyes gleaming. 'This was a play I had never seen before. It was an entirely new work.' This was enough to silence even Sherlock Holmes. He sat up and stared at Spenning as if examining him properly for the first time.

'A hoax, surely,' laughed Holmes.

'That ,of course,' admitted Spenning, 'was my immediate thought. A so-called new Shakespeare play is discovered almost every week. Yet here was one of London's most famous impresarios staking his reputation on the claim.' The professor continued with his statement.

'"Are you playing me for a fool, sir?"' I demanded.

"How dare you!" Somerville cried, rising to his feet.'

'So you believed it to be a fake?' I broke in.

'Yes, of course,' agreed Spenning, 'at least at first.' Somerville proceeded to remove a parcel from the inside pocket of his coat. He placed it on the table then carefully unwrapped it, unfolding one edge at a time. At once, I recognised the format and approximate vintage. It was a printer's quarto, similar in every respect to the Shakespeare quartos published around 1600. I pulled a pair of gloves from my desk drawer and with Somerville's permission, turned the first page.

'I can hardly bear it,' cried Holmes, clapping his hands in delight. 'What was its title?'

'The Jeweller of Florence,' said Spenning. Holmes repeated the title to himself. 'A kissing cousin,' he declared, 'of The Merchant of Venice.'

'So it would seem,' stated Spenning and, in fact, the publication date is similar, 1599, although it could have been written earlier.

'Or indeed three hundred years later!' added Holmes.

'Yes that occurred to me too,' conceded Spenning. 'But it appeared genuine in every respect. The pages are as time-worn as you would expect and the printer is J. R. [James Roberts] for Thomas Heyes, the same as for The Merchant of Venice. The inscription reads 'The most excellent history of The Jeweller of Florence being the true account of the marriage between Alessandra, daughter of the Duke of Florence and Flavio, master jeweller. With the obtaining of a necklace of pearls for the wife of the Duke and the comic interludes of Filippo the clown who appears in divers jocular scenes.'

'An intriguing summary,' opined Holmes. 'If it is a hoax, then it has the benefit of considerable artistry. Suddenly Holmes blanched and rose to his feet.

'Professor, please do not tell me it was upon your person when you entered the lake yesterday.'

'No, Mr Holmes, it wasn't.'

'Well let us be thankful for that!' declared Holmes, visibly relieved.

'So, tell me, professor,' my friend continued, returning to his chair. 'Where can we find this extraordinary document? I would most sincerely like to read it, fake or not.'

Spenning removed his spectacles and pressed his face into his hands. 'I have no idea,' he confessed.

'What?' Holmes shouted.

'It was stolen from my study on Tuesday afternoon and my career, and dare I say my life, is effectively over.'

We listened to the sounds of the street; a sparrow at the window; an argument between a newspaper seller and a deliveryman; a dog barking and a pair of horses pulling a brougham past the house.

'You have conducted a thorough search?' I asked. Spenning gave me a withering look.

'Dr Watson, I have torn the room apart!' He advanced on me with outstretched hands. 'Do you understand the gravity of my situation? Somerville entrusted me with the manuscript. He explained that only I could certify that it was genuine. He gave me until close of business on Thursday to conclude my examination of the quarto and deliver my verdict. There was nothing else for it,' Spenning concluded. 'I could hardly go to the police and report the theft of such an object. They would laugh me out of the place. So I resolved to break the news to Somerville face to face. I boarded the train at Oxford with my bicycle and a flask of tea and was on my way to his offices when I lost my nerve entirely. It was at this point, I believe, that I may have taken leave of my senses and ended up in the lake. The rest you know.'

'A singular predicament,' my friend remarked. 'However your deadline is not yet upon us and I believe there is merit in exploring your rooms for a clue. It would be infinitely better to face Somerville with the benefit of a lead than empty-handed.'

'I assure you, Mr Holmes, my own search has been entirely thorough.'

'With all due respect, you are a Shakespearian academic and I am the world's foremost private detective. You and I will have different ideas as to the definition of a thorough search. It is quite possible that there will be a detail – a dropped cufflink, ink from a nib other than your own or a trace of foreign scent in the air that has eluded you. It is such trifles as these that invariably provide the breakthrough. Now, if we are quick, we have an excellent chance of making the two twenty train to Oxford. Watson, will you be disposed to join us?'

'Most certainly,' I stated. 'What's more, I feel it is my duty as your doctor to keep a close watch. For one, you would do well to steer clear of open water.' No one appeared to find this amusing.

'Then we are resolved,' said Holmes rising to his feet. 'Professor, allow us to throw a few essentials into a valise and we will muster here in fifteen minutes.'

A brougham delivered us to Paddington in good time and I collected our tickets from the booth. I found myself wondering whether, after all these years at Holmes' side, I was significantly out of pocket.

25

Holmes and I had a somewhat lackadaisical attitude towards money, with no fixed fee for a client and no set book keeping arrangement between the pair of us. The thought quickly passed from my mind as I strolled back towards my companions.

The prospect of Oxford in the spring was appealing. It conjured images of cherry blossom against the weathered stone and ancient spires reaching up into the cumulous-filled sky. It was a place of youth and beauty, of brilliance and hopefulness. Above all, there was a sense of the future and the past in perfect balance. I recalled playing rugby there in the late 'seventies while at the University of London. There was a long and hazy night of revelry following a memorable victory on the field. Rusty Mayweather's dash from the ten yard line was quite…'

'Watson!' cried Holmes, 'our train!'

I snapped out of my reverie to see steam pouring from the locomotive at the end of the platform. My nostrils filled with the acrid stench of burnt cinders and a piercing whistle rang in my ears. We gathered up our things and sprinted to our first class carriage.

Once aboard, Holmes fell into his usual routine. He devoured The Times, then The Illustrated London News before even contemplating any discourse. Eventually, my friend lowered his paper and lit a Capstan, one of the new cigarettes he had acquired from Wills. He expelled a cloud of blue smoke that would have provided a splendid special effect for a West End melodrama.

'Tell me,' he said, addressing Spenning, 'did you speak to anyone about the play?' The professor pursed his lips and stared out of the window.

'Only one other,' he said at length, 'my star student, Oliver Standbull. He is quite beyond reproach.'

'I see,' said Holmes, in the manner of a prosecuting barrister, 'and when was this?'

'Tuesday afternoon,' replied Spenning, 'directly after my interview with Somerville. I believed he would be able to provide a valuable second opinion.'

'Have you seen him since the theft?'

'Yes, of course,' said Spenning, sitting forward. 'I asked him directly whether he had taken it to study in private. Of course I made it clear that I would understand if this was the case and that nothing more would be said of the matter. He told me he knew nothing. Indeed he helped me search the study.'

'He must remain a suspect,' warned Holmes.

'Impossible!' Spenning returned. 'He has the noblest mind and purest heart of any student I have seen.' Holmes narrowed his eyes and peered at the professor in the most curious way.

'How quickly nature falls into revolt,' he quoted, 'when gold becomes her object.'

'Henry IV had his view of things and I have mine. Virtue is bold and goodness never fearful.'

'Splendid!' applauded Holmes allowing himself a thin laugh. He was enjoying the game immensely. 'Of that I do not doubt and who am I to argue with the Duke in Measure for Measure? But let us not forget there is some soul of goodness in things evil.'

'Henry's son was as fond of his own voice as his father. But neither of them have met Oliver Standbull, and I am willing to vouch for his character. You will see for yourself when we reach the college.'

Oxford was a pleasant bustle compared with the madness of the capital. Some things remained familiar however: the hoi polloi rubbed shoulders with the moneyed classes in much the same way along the narrow pavements. The tradespeople in their flat caps stood by as tall, athletic looking gentlemen strode the streets in their academic gowns like the inheritors of the Earth. Small groups debated their way through the thoroughfares lost in the brilliance of themselves. Holmes marveled at the spectacle as he stepped out of the station.

'Ah,' he said, breathing in the air. 'Oxford. "It speaks with a thousand tongues to the heart; it waves its mighty shadow over the imagination."' Spenning raised his eyebrows, clearly impressed,

'A follower of Hazlitt?' he noted. 'I am no fan of him myself. As a philosopher I find him fanciful; as a grammarian I find him pedantic.' While the pair traded intellectual blows, I looked out on the great city. There was a palpable excitement about the place; as if those fizzing young minds had managed to electrify the air itself; there was a scent of blossom and evanescence like champagne.

'My dear Watson,' remarked Holmes. 'You are standing in a pile of horse manure.'

'So I am,' I noted.

A four-seater was summoned and Holmes and Spenning continued their badinage all the way to gates of Corpus Christi College. The sun and shadows played on the sandstone walls and ramparts, which seemed to crack and buckle from the weight of learning they contained. The professor greeted the porter with a nod. He was a Falstaffian character with a bulbous nose, ruddy cheeks and an outrageous twinkle in his rheumy eyes, as if he considered porter and port part of his duties too.

'Good day, professor,' he said, tipping his bowler. 'Will there be two extra for dinner this evening?' he asked. 'I'm told there's a good bit of venison in the offing.'

'Yes, very good,' muttered Spenning, preoccupied.

'You had another visitor while you were out, sir.'

'Oh yes?' the professor said, more interested.

'A strange character, he was, sir, a giant of man with uneven features and something of a limp. A black cape and a large felt hat, as if he was trying to hide himself. If I didn't know better I would say he had walked off the stage at the Sheldonian.'

'Did he leave any message?'

'None at all, sir. But his face said it all. A rapscallion if ever I saw one; eyes like bottomless wells. I didn't like the look of him one bit.'

Spenning thanked the man for his trouble, then led us down the ancient corridors to his study. It was a light, airy room full of curiosities. Besides the bookcases and the open volumes on the desk, there was a row of slender, porcelain jars lined up on the mantelpiece. On the walls were playbills for productions of Shakespeare's works. A poster for The Tempest was a garish watercolour with Ferdinand standing at the prow of a ship and Ariel like an angel flying above, accompanied by the legend: *Not acted this season!*

'His last great work,' the professor said lovingly.

'Quite,' agreed Holmes.

'Although it is so often rendered,' Spenning added, raising his nose in distaste, 'as vulgar music hall.'

28

'"But the isle is full of noises,"' countered Holmes, '"sounds and sweet airs."'

'Mr Holmes,' said Spenning, beckoning for us to sit down. If you ever tire of your detective work, I'm sure we could find you a position here in the department. Your mind is a cabinet of wonders.'

'My mind,' confessed Holmes, 'is a stranger place than I care to admit. It is strange even to me. I think of it as a set of rooms in a labyrinthine house. Residing in each room are characters from past adventures and unsolved cases. In some rooms there are dead men, in others villains and monsters. Other rooms are piled with books. Some doors open onto windswept moors or storm lashed seas. Others I have never opened. When I think deeply on a problem, I roam the corridors on this house thinking back on which door I may need to open. It is a simply a question of choosing which to open and, of course, finding the right key.'

'A mind as multifarious as that of the Bard himself,' marvelled Spenning.

'Now,' said Holmes, snapping back into the present. 'I believe Somerville smokes Turques Stamboul cigarettes. I wonder if he has left us one to try? Perhaps in the left hand drawer?'

'Remarkable,' said Spenning, pulling open the drawer in question. He produced a single cigarette and handed it to my friend. 'Now I suppose it is plausible you detected the scent,' he ventured, 'but how could you know about the cigarette, or the drawer for that matter?

'The Turque Stamboul,' Holmes began with the air of a visiting professor, 'is in fact almost odourless. But the ash residue is distinctive. And like any smoker of an unusual blend, Somerville would be an evangelist for his brand, which means he would foist one on an acquaintance whether he wanted one or not. You of course do not smoke, an abstinence I can hardly condone. Not wishing to cause offence however, you accepted the cigarette in your right hand. You are right handed are you not?'

'Yes, I am.'

'It was then perfectly natural that you opened the drawer on your left with your free hand, dropped the cigarette therein and closed the drawer again. Now, Watson, if you would be so good to hand me a match, I will sample this delicious blend for myself.'

'My dear Holmes!' I exclaimed striking the light. 'You have excelled yourself.'

'Simplicity itself,' he smiled in a cloud of delight.

'So,' Holmes proceeded, 'the manuscript.'

'Ah, yes,' sighed Spenning, as if, in the dazzle of Holmes' company, he had had momentarily forgotten his predicament.

'You kept it locked in the right hand drawer of your desk?'

'Yes,' agreed Spenning, by now accepting Holmes' powers of telepathy.

'And does the same key open both drawers?' my friend asked.

'No, there are two keys, both of which returned with me to my rooms. There are no copies. So worried was I about the quarto, I kept the key to the right hand drawer on a string around my neck. Of course now I only wish I had taken the play itself to bed with me.'

'And there was no sign of forced entry, either to your office or to the drawer itself.'

'None.' He slumped forward and stared into space, reliving the nightmare.

'And when you returned to your office you found both the door and the drawer locked?'

'Exactly; another reason the police would not look at the case. A play that could not possibly exist is stolen from a locked drawer in a locked room. Impossible!'

'Improbable,' corrected Holmes, 'but not impossible. How old is the desk?'

'An antique certainly,' answered Spenning.

'Is it possible,' enquired Holmes, 'that a previous owner of the desk retained a key?'

'Perhaps,' admitted Spenning uncertainly, shaking his head.

'The desk certainly predates you,' my friend returned, stubbing out the cigarette with an air of finality. 'We could make enquiries as to the previous owner. An older colleague would be my suspicion. But guessing is not a pastime in which I indulge. It is a fancy rather than a science and is unsupported by fact. I think of a case as being not dissimilar to a bridge spanning a valley. In order to reach the truth, you need a number of supporting facts. Without them, it will collapse into the ravine.' Presently there was a knock on the door.

'Come!' said Spenning with a surprising authority. A sullen, thin faced young man appeared from behind the door. He was little over twenty years of age, his hair long, curled and dark, high cheekbones with a snarl about the mouth. It was uncanny, but it seemed like a face that belonged to some distant age. It seemed possible that he was Italian in origin. Clothe him in ecclesiastical robes and he could have been a young Florentine priest in a portrait by Lorenzo Lotto. He took each of us in then addressed the professor.

'You asked to see me,' he intoned. His voice was unexpectedly deep and sonorous.

'Yes, but not now,' dismissed the professor. 'I have visitors as you can see.'

'Please,' smiled Holmes, 'do not vanish on my account.' He extended a hand in greeting. 'You must be the brilliant Mr Standbull. My name is Sherlock Holmes.' Standbull seemed unimpressed by this fact.

'Very well,' muttered Spenning. 'Come in and close the door behind you.' Standbull moved silently to the far end of the room and stood with both hands behind his back. He seemed strangely aloof, as if his dignity had been hurt by this slight reproach.

'You may speak freely with my student. As I have mentioned, he knows of the play and its disappearance.'

'Then you must have a theory,' Holmes proposed.

'I have no theory,' Standbull pronounced, 'except that the loss has thrown the professor into a purgatory. He will have no peace until the play is returned.'

'Professor,' said Holmes, 'humour me for a moment. Please hand me the keys to both drawers.' Spenning did as he was instructed. Holmes examined the two small keys for a moment in his palm, closed his fingers around them then presented them again.

'Now kindly take the key to left hand drawer.'

'It is impossible,' returned the professor. 'They are practically identical, as you well know.'

'Then how did you know which one you wore around your neck the night the quarto was stolen?'

'Key or no key,' cried Spenning in exasperation. 'The play must be found!'

'On that point we all concur,' sighed Holmes, peering again at the bill poster. 'I do not mind admitting I would give my diamond tie pin for a glance at a single page.'

'Then on that account, I am most happy to oblige,' said Spenning suddenly. He slid open a draw and withdrew two pieces of foolscap. 'You were saying about a tie pin?' he enquired. 'Before it was stolen, I had begun some work on the first act, beginning by copying it out in long hand.'

'By heavens!' I cried. Holmes and I rushed to Spenning's side and peered at the closely printed text. For a minute we read in silence.

Enter Vito

VITO
What pains you, Flavio?

FLAVIO
A lost cause.

VITO
No cause is lost until every stone is turned.

FLAVIO
If I could find a stone to match her beauty,
An orb as lustrous as the sun itself that
May please her eye as that first dawn
Invited Eve to gaze to heaven in delight,
No longer would I suffer so. I would place it in
The setting of gold, a burnished sky and
Her wonder would be at the wealth of my love
Entreating her to marvel at its faculty.
Nothing so much as perfection will do; no
Ornament will suffice. No, dear Vito, I must
Render unto her a bauble of matchless art
That gleams like the tear of proud Niobe.
Her thankfulness will be equal only to the
Priceless gift of requited love. Let me say this:
If such a stone was found, a star-splinter an
Emperor would covet, then I at last I will be

Released from this purgatory. Leave me a while.
1.2

DUKE
What music, sir, is this?

ANTONIO
Tis wedding music, my lord. They practice as larks at dawn.

DUKE
What happy pair will join in such delight?
Hannibal's elephants would not trumpet
With such joy as this. The trunks of England's
Trees would shake at such a cacophony.
This fanfare of angels, this well wrought sound
of heaven, has seeped through our vault of sky
and filled the twin cathedrals of our ears.
Fetch me those who engendered this row
I shall bless their matrimony, their solemn vow.

                          (They go)
SCENE 3

SILVIO
What foul weather has blighted our fair conceit!
The servant's flapping tongue forewarns the duke
Of a marriage. But yet he has not wind
That these nuptials are his own daughter's,
And that she is betrothed to the only son
Of his foresworn enemy. What dark skies
would come from this unseen tempest;
such squalls and that would wreck his heart.

MARCELLO
Soft, fair brother, he hath not the reason
Nor temperament to suspect; his season
Is always spring; serenity blossoms
In him as bitterness dwells in the spleen

Of the cynic; by the time he smells the rose
The altar will be clear, the candles snuffed.

SILVIO
Now where goes Flavio? These hours 'til our
Brother's union will I fear be fraught;
But for a stoup of wine to numb our nerves.

'Well,' said Holmes, at length. 'It's hardly Hamlet.' Spenning and Standbull glanced at each other. 'But then,' my friend added, 'it's not The Two Gentlemen of Verona either. In short, I believe it to be perfectly average Shakespeare. Mr Standbull, what is your opinion?' 'I believe it is a fake.'

'You seem quite certain,' remarked Holmes. 'And Watson,' he added, turning to me. 'What is the doctor's verdict?'

'I say that it is equal to his other works. That it is to say, I can ring very little sense out of it at all. Surely the professor's opinion is the one that counts.' Spenning stood up and removed his spectacles.

'Very well,' he began. 'As a text, I believe it to be of middling quality. It is overblown and the metre is faulty in places, but it is possible that Shakespeare was affected by the loss of his son, Hamnet, at the time of composition. If we place it next to The Merchant of Venice in the chronology then that is quite plausible. But if it is a forgery,' he concluded diplomatically, 'then it is still one of considerable artistry.' I could bear it no longer.

'To my ears,' I cried, 'only Standbull has nailed his colours to the mast!'

'Come, Watson,' chided Holmes, 'you could not say what ails a man without examining him first?'

At that moment, there was a shattering of glass and a stone skittered across the floorboards.

'Good lord!' I shouted, ducking behind the desk. 'Look, a note!'

Holmes ran to the window and peered through the shattered pane. I reached down and removed the scrap of paper wrapped around the stone.

'Your hearts I'll stamp out with my horse's heels,' I read, 'and make a quagmire of your mingled brains.'

34

'Henry VI, Part I,' muttered Spenning, sinking back into his chair, his face pale with fear.

'Lord Talbot,' said Standbull. 'One hundred percent certified Shakespeare.'

'There are dark forces at play,' warned Holmes, retrieving a piece of glass from the floor and inspecting it. 'Report the broken window to the police, request some protection, but say nothing of the play. Watson and I will return to Baker Street to consider the problem further. I shall wire further instructions in the morning.'

THREE

The Understudy

I was awoken that night by a fearsome storm. The sky groaned with thunder, the windows rattled in their frames and rain lashed like a horsewhip against the glass. I fought with my pillow for a moment then fumbled for my pocket watch. Striking a match, I saw that it was a little after three. The night was preternaturally cold and the flame was soon extinguished as if by its own accord. Suddenly the entire room was illuminated in a flash of blue lighting and to my horror I saw a figure seated at the end of my bed.

'Fear not, Watson!' a man cried. 'It is not your father's ghost; only your old conspirator, Sherlock Holmes.'

'Gracious, Holmes,' I cried. 'That was a cruel prank.' I clambered out of bed and lit a lamp. Only then did I see that my friend was soaked to the skin.

'Have you lost your senses?' I asked. 'You ventured out in this tempest?'

'When a dog has a scent,' he grinned, 'no amount of weather will put him off.'

'When a man absorbs this much rain,' I returned, 'no amount of beef tea will restore him.'

'I should be grateful for an opportunity to disprove that theory.' I knew Holmes would not sleep until he had shared his night's adventure.

Ten minutes later and my friend was warming himself beneath a tartan blanket, a steaming mug at his side, the fumes of his strongest, foulest pipe exsiccating his waterlogged system. I sipped at some hot cocoa and peered at the incorrigible detective.

'So what was it this time, Holmes?' I teased, 'perhaps a night at the opium den? Or were you high rolling with the Prince of Wales?'

'My dear Watson,' he said, 'such irony does not befit you. If you are to resort to speculation then at least afford me the dignity of employing my methods. What did you observe when I appeared at the end of your bed?'

'A great deal of water,' I replied wearily, feeling my patience tested by this familiar game of cat and mouse.

'What else?' I thought back to that ghoulish apparition that had emerged from the storm.

'A thin moustache,' I said slowly, the image growing clearer.

'Splendid. A theatrical touch I could not resist. Keep going,' he encouraged.

'A top hat in your hand,' I suddenly recalled, 'which you rarely wear.'

'Excellent, Watson. Can you name an occasion when I have worn it?'

'A concert?' I asked. Holmes' face remained impassive. 'The theatre!' I cried.

'Bravo!'

'Must everything be a parlour game?' I sighed.

'Life is a game,' replied Holmes, working his pipe, 'at which we go to great lengths to master the rules, only to discover that they have changed overnight.' I was only half listening however, now puzzled by an aberration in my friend's account.

'But what performance,' I put in, 'concludes at two o'clock in the morning?'

'There you have me, Watson.' Holmes leaned forward in his seat, like a much-loved schoolmaster about to regale a roomful of attentive students.

'The play I saw was Mr William Somerville's production of King Lear. As a man of letters, Watson, you will surely know it is one of the longest of Shakespeare's plays.'

'Surely only Hamlet is longer?'

'Incorrect!' scolded Holmes. 'Lear is only the seventh longest of his works. But at 3,499 lines it still leaves little left of your evening.'

'Even so,' I protested, 'all the blood would have been spilled by eleven.'

'And indeed it was. However I indulged in a little extra drama after the curtain fell. The performance itself was magnificent, I should say. Edward Adler in the title role gave his all. At times I felt he risked his own sanity upon the heath. The Fool was sublime. Cordelia would have broken the hardest heart. At the end of the performance, I walked out into the rain as if it had followed me from the heath. I hid myself in the shadows by the stage door and waited for the principals to emerge. Somerville was almost the last to exit, flanked by one of his lieutenants. He paused right next to me as he fought to keep his cigar alight in the downpour. They boarded a waiting brougham and I followed hard at their heels in a hansom. We proceeded north through the rain into Islington then stopped at the Old King's Head in Upper Street. I paid off my driver then followed them in. At first, I felt somewhat foolish. The two men sat over drinks talking shop. Gloucester it seems is causing them trouble. Andrew Galloway has a slippery grasp of the role apparently and has developed too fond a taste for wine. By all accounts he is rarely sober, although I would not have known it from my vantage point in the stalls. Presently, the two men were joined by a third: a large man in a wide brimmed hat and cloak, gleaming with rain.'

'The man at the college!'

'Precisely, Watson. With little prevarication, the three of them then disappeared out of a back door. Waiting a decent interval, I followed them into the back street only to find that they had boarded another carriage. With no time to summon transport of my own, I took my life in my hands and hitched a ride on the outside of the brougham.'

'Good lord!' I exclaimed. 'It is a wonder you were not thrown beneath the wheels.'

'It is not a sport I would recommend,' Holmes agreed. 'I felt every pothole, dip and divot between Islington and Highgate. That is not to mention the rain. It is possible that I drank of pint of the stuff before we reached our destination. I can imagine journeying to the bottom of the Atlantic would be a drier affair. They disembarked outside the cemetery. I followed them as closely as their own shadows before losing them in the darkness. It was two o'clock before the Highgate ghosts succeeded in scaring me away.'

'A devil of a night,' I remarked. 'So what have we learned?'

'A great deal,' he said cheerfully. 'We have connected Mr Somerville with the mysterious visitor at the college gate. We have a substantial clue that he has business interests beyond the theatre. We also know that there is something afoot in Highgate Cemetery.'

'But how does any of this relate to the lost play?'

'Just as Rome was not built in a day, Watson,' my friend returned, 'a case is rarely solved in a single night. Tomorrow, you and Spenning will accompany me to the theatre. We will then conduct an interview with the great impresario. Now we have some intelligence on our side, we have the beginnings of a case.'

'You have a theory, Holmes?' My friend's eyes twinkled with delight.

'It is too early to call it a theory,' he returned, 'but the events to date have certainly piqued my interest. There is enough, let us say, to elevate this problem above the level of the humdrum. Now perhaps you could be persuaded to replace this disgusting beef tea for a cup of Mrs Hudson's delicious cocoa? Honestly Watson, without her services, we are merely camping.'

I woke the next morning to a blushing sky of peach and crimson. I sat up in bed and stared for some time at the simple beauty of the burgeoning light between the dark chimney tops. But my mind was soon overtaken by another vision; that of the face of my late wife. I replayed the fateful events that led to her death; the recrimination I felt that not even I, as her husband and doctor, could do anything to save her. Who was that woman in Baker Street? Once again, I was drawn like a ghoul to the front window and peered down into the street. Of course, there was no trace. Holmes had brushed aside my questions about my sleepwalking and had prescribed brandy, fencing and chess as the best medicine, and in that order. I returned to my rooms to wash and dress, then taking up my book, I drifted back to my easy chair.

Holmes emerged over an hour later, looking preoccupied, muttering under his breath, as if reciting a poem. Deciding not to interrupt, I returned my attentions to the gobbledegook I was reading, the absurd adventures of my men from Mars. My friend slunk into his chair, prepared a pipe and continued to whisper his chants and incantations, his eyes closed in concentration.

'Do you smell something fishy, Holmes?' I asked, looking up.

'I'm naturally suspicious, Watson,' he remarked, 'if that's what you infer.'

'No, actual fish, fish,' I said, frowning, attempting to trace the source of the stench.

'As matter of fact I do,' he agreed. 'Herring if I'm not mistaken.' At this very moment, Mrs Hudson appeared in the doorway holding a tray with a long slim item wrapped in brown paper. 'I believe,' said Holmes, 'we have identified our culprit.'

'A gift for you, Mr Holmes,' she said, 'from a Mr Ernest Crummles. He's waiting downstairs.'

'Well by all means,' smiled Holmes, giving me a quizzical look, 'show him in.'

He was a slender man with a tall bowler hat, fulsome side whiskers, a long, grubby overcoat and a squint that suggested he was in need of a pair of spectacles.

'Over here,' said Holmes, clicking his fingers. Our visitor, who had been orientated in the wrong direction now corrected himself.

'Beggin' your pardon, sir,' he began, with a cough, 'I don't want to kick up a shine, but I didn't know where else to turn.'

'Well you turned in every direction except our own,' laughed Holmes. 'Now before you begin,' he said, interrupting himself, 'would you first indulge me a moment?'

'Of course,' the man stuttered.

'My friend, Dr Watson here, is always grateful for an opportunity to improve his powers of observation and deduction. Would you allow him a few moments to inform us of a few salient points about your profession and predicament?' I flushed at this invitation.

'I say, Holmes,' I faltered, 'it's really not necessary…'

'I insist!' he pressed. 'But take your time. Observation is an art that requires serenity of mind, wouldn't you agree Mr Crummles?'

'If you say so, sir.'

'I do!' returned Holmes. 'Now over to you, Watson. Do your worst!'

In truth, I relished the prospect. I could not count the times Holmes had made the most obvious deductions, casting me as the dullard in the corner.

'Well,' I began. 'It is plain to see that you are a costermonger, a seller of fish.'

'That's correct, sir,' he confirmed.

'Bravo, Watson!' congratulated Holmes, 'if a little obvious. What else?'

'You purchase your stock from Billingsgate Fish Market on Lower Thames Street,' I suggested.

'Right again, sir!'

'My goodness, Watson, you are flying!' I did not like my friend's patronising tone and did not dignify this with a response. However, now I was left looking for scraps. I scoured the man for any odd detail but his hair, face and clothes seemed ordinary in every respect. Then I had it. There was a tiny cut on the bridge of his nose.

'You have had an altercation with a rival fishmonger, which resulted in the snapping of your spectacles. You wish us to help settle a dispute.'

'Blimey,' the man whistled. 'You 'ave taught him well, Mr Holmes. It's as if you were there!'

'I take my hat off to you, Watson,' said Holmes, shaking his head in admiration. 'I could have done little better myself.'

'Perfectly straightforward,' I said with a small bow. Flushing with pride, I returned to my chair.

'Now,' said Holmes, stepping forward, holding up his pipe so that its noxious vapours rose like steam from an Icelandic geyser. 'There must be a reason you brought us a fish that is past its prime. You are a man who generally takes great pride in the quality of his wares.'

'I most certainly am, Mr Holmes,' he sniffed. 'I am not the least bit happy about the state of that herring.'

'This is precisely,' my friend continued, 'what brings you here.'

'Right again,' he marvelled. 'There's strange dealings down at the market and I don't like them one bit. And I 'aint the only one who's had enough of it, I can tell you. For years we've paid good, honest money for good, honest fish.'

'I can't say I've met a dishonest one, can you Watson?' I shook my head, but felt my friend's strain of humour was a little misjudged in the circumstances.

'But that's all changed now,' the fish seller went on. 'The prices have doubled and the quality has dropped through the floor. They're putting it down to a man they called Neptune.'

'Neptune!' Holmes exclaimed. 'Are they indeed?'

'That's right, sir. He's taken over the whole operation.'

'But can't you just go elsewhere?' I suggested.

'You don't know too much about the fish trade, do you sir?' he opined, casting me a withering look. 'That's where it all comes in; the fish that it. Anyways, one of my mates, Archie Frizzle, he kicks up a proper stink, demands to see this Neptune character. Says he won't hand over any more of his hard earned tin until he's gone eyeball to eyeball with the man. He goes to see him and we've haven't seen him since. Then some of his cronies pays us a visit down at The Rising Sun, where we all go for a daffy, a gatty and a ding dong. They warns us that if anyone goes blabbing to a rozzer we'll go the same way as poor old Archie. That's when your name came up, Mr 'Olmes.'

'I see,' my friend said, peering hard at the man.

'We got money, if that's what you need,' Crummles added hastily. Digging into the fathomless pockets of his breeches, he produced two great handfuls of coins, with shillings, pennies and farthings spilling between his fingers and collecting around his feet.

'Good gracious!' exclaimed Holmes suddenly, 'You're on fire!' Inadvertently, it seemed, my friend had set our prospective client's whiskers alight, which were now burning green and yellow in the most alarming fashion. I seized the decanter from the drinks tray and, aiming it at Crummles, gave him two smart squirts until I assured myself the fire was properly extinguished. The man appeared lost for words.

'My most sincere apologies,' offered Holmes. 'That was unforgivable.'

'No 'arm done,' he spluttered, blinking the water from his eyes. A noxious vapour filled the air. 'Now about this Neptune. Will you join me down at the market tomorrow night at eight? We've heard he'll be there and we fancy it may present a chance for you to observe him at close quarters.'

'Mr Crummles,' said Holmes, 'your statement is not entirely without interest. I accept your case and my friend and I will see you at Billingsgate at ten to eight tomorrow evening. We will meet you beneath the flying fish, do you know the spot?' There was the merest pause.

'Yes,' he muttered, 'yes, of course.'

I showed Mr Crummles to the door then returned to my friend, buoyed with my success. He was biting firmly on the stem of his pipe and inspecting me in a most amused manner.

'So you are not the only detective at 221b Baker Street after all,' I announced, with a certain satisfaction, pouring myself a small, celebratory glass of claret. 'But I say, Holmes, you really should watch what you do with that pipe of yours. You are a menace to the public health.'

'A first rate performance, Watson,' my friend applauded, 'You were accurate in all but two respects.'

'Oh, yes? And what were they? They could not amount to anything of great significance.'

'Well, that is all a matter of perspective.' I took a small sip of the delicious vintage.

'So what did I miss?'

'Well for one,' he began, 'Mr Crummles is a woman.' I spat my wine across the room.

'What?' I spluttered, the claret dripping from my chin. 'Impossible!'

'Unquestionably a woman,' Holmes smiled. 'My small test with the pipe told me that her hair was not her own. From the pungent smell, I detected horse hair as the key component, although I cannot rule out a percentage of yak.'

'Yak?'

'Quite so. Then there was the line of the bandaging used to flatten her chest, plainly apparent beneath her shirt.' I shook my head in a daze.

'And your other observation?' I asked weakly.

'Everything she said was pure invention. Not a single word of it was true.' I sat with my mouth agog. Once again, Holmes had rendered me an utter buffoon. Holmes strolled to the window with his hands folded behind his back and began his lecture as a schoolmaster might address his class after a disastrous exam performance. 'To give you some credit, Watson, her story was a colourful one. There was plenty of authentic detail and the little tale about Archie Frizzle was awfully good. Neptune as the gang master was a splendid touch. But she stumbled over the merest trifle. It is always the way. Do you remember I asked that we meet her beneath the flying fish? If you were watching closely, you will have observed that her face was a perfect blank. How would a costermonger of many years not know about the most famous landmark at Billingsgate Fish Market? Her cover was blown.

'Then who is she?' I demanded. 'And what does she want with us?'

'In fact, Watson,' Holmes continued, 'you are already well acquainted with her. You mentioned the sighting of your late wife yesterday morning. Well, it was a cruel stunt. The ghost of Mary Watson and Mr Crummles are in fact one and the same person – the actress, Elsie Pinner. It is my belief that she has been engaged to lure us into mortal danger. You escaped narrowly with your life when you ventured abroad in the fog. Your encounter with the policeman was the only thing that saved you. I am in doubt that an appalling fate awaits us at Billingsgate. If we were to arrive at the appointed hour, I'm sure as eggs are eggs we would have ended our days in small pieces, filling a pair of waste buckets buried beneath a quantity of scales, tails and fish-guts.' This was too much. With a numb feeling that enveloped both mind and body, I returned to the bottle of claret and mechanically refilled my glass.

That afternoon, we dined early ahead of our engagement at the theatre. Mrs Hudson's cucumber soup was enough to restore the humours of a condemned man but coupled with her pheasant mandarin, Holmes are I were in famous spirits by the time dessert arrived.

'Mrs Hudson, you have excelled yourself,' I declared, dabbing my lips on a napkin as a gooseberry fool was placed before us.

'Dr Watson,' she replied, 'I am all too pleased to cook for a man so long as his food does not end up on the floor.' Sure enough a serving of pheasant had found its way beneath the table.

'A treat for the mice,' remarked Holmes. 'Watson, I believe, is keen to adopt a pet.' Mrs Hudson raised an eyebrow.

'Not if he wishes to remain at 221b Baker Street.'

That morning, as the rain abated, Holmes had wired for the professor and Standbull to meet us, appropriately enough, at The Shakespeare's Head public house in Wych Street, near Drury Lane.

'Come Watson,' said Holmes, as I dipped my last sponge finger into the delicious, slightly sour concoction. 'We cannot keep our friends waiting.' A two-seater delivered us to the inn, where we found the two scholars loitering inside.

A glass of water lay untouched on the table in front of Spenning.

'I'm sorry,' he announced as we approached. 'I simply cannot go through with it.'

'My dear sir,' said Holmes, removing his hat and signaling to the barmaid, 'we have no choice in the matter. We must speak to Somerville if we are to locate the manuscript.' Standbull sipped moodily at his ale and stared at his tutor.

'Why?'

'Because whether he knows it or not,' my friend explained calmly. 'He holds the key to the problem.'

'Then perhaps we could delay for a week?' suggested the professor. 'Perhaps we could tell him I have been taken ill. Or better still that I have had to leave the country to consult with a foreign academic on the text. What do you say to that?' Holmes smiled and shook his head.

'There will be a moment's pain, I grant,' he acknowledged. 'But Somerville is an intelligent man. He will understand that the quarto must be retrieved with a minimum of fuss. He will also know something of my reputation for competence. As my friend Watson can vouch, I have retrieved documents of perhaps even greater importance than this.'

'Impossible,' muttered Standbull.

'I'm sorry?' Holmes questioned.

'What could be more important than a lost play by William Shakespeare?' My friend fixed him with a steely glare.

'There are more things in heaven and earth,' he warned, 'than in your philosophy.' Holmes and I drained our pints, then straightened our collars. 'I have sent a card ahead to the dressing room,' Holmes explained as we crossed the road to the theatre, 'begging five minutes of Somerville's time. I have not elaborated on the matter. I suggest that we all enjoy this splendid production of King Lear and forget about our interview until the hour is upon us.' Spenning looked every inch the condemned man.

We joined the throng at the entrance to the theatre and followed a procession of top hats into the foyer. A magnificent chandelier gleamed above us like a miniature solar system with a burnished sun at the centre. The place was alive with chatter and high spirits, a little

45

inappropriate I thought for a tragedy. Still, a night at the theatre is a night at the theatre, and, with the exception of the abstemious Spenning, we seized the opportunity to have another drink. Holmes had not spared any expense and secured us some splendid seats in the stalls. We gloried in the spectacle of London's most famous theatre bedecked in cream, red and gold.

Row by row, the seats filled until it was clear there would be a full house. Some of the staff, I noticed, looked a little anxious and presently it became apparent that there was some sort of hold-up in raising the curtain.'
'Good lord,' I remarked, glancing at my watch, 'I can see now why you did not return until three in the morning.'
'Patience, Watson,' Holmes returned. 'Artists cannot be rushed.'
'They can if their audience hopes to be in bed before midnight.'

Presently a small, rotund gentleman appeared on the stage and a hush descended on the crowd.
'My lords, ladies and gentlemen,' he announced. 'I apologise for the delay to the start of this evening's programme. One of our actors has taken ill and we are arranging for an understudy. We pray your indulgence while we attend to this and thank you for your patience.'
There were general groans and one or two stood up to leave, including Holmes.
'Another drink perhaps?' my friend invited. 'These shall be my pleasure.' With that he disappeared towards the bar.

Spenning and Standbull kept their own company and I was left to myself, filling my time people watching. I scanned the crowd for a familiar face and was pleased to discover our old friend Lestrade a few rows behind us. He acknowledged my greeting with a curt nod and a brief levitation of the brows above his dark eyes. Some ten minutes later and Holmes had still not returned.
'There must be quite a crowd at the bar,' I remarked. At that moment, the lights dimmed and a regal fanfare struck up. The play had begun. There were three characters on the stage; one taller than the other two, all dressed in the robes of court.

KENT
I thought the king had more affected the Duke of
Albany than Cornwall.

GLOUCESTER
It did always seem so to us: but now, in the
division of the kingdom, it appears not which of
the dukes he values most;

The voice and manner was unmistakable. Behind Gloucester's face paint and beneath the yellow tunic was none other than my friend, Sherlock Holmes. I glanced across at Spenning and Standbull, who looked no less flabbergasted. Glancing over my shoulder I could see that Lestrade was equally taken by the unexpected turn of events. I could see no sign of a book or crib sheet and unless he was employing some trick, it appeared Holmes had the part committed entirely to memory.

He was utterly spellbinding. While I am no objective or expert judge of such things, Holmes struck me as simply magnificent. His speaking seemed to contain great depth and subtlety, as if he had rehearsed for months. I have written in the past how Holmes, with his emphatic manner and magnetic presence could have forged an alternative career on the stage, but it was now unfolding before my eyes. He reached a particularly menacing line and seemed to address it directly to the audience:

We have seen the best of our time:
machinations, hollowness, treachery, and all
ruinous disorders, follow us disquietly to our
graves.

It was unsettling in the extreme. At the interval I fought my way through the crowds and attempted to get backstage. However minders blocked the way at every turn and I resigned myself to leaving the mystery unsolved until the end of the evening. I did however manage a quick word with Lestrade in the bar.

'Remarkable, Watson,' he said, clasping my hand. 'Still, I suppose we knew he had it in him; he is one of the world's natural showmen.'
'I sometimes believe,' I marvelled, 'that there are no limits to the man's abilities.'
'I wouldn't go that far,' warned Lestrade, burning his lips with a glass of scotch. 'I have a stack of unsolved cases at Scotland Yard that if piled one upon the next would reach half way to the moon. If Sherlock Holmes has energy to spare, then I suggest you ask him to drop in to see me at his next convenience.'

The next two hours passed in a blur of wonder and trepidation. Try as I might, a small part of me doubted Holmes' ability to keep up this astonishing feat. At any moment, I half-expected that look of terror that sometimes forms on an actor's face when the next line evaporates from his memory. And yet, I should not have concerned myself. He threw himself into the part as if it had been his life-long vocation. I steeled myself for that cruel scene where his eyes are gouged, but nothing could prepare me for the pity and the pathos that Holmes evoked as he crawled towards the cliff's edge at Dover. Several members of the audience were weeping openly.

But somehow his performance was beautifully measured; full of consideration for his fellow actors. Never once did he attempt to steal a scene that was not rightfully his, nor try to twist the play into the Tragedy of the Duke of Gloucester. By the final curtain, mine were tears of admiration for this man's ability to amaze. He joined hands with the cast and held his head aloft with a look of unmistakable pride. As he was afforded a standing ovation of his own, it was, I felt sure, a schoolboy's dream finally realised.

We were reunited in the bar and I shook my friend warmly by the hand.
'My dear, Holmes,' I began, 'words fail me.'
'That would be a first, Watson.' Traces of grease paint and stage blood still clung to his pale, lean features but I rather fancied that he wore them as trophies.
'You were remarkable,' I managed, momentarily star-struck in his presence.

'Merely, perfunctory,' he dismissed, with not a little false modesty. 'Now we have an interview to conduct with Somerville. Perhaps, after this small endeavour, he will look more favourably upon our predicament.' Spenning looked unconvinced and shrank visibly as we made our way to Somerville's office.

'Take heart,' my friend urged as we approached the end of the corridor, 'what's the worst that can happen?'

'Murder?' suggested Standbull, in his laconic way, which earned himself a frown from Holmes. I could smell the cigarette smoke before the door was even open. I took a deep breath then knocked smartly.

'Enter!' a voice roared from the other side.

Somerville was a great bear of a man with huge, black whiskers and the red jowls of a bon-viveur. He wore a green velvet waistcoat that rolled like a meadow across the great expanse of his stomach. Laughter lines were worn deep into the creases of his face, although the eyes themselves retained a cold clarity otherwise at odds with his buffoonish air.

'My dear man!' he cried as he caught sight of my friend. He rose to his feet and embraced Holmes like a lost brother. Releasing him momentarily, he gripped him by the shoulders and stared directly at him. 'How can I repay you? The day was saved.'

'Think nothing of it,' said Holmes.

'I have seen better Gloucesters, I admit,' Somerville continued, wagging his finger, 'but none with your uncanny intensity. It was an intriguing performance, Mr Holmes and all the more remarkable for being off the cuff. You must have a memory like a well. How can anyone account for such a feat?'

'Quite easily,' explained Holmes. 'It was clear to me that your Gloucester was teetering on the very edge during last night's performance. I predicated correctly that his health would not hold out for another 24 hours. I simply spent two hours with some Persian tobacco, a pot of strong coffee and a copy of the Oxford Edition of King Lear. I am, shall we say, a quick study.'

'Well, well,' chortled Somerville. 'And you have brought friends too.' He suddenly stopped and peered at the professor.

'Good lord,' he cried. 'Spenning, is that you? I hardly recognised you. You look dreadful. I fear our stage blood was rather too realistic for your temperament. In the old days we used the blood of a newly stuck pig. There was nothing like it; although it did tend to congeal somewhat about the feet. You must be here to return the item I asked you to inspect.'

'Quite,' managed the professor.

'Quite what?'

'Shall we sit?' suggested Holmes.

'We have come regarding the quarto,' began Spenning in a faltering voice.

'The quarto?' repeated Somerville, as if it was the first time he had heard of such a thing. 'Is there something you wish to discuss in private?'

'We are all fully aware of the particulars.' Holmes assured him. 'Dr Watson, my associate, can be trusted completely; Mr Standbull is Professor Spenning's brightest student and has studied the play at length.'

'Do you have something to tell me?' Somerville asked quietly.

'It appears,' said Spenning, adjusting his spectacles, 'that the quarto has been stolen.' Somerville stared directly at him, utterly impassive, as if under some curse. I glanced over at Holmes then back at the impresario. I noticed that the man's shoulders were beginning to tremble. Soon his arms and torso also began to quiver in a similar way, like a volcano moments before an eruption. I saw Spenning's Adam's apple rise and fall. He took a cautionary step backwards. Somerville suddenly swept the papers from his desk.

'Stolen?' he bellowed. 'The most important discovery of the 19th century! Stolen?'

'Yes,' stuttered Spenning, 'I'm afraid that appears to be the case.' Somerville's face turned from red to a horrible shade of dead man's purple. He advanced on the hat stand and hurled it to the ground. 'I told you to guard it with your life!'

'I did!' protested the hapless man.

'Then why are you still alive?!' Somerville rushed forward with his hands reaching for the professor's neck. It was only Holmes' intervention that prevented certain death.

'Release me, Holmes,' he shouted. 'This has nothing to do with you!' Somehow my friend managed to coax the producer into a chair.

'If it is any consolation,' Holmes began. 'I have agreed to take on the case.'

Somerville breathed like an asthmatic. With unsteady fingers he lit a cigarette and smoked it with a fury. He swiftly followed this with another, continuing to fix the cowering professor with a murderous glare. Soon smoke appeared to drift from his every pore. Indeed, it was as if he was a piece of smoking coal that had been lifted with a pair of tongs from the fire.

'I should have known better,' he growled, 'than to entrust my play to an academic. There are men who make their mark in the world and then there are those that lurk in the shadows.' Standbull returned Somerville's furious look.

'How dare you stare at me, young man,' threatened Somerville, redirecting his ire at the student. 'You would do better to choose Mr Holmes here as your mentor instead of this…' he searched his mind for the *mot juste*; 'dung beetle!' There was a light knock at the door.

'Not now!' Somerville bellowed. The visitor went on their way.

'So, Mr Holmes,' he demanded. 'Who has my play?' My friend reached into his pocket and withdrew a silk handkerchief.

'Mr Somerville,' he began, handing it to the producer, 'you have the beginnings of a cold and should not be exerting yourself in this way. You would do well to avoid foolish excursions in the rain.' Somerville cast him a curious look. 'You have a new pair of shoes,' Holmes observed. I have observed the box in the corner containing your receipt. Is it possible that your previous pair were destroyed in the mire of a foul London night? Allow me three days and I will return your play, but first I need to know what you were doing in Highgate cemetery at two o'clock in the morning.' Somerville looked as lost as Lear on the heath.

'What possible business is it of yours,' he growled, 'where I go and with whom I speak? I ought to have you all arrested.'

'On what possible charge?' asked Holmes.

'Theft? Spying? Take your pick!'

'I am simply struggling to understand,' stated Holmes calmly, 'what business must be conducted after midnight in a cemetery.'

'You are a resourceful fellow, Mr Holmes,' he said, in rather menacing tones, 'I will give you that. Now listen; I am a reasonable man. I have one wish and one wish only, and that is that the play is returned. I am prepared to grant you forty eight hours to return the play with no questions asked before I turn the matter over to my associates. I do hope, for all your sakes, that any unpleasantness can be avoided. I suggest you begin your enquiries with Mr Arthur Tickler.'

'This Mr Tickler,' said Holmes. 'I assume it was he who supplied you with the quarto in the first place?'

'I have nothing more to say,' said Somerville, turning his back. 'Good evening gentlemen.'

FOUR

The Steel Trooper

'Will you be answering any of this, Holmes?'
I patted a thick wad of correspondence pinioned to the mantelpiece
with a jack knife. The cream envelope at the very top of the pile had
not yet even been opened. 'This one says War Office,' I remarked,
turning it over. 'It looks like official business.' My friend was
preoccupied with the workings of an ancient stove, upon which he
intended to brew a pot of coffee.
'Holmes?' I repeated. 'Are you listening?'
'None of my business is official, Watson,' corrected Holmes. 'That
is how I operate: unofficial and off the record. That is, of course,
until you place it on the record.'

Spenning had returned to his college to fulfil his teaching obligations
leaving Holmes and I once more with the run of 221b Baker Street.
Despite our new deadline, my friend seemed in no great hurry to
track down Mr Tickler.
'I have a suggestion,' I said brightly. 'Instead of tinkering with that
contraption, why don't we just ask Mrs Hudson to bring us our
coffee? It could be here in five minutes.'
'Whatever for? In a moment or two, we will have a ready supply of
our own. It's just a matter of adjusting the valve, like so.' A washer
dropped to the floor and rolled under my armchair.
'You've been at it for over an hour,' I protested.
'A little patience,' Holmes sighed, with just a trace of exasperation,
'is a small price for a decent cup of coffee.' It was then, I realised
that Mrs Hudson was standing in the doorway.
'A parcel for you, Mr Holmes,' she announced. 'It was delivered by
one of those little urchins. A remarkable little beggar he was too.'
'One of the Baker Street Irregulars, no doubt,' I ventured.
'No I don't believe so, doctor,' she said, placing the parcel on the
coffee table. 'I know them all too well. Must be one of the new ones.
But then, beneath all that grime, I doubt his own mother would know
him. He had a nasty cut across his chin too. Poor soul. Sh   all I
bring up the coffee?'

'No thank you,' Holmes replied curtly.

'Yes please,' I corrected.

'Very good, doctor.' My friend continued to tinker with his device.

'Well,' I said, at length. 'Are you going to open the parcel? I'm afraid it won't fit on the mantelpiece.' He removed the bolt, which was gripped between his teeth.

'Why don't you do the honours, Watson?'

I snipped the string then carefully sliced the brown wrapping with Holmes' pearl handled paper knife. Inside were two wooden boxes, each fashioned from polished mahogany.

'I haven't forgotten your birthday again, have I, Holmes?' I joked, while I performed this work.

'Birthdays are merely units of decay,' pronounced Holmes, still refusing to give up on his stove. 'You know very well that I never celebrate them, unless there happens to be a serviceable production of Twelfth Night.'

'Very well,' I reasoned, 'then I believe someone has just bought you a new pair of shoes. Perhaps a late thank you from the insufferable tenor we assisted in Chelsea?' I cleared away the remaining paper.

'Why do you say shoes?' enquired Holmes. 'It could equally be a set of bookends or a pair of revolvers.'

'One box is marked LEFT and the other RIGHT.'

'Most singular,' remarked Holmes, his curiosity stirred.

'On the contrary,' I parried. 'There are two boxes.'

'You deprive the London stage of your wit, Watson.'

'Well, what shall it be,' I asked again, 'left or right?'

Holmes lowered his spanner and walked over to examine the caskets. I saw a flash in his eyes that suggested he saw the prospect of a new case, or even, perhaps, a case within a case.

'I am naturally suspicious, Watson,' he said. 'As anyone would be who has handed a man over to a   hanging judge. Criminals have associates and regardless what you think about honour among thieves, some remain strangely loyal to the end. Favours repay other favours even when the protagonist is feeding the worms. And vengeance has an allure all of its own.'

'You don't suspect some explosive device?'

My friend lifted the box marked RIGHT, weighed in his hand, examined it carefully in the light and sniffed the lid.

'It was packed by an unmarried man with small hands,' he said. 'He prepared this box first. He is a cigar smoker and a fellow violinist.'

'It is as if you watched him at work.'

'Nonsense. It is simplicity itself. He has told us as clearly as if he has written a note. You will see the alignment of the fingerprints; the relative position of the thumb and the curiously blank fingertips where the calluses have formed.'

'But what of this claim that he is unmarried.'

'There,' said Holmes, angling the box for my benefit. You can see for yourself the clear print of the whole ring finger on the left hand. No wedding ring. The minute traces of cigar ash carry the unmistakable signature and scent of the Gurkha brand.' For a moment he peered intently at the base of the box, presented it to the light then quickly compared it with the other.

'A clue?' I asked.

'Too early to say.'

'But is there any danger?'

'Danger is everywhere, Watson,' my friend declared and flipped open the lid.

It was to Holmes' credit that he did not drop the box. Inside, on a lining of purple velvet was a severed human hand. My friend lowered the casket to the table and sat down in his armchair, peering intently at the extremity.

'The right hand of an adult male,' he said. 'He was already dead when it was removed. Am I correct, Watson?'

'Yes,' I spluttered.

'Come now,' chastened Holmes. 'You must have attended a hundred autopsies. This can't be such a shock.'

'Something of a surprise, though, would you not admit?'

'Granted, Watson,' he nodded. 'Now,' he continued in a matter of fact way, 'I would say it was a well-built man of forty; a Spaniard or Italian.'

'No note or letter?' I asked.

'None.'

'And we can guess at the contents of the second box.'

'You know my opinion of guesswork, Watson,' he frowned. 'That is a sport they play at Scotland Yard. We are engaged in another business entirely.'

Holmes fetched a cigar from the coal scuttle, no doubt prompted by the alluring scent of the Gurkha lingering on the wood. He did not appear to be in an especial hurry to open the second casket, and if I did not know him better, I would say he was enjoying the suspense.
'Well I suppose it's my turn,' I said and reached out for the box. I lifted the catch and opened the lid. My nerve proved not as steely as Holmes'. I cried out and instinctively withdrew my arm. With lightening reactions, my friend caught the box mid-flight, but not before its contents spilled to the floor. I stared in horror.

A mechanical hand, anatomically correct in every respect writhed inside the box, unfurling and flexing its fingers before tightening into a fist. It repeated the motion several times, before slowing to a stop.
'Watson!' my friend cried. 'Calm yourself! It is nothing but a child's toy; a simple clockwork mechanism. You are easily rattled today.' I continued to stare at the hand.
'It is uncanny,' I whispered. 'That is no plaything.' Perhaps for my benefit, Holmes returned the object to its case and closed the lids of both caskets.
'A singular morning, Watson,' Holmes remarked. 'In the absence of any other explanation, perhaps you would be so good as to pass me the letter from the War Office you found on the mantelpiece.' I lit a cigar of my own, then with some difficulty, removed the blade from the centre of the letter. I read aloud.

Mr Sherlock Holmes Esq.

Dear Sir,

I understand that as London's pre-eminent consulting detective you are constantly engaged. But I write to you by way of last resort and beg that you give my case priority.

On Tuesday last I received a letter from an acquaintance from my school days suggesting a meeting. Thinking it impolite to refuse, I agreed to a short interview at the War Office.

While in my company, the man, a Mr Aesop Bell, whom I did not recognise in the slightest, demonstrated an unusual machine for which he made the most extraordinary claims. While all good sense should have told me to send him on his way, he lured me into a rash business transaction, which I now wish to reverse. I wrote to him and begged to be released from our agreement.

This morning, by way of reply, I received two boxes, which I will send for your appraisal. I sincerely hope that you read this letter first to avoid the unpleasant shock I myself received upon opening them. Inside you will find a pair of hands; one mechanical, one human.

The nature of the transaction and my personal acquaintance with the man prevent me from seeking assistance from either my superiors or the police.

I therefore seek your urgent council to avoid public disgrace, financial ruin and the certain loss of my commission.

I will call upon your office at 10 o'clock on Friday morning.

Very truly yours,

Captain Hercules Winter

Retiring his cigar to the ashtray, Holmes ventured over to his volumes of biographies. Heaving down the file containing the entries with the letter B, he turned to the appropriate page.

'Well, Watson, we have an Edgar Bell and a Phillip Bell,' he said, running his slender finger down the entries. 'Those morally, and now financially bankrupt brothers caught selling shares in a non-existent gold mine, but no Aesop. It appears this man has yet to make his mark in criminal circles, or more likely, that he has succeeded in avoiding attention entirely.' We have a half hour before the captain arrives and I suggest using the interval to ensure these splendid cigars do not go to waste. As a military man, I expect him to appear precisely when he says he will. Let us not squander the time remaining in idle chatter.'

Exactly thirty minutes we heard the familiar jangle of the door below. Holmes had entered that strange hypnotic state, peculiar to him, neither waking or sleeping, during which he smoked with heavy lids, peering into the mid distance, considering I believed, the strange events of the morning, balancing fact with supposition; observation with deduction. At the sound of the bell he was roused into action. He leapt to the window and peered down into the street.
'Yes, there he is now.'

The captain was not the man I expected. To begin with the most painfully obvious point, he was almost the definition of half a man. As a result of some misadventure, he had managed to lose both his left arm and his right leg. In every other respect, he was a dashing, moustachioed officer of thirty five. His jaw was firm, his nose proudly Trojan in aspect, and he had a gleam in his eyes that remained undimmed despite his notable setbacks.

'Captain Winter,' said Holmes, 'we have been expecting you.' The officer examined the unholy mess that concealed the floor of our sitting room, registering his silent displeasure. 'Forgive me,' added Holmes, following the man's gaze. 'We never clear up for visitors and I am entirely to blame for the disorder. My long suffering friend, Dr Watson has long since given up trying to reform me. Now tell me, how is that new cane of yours? The old one was too short, was it not?' Winter stared at Holmes and then back at his walking stick.
'As a matter of fact it is new,' he confessed. 'The old one gave me terrible back pain.'
'I note,' Holmes remarked, 'that the sole of your shoe has been lowered to accommodate the shorter stick. Alas, this has still not provided sufficient compensation. I also note that nasty blister on your hand where you had to lean upon it has not yet entirely healed.'
'It is of no consequence,' he said. 'Now I see that my parcel arrived safely.'

'Delivered by hand,' I quipped. Both Holmes and Winter peered at me.

'Perhaps,' I added hastily, 'you would like to take a seat?'

The soldier leant his silver tipped cane against the writing desk and briefly inspected the framed portrait of General Gordon.

'No finer soldier has ever lived,' he remarked. 'He believed in reincarnation, you know. Odd thing for a practical man like him, don't you think? Still, who knows? Perhaps he is one of those ten year old boys running down there in the street. What's your view on the matter?'

'I have no proof of reincarnation,' replied Holmes. 'But the belief is a colourful one, and I am all for making the world a more interesting place. To live in a world without wonder is a poor existence.'

'Would you care for coffee?' I asked our guest.

'Thank you, but no,' he returned, observing the cold pot next to the dismantled stove. 'I would prefer an answer to the question I posed in my letter. Based on the evidence, are you willing to take my case?'

'I am a consulting detective,' remarked Holmes. 'It would be curious of me to decline one with features as singular as these.'

'Thank heavens,' said Winter, looking visibly relieved. 'I have no other recourse.'

'Now I require a full statement of the affair with particular attention to the details of your interview with Mr Bell.'

'By all means,' agreed the captain.

'Before you begin,' my friend added, peering at him through hooded eyes. 'Am I correct in assuming that you were bullied as a child by this Aesop Bell?' The Captain looked astonished.

'Yes or no?' questioned Holmes.

'Yes, but . . . how?'

'It makes perfect sense. You had no kinship with this fellow or contact with him since your schooldays. You can hardly spare the time for the meeting, and yet something compelled you to agree to meet him.' Winter's eyes smouldered.

'Yes,' he snapped. 'He was the perfect devil of a boy. Well, what of it? That's ancient history now. And besides, I do not believe it was the same man.'

'Perhaps not,' returned Holmes. 'But is it not possible that your new acquaintance knew something of your history with Aesop Bell?'

'Will you allow me to begin?' Winter asked in exasperation.

'By all means,' answered my friend.

'I was working at my papers, arranging for a consignment of Martini-Henri rifles to be despatched to Colonel Sir Francis Scott. You will be aware, gentlemen, that he and his expeditionary Force are presently engaged in Africa on the Gold Coast.' I nodded.

'Go on,' pressed Holmes.

'It was at that moment that my batman announced that my visitor had arrived, some minutes early. Before I could issue instructions to detain him while I completed my duties, the man appeared at my door. Beside him was an enormous wooden crate on a wheeled contraption. It seemed stupendous that he had managed to get the consignment up the stairs to my office on the third storey.

'"It has been some time, Winter," declared Bell. He was a short, swarthy, man, somewhat Napoleonic in stature. He had the unswerving confidence of an undefeated general and the shiftiness of a cove. His hair too was like the Frenchman's: dark and thinning, fastened to his scalp with sweat.

"I do not recognise you, sir," I informed him, rising to my feet; or rather my foot.

"The years," he began, noting my obvious deficiencies. "Have not been kind to either of us."

"Then tell me about old Hargreaves," I demanded. He was a notorious master at Ludlow.

"That old bluffer!" he cried. "I remember him flashing the gab. Fancied he knew a thing or two. But he was deaf as a post. You remember that time his back was turned? We all cleared out and he didn't notice until we were long gone. He had our hide for that." I smiled despite myself at this memory.

"Well, Aesop," I said relaxing back into my chair. "It has been a long time. Have a drink won't you?" I poured him a tumbler of brandy and we settled down to talk. I noticed that he had a strange tic; he blinked incessantly, as if he was constantly dazzled by some bright light.

"So," I began, closing my file of papers. "What brings you here?"

"I heard about your misadventures in the Sudan. An old trooper told me you are one of the bravest men he has ever known."

"That was gracious of him. Do you recall his name?"

"Bennett. Christian Bennett."

"I know the man. He has a splendid singing voice and magnificent whiskers, if my memory serves."

"The very man."

"Please proceed."

"I have developed a line of work which may be of interest to you, both professionally and personally. What I am about to tell has the potential to change the world. It will transform modern warfare and secure the British Empire for centuries to come."

"Quite a claim," I put in, lighting a cigarette and hardly bothering to suppress a smile.

"For too long," he said grandiosely, "our expansionist policies have been carried out at the expense of British lives. Wellington himself was sickened at the way his men died in square at Waterloo."

"The world has moved on since then," I said, tapping the table impatiently. "Now if you don't mind coming to the nub of the matter..." Bell's eyes flashed with anger.

"Was the man who invented gunpowder given such sort shrift?"

"I imagine," I remarked, "he came to the point a little more quickly."

"Very well," he glowered. "I can see that a demonstration will be necessary." He pulled a length of string attached to the front of the crate allowing one side to fall to the floor. Inside was a bulky object covered by a large tarpaulin. "May I present," he said, gripping the edge of the cloth, "the future." Like a travelling showman, he whipped off the cloth to reveal a large steel box.

"What have you brought me," I scoffed. "A tin of bully beef?"

"Patience!" he demanded.

"I have an exceptionally large workload," I retorted, rising to my feet. "I am afraid you have exhausted my patience, sir, school chum or not." Glaring at me, he pulled a lever on the side of the box. I heard a whirring of cogs and a spherical object began to rise from the top. Presently, I saw the iron cast of a man's face and torso. To my horror, I recognised it as a likeness of Trooper Bennett; the very man we had just been discussing.

"What is the meaning of this?"

"Ah, Winter, do I now detect some interest?" he cried, delighting in his own machine. He pulled another lever and a pair of arms unfolded outwards. He turned to address the machine.

"Trooper Bennett!" he commanded. There was a clanking and the neck and head turned slowly towards Bell. "Trooper Bennett," he called again. "Shake my hand!"

I watched in some disbelief as the right arm slowly raised. The fingers of a horrible mechanical hand placed themselves in Bell's own.

"A marvel is he not?"

"A grotesque toy," I returned. "This can hardly have Bennett's approval. He is a straightforward man and would have nothing to do with such foolishness."

'I regret to inform you,' Bell went on, with mock sincerity, "that the man you knew as Bennett is no longer with us; at least in his old form." I was aghast. "No doubt you heard he suffered a spear wound to the stomach at Abu Klea?"

"I had not," I informed him curtly.

"He held on bravely, but the wound proved fatal. With blessing of his commanding officer, I took this cast from his face after he was repatriated.

"I can hardly imagine you informed him of your intended purpose."

"My purpose," Bell said in defiance, "is that no British soldier need ever again perish on the battlefield. Allow me to continue my demonstration." He gestured towards a ceremonial sword that hung on the wall. "May I?" I nodded my assent, curious more than anything.

He held the sword in front of the automaton and then went to strike it. Immediately its right arm lifted to parry the blow, the other seizing it from Bell. Before I could react, Bell reached into his jacket and withdrew a revolver.

"Good God, man," I shouted. "What in heaven's name?" Before I could finish my sentence, he had fired at point black range. The bullet ricocheted across the room and lodged in the far wall, but there was barely a mark on the machine's gleaming body. My batman rushed into the room.

"I heard a shot," he began.

"That's quite all right, Briggs," I said. "Just a misfire."

62

"Well?" asked Bell after Briggs had left us.

"I think you're a madman," I said. "But by the same token, I can't say I'm not impressed. Now tell me how the trick is done."

"There is no trick," he replied, "only science. Inside this machine are a series of densely wound coils; working on the same principle as clockwork. The mechanism is so advanced that five minutes of winding supplies the machine with sufficient potency for a day's worth of activity."

"But how is it sentient?" I asked.

"It senses movement and light, exactly like a photographic camera."

"And your voice command?"

"It works on a system of sound vibration. Certain frequencies deliver particular responses." I carefully inspected the machine, looking beneath the table for sign of a stooge hiding inside. But there was nothing beneath or behind the head and torso.

"I know what you're thinking," Bell smiled. "I assure you this is no circus of the strange. We are not a double act. He lifted a hatch near the top of the machine's forehead and ran the blade of the sword clean through." I frowned, baffled by what I had just witnessed.

"And how do you explain the bullet?"

"The metal casing is a new alloy: Lundorium. It is ten times more formidable as steel." By this time I was dumbfounded. It appeared nothing short of wizardry.

"Captain Winter," Bell declared, seeing that now was the moment to reveal his hand. "I represent a consortium of businessmen and engineers. Using technology pioneered in secret by the Swiss, we are prepared to offer this machine to the government who offers the highest price. Naturally, patriotism compels me to give first refusal to the British."

"You mentioned some personal advantage," I added. "I sincerely hope you are not about to offer me a bribe."

"Nothing of the kind," laughed Bell, his arm around the shoulder of his metal monster. "I merely wanted to inform you that our organisation has used the same advances to pioneer prosthetic limbs with the same capabilities."

'A singular offer!' Holmes remarked in his laconic way.

'You can imagine I was much moved by this. The machine was

63

remarkable in every respect and I did not doubt that he could do as much for me.'

"And what is it," I demanded, "you want in return?"

"Simply an undertaking from the War Office to commission 100 units."

"And the cost?"

"It cannot so easily be put into pounds, shillings and pence. But a fee of five thousand pounds will allow me to take this off the tables of the war rooms of Europe. When you are delighted with your order, we can discuss mass production. The prosthetic limbs would be a gratuity. There is one more thing. I require an immediate answer, or I board the first ship to Calais and from there I proceed to Berlin."

I was thrown into turmoil; I could see that it would be remarkable benefit to our war machine. Furthermore, I saw a future for myself fully restored to life.

"It is not so easy," I cried. "The War Office does not move as swiftly as that. There are procedures..."

"Then I regret," he said, beginning to pack away the steel man, "that we have little more to say to each other."

"Wait," I said, staying his arm, "I can write a cheque for a thousand pounds now and wire you the remainder when the paperwork is complete." He paused. "Make it two thousand and we have a deal." I implored him to reduce the amount, but he would not move on the sum. I finally acquiesced and hurriedly wrote him a cheque. He gave me an address where I could reach him.

'You did not,' enquired Holmes, 'consult with another officer?'

'I did not,' he said, staring out of the window into the sunlit Baker Street. 'If truth be known, I did not want to share credit for this remarkable discovery.' Holmes winced.

'I do not sense a happy ending to this tale.'

'Nor I,' added the captain. 'Two hours later I realised how utterly rash and foolish I had been. My judgement had been clouded by a delirium of hope. I hastily wrote a letter cancelling my order and requesting the return of my cheque. By return, I received the parcel you see before you.' Holmes peered into the middle distance while he waited for Winter to conclude his statement.

'You find yourself in an astonishing predicament, captain, but your case is not a hopeless one. You will know yourself how Rome recovered after three successive defeats at Cannae at the hands of Carthage. They came back to become the rulers of the known world. You too can restore your position.' Winter did not look entirely consoled by this lesson from history.

'It is clear,' I put in, 'that this man is a charlatan and a confidence trickster.'

'Far from it,' scolded Holmes. 'We know little about him or his invention. What we have heard is impressive enough. There is some dark purpose at work here, Watson. It warrants our investigation. If this pair of hands are the bait, then we are the trout swimming up to take it.' Holmes leapt to his feet, seizing his hat and cane. 'Captain, do you still have the address?' He confirmed as much.

'Watson,' see if you can find us a brougham. 'Let us see if man can defeat machine!'

Leaving instructions with Mrs Hudson that we would be back by dinner, we negotiated the seventeen stairs to street level in ponderous fashion. Winter winced as he lowered himself down each step refusing all offers of assistance. While I lingered at the front door, I heard a sharp whistle from the street. Holmes appeared to be taking advantage of the delay by seeking out that irrepressible scallywag, Wiggins, the head of the Baker Street Irregulars. My friend scribbled a note and pressed it into his hand, followed closely by a coin of the realm. I could see Wiggins attempting to bargain for a higher rate, before Holmes sent him on his way with a clip around the ear.

Clattering through the streets of south London, it was as if we were travelling through a carnival or wedding; pink and white blossom burst from the trees. I caught Winter staring at a group of soldiers lounging outside a piano sellers at Clapham Junction. It was not hard to read his mind; no doubt he was considering his life before his injuries. Holmes looked equally lost in thought; his imagination charged with the possibilities of this new case. One thing troubled me.

'You cannot possibly believe our man will still be at the address?'

'Why ever not?' asked Holmes.

'He has his thousand pounds. Why risk arrest for the sake of more? Under normal circumstances, surely the severed hand alone would be enough to bring down the full force of the law.'

'These are normal circumstances,' said Holmes. 'And you forget Watson, that he has Winter in his power. Besides, there is the potential for considerable financial advantage.' He leaned forward in his seat and peered with delight through the window. 'Gentleman,' he said, 'we approach our destination. I believe we are travelling once again in the footsteps of our Roman invaders; this is the old Chichester road; they knew it as Stane Street.'

The carriage veered into a side street and we found ourselves in front of a row of formidable town houses. The brougham slowed to a stop and the horses neighed and whinnied their disapproval, as if dissuading us from getting out. Winter declined our help, lowering himself to the ground and leaning hard on his cane. He was a proud man who endured his difficulties without complaint.

The garden was overgrown, the boot scraper rusted and paint peeled from the window sills. But still the house had a certain faded grandeur. Certainly the neighbouring properties looked prosperous enough. The steel knocker I noticed was of a singular design; it resembled a horse's head with a spectacular headdress of feathers.

'We should be on our guard,' I said feeling the reassuring weight of my service revolver in my jacket pocket.

'Expect the unexpected,' said Holmes, 'and you will be surprised by nothing.' He then knocked three times. The street was almost deserted; a cat skulked by the front gate.

Just as we were about to turn away, I noticed a shadow in the corner of my eye. A vagrant with a bristled chin and decaying blue frock coat shambled up to us. One of his eyes was half closed. With the other he peered quizzically at Holmes.

'You don't want to be knocking there,' he muttered. 'No good will come of it. Now how's about a bit of kindness for an old showman? Ignatius Solomon's the name. Here's my card.' My friend took the old card, glanced at it, then handed it back. He peered at the odd fellow with a mixture of curiosity and amusement.

'I thank you for your warning, Mr Solomon' he said evenly, indicating for me to part with another coin, 'however we have an interview at this house that cannot be deferred.' The man received his shilling as if it were a prized jewel, peering at it on his palm.

'Then, gentlemen,' he said at last, making a facetious little bow, 'I shall leave you to your business.' He scurried away down the path. I glanced at Holmes, then back at the door.

'What is London, Watson,' my friend remarked, 'if not full of colour.'

Presently the door swung open, as if of its own accord. The interior seemed conventional enough for a middle class house in these parts; there was a black and white tiled floor, a hat stand and polished wooden banister. Dark oil paintings adorned the walls, including I noticed, a reproduction of the famous painting of Ophelia by Sir John Everett Millais.

'A somewhat gloomy welcome,' I remarked.

We made our way warily through the house and into the drawing room. No sooner had we entered when the door closed behind us. I had the eerie sensation that we were being watched.

'I don't like this one bit, Holmes,' I confessed. Winter, I noticed, swinging forward on his crutch, was wielding a revolver of his own.

'Bell!' he shouted. 'It is I, Captain Winter.' At that moment, the grandfather clock struck the hour and I leapt a clear foot into the air.

'Calm yourself, Watson,' said Holmes. 'There are three of us and only one of him. Strength in numbers!' At that moment the far door swung open and a strange apparition appeared before us.

The gleaming steel head and torso that Winter had spoken of, approached us, borne on a wheeled cabinet of some description. Its movement was accompanied by a strange, whirring clockwork sound. It came directly towards Winter, stopping barely a foot from him. There was a clunk from somewhere inside the chest cavity and the distant, scratchy sound of a recorded voice began to play.

'Greetings, Winter,' the voice began. 'And greetings to your friends too.' My blood froze at this.

'A phonograph cylinder!' Holmes exclaimed. 'Marvellous!'

'I am pleased that you have reconsidered my offer. It still stands, although now, because of the time lost, I must insist that the full sum of five thousand pounds is paid. For this I am willing to provide the first twenty units.' The voice fell silent.

'What am I to do?' whispered Winter.

'Do you wish to place the order?' asked Holmes.

'I know what you are thinking,' the voice continued. 'Am I still willing to provide the prosthetic limbs?' Winter and Holmes exchanged a look. 'I am a man of my word.'

The first door open once again and a second machine entered. It moved directly forward to a wooden chest, which sprang open to reveal a metal arm and leg.

'This is monstrous!' Winter cried. 'I cannot bear to see this good soldier's face in a steel mask. It is the living dead.'

'It is what Trooper Bennett would have wanted,' the voice said, as if it had registered Winter's remark.

'This is trickery!' I shouted. 'Holmes, unmask these fiends. Where are they?' I spun around looking for the controlling mind.

'Bell!' I shouted, 'where are you hiding!'

'I see you have made yourselves at home, gentlemen.'

We spun around to be greeted by the sight of a magnificent woman sailing into the room. In expansive green skirts, white cuffs that bloomed at her wrists and a bonnet like a main sail, she resembled in almost every respect a ship of the Spanish Armada separated from the rest of the fleet. She was a little over sixty, of refined stock and held her chin in the air as if permanently inspecting the ceiling for signs of damp. The beginnings of a wattle was forming on her neck.

'Forgive us, madam,' Holmes began in that wonderful ingratiating way he had with women. He gave a little deferential bow. 'We are here at the invitation of a Mr Aesop Bell.'

'Then it is my nephew you seek,' she declared. 'I imagine he is trying to interest you in these tiresome machines.'

'Exactly so,' Holmes smiled. 'Does Mr Bell live here with you?'

'Only when he is not gallivanting across the continent. I have given up trying to keep track of his comings and goings. I keep my mind on higher things.' She made her way to an armchair, removed her shoes, folded herself down on one of the cushions then clicked her fingers. At once, one of the machines moved to a drinks cabinet, extended its arms, lifted a jug with one hand and a glass with the other and poured her a measure of gin. Dutifully, it brought the glass to her side.

'I suppose,' she admitted, 'they have their uses. "There is nothing like staying at home for real comfort." Do help yourselves gentlemen.'

'Did your nephew leave any instructions,' asked Winter.

'Of what kind?' she snapped.

'Relating to an order for these machines?' The woman placed a finger to her lips as if trying to remember.

'Austen,' I spluttered.

'I'm sorry?' questioned Winter.

'You quoted Jane Austen,' I repeated. '"There is nothing like staying at home..."'

'Excellent,' the woman congratulated, her eyes brightening. 'Do you read Jane?'

'A little,' I confessed, 'although, I confess I prefer science fiction.'

'"Our half of the world,"' she quoted, '"cannot understand the pleasures of the other."'

'I wonder,' I added, perhaps unwisely, 'if she considered ever setting a story in space?'

'Jane Austen in space?' she repeated, somewhat appalled. 'That, I very much doubt.'

Holmes seemed very much amused by her condescending manner.

'Tell me,' asked Holmes. 'Do you think of Hamlet as a man obsessed by his mother?'

'Why do you ask,' she said, suddenly interested.

'Just that you will be playing Gertrude shortly and you are bound to be giving the matter some consideration.'

'Whatever gave you that idea,' she asked coquettishly, taking a sip of her gin.

'There is a copy of the play on the table and the creases indicate where it has been left open: at Gertrude's soliloquies. Besides, it is the only conceivable part for a woman of your vintage.'

69

'Of my vintage!' she scoffed. 'Mr Holmes, it is only a few years since I played Ophelia.'

'Ah, so you know who I am, then?' said Holmes in delight. She blushed a little.

'Well, yes, I am familiar with some of your cases,' she admitted. 'I confess I enjoyed reading about that ridiculous business of the blue carbuncle.'

'A little low brow for your taste,' I suggested.

'Let me call it a guilty pleasure, doctor.'

'Enough!' cried Winter, glowering at the woman. 'Your nephew has stolen a sum of money and I demand its return.'

'That is not,' she returned imperiously, 'the version of the story I heard.'

'Then where is he? Perhaps he can explain himself.'

'He is engaged on business,' the woman said crisply. 'I am not at liberty to say where. I have no other information and if you have nothing else to add, then I would suggest you leave. This conversation has suddenly become a good deal less amusing.'

'We will not leave until this matter is resolved,' declared Winter.

I became aware of a quiet whirring sound. The steel trooper directly behind the woman, previously inanimate, now began to move slowly towards her.

'Holmes,' I shouted, 'look out!'

The automaton raised its arms and closed them around the woman's waist. She shrieked in terror.

'Do something !' she cried. 'Unhand, me, you beastly machine!'

Instinctively, I drew my service revolver. Winter too, hobbled forward, although I was unsure as to what purpose. Holmes himself I noticed, remained curiously unmoved.

'I am sorry that it has come to this,' we heard the recorded voice resume. 'But my aunt, as you have discovered, is a dreadful bore. She is also entirely expendable. If you do not provide the full amount of five thousand pounds, I am rather afraid that she will suffer as a result. I will give you an hour to raise the necessary funds. You have seen what my machines can do. Please do not attempt to involve the police or any other authority.' The woman fell limp in the metal arms.

'Confound it, Holmes,' Winter cried, striking the table in anger. 'We have no choice.'

I peered at my friend, awaiting his response. Presently, he broke into a broad grin. He began to clap, slowly, then rose to his feet in a one man standing ovation.

'Bravo!' he cried. 'Truly, it was first rate. Watson, you will see nothing finer this year on the West End stage.'

I peered at my friend, believing that he had finally taken leave of his senses.

'You can dispense with the act now, Miss Kemp,' he advised. I saw her open a single eye, glance around for a moment, before shutting it again quickly.

'Watson,' said Holmes, striding forward in that masterful way of his. 'Allow me to introduce Miss Henrietta Kemp, or as her public knows her, Patricia Wells. Her Ophelia was indeed magnificent. I saw it myself as a boy. She carried her terrible fate with great grace. Fewer know however, that she is in fact Captain Winter's mother.'

'His mother?' I stuttered, utterly bemused. Winter was ashen faced.

'Captain Winter, you should be ashamed of yourself. Not only have you destroyed your reputation as one of the brave men of the nation, but you have dragged your delightful mother into your rotten scheme.'

'What scheme?' I demanded.

'A scheme to extort a vast sum of money from the War Office.'

'But what of Aesop Bell?' I demanded. 'Surely he is the villain of the piece?' Again, Holmes flashed his thin smile.

'There is no Aesop Bell.' I felt my jaw slacken. Not for the first time in the company of my brilliant friend, I found myself dumbfounded.

Winter poured himself a measure of whiskey and drank it down.

'The captain here,' explained Holmes, 'is a man of considerable ingenuity; he is also possessed of a theatrical streak himself.'

'But how…' I began. My friend selected a cigarette from a silver tray and put it to his lips. He offered them around the group, but

71

received no response.

'As you like,' he shrugged. 'My suspicion was first aroused by the boxes containing the appendages. You recall that I remarked that they could easily contain a pair of revolvers? Well in fact, that is exactly the case. They were ceremonial presentation cases for retired officers. Winter, as a procurement officer had access to a ready supply. If he had inspected them more closely, they carried the letter WO on the base, along with a serial number. The numbers were in direct sequence.'

'Naturally, it also puzzled me that such a man with a name as distinctive as Aesop Bell should have escaped my attention these many years. You will remember, Watson, that he does not feature in my archive or volumes of biography. In my experience, the criminal mind invariably enjoys a certain level of notoriety.'

'But there are witnesses!' I said. 'We need only to walk over to the War Office to take the testimony of Winter's own batman. It is a simple case of finding out if Bell visited that day.'

'I have already taken that liberty,' smiled Holmes. 'You remember my brief conference with Wiggins; I left him with a series of precise instructions and a small fortune in bribes. The first was to obtain a facsimile of the relevant page of the visitors' book at the War Office. I have the copy of it in my hand.'

'Miraculous!' I exclaimed.

'Nonsense. It was nothing more than diligence. No man named Bell visited that day. I saw Winter clenching his fist as Holmes continued his homily.

'You recall the brush with the vagrant outside the door?' he asked. 'If you had observed more carefully, you would have noticed it was none other than my old friend Shinwell Johnson whom you know that I employ from time to time for such matters. He brought the evidence directly to me. He was also able to supply the name of the owner of this house. I understand that this took a little more persuasion, but the name on the deed is none other than Captain Hercules Winter himself. Is that not true, captain?'

'You are a fool, Sherlock Holmes,' he sneered.

'I have been called many things,' my friend replied coldly, 'but never that.'

Mrs Kemp (or was it Mrs Winter?) was following this discussion with interest from the arms of the steel trooper. All trace of fear had left her.

'You underestimate my son, Mr Holmes,' she warned.

'On the contrary,' said Holmes. 'What remains unexplained is the mysterious technology he has acquired. What secret lies behind these automatons?'

'That, you will never discover,' cried Winter leaning on his crutch and backing away from us.

'In any event, Captain Winter,' cautioned Holmes, 'I recommend you take great care. Here is a man, Watson, eaten up with bitterness and self loathing. Unable to bear his disfigurements he constructs a scheme to defraud the very government that sent him to fight.'

'But,' I replied, 'we have seen these machines with our own eyes.'

'No doubt you have heard, Winter,' Holmes declaimed, 'of that piece of wisdom from the great German, Nietzsche. "He who fights with monsters might take care lest he thereby becomes a monster."'

Holmes advanced fearlessly on the machine gripping the actress. He seized a panel at the top of the breastplate and tore it away. The mask and torso fell away and clattered to the floor.

I was aghast. Staring out was the face of a ghost, or at least that was my impression. His skin was deeply lined and had a deathly pallor. His eyes were yellow and rheumy and utterly devoid of hope. But most startling of all, a great part of his forehead was missing. He stared back at us expressionless. It was only then that I realised that he bore the same face as the steel trooper.

'Good god!' I cried. 'It is Christian Bennett!'

'The very same,' confirmed Holmes.

'You poor devil,' I said, overcome with pity. 'Holmes, you must help me extricate him from this contraption.'

'Wait!' shouted Winter.

'You are a monster, sir!' I bellowed.

'Not at all,' he said coldly. 'I rescued this man from the gutter. But you are right in one respect. Trooper Bennett did not die in a foreign field, but it may have been better for him if he had. He lost both legs and his health had already gone to ruin. I took him in and offered him a business proposition. If he was willing to be my accomplice, I would keep him from the streets. His unique physical attributes made him ideal for my demonstrations. The wound to his head was particularly useful in disproving any foul play.'

'Then these machines are a sham,' I said.

'Do not be so hasty,' said Winter. 'I have pioneered certain advances. Yet I realised that if I was to secure my orders, I would need to accelerate my programme.'

'You will have noticed Watson,' put in Holmes, 'that only one machine was capable of complex functions. The others are mere toys drawn by invisible wires.'

'This is outrageous,' I said. 'You are keeping this man prisoner.'

'Nonsense,' said Winter coolly. Trooper Bennett is permitted the occasional cigar. His deployment is unusual, I grant you, but he is merely following orders, as he has always done.'

'Is this true?' I asked of Bennett. He made no attempt to reply, his spirit clearly broken.

'I have heard enough,' I muttered. 'This man needs medical attention. Holmes, we should call Lestrade.'

'That will not be necessary,' said Winter with a certain *sang froid*. He aimed a gun directly at Holmes' head, then strolled over and placed a weapon in the trooper's hand. 'Bennett,' he cried, do not release my mother. That is an order.' He then turned to me, a cold sneer forming on his lips. His transformation from hero to villain it seemed, was now complete.

'Dr Watson,' he warned, I recommended that you keep you hand well away from that old service revolver of yours. Can I rely on you, as one old soldier to another? '

'No, you cannot rely on me,' I growled. 'I have borne my own wartime injuries without complaint, you should have done the same.'

'Injuries?' he scoffed. 'When a limb is blown off, that is when you can talk of an injury. Yours was nothing more than a Blighty wound.' As he spoke, he hobbled towards the open chest. He began to strap on the prosthetic arm and leg that lay there.

'You might well have turned your talents,' suggested Holmes, 'to providing such services to your fellow veterans.'

'I have cared for Bennett in my own way,' he protested, attaching the arm, which was skilfully fashioned from wood and steel. 'You forget, Mr Holmes, I am a businessman, not a charity worker.' By some means, I noticed, he was able to both bend the arm at the elbow and flex the fingers of the hand.

'Ingenious, is it not?' he smiled. A very different man stood before us.

'An impressive rehabilitation,' remarked Holmes. I could not help but agree.

Presently, there was a shattering of glass. Three or four policeman crashed through the bay window and bowled into the room. They were followed by the thin, austere Lestrade, who picked his way more carefully through the broken shards. He gazed around at the spectacle: Bennett, still strapped into his wooden cabinet, his steel body armour open like a door; Winter, himself, half man, half automaton; the aging actress now looking defiant.

'Why, Holmes,' he remarked drolly, 'this is bizarre even by your standards.' Before he could make his arrest however, Winter sprung forward with astounding agility. Two of the constables dived and missed him. Lestrade fired his pistol, but succeeded only in destroying a small statue.

'I say!' protested Mrs Kemp, 'that was Roman!' We saw Winter hurl himself through the open window and heard the clatter of his steel leg against the paving stone as he made his escape.

'We will speak further,' said Lestrade then disappeared through the window in Winter's wake.

By the time Holmes and I had returned to our rooms, the dying sun had turned Baker Street to gold. The windows and roof tiles glinted and molten rivers of light flowed across our hearthside rug. The stove still lay in pieces on the floor. The pile of correspondence, which remained unanswered on the mantelpiece looked no less forbidding.

'What secrets wait within those envelopes, Watson?' asked Holmes. 'What desperate spirits have inscribed the letters 221b in the hope that we may be able to assist them? We cannot help them all. Even if there was time left in the universe, I would not care to help them all. I am unable to work on the mundane, the common place. Mine is a magpie mind, attracted by oddity, by the brilliant, the strange and absurd. Call it a perversity, Watson, if you must.' I shook my head.

'I have just three questions,' I said, blowing on my tea. 'The easiest first, if I may?'

'Throw the spear, my dear Watson.'

'How did Lestrade know? Was he there all along?'

'Simplicity itself,' smiled Holmes. 'I sent Shinwell Johnson directly to Scotland Yard to summon him. Or rather, he glad-handed someone else to actually speak to Lestrade. Johnson would not dare set foot in that place himself.'

'All well and good,' I said, satisfied with the reply. 'Now the more singular puzzle. Why did Winter involve us in the first place? Why did he not simply steal the money?' Holmes smiled and sank deeper into his chair, his pipe smoke rising in a thick, white column.

'He required a reliable witness,' explained Holmes. 'If I could vouch that he gave up the money against his will, it would make Aesop Bell the villain of the piece. Winter could make his escape, then return at some future date, claiming he had been held against his will, his reputation intact.

'But what a perfect dullard he is, for believing he could outwit you.'

'Watson,' laughed Holmes, 'my dear Watson. Not everyone shares your good faith. You are truly a rare breed, my friend.' He gazed out of the window at the sheets of gold that coated the rooftops.

'Captain Hercules Winter is guilty of the sin of hubris,' my friend declared, 'that most Shakespearian flaw. Despite, his disabilities, he believes himself above all others. Pray that Lestrade brings him to swift justice, Watson, for I fear that he is capable of significant mischief. Still, this is not a wholly unsatisfactory end to the episode. Thanks to your connections, Watson, Trooper Bennett will now be safe in the care of the Sisters of Mercy. Mrs Winter I believe will be forgiven for her small part in the crime. Besides, it would be a great shame for the producer of her Hamlet to lose his Gertrude at such short notice.'

'But one last question remains, Holmes.'

'Yes?' he enquired.

'The hand,' I said.

'Ah, yes, the hand.'

'You and I will pay a visit to Highgate Cemetery in the morning, to see if we can return it to its rightful owner. Now do pass the Claret, Watson.'

FIVE

The Ghosts

'Lend a hand, Watson.'

I frowned at Holmes as he passed the wooden box to me. It was unlike him to make such a puerile remark, but nonetheless it seemed to please him immensely. A light mist hung over the West Cemetery at Highgate as if the spirits of the dead were themselves rising from the earth. The place was almost deserted. Our only company was a dour looking man with a grizzled face, black suit and cheap cigar smoking from his lip. He stood just beyond the gate, leaning heavily on a shovel. Quite reasonably, we took him for the gravedigger.

'A bit early to be visiting, gentlemen,' he said, eyeing us suspiciously.

'The gates are open are they not?' challenged Holmes.

'Certainly they are,' he growled back. 'So are you paying your respects or surveying a plot of your own? No flowers, I note.'

'My friend here,' explained Holmes 'is a student of architecture. I plan to show him the Circle of Lebanon.' The man nodded slowly, looking unconvinced.

'Yes,' I agreed, falling in with my friend's scheme. 'We thought we'd get here early to beat the crowds.'

'Crowds?' the man laughed. 'The crowds are under the ground.' He paused and surveyed the stones tangled in the ivy and grass. 'Well, they're not such a bad lot; they don't give me no trouble, anyway.' I caught him staring at the box under my arm. 'So what have you got there,' he asked. I was momentarily flummoxed.

'His breakfast,' Holmes smiled. 'Would you care for a cold sardine?'

We left the man to his duties and made our way into the cemetery. The path wended along an avenue of lush greenery, wet with morning dew. It was a place of sleeping angels, decaying stone and shy cherubim hiding in the long grass.

'Do you feel we're being watched?' I enquired.

'Only by the gold-crest and the cuckoo,' my friend returned cheerfully.

'What exactly are we looking for, Holmes?'

'We will know it when we see it,' he said. 'I am attempting to pinpoint the precise spot I lost Somerville that night after the theatre.'

We headed deeper into the labyrinth, Holmes glancing left to right into the undergrowth, scanning the names on the moss covered stones. Almost every monument was enveloped in ivy, the creepers curling around each stone bird, angel and vase. Presently I noticed a small red handkerchief tied to a vine, some sentimental token perhaps left for one of the deceased. Holmes saw it too and peered intently at the ground around it.

'A curious object to see in a cemetery,' I remarked. 'Perhaps it was a cold that finished him off?'

'Over there, Watson,' he whispered, then stepped off the path and into the trees.

The shadows of night still lingered in the darker corners and I was a little unnerved by the sound of our footsteps as we made our way through this city of ghosts. For here, surely, was man at his most pathetic, attempting to resist the horror of oblivion. But most of the names were now worn away; those monuments that remained were being slowly dragged back into their earth by the creeping fingers of weeds and vines. I glanced around to see if indeed we were being followed, then joined Holmes as he journeyed into the underworld.

My friend and I stepped over the slippery stone until we were both standing before a nondescript looking grave. Holmes tore away the ivy, then removing another handkerchief from his pocket, rubbed at it until we could make out the inscription.

SUSAN MACBETH
(1713-1764)
She should have died hereafter.

'Well, well,' remarked Holmes, standing back.
'A dismal epitaph,' I muttered.
'You think so?' he asked. 'Its author was held in some regard.'
'Really?' I asked. 'It seems rather mundane.'

'Perhaps that is because it has been truncated. It is a line from Macbeth, of course. "All our yesterdays have lighted fools the way to dusty death."'

I frowned. 'We seem truly haunted by the Bard of late,' I said. 'But this grave can have nothing to do with our enquiries. Look at the dates. The hand could not possibly have been preserved all these years.'

'Of course, you are right, Watson, unless of course, Susan Macbeth has another bedfellow.' I stared at my friend aghast.

'Truly, Holmes,' I said. 'I cannot stand this place.'

'Ours is a strange vocation, Watson, I grant you,' he admitted. 'Yet from the darkness we may glean some light. Now help me with this, there's a good fellow.'

The headstone stood at one end of a large stone casket. A great crack ran down the length of the lid and one side was partially caved in. Holmes pulled at the side slab and immediately it fell back on the grass to reveal a hollow interior. A field mouse scurried out of the darkness.

'Look there, Watson,' my friend said with satisfaction. 'The ground has been disturbed.' Sure enough the base was lined with freshly turned earth. 'That soil has not laid undisturbed for 120 hours,' he observed, 'let alone 120 years.'

'Surely this tells us all we need to know,' I said, somewhat hopefully. In truth, I knew that once Holmes was set on a course, he was unwavering.

'Come now, Watson, we have progressed this far, we may as well get to the heart of the matter, regardless how distasteful. It feels remiss now that we did not bring a shovel of some description.

'We could hardly have concealed a spade,' I reasoned.

'It is indeed a pity that we cannot call upon the services of our new friend.'

We scooped a few handfuls of dirt away with our hands, but it was soon clear the task was a hopeless one. I heard footsteps.

'Hush now, Watson, I do believe this is our man coming now.'

As if on have cue, the gravedigger came trudging up the path, looking this way and that as if searching for something. It occurred to me that, suspicious of our motives, he was shadowing us.

'Don't move, Watson,' Holmes urged. 'The best concealment is to remain completely still.' We relied then, on the dim light and the foliage to conceal our position. He moved a little way past us, and then, alerted perhaps by a minute sound, or sixth sense, he stopped. I held my breath; Holmes narrowed his eyes. The man then leant his shovel against a tree and left the path, venturing into the graves on the opposite side.

'Fortune smiles on us,' whispered Holmes. Then, as nimble as a fawn, he stepped lightly back across the grass, ivy and the broken graves to the path. He swiped the spade and just as swiftly returned. 'Now into the grave, Watson, quick as you like.'

I stared at my friend in horror.

'There is no time for argument!' he urged, then bundled me in and rolled in himself. Together we heaved up the stone slab on our left until Holmes, myself and the spade lay together, entombed.

For a time there was nothing but the sound of birdsong and the scratch of a rodent returning to its nest. Then we heard the low curse of the gravedigger.

'Blast it!' he cried. 'I swear this was the tree.' It must have seemed strange indeed for his spade to vanish in such a fashion. 'Which of you spirits have swiped it?' he demanded. We listened to the same silence. 'I don't mean you no harm,' he added in more emollient tones. 'I 'aint going to disturb you.'

Once more we heard the crunch of the gravel as the man retraced his steps. Inside the tomb the air was dank; a bitter combination of damp and Holmes' strong Persian tobacco. My friend lay deadly still, as if in some trance but I soon caught the reassuring flash of his eyes as they reflected the dim light. I breathed in short gasps, wary of an involuntary cough or sneeze.

'Do you think it's safe...' I began, before Holmes kicked me into silence. The footsteps were getting closer. I could hear his heavy boots on the grass and stones as his made his way towards us. Holmes gripped the spade in case we had to defend ourselves.

'Who are you?' the man roared. 'Grave robbers? Devil-worshippers?' Our situation was becoming parlous. 'I'll tell you what you are,' he called. 'Cowards! Come and face me like men.' I do not mind admitting I felt ashamed. He was a decent fellow going about his work.

It was a full hour before Holmes permitted us to rise from the dead. During that time, I reflected soberly from the darkness of my chamber on the sheer joy of existence; the feeling of the sunshine on the skin, the taste of a cooling cup of tea; the pleasing music of children laughing in the streets. As Holmes and I clambered out, stiffly surveying the graves and trees around us, I breathed deeply of the wonderful, sharp, clean air. The cumulous clouds suspended above me held an unimaginable beauty.

'If you don't mind me enquiring, Holmes,' I interrogated, 'what occupied your thoughts as we lay there?' He paused and gazed obliquely around him.

'I was making some mental notes,' he said, 'for a monogram I am preparing on The Analysis, Construction and Weave of Textiles in Crime Detection.'

'Great Heavens, Holmes,' I exclaimed, 'are you flesh and blood?'

'Alas, yes. Personally I found the conditions quite satisfactory for such work.'

After ten minutes we found ourselves entirely alone once more. But there was no time to be squandered; my pocket watch informed me it was close to nine and the day's visitors would soon be upon us. While I stood sentry, Holmes set to with the spade and began to turn the earth. Barely a minute later he stopped and called me over.

'I believe we have found what we came for,' he announced. Less than two feet down, a man lay face up in the soil. It sickened me that we had laid above him just a few minutes before. Even caked in soil, I could tell his clothes were fashionable and cut from expensive cloth.

'Look there, Watson,' said Holmes.

His right arm stopped short at the wrist. The face was a ghastly white; decomposition had not yet begun. He had striking Latin features, dark brows, strong bones and a certain dignity remained. He fitted perfectly the profile Holmes had identified in Baker Street: a strongly-built man of forty.

'Do you recognise him, Holmes?' I asked. He peered intently at the unfortunate fellow.

'Perhaps,' he said at length. Like a jack daw, I saw his eyes suddenly alight on the edge of a small object gripped in his hand.

'I say Watson, look there.' Holmes prised open his fist and removed what looked like a tiny wrought iron key. 'A familiar object,' he remarked, holding it up to the light.

'The key to Spenning's desk!' I exclaimed.

'So it appears, but let us not get ahead of ourselves.'

He produced a silk handkerchief, wrapped the key in it then dropped the package inside his pocket. 'Undoubtedly, this has a story to tell.'

'We cannot possibly take it,' I declared. 'It would prove our friend right. It would make us nothing but grave robbers.'

'We shall return it at the appropriate hour,' said Holmes. 'But for now, let us return the missing hand to the grave and alert Lestrade. He can help us identify the body.'

An hour later we stood beside the fully dug grave, with the emaciated police inspector, Lestrade, a cohort of his men and the gravedigger reunited with his shovel.

'If you'd said who you were,' the worker grumbled, 'I would have gladly helped without the need for a game of hide and seek. To think of me accusing Sherlock Holmes of grave robbery! But for the life of me, I still can't think how you gentlemen disappeared after you took my spade.' Holmes raised his eyebrows.

'We were never far away,' he said. Lestrade shook his head.

'It puzzles me, Holmes,' admitted Lestrade. 'From a one legged man in Clapham to a one handed man in Highgate, however did you make the link?'

'Quite elementary,' my friend pronounced, without elaborating.

A few routine enquiries amongst Holmes' underworld contacts brought us to the lair of Arthur Tickler. Our hansom pulled up adjacent to a series of commercial units built into a row of crumbling brick arches. Each was possessed of its own peeling wooden door and grimy windows revealing nothing but the darkness within. Tickler's was the last of these and the most mysterious. Holmes rapped three times with his cane and we waited in the light rain shower for the owner to appear.

'Not quite the King's Road,' I remarked, glancing down the line of grotty premises.

'Remember, my dear Watson, 'that Aladdin's Cave was not located in Mayfair. If you deal in extraordinary things, it is wise to be inconspicuous.'

At last, the door opened. A boy of fifteen or so appeared, dark skinned and dressed in a dusty red tunic with gold braiding. Instinctively, he glanced left and right before uttering a word.

'What is your business?' he demanded.

'The shopkeepers in the King's Road,' I ventured, 'certainly have better manners.'

'My name is Sherlock Holmes,' my friend said. 'And you must be Alim Sadiki.' The boy appeared taken aback.

'How do you know this?'

'I can see that you are both wise and faithful.'

'What sort of man are you?' he demanded. 'You speak like a sorcerer.' He furrowed his brow. 'Or a confidence trickster.'

'I am neither,' Holmes assured him. 'I seek only an audience with your employer, Mr Tickler.'

'He is not my employer,' corrected the boy. 'He is my associate.'

'Forgive me,' Holmes replied.

'Very well,' said the boy solemnly, 'step this way.'

'Enter, friends!' a man announced, before turning to the boy. Tickler was of average height, mid-forties, somewhat jowly, devoid of hair except for a pair of fine grey mutton chops and a thin brown covering above the ears, which he had combed forward. His face appeared to be set in a permanent grin, his cheeks dimpled and cherry red.

'Alim,' he said indignantly, 'we must not keep our customers waiting.' The young man frowned, then disappeared behind a blue velvet curtain into a back room. 'Arthur Tickler, at your service.'

'Sherlock Holmes and this is my friend, Dr Watson.'

'Honoured, I'm sure,' he said, bowing low. 'Now, please forgive my associate. He is naturally suspicious.'

'Not at all,' began Holmes. 'Suspicion is a finely evolved human instinct and an entirely wise precaution.'

'I can tell that nobility runs through your souls,' Tickler went on. 'I can also tell that something special has brought you here. But first, will you take some apple tea?'

'Why not?' I said.

'Tea!' shouted Tickler, clapping his hands. 'Alim, bring some tea!'

'I am not your tea boy,' his partner replied from behind the curtain, 'I am your associate!'

The shop was a stupendous jumble of the curious and strange; exotic objects filled every shelf and surface. Narrow aisles were established between the assorted paraphernalia that allowed some passageway. Oil paintings and framed playbills were leant up against watercolours; porcelain rested upon ancient gaming tables, chairs in various states of upholstery butted up against cabinets filled with the gold clocks and the busts of Roman emperors. A large old fashioned handbag stood open on the floor beside a brittle looking fan of intricate design.

Tickler was reading a play: An Ideal Husband, by Oscar Wilde, which he laid face down on his table as we entered. A gold watch chain was threaded through his black waistcoat and he wore a large, ostentatious green ring on his left ring finger.

'Ah, doctor,' he said, following my gaze. 'I can see my emerald caught your eye. It once belonged to a Madagascan pirate.'

'Indeed,' I said, suitably impressed.

'The rest of his fortune, I fear, lies on the floor on the Indian Ocean.'

'Along with his bones?' suggested Holmes.

'Perhaps you already know the story. Now what is your fancy, gentlemen? I am a man who can procure what others cannot: the rare; the precious; I make the unobtainable obtainable.'

'For instance?' challenged Holmes.

'For instance,' said Tickler, reaching beneath his counter, 'may I present the gout stool once owned by Dr Johnson. He suffered terribly, the poor man. But what taste!' He produced an extraordinary hinged contraption with a delicately patterned L-shaped cushion. 'Then there is this.' He reached down once again and produced a plain wooden goblet.

84

'This simple vessel,' he said, in tones of wonder, 'was found in a central square in Jerusalem. It is two thousand years old. Every person who ever walked in Jerusalem would have drunk from it.'

'Remarkable,' I said, inspecting the object.

'It is entirely reasonable therefore, to suppose that this was touched by the lips of Jesus Christ.'

'Upon my word!' I cried.

'On the subject of religion,' said Holmes, inspecting a small figurine. 'What took you to St Paul's this morning?' Tickler raised his eyebrows. 'It is not a Sunday,' my friend continued, 'and you do not strike me as a particularly devout man.' The man looked perplexed.

'My associate informed you, I suppose?'

'Not at all,' smiled Holmes.

'I detected the scent of burnt wax on your clothes. I happen to be familiar with the particular kind of spermaceti, or whale oil, they use for the candles there. It is strange isn't it, to think that the cathedral of God is lit by the great monsters of the deep. Their live in darkness, yet yield a most brilliant light.'

'A remarkable observation, Mr Holmes,' congratulated Tickler. 'You are quite correct. I had a private meeting with a Minor Canon on Ludgate Hill about a curious object that came into their possession.'

'How private was the meeting?' enquired Holmes. 'Can you share the substance?'

'I can do better than that,' he said, reaching into his jacket. He produced a slim leather case from his jacket pocket, undid the catch with his fingertip then flipped the lid to reveal a drawing tool of some description.

'Gentlemen,' he said, his eyes gleaming. 'What you see before you is the corner rule that Christopher Wren himself used to design St Paul's Cathedral. I have a client who is an architect. He has been without a commission for some months and believes that an item of such providence will revive his fortunes.'

'You must have paid a high price.'

'I prefer a system of barter,' said the dealer. 'Everybody wants something. The Minor Canon was happy to settle for the miraculously preserved thumb of an early Christian saint, which came into my possession by a strange turn of events some months ago.'

'Yours in a unique calling,' I murmured.

'So, what is your desire?' he asked, pressing his fingers together. 'No doubt you know something of my reputation, otherwise you would not be here.'

'We seek nothing more than information,' said Holmes.

'I pride myself on my discretion,' he said.

'Nonsense,' scoffed Holmes. 'You have been remarkably indiscreet in the last five minutes alone. Perhaps you recall a little known play by Mr William Shakespeare by the name of The Jeweller of Florence.' Tickler pursed his lips and raised his chin a little in a small show of recalcitrance. He patted his pockets for his tobacco pouch.

'I am certain I would remember such a transaction,' he muttered, then turned towards the back of the shop. 'Alim!' he cried. 'Bring me my tobacco!' The youth re-emerged.

'You forget I am your associate and not your servant,' he said calmly. 'Your tobacco is exactly where you left it, in your left breast pocket.'

'So it is,' said Tickler, rediscovering his stash. 'Some clients insist on absolute secrecy,' explained Tickler, 'that is often part of the arrangement.'

'So I assume,' continued Holmes, 'that was a condition imposed by Mr William Somerville?' Tickler smiled then threw up his hands. 'I am bound by my word,' he said. Holmes paced around the shop.

Presently Alim floated through the blue curtain like a magician's assistant, bearing a tray of tiny glasses and a steaming pot of tea. 'Ah!' exclaimed Tickler. 'Not a moment too soon. I assume gentlemen, that you have not yet sampled the delights of apple tea? You must drink it scalding hot and with plenty of sugar.' The beverage was served with great ceremony while Tickler dropped dollop after dollop of sugar into the glasses. 'I discovered it in Turkey while on a business trip and now rarely drink anything else.' He distributed the tumblers then raised his own. 'Your good health,' he said, and sipped at the liquid. 'Now,' he continued, 'I have made a solemn promise not to divulge any information, but I do not believe

86

my associate is bound by the same conditions. I will be in the back if you need me. Good day gentlemen.' The young man stared at us.

'We understand that you procured a play for a Mr Somerville,' began Holmes. 'It is a remarkable piece of work entitled The Jeweller of Florence.' Alim remained entirely impassive. 'I recall nothing,' he said, smacking his lips.

'Watson?' my friend gestured, 'do you have your wallet with you?' I produced a white five pound note and laid it flat on the table.

'Nothing doing,' said Alim. Holmes smiled.

'I see Tickler has taught you well.'

'It is I who taught him. I was born into a family of merchants. The bazaar was my nursery; I learned to barter before I learned to walk.'

'Then perhaps this might persuade you,' my friend said. He reached into his jacket and removed a piece of cloth. He unrolled it with a flourish to reveal a fine quill.

'The instrument with which Charles Dickens wrote Great Expectations,' announced Holmes. 'I also have a letter of authenticity.'

'Good heavens!' cried Tickler who had evidently been listening from the other side of the curtain. 'However did you come to possess such a thing?'

'I received it as a token of thanks from one of his sons,' my friend explained sipping at his tea. 'I once settled a trifling matter on his behalf.'

'Our negotiations have taken a singular turn,' said Tickler.

'My negotiations,' insisted Alim.

'Naturally, naturally!' said Tickler, giving the quill a covetous look.

'Then you are ready to talk?'

'We are always ready to talk under the right conditions!' said Tickler.

We adjourned to the back room and were shown to some comfortable chairs draped in extravagantly patterned cloth and arranged around a low table. It was clear this was where the dealer conducted his most serious business. Tickler once again raised the tiny glass to his mouth and scalded his lips with the sweet tea. He winced, then placed it back onto the table.

'A curious business,' he said, shaking his head, 'even by my standards. She was like an empress when she walked in here. And in a way, she was. Her name was Florenza De Medici. Yes, Mr Holmes, you heard me correctly, a Medici. She appeared one evening last winter; I would say February if I was pressed. It was just past midnight and there was snow still on the ground. I was working at my ledger and had just dozed off when I heard a clattering in the next room. At first I thought it was my associate creating the disturbance with his preposterous folk dancing. Then I remembered that he was away on some business and I realised that the noise was coming from the other side of the front door. I struggled up, threw on my gown, lit a candle and prepared to give whoever it was a piece of my mind.'

'I'm sure you did,' said Holmes. 'Please go on.'

'Well, Mr Holmes, I can tell you, she was like the angel of death herself, dressed all in black and right bang up to the elephant with immaculate war paint and a hat that towered above her head; a splendidly haughty manner to boot.'

"Signor Tickler?" she asked. She had a thick, breathless Italian accent.

"Who are you?" I demanded, regaining my composure.

"A Medici," she pronounced, as if this was explanation enough. I invited her in. She glanced behind, taking care that she was not being followed. Once the door was closed, she pressed her back against it.

"Signore," she announced. "I understand that you are a man who deals in things that do not exist; things that cannot be obtained."

"So it is said," I confirmed with some pride. She produced a parcel from under her coat.

"I have something that does not exist." She looked around for some suitable surface to show me her treasure. "Do you ever clean?" she asked, impertinently.

"I live my way, I told her, "you live yours." I cleared some space on this very table. Well, Mr Holmes,' he said, a faraway look in his eye, 'it was one of those moments you wait for all your life.' She untied the string with those long, elegant white fingers, all glistening with gems, and then there it was, The Jeweller of Florence by William Shakespeare. Well what do you say to that?'

'What indeed!' my friend agreed.

'Well, I stared at this artefact for some considerable length of time. I have seen some remarkable treasures in my time, Mr Holmes, but I have also seen some remarkable fakes.'

"How did you come across such an item," I said at last, being careful to inject, I hoped, a note of cynicism in my voice. This is quite vital for keeping down the price. "You will understand," I added, "that without proper providence, an object can lose much, if not all of its value."

"I have had a most difficult day," she told me. "Fetch me a glass, pour me some wine, and I shall explain."

'I liberated a good bottle from my store, a Chateaux d'Yquem 1889. If ever there was a moment for such an extravagant gesture it was then. It is all about establishing the right atmosphere for the transaction. She placed both her hands around the goblet and drank deeply, then flashed those dark eyes at me. Well, Mr Holmes, I am man of flesh and blood and on any ordinary day, they would have succeeded in distracting me from my business. But this was no ordinary day. I was fixed on a bigger prize.'

"It is possible," she began, "that you know something of my ancestor, Ferdinando I de'Medici. He was the son of the great Cosimo I of Florence; a cardinal and eventually the Grand Duke of Tuscany. He was, as is consistent with the male line in my family, a ruthless, and perhaps a cruel man. Even by the standards of the day, there are many things in his history of which I am not proud. But of this I am certain. He was, at heart, an artist; not a painter or a sculptor, or a poet, but none the less, an artist. This manifested itself in his collecting. He was a man of infinite curiosity and boundless appetites. He created an unrivalled collection of sculpture, bestowed patronage on the poets and composers and commissioned great mosaics: the intricate *pietre dure* created from precious stones. As a man who deals in fine things, you will know he employed the finest craftsmen alive. They say he loved to spend time in the workshops of the masters, watching as they fashioned wondrous things.

"Above all, he was obsessed by the idea of artistic genius. As a man of the court, naturally his principle entertainment was theatre. The re-enactments of battles on the Arne are legend. But he was a man of the world and his interests extended far beyond the shores of the Mediterranean. He dreamt of establishing civilisations in the new world, creating great cities in Brazil. He had heard of this man William Shakespeare, and had his plays translated and enacted for him. He was fascinated by the playwright's mind; how he could conjure a man from the air and make him as real as you or I. But it was not enough simply to hear his plays; the same words that had been heard by countless others. The Medici was a family of limitless wealth and power. Nothing was impossible for them and once set on a course, he could not be easily swayed. Through his brokers he sent word to England that he would commission this playwright at whatever cost. He wanted a play that would be no less dazzling in its insights, eloquent in its poetry or breath-taking in its ambitions than any other of his great works. For this, he would pay handsomely. But there was one condition: it must be his and his alone.'"

'But Holmes,' I spluttered, 'this is incredible!'

'I could not believe it myself,' Tickler agreed. 'In fact, at this stage, I refused to believe it. But I recharged her glass and she continued her tale.'

'"A fee was negotiated, it is believed through Richard Burbage, the actor and one of Shakespeare's closest associates. No one has recorded the sum, but it must have been stupendous. Around 1596, he was writing four plays simultaneously. How could he write another?'

'More prolific even than you, Watson,' my friend noted.

'The family legend has it that he wrote it in a furious burst over three days. At the end of it he drank a bottle of Spanish wine and then slept for a day and a night. A single copy was printed in conditions of the greatest secrecy.'

'A single copy?' Holmes, queried. 'That seems most unlikely. Surely vanity would dictate Shakespeare would keep one for himself.'

'He was bound by the terms of the agreement.'

'There is a not one shred of evidence for all this,' I broke in.

'Was the play not evidence enough?' replied Tickler. Besides, there is evidence too of a windfall. In 1597 Shakespeare suddenly finds the money to buy New Place, the grandest house in all of Stratford. How could a simple player find such riches? Like you, I was stunned. But then cold reason took hold.'

'"Why are you offering this to me?" I demanded of the woman. I suddenly sensed a great scam; a swindle orchestrated by one of my enemies or disgruntled customers. I glanced up at the window but saw nothing but the bright sickle of the moon. Again, she drained her glass. It was clear her nerves were shattered.

"I have my reasons," she told me. "The fortunes of my family have dwindled since the time of Ferdinando. The great age of the Medici ended in 1743 with Anna Maria Louise de Medici. Since then the family was scattered across the world. We eked out a living any way we could. My own family remained close to Florence, living frugally in the hills. We had some simple luxuries of course, but have never forgotten our birth right and the many great secrets of the Medici. Now we find ourselves in a most desperate plight. In a final, foolish enterprise, my family pooled its resources; we sold our remaining pearls and gold and risked it all on a single splash on the money markets. We were told it was safe stock with guaranteed returns that would restore us to our former position." She pulled a silk handkerchief from her sleeve. "Mr Tickler," she said, looking me right in the eye. "You know the meaning of hubris. It will not surprise you to discover that we lost everything." She folded the handkerchief and pressed it into the corner of each eye. There was still great pride there, I can tell you. But I remained sceptical, Mr Holmes. She was a finely dressed woman for a pauper. I took a deep breath.

"Perhaps you here on false pretences," I told her. "You must understand the way I work. I do not pay vast sums for my treasures. I do not have such sums at my disposal. I operate a system of exchange."

"So I understand," she replied.

"Then what is it you want?"

"You have in your possession something that belongs to me."

"I assure you madam," I instructed, "that is not the case."

"Then tell me, Signor Tickler, what do you know of the mirror with the green face?" I narrowed my eyes, unwilling to give anything away. In actual fact, I had nothing to give away as I had no idea of what she was referring to.

"One of the great treasures of the Medici was lost more than a century ago. My family has spent years searching for it and it has led me to your door." As you can imagine, I was somewhat surprised by this statement.

'She stared accusingly, as if I was holding something back.
"I assure you madam, I have no idea what you are talking about."
"Then my visit is wasted." At this moment, there was an appalling thud against the door, as some brute strength was attempting to force its way in.
"By thunder!' I shouted. "Who in heaven's name is that?" There was a second crash and by the alarming way the hinges sprung loose from the wall, I could see the door was not going to withstand a third. "Get inside that chest," I commanded and with less decorum than perhaps she was used to, I flung open the lid and pushed her inside. She clutched the precious manuscript to her person.

'I stepped somewhat reluctantly into the front of my shop, pulling the curtain closed behind me. I am a man of business you understand. The door finally crashed down and a brutish figure appeared before me: six foot, swarthy and moustachioed like a Spanish naval captain.
"Tickler!" he roared. I stood my ground, doing my best to control the tremble in my knees.
"Who are you?" I returned.
"Duke Alberto Borgia," he growled in a thick Italian accent, "sworn enemy of the Medici." Slowly he withdrew a silver dagger from his cloak. "Where is she?" he demanded.
"There is no one here but me."
"You lie!" he swore, then lunged towards me. I leapt backwards and threw a table between us, looking frantically for some means of defending myself. Then I saw it.
"That's no knife!" I exclaimed, then reached up and tore down a cutlass from where it was mounted on the wall. "This," I cried, "is the sword of William Kyd, the legendary English pirate. You will leave my shop or taste its blade, sir!"
"You dog!" he shouted, and hurled the knife at me, slicing my ear.
'You will see,' he said, pointing to the wound, 'where it almost took it clean off.'
'Neatly stitched,' I noted. 'But how did you escape?'

'Now he was disarmed, I look my chance. I lunged at the fellow with Kyd's sword, succeeding in nicking him on the chin. Yet I had underestimated the man. He wiped the blood from his face with the back of his hand, spat on the floor, then produced from his belt a mighty blade. Without taking his eyes from my own, he sliced my cutlass clean in half. I stared at the truncated blade in astonishment.
"That was a treasure beyond worth!" I cried.
"Tell me where she is!" he cried, the point of his sword pressed to my chest. I was in a lean position.
"You are a cultured man," I bargained, "and I am a well-connected one. If I cannot give you what you want, perhaps I can offer something else? You will be aware no doubt, of the lost emerald of César Borgia. He was said to be wearing it on the battlefield set in a ring the day he died."
"You are not fit," Borgia snarled, "to breathe his name! I saw her enter this place; she is here and I will find her if I have to tear your shop apart brick by brick."

'It was then that I was handed an astonishing piece of luck. Almost directly below my hand, was a long, thin wooden box. Flipping open the lid I retrieved the artefact inside.
"This," I warned, "is the gladius of Marcus Vipsanius Agrippa, the greatest general of Roman Empire!" I swung the ancient blade and parried Borgia's sword, at the same time hurling the wooden box into his face. I scrambled up onto a chest to give me the upper ground then considered my next move.

"So now you die!" he bellowed, and charged at me, thrusting with his sword. I leapt desperately into the air, and caught hold of the chandelier. Still clutching my Roman sword, I swiped at him from above, wounding his arm. I heard him shout in pain just as the light fitting gave way and I came plummeting down directly upon him. Then everything went black.'

I sipped at my apple tea, now unpleasantly cold.
'Whatever happened next?' I asked, quite riveted by his account.

93

'I felt cold water splashing across my face, blinked and then opened my eyes. Facing me was Medici, her cheeks flushed. Beside me, the Borgia lay dead.

"You fought bravely," she said. I could scarcely believe it was over; even less that I had defeated such a foe.

"Did I...?" I began.

"No," she corrected, stepping back. "It was I." I gasped as I saw the jewel encrusted helm of a small knife protruding from his back.

"Is this," I managed weakly, "a dagger I see before me?"'

Tickler paused. 'Now I tell you all this, gentlemen, in the strictest confidence. From what I know of your activity, not everything you discover in the course of your enquiries finds its way to the Scotland Yard. I know enough of the law to know that I would be on safe ground. A man breaks into my shop and I defend myself. It is a simple enough defence and if I know the law, it would serve for her just as well.'

'Quite possibly,' said Holmes thoughtfully, 'and yet you did not report any of this. That would go against you.'

'We thought it better to keep quiet,' Tickler explained. 'I have friends in all professions in London, including gravediggers. It is not so hard to hide a body where others already lie.

'Concealing a body is no small matter,' I put in.

'Be that as it may,' Tickler said. 'As I lay there recovering my wits she showed me the object she was seeking: a mirror with a stem of gold, with more around the glass. On the reverse was a whimsical face wearing an enigmatic smile, fashioned from a green tinted alloy. Uncertain of its providence, it had languished in my shop for years and I had paid it very little notice.'

"This," she said, peering at the thing in wonder, "is the second of a pair. It was fashioned in the workshop of Alberto Parigi and has been lost for two hundred years. I was told by a dealer in Rome it was in your possession."

"But what is this knick-knack," I asked in all truthfulness, "next to a great lost work of Shakespeare?"

"It is my belief," she said solemnly, "that the play will never be authenticated. As such it is worthless to me. And yet this, as a pair, can be sold to pay our debts, purchase our family home in the city and restore our reputation. Give me this and the play is yours."

"You said yourself it could be a fake."

"You have only my word as an honourable woman from an honourable family. The risk is yours."

"I weighed all this up, Mr Holmes. The exotic woman, the dead Borgia and the play; above all the play! I picked it up again, coveted its frontispiece and gazed upon that immortal name. I am a dealer in the unimaginable, the unobtainable. It was too much to bear; I had to possess it. But I am a fair man, too.

"Very well," I said. "I am ready to strike."

"Be warned," she warned. "This is a deadly play. Since it came into our hands from another branch of the family it has brought us nothing but bad luck. Our enemies have pursued us. You have seen yourself what they can do. Perhaps this is what they seek."

"I understand," I replied, "but for this, I am prepared to take that chance."

'We shook hands on it. I told her I would dispose of the body and with a final flash of those dark, Latin eyes, she turned and vanished into the night.

'Remarkable,' I whispered.

'Yet there is one thing more,' he said, his face darkening with anger.

'She stole something from me.' He reached inside his shirt and pulled out a gold chain. Something had been torn away from a setting at the centre.

'A small diamond shoe,' he said. 'I have never known its origin, but it was a work of the most astonishing craftsmanship. It had become my talisman.' Glistening, I saw a tear begin to well in his eye. "I wore it around my neck for twenty years. The mirror with the green face was nothing but a ruse. This was the treasure she sought. For all I know, the play is a counterfeit. I contacted my friends in the theatre business and was glad to sell it to Somerville."

Holmes rose to his full height.

"Tickler,' he said. 'I thank you for your candour. Dickens' quill is yours and I ask for nothing in return. But I regret to inform you that your friend Alberto Borgia, brief resident of Highgate Cemetery was discovered this morning.'

SIX

The Derby

The window was slightly ajar and a strong breeze stirred the fetid air of our sitting room at 221b Baker Street. Holmes and I, reclining after a long lunch, stretched our legs before the empty hearth. I folded my newspaper and absorbed myself in a long and rather tiresome article about army supply problems. Had it not been for our run in with Captain Hercules Winter I would have no interest in the matter, having put my own military days firmly behind me. However I felt it might somehow provide some useful information pertaining to our case. I soon found my attention wandering.

'I say, Holmes,' I remarked, 'Rosebury's government is looking a little shaky. Do you know, I'm not sure whether his heart is in it anymore.' Holmes puffed evenly on his pipe while perusing an American periodical entitled Gleanings in Bee Keeping Culture.

'I have had no dealings with the man since his days on the London Council,' Holmes muttered, turning a page. 'If I recall correctly, a valuable set of minutes went missing, which would have meant his certain resignation as Chairman. If you recall, I managed to locate them before he was forced into such a position. A brilliant and charming fellow but a disastrous Prime Minister I fear; too many interests to focus on the matters of the state: something of a renaissance man. The fate of nations can seem awfully tiresome to a man who has hobbies.'

'Did I hear somewhere that he owns a racehorse?' I enquired. 'Was it Ladas or Sir Visto? Possible he owns both.' I rifled through the sports pages in search of the answer. 'That's right, I muttered. Sir Visto is highly fancied in this year's Derby.' Holmes laid his periodical flat on his lap.

'All this racing talk brings back memories of that curious incident in Dartmoor with Silver Blaze and his trainer.'

'A perplexing affair,' I remarked, sitting up in my chair. 'Seeing as we are at something of an impasse with the search for our play, what do you say to a day at the races?'

'A tax on the foolish,' dismissed Holmes. He must have seen my face fall. 'Still,' he said, tapping his pipe, I have heard Somerville is something of a sportsman and I have no doubt he will be there. Perhaps it will give us an opportunity to observe him at close quarters.'

'Splendid,' I said, tucking my handkerchief into my sleeve. 'Do you have the key to your bureau? I feel my cheque book is about to receive an airing.'

The morning of 29th May, Derby Day, was as fine and bright as any that year. It seemed to me an auspicious sign. I treated myself to a new collar and retrieved my straw boater from the top of my wardrobe where it had languished since the previous summer. Stepping lightly into the sitting room I was arrested by the sight of Holmes standing by the window, his back to me, a newspaper rolled in his hand, as if he had successfully murdered a fly.

'I say, Holmes,' I began. 'Do you think I could get away with the straw boater or should I stick with the bowler? It can get awfully windy on the Downs.'

'I believe,' muttered Holmes without turning around, 'that it would be instructive for you to read this.'

'What have you got there? The weather forecast?' He handed me the baton and I unrolled it.

'Good god!' I ejaculated. 'Spenning!' I scanned the short report.

OXFORD PROFESSOR VANISHES; POLICE BAFFLED
Professor Telemachus Spenning, reader in Shakespearian studies at Corpus Christi College, Oxford was reported missing yesterday. He was last seen at dinner. Provost of Corpus Christi College, Professor Eugene Noble said that he was a reliable, well liked and respected member of the faculty and was unable to explain his disappearance. Spenning's student, Oliver Standbull, described as 'outstanding' by Professor Noble, is also missing. Police have said they are examining leads but at this stage are refusing to link the two incidents.

'Our case has taken a singular turn,' noted Holmes. 'However losing clients is not the disaster it might at first appear. I invariably find that

97

they have little to offer in the way of information and less in insight. In fact, is it is infinitely more straightforward to examine a case without the encumbrance of emotion and vested interest.' I lowered the paper, once again feeling rather crestfallen.

'I suppose then, it is a train to Oxford?'

'Nonsense,' my friend retorted, 'Let's allow Scotland Yard to chase its tail for the time being. If we are quick about it we shall make the 8.14 from London Bridge and be at Epson Downs before the first riders are out of the Paddock.'

'Splendid!' I cried.

We joined our fellow pundits on the platform, each sporting a flat cap or boater and all clutching a copy of Sportsman or Sporting Life as if their very existence depended on it. To a man, they exuded that sense of irrational optimism that possesses every gambler, believing themselves privy to inside information. Most were in high spirits and several policeman were keeping order, confiscating a bottle here and settling a small dispute there. One of the constables, the owner of a particularly luxuriant sand-coloured moustache and side whiskers, turned to acknowledge Holmes.

'I didn't have you down as a gambler, Mr Holmes,' he called.

'You are quite right, Bartlett,' my friend returned. 'I deal only in the business of certainties. However that does not preclude me from enjoying the spectacle of a thousand Londoners casting their money to the wind.'

'Very sensible, Mr Holmes!' the constable returned.

'By the by,' added Holmes. 'Please accept my congratulations on the birth of your daughter,'

'My daughter?' he asked. 'How could you possibly know?'

'You have a tiny amount of baby mewl on your sleeve' indicated Holmes. 'Then there is the small posy of wild flowers in your pocket and the unmistakable twinkle in the eye that is the sole preserve of the new father.'

'Extraordinary, Mr Holmes!'

'Elementary,' my friend corrected.

We had treated ourselves to first class accommodation for the short journey from London Bridge. A pair of gentlemen were quietly conferring over a newspaper, clearly engaged in a similar conversation to those we had overheard on the platform, albeit in a more civilized fashion. Holmes and I smoked our cigarettes, shook out our own papers and waited for the guard's whistle.

'Who do you believe has Spenning?' I asked, as we got underway.

'Is Winter wrapped up in this?' Holmes looked quizzically at me.

'My dear Watson,' he said. 'You are familiar with my methods. I pronounce only after assembling the facts. We may just as well speculate on the winner of the Derby without first consulting the form.'

'In that case,' I said, 'I see you have glanced at the newspaper. Have you formed a view on the winning horse?' I noticed the two men were now listening in on our discussion.

'Naturally,' said Holmes, expelling a cloud of smoke. 'If I was possessed of a king's ransom, I would place it on Sir Visto.'

We waited for crowds to thin on the platform before disembarking. Given that it was a fine day and we were still ahead of ourselves, we resolved to continue the journey on foot, passing the illegal bookies and an extraordinary one-eyed street vendor, hawking newsprint, parasols, soda water and confectionary. All of England it seemed, had convened on Surrey, as if participating in a mass experiment to test whether the country's entire population could fit inside a single county.

'Playwright in Pentonville!' the newspaper vendor caterwauled. 'Wilde gets what he deserves!'

'I say, Watson,' said Holmes. 'Would you hold on a moment?' My friend advanced on the man, tapped his cane smartly on the road ahead of him, then whispered something in his ear.

'You want to buy the whole bleedin' lot?' the man asked. I saw Holmes nod, then hand over a sovereign.

'And how do you intend to transport them?'

'I don't,' returned the detective. He dropped a handful of what appeared to be a strange, green dust over the newspapers, flashed a match into life then watched in satisfaction as the entire pile went up in flames. Holmes returned to my side and we pressed on without a word.

Piling through the gates, we were swept along on a human tide to be met by a clamour of wild eyed racing fans. The spectators in the grandstand seemed to number in the tens of thousands. The edifice glistened brilliantly white, rising up like the Hanging Gardens of Babylon, teaming with the rich, the hopeful and the deluded. The Union Flag snapped at its pole at the top of the pavilion.

'There cannot be a soul left in all of London,' I marvelled. 'If ever there was a day to break into the Tower and steal the Crown Jewels, it would be today.' Flat carts and four wheelers lined up on the grass and the great and the good stood upon them in their top hats and tails craning to get a look at the early runners. The air was filled with the shouts of bookmakers as they called the odds, the whoops of coarse young working men mingling with the chatter of the middle classes as they compared hats and frocks. The sun glinted from the white boards displaying the runners and riders.

We placed our bets and found ourselves a vantage point on some upturned wooden crates. Holmes produced a pair of opera glasses from a leather carrying case and scanned the horizon for points of interest.

'I believe that's Sir Visto over there,' I said, squinting into the middle distance. 'He looks on form to me. I can see him gleaming from here.

'Don't worry about him,' remarked Holmes. 'We knew he would be here. More noteworthy is the Prince of Wales over there in the Royal Box.'

'Well,' I replied, 'he of all people can afford a flutter. I wonder whether Rosebery is with him.'

'Yes, I expect he is. It does make one wonder,' Holmes mused, 'who is running the country while the great and the good have their minds on the nags.'

'I heard somebody say that Rosebery had three aims in life,' I said, 'to become Prime Minister, marry an heiress and own a horse that won the Derby. Perhaps today he will get the hat trick.'

'I heard he doesn't enjoy the race itself,' said Holmes. 'It makes him nervous.'

'It makes me nervous and I have only a pound on it!'

'Well, well,' said Holmes, lowering his binoculars. 'Unless my eyes deceive me, I've just spotted Mycroft in the stand!'

It was soon apparent that horse racing was merely one, and perhaps not even the most important part, of Derby Day. A carnival atmosphere was sweeping the crowd. Acrobats tumbled past; stilt-men teetered over us with strange, painted faces and minstrels strummed melancholic songs as they wandered gaily through the throng. The intoxicating smells of manure and toffee apples, cut grass and beer served to befuddle the senses, no doubt increasing the bounty of the bookmakers as the race goers recklessly backed the outsiders, and equally foolishly herded after the favourites. Holmes seemed to relish the cornucopia.

'Every stripe of humanity is here,' he cried, sidestepping a discarded tray of cockles. 'For one day, class is perfectly meaningless. The grey beards of club land and the swashbuckling guardsman mingle with tatterdemalion, the costermonger, the cobbler and his wife looking for a little holiday madness. They are united by a mutual ambition to abandon good sense and give themselves over to pleasure. It is a glorious vision of a classless society.'

'A fantasy!' I cried.

'You see it with your own eyes!' my friend retorted. 'What's more it's in the air! Can you not smell the cheap smoke of the Penny Pickwick cigarettes mingling with the costly vapours of La Ferme? It is the scent of England at play.'

'Can you still see Mycroft?' I asked.

He returned his opera glasses to his eyes and scanned the stands.

'Yes, he's there all right,' my friend confirmed, 'although I still cannot think why.'

'Excuse me, gentlemen, do you mind?' I turned to look for the owner of this distinctive American accent.

'My apologies,' I said, raising my hat. 'I say, Holmes, I do believe we are rather getting in the way.'

We were standing in front of a camera of some description, mounted on a tripod and being operated by a man of forty with a handlebar moustache, high forehead and quizzical eyebrows.

'Ah,' exclaimed Holmes, surveying the contraption, 'the moving picture!'

'Birt Acres at your service,' the man said, touching the brim of his hat.

'A magician of the modern age,' said Holmes.

'You are too kind, sir. It is true, I am the inventor of the kinetic camera.'

'A splendid fairground attraction,' I said.

'I beg to differ, sir,' the man argued, with a sudden seriousness. 'Be in no doubt, gentlemen, that the invention of the moving picture is of no less significance than the advent of Caxton's Printing Press. It will allow us to preserve a day such as this for all time. Take that boy in the distance who has dropped his candy floss to the ground. That moment has been caught for posterity; it will be seen in future ages long after the boy has grown old and died.'

'A sobering thought,' reflected Holmes. 'But we ought to be grateful at least that an Englishman can be credited with this invention.'

'English?' I questioned.

'Certainly,' said Holmes. 'No American would call cotton candy *candy floss,* nor would he knot his necktie with a double Windsor.' The man smiled at these remarks.

'Then perhaps I could attempt a little deduction of my own,' he remarked. 'You are none other than the celebrated Mr Sherlock Holmes of 221b Baker Street, which must make you the faithful Dr Watson.'

'The very same,' my friend admitted, bowing low.

'It would do me the greatest honour if you were to permit me to capture a few moments of you both on 35mm film.' This offer appeared to please Holmes enormously.

'Any objection, Watson?' he asked, dusting his sleeves.

'None at all,' I replied.

Acres disappeared behind his machine and set the thing in motion, rotating a handle, while Holmes and I moved stiffly about, pretending to interest ourselves in the programme, while adjusting the flowers in our lapels.

'Not easy performing for the camera,' I admitted as Acres remerged.

'No,' the American concurred. 'It can turn the most animated of men into automatons.'

'That does not sound like a favourable review,' Holmes smiled thinly.

'Still, I am most grateful,' continued Acres. 'One day a fee paying member of the public will exclaim, "I saw the great Sherlock Holmes live and breathe before my eyes. He lives beyond the pages of a book!"'

'That does not bode well for the sale of my stories!' I replied.

'Who knows what the future will bring,' he concluded.

Finally, we were within shouting distance of Mycroft. He was dressed in an absurdly tight-fitting white striped blazer, with a matching pair of pantaloons and straw boater. Chewing thoughtfully on a drum-stick, he stared into the distance entirely oblivious, it seemed, to the excitement of the crowd and mutton-eared to our cries.

'Sherlock, Watson,' he remarked, nonplussed at our sudden appearance. 'I wondered how long it would take you to reach me.'

'Are you here on account of some bet?' his brother enquired.

'Isn't everyone?' Mycroft retorted. I couldn't help but smile. 'Have you lunched?' he added.

'Lunch?' I repeated, 'we have only just swallowed down breakfast!'

'Breakfast is a forgotten memory,' he said mournfully, 'and lunch is a distant dream. I have packed a few simple provisions to tide us over.' He flipped the lid of a sizeable hamper. 'A few morsels to sustain life and limb,' he muttered. 'Some pressed beef; a little cream cheese and dressed crab. Little more than appetisers.' I stared at the array of treats, which more closely resembled the window display of the Food Hall at Harrods than a picnic.

'Well Mycroft,' pressed Holmes. 'Short of the closure of the Diogenes Club or the end of the world, whichever is the least likely, what the devil are you doing here?' His brother sighed and reached into the inside pocket of his coat.

'This note was intercepted by one of our agents,' he revealed, passing it to my friend between two chubby fingers. It was a single sentence scrawled in black ink on a scrap of newspaper.

A Hereafters Shovel Him Ins

Holmes peered at this statement with great interest, a smile beginning to form on his lips. 'What do we know of the messenger?' he enquired.

'Not a great deal. It was a boy of ten years of age, who managed to slip away before our man could pursue any line of questioning. He was caught trying to sneak in early this morning and I was summoned to decipher the note.'

'Summoned by whom?' demanded Holmes, reddening at the cheeks, presumably peeved he had not been called upon himself.

'By Lestrade.' Holmes seemed all the more put out.

'I think possibly, Sherlock,' counselled Mycroft, 'they wished to keep this a governmental matter.'

'Well,' said Holmes, with a supercilious air. 'What is the government's take on this?' Mycroft took a thoughtful bite on his chicken, then dabbed his lips with his handkerchief.

'The government believes the author of this note has a poor command of grammar.' Holmes held the scrap up to the light.

'If I'm not mistaken this is the newsprint of a local paper. You will note that the fibre is coarser than you might expect from The Times for example. My suspicions are raised further by the reference to Boar's Hill, a delightful spot overlooking Oxford. If this is not a scrap of the Oxford Journal I would be very much surprised.'

'Marvellous!' I exclaimed.

'Quite elementary,' corrected Holmes.

'But what of its meaning?' I asked. 'The sentence sounds somewhat threatening.'

'That is exactly why Lestrade has raised the alarm. With the Prime Minister and the Prince of Wales in attendance, I suspect he is taking no chances.'

'So, what of it?' I asked.

'It is certainly an anagram,' pronounced Mycroft. 'Yet I have not so far managed to untangle it.'

'Well, two Holmes are better than one,' I suggested. Mycroft raised his eyebrows; his brother's knitted themselves into a frown.

'On the face of it, it seems a singular puzzle. But taken in stages, it is quite straightforward,' said Holmes. 'Let us alight first on "Him Ins."' This will lead us reasonably to "himself." We then need to find a name or noun to connect with this construction. But a name surely would be too dangerous to include in such a childish game. So let us look for something else; an animal for instance.'

'A raven perhaps?' suggested Mycroft.

'Splendid!' shouted Holmes.

'Or a horse?' I put in.

'Equally good!'

'And now a verb or an adjective?' I was flummoxed.

'But Watson, you have already arrived at it,' cried Holmes with delight. 'The raven himself is horse.'

'A raven is a horse?'

'So it appears.'

'Then it is a harmless racing tip!' I laughed, and seized up a copy of the racing paper and scanned the names for a horse called Raven. 'Nothing at all,' I admitted, somewhat deflated.

'Of course not,' smiled Holmes. 'The correct solution is "The raven himself is hoarse" as in 'without voice.'

'Ah,' I said. 'Now you mention it, it sounds awfully familiar.'

Holmes stretched out a hand and declaimed to the heavens.

'The Raven himself is hoarse/That croaks the fatal entrance of Duncan.'

'Good lord!' I shouted. 'More Shakespeare!'

'Excellent, Watson. Once again, it is Macbeth. Act I Scene V to be precise.'

'But whatever does it mean?'

'Come, come, my dear Watson,' admonished Holmes, 'You are supposed to be the man of letters. These are the fateful words of Lady Macbeth, hatching her despicable scheme to murder the king.'

A terrific roar went up from the crowd as a race began and the horses got away. It was soon impossible to hear each other above the din and Holmes gestured for us to make our exit. With great difficulty, we extricated ourselves from the stand, Mycroft lugging his hamper behind him. Once down in the almost deserted public bar, Holmes called his council of war.

'Well, Mycroft,' he said. 'Which is it, the Prime Minister or the Prince of Wales?' I stared at my friend, not for the first time failing to comprehend his meaning. The elder brother pondered the note for an eternity.

'It is Rosebery.'

'Then there is not a moment to lose!' Holmes flew towards the door, his great coat whipping around his rake thin frame. I glanced at Mycroft who indicated with a low bow and an extended hand for me to give chase.

The day was reaching its apotheosis. The sun blazed over the sweeping downs and the sound of the hordes waving their betting stubs was like the roar of a tempest. The main race was underway. The Prime Minister's horse, Sir Visto was storming the field, his glossy flanks gleaming with sweat. Holmes skidded to a halt and stretched out his arms, as if for balance. He began to scan the crowds, turning his head in minute increments. He had the stillness of a hawk, pinned to the sky, awaiting its kill.

'Over there, Watson!' he shouted suddenly, pointing into the far distance. From a standing start Holmes bolted away like an Olympian and once more I was left in his wake.

I followed Holmes into the melee, keeping up as best I could. The villain of the piece had made himself known: a great bear of a man who was lumbering towards a small group of men close to the paddock. He wore a long, black cape and matching felt hat. Realising he was being pursued, he skilfully weaved into the crowds, disguising his bulk among the race goers. I apprehended a bobby en route, a pork-bellied, moon-faced fellow with fiery, red whiskers.

'I say, you there!' I cried, 'Would you care to assist Mr Sherlock Holmes?'

'Of course!' he replied and placing a steadying hand on his custodian helmet, he joined the chase.

'What's the game?' he asked, puffing at my side. 'A pickpocket is it?'

'We believe someone means to murder the Prime Minister.'

'Great heavens,' he replied. 'I should inform my superiors.'

'No time!' I yelled.

For a while, both the pursuer and pursued disappeared completely. Then I saw the brigand break free and for the first time caught a glimpse of his face. He had a prognathous jaw and a horrifically pale, blank expression. I fancied he caught sight of me and for a second I stared into his empty, inky black eyes. It occurred to me that there had been some appalling mistake; that this was an actor made up as a monster from an entertainment. These suspicions quickly vanished when I caught sight of the Lancaster pistol in his hand, one of those fast firing types we used in Afghanistan. It was not a weapon to be trifled with. Using his superior speed, Holmes reached the Prime Minister's group first and in a moment had them down on the ground, a cordon of police officers closed in around them. It was obvious that the Prime Minister was among the men. My friend then turned and faced the brute as he bore down on them.

I had the privilege to observe Sherlock Holmes at close quarters over many years. Yet at no time did I feel I ever had the measure of the man. Each new day in his company was to be astonished at the infinite well of his mental and physical resources.

At the critical moment, when it seemed inevitable that this was indeed the end of my dear friend, something truly wonderful occurred. Sherlock Holmes suddenly ascended into the air. I saw him rise like an apparition, a minatory look of grim purpose stamped on his features. The villain stopped in his tracks and stared up at this fearsome sight. When Holmes was a clear six feet off the ground, he began a terrifying decent, swooping down on the brute before he could discharge his pistol. Holmes delivered what appeared to be a single blow to the man's neck and I saw them both drop, apparently insensible to the ground.

The means of Holmes' flight was now apparent. A pair of wooden stilts (no doubt borrowed from one of the burlesque performers we had seen earlier) lay at either side of the detective. He had hidden them ingeniously within his coat. However my first concern was for his well-being. Was it possible that a bullet had somehow been fired, the sound muffled by the roar of the crowd? With no little alarm, I scanned his body but found no blood or trace of an entry wound. I suddenly felt a cold hand on my own.

'Fear, not Watson,' Holmes assured me, 'merely a small concussion. I came down on him perhaps a little harder than I anticipated. He raised his head, glanced over at his adversary and managed a wan smile. 'I am pleased to discover he came off much the worse. Now I would suggest that he is restrained at the earliest opportunity.' Indeed three policemen took it upon themselves to apply that old fashioned but ever reliable tactic known to the law: sitting on the villain until reinforcements arrive. Remarkably, the drama had attracted almost no publicity. Sir Visto crossed the line at 9 to 1 by three parts of a length and was met with an uproarious reception.

We watched as the rogue was bundled away by a burly sergeant and two constables, one of them collecting the man's strange hat from the ground. I did not know exactly what Holmes had done to him, but the man seemed barely conscious that he had been apprehended, slurring and hardly capable of keeping his eyes from rolling loose in their sockets. My friend peered at him intently and then whispered something in the sergeant's ear.

'Certainly, Mr Holmes,' he assured him. 'We'll call you when you we get some sense out of him.' Holmes narrowed his eyes, smoothed back his oily hair, dusted his cuffs and straightened his cravat.

'Well, Watson,' he said, that singular gleam suddenly returning to his eyes, like the first stars of the night sky, 'I believe I have the bones of a theory. It is a rough hewn, certainly, but a theory none the less.'

'Then pray share!' I urged, offering him a match for his pipe.

'Tut, tut, Watson, you are well enough acquainted with my methods to know that I will not share a theory until it is complete. It would be like removing soufflé from the oven before it is ready. A half baked soufflé is no soufflé at all.' I sighed at this typically circuitous exchange.

I turned to find myself face to face with the Prime Minister. Rosebery's still, melancholy eyes bore an expression of perfect ennui.

'What a tiresome distraction,' he apologised, placing his hand in my own. 'I do hope it has not spoiled your day. Did you back the winner?' For a moment I was dumbfounded.

'As a matter of fact, I did!' I confirmed, suddenly remembering the betting slip in my pocket.

'Good show,' he said. 'It is very becoming of a British subject to show loyalty to his Prime Minister.'

'Not to mention profitable!' I added. He turned to my friend and handed him a small item.

'You have my gratitude, Mr Holmes,' he said, bowing slightly, 'then waved over one of his people.

'You will ensure of course that these gentlemen are properly looked after for the remainder of the day.' His private assistant stepped forward, an elderly man with feathery white, overhanging eyebrows and an equally thick thatch of white hair.

'You have been clever enough,' he twinkled, 'to make friends with the Prime Minister. This way, gentlemen, if you please.'

My friend and I were ushered along a dimly lit corridor deep within the stands, lined with paintings of thoroughbreds. Finally we arrived before a mahogany door that swung open as we arrived. No expense had been spared in the room's decoration; a gold table stood upon a Persian rug and a pair of chaise lounge waited invitingly. If Cleopatra was in attendance at Derby Day, she would scarcely have cause for complaint. A deferential fellow in a white steward's jackets and perfectly bald pate bowed low and enquired what refreshment we might like to take. After our exertions we were all too pleased to accept the hospitality and made ourselves at home in the luxurious den. While the man disappeared to fix our drinks, I took Holmes to task on the day's events.

'So if you won't reveal your theory,' I began, 'will you at least furnish me with the answers to some basic questions?'

'Throw the spear,' Holmes invited.

'Well,' I continued. 'For one, how did you spot our darkly dressed adversary in a crowd of thousands?' Holmes smiled and pressed his fingertips together.

'It was the simple power of good observation. So many people can scan a horizon and see next to nothing. The trick is to divide the horizon into quadrants. Observe and record all of the detail you see before moving onto the next. The next trick is to work from right to left, rather than from left to right. Your brain will work harder, absorb more detail and thereby provide more satisfactory data.'

'Wonderful!' I said.

'Perfectly simple,' corrected Holmes, sparking his pipe into life. 'We merely need to reawaken the powers we acquired in primeval times; the skills of the hunter.'

'Quite,' I agreed. The steward arrived with champagne flutes.

'Why not leave the bottle?' I suggested.

'Very good, sir,' he said, departing and then closed the door behind him.

'Now Holmes,' I said, sipping at the elixir, 'I must insist on knowing the identity of the Prime Minister's assailant.' A plume of creamy white smoke rose from my friend's lips and he watched it curl towards the stucco ceiling and around the crystal chandelier.

'What makes you believe I know his identity?' he enquired.

'I saw that look on your face.'

'Well I can tell you this much. I both know his identity and at the same time, know nothing at all about him.'

'Honestly, Holmes, you are the most infuriating fellow!'

'It seems therefore,' he drawled, 'you have made an odd choice of companion.'

'On the contrary,' I retorted. 'There is no man alive who I admire more, despite your ghastly habits.'

There was a single knock at door.

'I say,' I muttered, 'do you think you could give us a moment?' It opened regardless, to reveal the corpulent figure of Mycroft. He stood in his tightly fitting suit, his slim, elegant, brown shoes incongruous with his massive frame.

'My dear, fellow!' I cried. 'Why, do come in.'

'I see you have started without me.'

'Plenty to go around,' I reassured him. He strode in and deposited a bundle of pound notes from his pockets onto the sideboard.

'I see you backed the winner too,' I noted, pulling up an armchair.

He sloshed some champagne into a mug, helped himself to a beef sandwich then collapsed heavily into the chair like a hot air balloon crash-landing in a field.

'Tell me, Mycroft,' said Holmes from his reclining position. 'How did you know the note alluded to Rosebery and not to the Prince of Wales?' His brother raised an eye brow and took a bite from his sandwich. We waited an age for him to reply.

'I didn't,' he finally announced. 'It was a guess.' Holmes bolted upright.

'A guess!' he shouted. 'Since when did you leave the fate of nations to guesswork? Go back a thousand generations and you will not find a Holmes who believed in such foolishness.' He took another mouthful of sandwich, then washed it down with that the excellent champagne.

'Even I could tell, Sherlock,' he said, 'that the matter was pressing. Sometimes an uninformed decision is better than no decision at all.'

'I cannot say I agree with you,' announced my friend. 'I would say that luck played an unacceptably large part in today's outcome.' I eyed the substantial sum of money.

'Amen, to that!' I added.

'The question remains,' I pressed. 'Who is the fiend who attacked Rosebery?' Sherlock Holmes picked a stray hair from his jacket and examined it.

'The police will discover nothing about him. He will remain in their custody as impassive as mannequin's doll. If they keep him until the end of his days, they will learn no more in their last hour with him than they did in their first.'

'And yet you say, you know his identity!' I exclaimed, exasperated. 'How can this be?'

Three lines were tattooed upon his arm: 'Be not afeard.'

'Clearly some sailor type,' I said. 'In all probability it was tattooed one drunken evening while on shore-leave. What does it tell us?'

'It is an archaic construction, is it not?' I frowned.

'What are you getting at, Holmes?'

'"Be not afeard; the isle is full of noises,"' my friend intoned. '"Sounds, and sweet airs, that give delight and hurt not."'

'Ye Gods!' I cried. 'The Tempest!'

'But whose line is it?'

'Prospero's?' I guessed.

'Wrong!' shouted Holmes, like an indignant schoolteacher.

'Ariel?' I fretted.

'Try again, Watson.'

'Caliban?'

'Thank you, Dr Watson. Now go to the back of the class.'

My friend and I sat in a darkened room, light flickering across our faces, each of us smoking impassively as the Projecting-Kinetoscope clattered behind us. On a large white sheet hung from the wall was a shaky, grainy but still undeniably moving picture: the first cinematic depiction of the great detective, Sherlock Holmes. Alas the appearance was ham-strung by an appallingly wooden performance from one Dr John Watson. In the film, my friend and I were pretending to converse on some subject or the other. It wasn't faintly believable. The film ran to white and finally snapped to a halt.

'Would you like me to run it again, gentleman?'

'Honestly, Mr Acres,' I sighed. 'Much as I admire the wizardry of your machine and your own considerable artistry, I cannot bear to see myself for a second longer. In thespian terms I am hardly the equal of Mr Holmes.'

'Come Watson,' my friend cajoled, 'you are too hard on yourself. Mr Acres, it is nothing short of miraculous! Let us have it again.'

Once more I had to suffer the two of us posturing in the foreground, while behind us the race goers went about the business in their flat caps, top hats and boaters. It ran at an unnaturally fast speed, which lent it a slightly comical dimension.

'History,' declared Mr Acres 'can now step from the page. Future generations will be able to see for themselves that most famous of double acts, Sherlock Holmes and Dr Watson.'

'In which case,' I said, 'I request that you burn it now!'

'Wait!' cried Holmes. 'Would you be so good as to take us back five seconds or so.'

'Certainly,' Mr Acres obliged.

'There. Stop it there.'

'Do you recognise that man above your left shoulder, Watson?'

'Good Lord,' exclaimed. 'It's Somerville.'

'The very same. And look who is standing beside to him.'

'It is the brute who made an attempt on Rosebery's life. So they are in cahoots!' My friend narrowed his eyes and peered hard at the screen. He then collected his cane and returned his hat to his head.

'A most impressive demonstration,' congratulated Holmes, shaking Acre's hand. 'I predict a great future for your device. The masses will flock to it while the criminal classes will cower from its lens. One day it will provide powerful testimony in a court of law.'

SEVEN

The Dancing Bear

The flowers were out in Baker Street. They bloomed from the window boxes, blossomed from the bonnets of the fashionable ladies and flowed in a colourful stream on the carts and barrows that made their way up and down our famous thoroughfare. The sun illuminated my copy of The Illustrated London News and a good cigar lay smoking in the ashtray. With my tea cooling at my side and my breakfast of Yarmouth bloaters still a pleasant memory on my lips, it appeared I had alighted upon a moment of perfect tranquillity. It was then I heard yelp of pain from Holmes' room.

'Good God, Holmes,' I shouted, 'whatever is the matter?'

He appeared in the doorway, clutching the side of his face, blood trickling through his fingers. I threw my paper aside and leapt to my feet in alarm.

'Fear, not Watson,' he grimaced, 'merely a shaving wound. My mind was occupied elsewhere while my fingers went about their clumsy work.'

'Astonishing!' I cried. 'I have just this minute been reading of the invention of a safety razor, patented in the United States.' My friend lifted his hand from his neck, revealing no wound at all. 'My little joke, Watson,' he laughed thinly. 'It is merely ink on my fingers. I knew that article would attract your attention given your propensity for the strange and new.'

'Holmes,' I said, shaking my head. 'If you are possessed of a sense of humour, which is by no means a certainty, it is a peculiar one.'

'No doubt,' my friend said, wiping his hands on a rag, 'this safety razor will take ten years to find its way over here. Mark my words, Watson, while London remains the capital of the civilised world we are at risk of losing our lead. Our American cousins I fear are more open to new possibilities than we dinosaurs of the old Empire.'

Presently Mrs Hudson appeared and saw the ink on Holmes' hands.

'Are you hurt, Mr Holmes?' she enquired with some concern. 'Has the doctor looked you over?'

'No collateral damage, Mrs Hudson,' he assured her. 'And no, I have

113

not let Dr Watson inspect me. It would only give him an opportunity to confirm his suspicions that I am a cold blooded creature.'

'There is a gentleman at the door who wishes to see you.'

'Do we have a name?' my friend asked.

'Only this,' she said, and handed over what appeared to be an animal's claw.

'A singular calling card,' noted Holmes. 'Well, he has succeeded in gaining my attention. Please show him up.'

A stout, bald headed man with European features and a heavy brow appeared in the doorway. He towered above Holmes and was as wide again. My first impression was that he was superbly pungent. It was a smell of the most astonishing depth and complexity, one part cinnamon, one part liquorice and one part cow dung. His luxuriant moustache was coiled into points at each end, but he was otherwise entirely clean shaven. His coat was hewn from heavy, dark oily leather, fastened with large brass buttons. Around his shoulder on a length of cord was slung a small, wooden flute of some description. In his hand was a tall, leather hat, of the variety perhaps more commonly seen in the American mid-west. His dark, careworn eyes seemed to suggest a lifetime of hardship.

'I see you are a Slav,' said Holmes. 'May I surmise that your home is to be found among the High Tatras mountains?' The man furrowed his brow in suspicion.

'Then you already know of me,' he asked in faltering, thickly accented English.

'Not at all,' dismissed Holmes. 'I have never come across you in my life.'

'Then how is it you know this much?'

'You own a particular set of features common to your countrymen,' my friend explained, 'although that alone would not be enough to place you. I happen to have written a monograph on the instruments of eastern Europe, an exercise which has equipped me well enough to identify a koncovka when I see one.'

'But how do you know I am a mountain man?

'Your instrument is made from the wood of an elder is it not? I happen to know the best elder is found in your part of the world.'

'You speak the truth,' he said, staring at the detective, as one might look at a medium after she has read your mind.

'Please,' Holmes invited, 'won't you take a seat and tell me all about the bear.'

'Bear?' I enquired.

'Naturally,' said Holmes. 'This man is a bear tamer and the keeper of a Brown Bear; the *ursus actos*. No doubt, he is, what the public will recognise as, a dancing bear.'

'This is true also,' the man confirmed. 'I raised my poor, dear Gregor from a cub. He and I have travelled the length of Europe, living on the kindness of strangers, the beasts and berries of the hills and the discarded scraps of the townsfolk. We have performed in the courts of great kings and in the slums of Paris. We go wherever there is an audience. We are inseparable.' I glanced out of the window and down into the street.

'Then, unless he is waiting downstairs with Mrs Hudson,' I put in, 'where is Gregor now.' The strange man stared at me, as if I had wounded him to the core then began to weep.

'My own dear, Gregor!' he sobbed. 'What is to become of him?'

I glanced at my friend who raised his eyebrows then busied himself with the book that was lying open on table: a miniature, leather bound copy of Henry IV Part I. For a man such as Holmes, emotion was something of a foreign language, and one he was disinclined to learn. I produced a handkerchief and offered it to the bear tamer.

'We do not yet know your name, sir,' I pointed out, attempting to change the subject. He peered at me, wiping away the tears with the back of a hand. For a moment his eyes glazed over, as if he was unsure where he was. He then stood to his full height, suddenly resolute.

'Olo Bosko,' he said, extending his hand to Holmes. 'My name is Olo.'

'Then Mr Bosko,' Holmes said, warily eyeing the hand without going as far to touch it, 'I know enough about the people who ascend the seventeen steps to our rooms at 221b Baker Street to know that you are in a certain degree of trouble. My name has been recommended to you. "Out of these nettles, danger, I pluck the flower safety!" But first I need data. All of the data you have. Dr Watson, here, is the most trustworthy man in London. Nothing you say will venture beyond these walls, isn't that so Watson? Well, at least for now. Now, doctor, if you would be good enough to pass me the Persian slipper, I will make a pipe and Mr Bosko can begin his account.'

The Slav lit a pipe of his own, an ancient, long stemmed antique implement, sticky with grease and soot.

'Very well,' he began, 'you shall hear my tale. Gregor and I arrived by boat near a place called Broadstairs just before Christmas. We were put ashore by an agent who knew how to land a bear in England without attracting attention, no easy thing I assure you. We dressed Gregor in a bonnet and threw a blanket over him. He rode with me in a carriage to London. We were stopped by a constable by a toll gate who asked us our business. I explained I was a merchant from Poland, travelling with my wife. He waved us through.'

'An audacious bluff!' I marvelled.

'You see it was very dark, doctor,' Bosko explained.

'No doubt!'

I was lodged in a boarding house in Bow. It was, how do you say...?'

'Squalid?' offered Holmes.

'Yes, squalid,' agreed Bosko. 'I am a humble man, but still, I have my standards. Gregor was imprisoned in the backyard, tied to a post, enclosed by walls and covered with a tarpaulin to avoid attention. But it did not take long for the boys of the neighbourhood to discover they had a strange new neighbour. At first they taunted him. He did not rise so easily. Gregor is trained and did not respond to their jibes. But after a while, it is always the same: they begged me to present him to them. It was time for the show to begin.

Bosko leapt to his feet and seized his flute. Presently a mellifluous air began to float from the instrument, beguiling in its melancholy beauty. Holmes smiled his appreciation. Then, continuing to play, the bulky Slav began to galumph around the room in an impersonation of his beloved bear.

'Go on,' interrupted Holmes, less impressed, it seemed, by this display. 'You a remarkable musician, but I do not care much for the Slovenian folk dance.'

116

'Our first performance drew crowds from ten streets away. Gregor danced like a member of the Bolshoi and my hat was full. I realised we had found a new life for ourselves. Our revenues increased over several weeks and I believed we would never have to leave London. But now this; now this!'

Mrs Hudson cleared her throat.
'Excuse me, gentlemen,' she broke in, 'but Inspector Lestrade is waiting downstairs.' Olo's eyes flashed with fear.
'You must send him away,' he cried.
'Impossible,' said Holmes calmly. 'Lestrade is one of the few men we can deal with at Scotland Yard. He is not blessed with imagination but he proceeds with a singular determination, if not always in the right direction.'
'Then you must conceal me,' he said, his eyes darting around the room as if searching for a hiding place. 'The police believe I am responsible for a murder.' Holmes raised his eyebrows.
'Perhaps,' I offered as a compromise, 'Mr Bosko could wait in my room while we talk with Lestrade?'
'You have acquired a sympathiser in Dr Watson,' noted Holmes. 'As things stand, these are unconnected matters.' We therefore squirreled the Slav away while Mrs Hudson showed the inspector up the stairs.

Lestrade stood clutching his bowler in the doorway, his ferrety eyes twitching this way and that in their dark sockets. He lived a life of suspicion in a world where nothing and no one could be trusted.
'Thank you for seeing me a short notice, Holmes,' he said, glancing about the room. 'May I sit?'
'By all means' invited Holmes. 'I am never happier than putting the hounds of the law on the right scent.'
'Speaking of which,' noted Lestrade, clearing a space on the couch. 'If you don't mind my saying, there is the most astonishing smell in here.'
'Ah,' said Holmes. 'It is perhaps an exotic new brand of tobacco with which I am experimenting. The Three Castles brand has become rather bland over the years wouldn't you agree? I have conducting experiments with an Anglo Egyptian variety which is giving all indications of superseding the Persian in my affections.'

'I see,' said Lestrade, rather unconvinced, I thought. 'Well, I will come straight to the point. There has been grisly murder in Whitechapel. Even by your standards, it has something of the macabre about it.'

'Try me,' smiled Holmes.

'Well it appears the murderer is not a man, but a bear.'

'Indeed!' he said, with feigned nonchalance. 'But perhaps the word murder is a little strong for a dumb beast?' suggested Holmes. 'It was an unfortunate accident, no doubt.'

'On the contrary,' said Lestrade. 'It is our belief that this is a highly trained animal operating on the instructions of its master.'

'Another escapee from London Zoo?' I enquired. 'Really, someone ought to do some locking up at locking up time. What of the victim?'

'Well, that's just it. I'm afraid he's a friend of yours: a Professor Spenning.'

'Heavens have mercy!' I shouted, leaping out my seat. 'Spenning?'

'The same,' Lestrade confirmed. 'He was found dead in the street by a charwoman. It will take weeks for her to recover. Even the first constable on the scene found the sight difficult to stomach. The professor had been diced; there is no other word for it, poor fellow. Only his spectacles and papers were left to identify him. But it's him alright.'

We sat for a moment in silence, deeply affected by the news. It seemed an appalling complication to what had begun as a diverting, but rather innocuous case.

'So much for my client,' harrumphed Holmes. 'What of the animal?'

We found the beast performing in the next street with his ne'er do well master, a foreign fellow who had somehow covered his tracks by the time we arrived. There wasn't a drop of blood to be seen.

'So what makes you so sure it was the bear?' I asked.

'The wounds tell their own story. There are two sets of five lacerations across his body. Besides, we brought in Nicholas Kibble, the head keeper at London Zoo, who confirmed it all.'

'Hard to argue with Kibble,' mused Holmes. 'He is a man who knows his onions. I suppose there were no other bears at large?'

'Not that we could find.'

'Then, aside from the lack of evidence,' my friend concluded, 'the lack of motive, the lack of witnesses and the entirely circumstantial coincidence of a bear in the next street, it is a clear cut case. What assistance could you possibly require?'

'Then how,' parried Lestrade, 'do you explain the lacerations?'

'There is always an explanation, but it is rarely the one you first suspect. What action have you taken?'

'We have the bear in custardy, but the tamer has gone to ground. He saw us and made a run for it. In the eyes of the law he will answer for the crimes of his animal. These street performers appear from nowhere and slip away just as easily. He could be aboard a steamer to New York by now.'

It was at this moment that I noticed the claw resting on the glass table top. Holmes too had spotted the danger.

'There is just one thing that troubles me,' my friend put in, 'and it is this. Accompany me to the window if you would, Inspector.' Lestrade duly followed him.

'Take a thoroughfare such as Baker Street,' Holmes expounded. 'It is overlooked by a hundred windows. How is it, in the deadly quiet of the night, that such barbarism take place without attracting attention?' With the inspector safely engaged, I slid the bear's claw across the table, dropped it into my hand and thence into my pocket. 'Surely such an end would not be a quiet one. What of the screams and desperate calls for help? What of the fierce utterances of the beast as it went about its bloody work? Unless the good souls of Whitechapel sleep the sleep of the dead, your explanation sounds fantastical.' The inspector looked not a little annoyed.

'Then what alternative theory do you propose?'

'It is merely a case of eliminating the impossible,' continued Holmes, throwing me a glance. I nodded an indication that the coast was now clear. 'Perhaps if you would allow me to inspect the scene, it may be that I can cast some light on the subject. Give me a moment to throw some water on my face and I will join you outside. Dr Watson, I'm sure, will accompany us and together we will provide all assistance in our power. My feeling is that while this bear remains alive, the bear tamer will not abandon him. Mark my words, inspector, our man is but a stone's throw away!' I marvelled at Holmes' audacity. With Lestrade safely outside, Olo Bosko emerged gratefully from his hiding place.

'A thousand thanks ...' he began, ringing his hands together. 'May the blessings of Saint Jude be upon you.'

'The Patron Saint of lost causes?' laughed Holmes. 'Come, my friend, I think you can afford to be a little more hopeful than that.' My friend busied himself scribbling on his notepad. He tore out a leaf and handed it to the Slav.

'Now,' instructed Holmes, 'here is a place you can lie low for a couple of days while we straighten this out. Ask for a man named Shinwell Johnson. He is a devious, repellent-looking fellow who is as shy of bathwater as he is of the law. Pass on my felicitations and thank him with this bank note on my behalf for his recent services. He will keep you out of harm's way.'

Within ten minutes, Lestrade, Holmes and I were bolting along Whitechapel High Street in a four wheeler, gripping the door handles for dear life as we turned sharply into Commercial Street.

'I've offered our man an extra coin for every minute he takes off the journey,' explained Holmes. 'No doubt, Lestrade, your men will have thoroughly trampled the crime scene before we arrive.'

'We have been as careful as we can,' assured the inspector.

'Which is rarely careful enough,' sighed Holmes.

Presently, we saw two constables guarding the end of the street and beyond them a canvas tent which stood over Professor Spenning's remains.

'"Now there is only death's eternal cold,"' Holmes quoted grimly. The policemen nodded us through and we approached the tent, on my part, with no small degree of trepidation. As a family doctor, rheumatism and the common cold were more regular complaints than a mauling from a bear.

'You've seen worse,' warned Lestrade, lifting the flap, 'but not often.'

As ever, my friend went his own way, walking straight past the tent and along the street, glancing up at the second floor windows then down at the ground.

'I say, Holmes!' called Lestrade. 'Surely you wish to inspect the body?' The detective turned on his heel.

'Inspector,' he admonished, 'you have already provided me with a colourful description of the contents of that tent. I am far more interested in what the hebetudinous bumbledom of Scotland Yard may have missed in its excitement. In his flight, did the assailant, or his keeper, if we are to follow your logic, leave anything behind that might provide a clue to his identity? Forgive me, Lestrade, but until I have conducted a full audit of the data, we are operating in a vacuum. Lestrade glared at him.

'Very well, Holmes,' he said. 'You have your methods and I have mine. Now doctor, perhaps you would be able to provide a medical assessment?'

'I'm perfectly happy to wait for Holmes,' I assured him.

At this moment, a curious, smiling man emerged from a side alley. He was well into his third age, with missing teeth, a nose richly veined with red capillaries and great clumps of greasy white hair protruding from beneath his crumpled top hat. He was strangely familiar. But the most singular aspect was his elliptical gait, a hobble so exaggerated it was almost as if he danced as he made his way down the street. I raised my own hat as he passed and he returned this greeting with a wheezing noise, his tongue lolling slightly over the wreckage of his dentistry. He peered at me with the most unsettling eyes, one clouded, one clear, that appeared somehow strangely intelligent and all knowing.

'Good God, Lestrade,' shouted Holmes. 'Who's the gigglemug? I thought this street was closed?'

'I can hardly keep the residents prisoners in their own homes!' the inspector protested. My friend shook his head and continued his investigations. I turned and saw that the man had vanished as swiftly as he had appeared.

Holmes suddenly stopped, crossed the street and knelt down.

'A clue?' I asked.

'Perhaps, and perhaps not.' He produced a small, green brooch.

'Is it jade?' I asked.

'Plaster of Paris,' said Holmes, 'a worthless trinket.' We returned to Lestrade. 'Now,' he stated, 'we are ready to inspect the body.'

It was as grisly as expected. Spenning lay on his side next to his bicycle, his tweeds cut to ribbons and his face torn horribly into strips. I examined the wounds and they appeared consistent with the animal attacks I had seen in Afghanistan. What's more, there were undeniable traces of animal fur, coarse brown and to my eyes, convincingly bear-like.

'What did Kibble make of the hair?' I asked.

'Bear,' came the inspector.

'Still, I cannot imagine,' I put in, 'what might have provoked a tame animal to suddenly molest the professor. By the same token I am intrigued as to what business an Oxford Professor of Literature might have in the slums of the East End. There cannot be much call for his line of work here.'

'Excellent reasoning, Watson,' commended Holmes, extracting a single length of hair from the body and dropping it into an envelope. 'I might have asked the same questions myself. Do you have an answer, Lestrade?' The inspector narrowed his rat-like eyes and peered down at the body.

'Every man has his own business, Holmes. But when the evidence is as compelling as this I cannot see the point in delving deeper. Find me another bear and another bear tamer and I would be happy to interview them. Now, there is a reason you are here. Can you help me locate my man?'

'Perhaps, inspector, perhaps,' my friend said in a distracted way. I assume you have made enquiries at his lodgings?'

'Naturally.'

'Lestrade,' Holmes announced, 'it is my firm belief that neither the bear nor its master had a thing to do with this murder.'

'Preposterous!'

'Give me a day and I will prove it to you.'

We left Lestrade brooding over his corpse, no doubt furious at Holmes' incalcitrance, then made our way to the end of the street. On the corner lingered a group of three old crones selling matches. Each was wizened and stooped; they wore black shawls over their white hair and expressions of perfect, downcast misery.

'I say,' I suggested cheerfully, handing over a coin, 'you might do better if you worked different patches.' It was then that I noticed their blank stare. I staggered backwards, stumbling on the curb, recoiling from the eyes peering back blindly at me, all clouded white with cataracts. The women nearest to me shot out a thin, white hand, and seized my wrist in her cold clasp.

'"By the pricking of my thumbs,"' she hissed, '"something wicked this way comes!"'

'Get away from me,' I shouted, and they burst into a horrible cackle.

'Come Watson,' Holmes laughed, watching the spectacle with his arms folded. 'Leave these good ladies to their trade.'

'Yes!' taunted one as I staggered away. 'Leave us to our trade!' One of them clapped her hands together a tongue of flame appeared to leap from her hands. I stared agape.

'What did you make of all that, Holmes?' I gasped as we leapt into a hansom.

'I believe they were making fun of you, Watson. Now I don't suppose you have a light?'

The afternoon slipped into dusk and the gas lamps began to burn the edges of the sky. As we weaved our way back through the city, the cloud cleared to reveal a glitter of stars, like sapphires scattered to the wind. We stopped in at Shinwell Johnson's lodging on our return to Baker Street and a bilious place it was too: a brick hovel built in the gap between a railway arch and workshop. Putrid grease seemed to seep from its very walls; moss and lichen attached itself to the windows and it was through one of these that we saw Shinwell's shifty eyes peering out. A moment later and the door opened an inch. Holmes pushed against it and we stepped into the gloom.

To our surprise an appetising aroma greeted us. Bosko was warming himself by a meagre fire.

'Mr Holmes!' he said, rising from his chair. In his hand was a poker, on the end of which was a sausage of some description, which he was slowly turning over a low fire.

'Domace Klobasy,' he explained, following our gaze. 'It is very good. The secret is the sweet red pepper. I carry a sausage in my pocket at all times. Would you like to try?'

'For a bag o' mystery,' muttered Shinwell who was tucking into a plate of his own, 'it 'aint half bad.'

'Thank you, but no thank you,' declined Holmes. 'We have seen enough diced meat for one day.'

'As you like,' shrugged Bosko, and took a bite from the end. 'So you have cleared up everything?' he asked, brightly.

'Not exactly,' admitted Holmes.

'I should be asking more for sheltering a wanted man,' grumbled Johnson.

'You are wanted man yourself,' scoffed Holmes. 'You are hardly in a position to bargain.'

'Now Bosko,' my friend said, turning to the Slav, 'I will be back in a day's time with news of your freedom and an apology from Scotland Yard. In the meantime, I suggest that you and Shinwell here continue to enjoy each other's kitchen secrets. But before we bid you adieu once more, I have a question relating to the missing claw.'

I dug into my pocket and felt the sharp point and coarse leather tassel. I pulled it out and held it in my open palm.

'When did Gregor lose this?' Holmes asked.

'Four years ago, in a fall in the Pyrenees.'

'Well it may well turn out to be a very lucky charm indeed.' A smile began to crease the edges of my mouth.

'Splendid, Holmes!' I cried, as the realisation dawned on me. 'A bear with nine claws! The wounds on Professor Spenning's body do not match.'

'Precisely, Watson; it was my first thought, but an inspection of the body was necessary to confirm the theory. Do you mind if we hold onto it for a few hours more?'

'By all means,' agreed Bosko, his face lit by the flames.

'Then who did murder Spenning?' I asked.

'All will become apparent,' remarked Holmes. 'Patience is an admirable gift.'

I was all too pleased to leave the seedy streets of Bow behind as once again, we engaged the service of a London cabbie. I was relieved too to be heading back to the homely comforts of 221b Baker Street. With the latest instalment of Hardy's gloomily compelling saga, Jude the Obscure to read in Harper's and an unopened single malt, I planned a quiet conclusion to an unsettling day. My friend, however, seemed preoccupied, brooding beside me.

'Surely, Holmes,' I cajoled, we have solved the curious case of the

124

dancing bear. The solution seems so straightforward it barely seems worth a chapter in our chronicles.'

'You will recall, Watson,' my friend said, turning to me, his face half in shadow, 'my words of caution from the Boscombe Valley affair: "There is nothing more deceptive than an obvious fact."'

'It was,' I agreed, 'a strange way to begin an adventure, to be handed the solution by the client himself.' Holmes reached into his pocket and withdrew the brooch he had discovered earlier.

'A light, Watson, if you please.' I struck the sulphur and my friend moved the trinket into the light, turning it over.

'Do you see those initials?' he asked?

'H.R.,' I read.

'Harold Rosenblatt,' muttered Holmes.

'A friend of yours?'

'The manufacture of costume jewellery,' he explained. 'Almost everything on the London stage, from a fake sword to a phony diamond is manufactured by the man. Within his own, limited sphere, he is an artist or sorts. While fulfilling my duties as an understudy I saw those initials everywhere.'

'So what's your inference?'

'It is a curious item to find on the streets of Whitechapel, would you not agree?'

'Could it be,' I proposed, 'that it was dropped by a down at heel actress? It hardly seems impossible.'

'Certainly, Watson. In fact, I saw an identical brooch being worn by our friend Elsie Pinner, the actress who played Desdemona this winter just passed.' I furrowed my brow.

I saw little of Holmes that evening. He left our rooms informing me he intended to visit Rosenblatt, the theatrical costumer and then call in on his brother, a rare occurrence at such a late hour. Yet even in his absence, his personality dominated the room. His papers spilled across the floor; the violin lay with its bow on the desk where he had left it, distracted by some book or other. A glass vessel stood half filled on the acid stained tabletop. His monographs lined the shelves and there were bullet holes around the mirror, where he had fired in a fit of joy when arriving at the solution of the memorable Adventure of the Albino Unicyclist. Sherlock Holmes gave these rooms meaning; without him they would be merely be the anonymous chambers of a man destined to be lost to history. A harvest moon rose above Baker Street, an exaggerated, swollen version of itself, preternaturally bright, giving the sitting room an ethereal glow. I found myself peering from our first floor window into the street, watching the long shadows and dreaming once again of Mary's ghost.

Next morning there was no sign of my friend. He eventually rose at one, as if this was perfectly common practice and sauntered into our sitting room, his nose in Henry IV Part I. He wore his large blue dressing gown, the stem of a pipe peeking out of one of its capacious pockets.

'A splendid moon last night, wasn't it Watson.'

'Well, yes it was as a matter of fact.'

'I cannot help but notice, 'he gestured, 'that you stood just to the left of the window admiring the moon, lost in your thoughts between a quarter to nine and ten to nine. You then moved to the drinks cabinet and poured yourself a measure of Gordon and MacPhail's single malt, adding no water. You drank it as you circumnavigated the room in an anticlockwise fashion, pausing to skim my monograph on the identification of bicycle tracks field and moorland. It is by the way, now misfiled behind a more recent study on the detection and tracking of horseshoes deliberately fitted backwards.'

'It is as if you were here watching me!' I marvelled, shaking my head. 'But how could you possibly know?'

'Four simple observations,' he announced with a flourish, 'the level of the whisky and soda: one lower by a quarter inch, the other unchanged; the indentation of the rug and carpet, the slight protrusion of the volume on the shelf; the marks left by your glass here, here and here.'

'Remarkable!' I cried.

'Elementary,' he corrected.

'Now what time do you call this, Holmes?' I said, tapping my watch, feeling as if I ought to take him to task. Even if you returned past midnight, you must have still slept a full twelve hours.'

'It is no secret that I value my sleep. It is the most perfect and natural state. It is where the mind begins its most sublime machinations, conjures its most fanciful notions and leads us to our darkest, most innermost sanctuaries. Now, despite the hour, do you think a kipper is out of the question?'

'You wanted to see me?' asked Lestrade officiously, putting down his pen and rubbing his dark, tired eyes. It was an hour after Mrs Hudson begrudgingly prepared Holmes his late breakfast. We were standing in the Inspector's office at Scotland Yard, a chamber of gloom, lined with filing cabinets and thick bundles of unsolved cases. It felt as if the floorboards would buckle beneath the weight of criminal endeavour.

'Lestrade,' mused Holmes. 'I sometimes wonder whether you take enough delight in catching your man.'

'Delight?' the inspector repeated, handling the word with distaste. 'I take no delight in my work,' he stated, reaching into his pocket for his cigarette case, 'only the satisfaction of knowing that justice has been served.'

'For my own part,' added Holmes, 'I would have little interest in upholding the law if there was no pleasure to be had in the process. I sometimes feel that your efforts and your results do not always tally. Often a very specific observation or intervention, the work of a moment, can yield greater rewards than a hundred hours of drudgery.'

'Have you called in specifically to criticise my methods?' Lestrade asked wearily. 'If so, I can tell you that I have plenty of that from my superiors.'

'Only friendly words of advice,' twinkled Holmes.

'You have your methods and I have mine,' opined Lestrade, touching a flame to the end of his cigarette. 'My philosophy is that application will eventually be rewarded.'

'In my experience,' continued Holmes, 'a criminal will only be caught when he reaches the point where his greed exceeds his control of risk. A man's carelessness invariably increases in direct proportion to his appetites.'

'Is there a point to any of this?' asked Lestrade wearily.

'I can tell you where to find your bear tamer.' Lestrade blinked and then stood up, his knuckles pressed down on his desk, leaning forward accusingly.

'Is this something you have only just learned or am I to believe that you have been withholding information? Why didn't you tell me before?'

'You never asked.'

'Don't play games with me, Holmes,' he warned, reaching for his jacket. 'Take me to him at once.'

'I need to show you something first,' he said.

'Watson,' he invited, 'will you do the honours?' I stepped forward and deposited a heavy, leather case on Lestrade's desk. Holmes flipped the catches and reached inside, withdrawing two fearsome metal implements; a pair of jagged steel claws, each fitted with a rounded handle.

'What's the meaning of this?' demanded Lestrade.

'Here are your murder weapons,' Holmes stated. 'They are known in the trade, rather unimaginatively, as the bear paw claw.'

'What trade?'

'An excellent question,' said Holmes. 'The answer is the catering trade. They are used by cooks to dice meat. Nothing, it appears, has improved on nature's own ingenuity.' Lestrade frowned, looking unconvinced. 'Watson and I both examined Spenning's body. The wounds are perfectly straight; if the man was attacked by a real bear, the incisions would taper inwards; the middle wound would also begin higher than the others. In this case, they all begin at exactly the same point.' Lestrade gave Holmes a dismissive look.

'That is not the sort of detail that will interest a hanging judge.'

'Then perhaps he would be interested to know that there were ten long incisions in Spenning's body, rather than nine. If you check the beast in your custody, you will discover he has only nine claws. Here is the tenth.' He tossed the bear claw onto the desk. The inspector held it up to the light and nodded thoughtfully.

'I am prepared to admit there may be something in this,' he confessed. 'But even if what you say is true, it puts us back to where we started, knowing nothing.'

'If you excuse the pun,' said Holmes. 'We may not have to start quite from scratch.' He held up the jade brooch.

'I discovered one other item of interest at the murder scene,' he said.

'Impossible,' dismissed Lestrade. 'My men combed every inch of that street.'

'Then I suggest,' my friend put in, 'that next time they use a finer toothed comb. This brooch is a piece of theatrical jewellery. It is my belief that it was worn by the killer.'

'A wild speculation,' stated Lestrade. 'Simply on the basis that it was found near the body?' It could have been dropped by anyone at anytime.

'I made some enquiries,' said Holmes, 'and discovered it is one of a kind. Its manufacturer, Harold Rosenblatt made it to order for a recent production of Othello. It was worn by the actress who played Desdemona, a woman by the name of Elsie Pinner. If I remember correctly you saw her wearing it with your own eyes!'

'I also suggest that she had an accomplice, an older man who Watson has met twice.'

'Twice?' I asked.

'Yes,' said Holmes. 'Do you not recall the toothless tramp that morning in Baker Street? He has a habit of appearing with the woman.'

'Of course!' I replied. 'It was the same man.'

'Do you two fellows never speak?' asked Lestrade.

'They are both members of an elusive society,' said Holmes. 'Infiltrate the society and we will capture them all in one fell swoop.'

EIGHT

The Problem of the Hourly Message

'What time do you have, Watson?' my friend asked.
'It is five minutes since you last enquired,' I returned wearily.
'The precise time,' he specified. 'I have been doing a small calculation in my head about the time it would take a one legged man to walk the distance between Whitehall and Baker Street. I would be grateful if you could help me confirm my theory.' I glanced at my fob watch then slipped it back inside my pocket.
'It is precisely four minutes past eleven.'
'Excellent!' he cried in triumph, then slipped back into his seat with an air of satisfaction.

Holmes and I were enduring what appeared to be an interminable crawl through London. Finally, after navigating past the scene of upended omnibus, a dead horse and for all I know a spilt applecart, our growler finally deposited us outside the door of 221b Baker Street. The scent of Mrs Hudson's cooking was enough to restore our flagging spirits as we stepped inside and discarded our coats.
'Lunch smells marvellous,' I called, returning my brolly to its stand.
'I shall be serving in twenty minutes sharp!' she reported back.
'Very good,' I returned.
'A curious combination,' remarked Holmes pausing to sniff the air.
'I wait with interest.'

Mrs Hudson did not disappoint. A delicious hare soup was followed by sheep rumps and kidneys in rice, served with beef olives.
'Well,' my friend remarked. 'Our landlady has certainly raised her game. I doubt very much that the King of Persia is dining in such style.'
'Is it all to your liking, gentlemen?' Mrs Hudson wiped her hands on a cloth. I nodded and swallowed a final mouthful of rice.
'I'd say!'
'I'm experimenting with some new dishes ahead of a friend's birthday,' she explained.
'Any time you feel the need to experiment,' I volunteered, 'please

consider us game.'

'Thank you, doctor. I like a man who enjoys his food. Unlike you, Mr Holmes, who, with the greatest of respect, would benefit from a little feeding up. Now would you have room for a little dessert?'

'Plenty,' I assured her.

'I have perfected what I believe is called the floating island: meringues adrift in yellow custard.'

'Mrs Hudson,' I said lifting a spoon in readiness, 'It is my sincere belief that you were sent to us from heaven.'

No sooner had I raised my spoon when I heard a single rap on the front door.

'I'll answer,' I informed Mrs Hudson, knowing that she was engaged in more pressing matters. With a decidedly heavy step, I descended the seventeen stairs and opened the door.

'Telegram, sir,' reported a flame haired young boy. I proffered a coin and hurried back to my pudding. Such was our interest in Mrs Hudson's floating island that we neglected to inspect the message until our coffee arrived. Holmes glanced at it, then read it again with an increasingly furrowed brow.

'The game is afoot, Watson!' he exclaimed, pushing it across the table. 'What do you make of this?'

'Yea mayo duly. Bile wilt mutton'
Best Hen Pen

'Baffling,' I said. 'Does it pertain perhaps to some unpleasant business relating to Irish sheep?'

'I think not,' replied Holmes then retrieved a grease pencil from his pocket. He made a series of strident marks on the slip of paper, tapped the end a few times against his teeth then finished his work.

'There,' he said, with an air of satisfaction. 'QED: Quite easily done.' I read Holmes' scrawled note.

'You may delay. But time will not.'
Best Hen Pen

'An anagram!' I cried, 'of course.'

131

'That, I fear,' remarked Holmes, 'is only half the puzzle.'
'Then it is a threat of some description?'
'If I had a penny for every threat I have received Watson,' he muttered, 'I would be the owner of a large farmhouse in Sussex rather than a tenant at 221b Baker Street.'
'Should we call Lestrade?' I asked. Holmes gave a mirthless laugh. 'I am uncertain what assistance the inspector could provide. Besides, I think by now, Watson, we are more than capable of looking after ourselves.' I considered this for a moment, suddenly feeling unable to finish the pudding.
'But who is this Best Hen Pen?' I asked. 'He must be a brash fellow to supply his name. Perhaps he will show his face this afternoon.'
'Yes, perhaps, he will.'

My friend busied himself with a dictionary of quotations, running his bony finger down each page until he struck gold.
'There it is,' he exclaimed in triumph. 'Benjamin Franklin. Did you know, Watson, he was a marvellous chess player?'
'I did not,' I confessed. 'Presumably he founded the United States in his spare time.' Holmes bit down on the stem of his pipe and took up his pearl handled paper knife, turning it slowly in his hand.
'I am very much taken,' Holmes reflected, 'by the idea of the polymath. The greatest enemy of every man is time; the second is his fear of failure. Most men do not take up the greatest challenges for fear they will have not have the time or the ability to see them through. It is true to say that the polymath, possessed of his keen intelligence, inquisitive brain and bullish temperament has no fear of time or failure. To him the world is an endless horizon of potential and possibility. He is led by his curiosity and unfailing belief in his own powers. He puts himself above time and laughs at the imagined constraints imposed by convention. He creates his own universe and abides by his own rules, ignoring the boundaries imposed by more conventional minds. If such a man decides one day that he wishes to learn to fly, then he will put his mind to it and achieve his goal. One fine day, not so far from now, one such polymath will do just that. By inspiring those around him with his irresistible optimism and through his own supreme example, he achieves what others cannot. That is how Benjamin Franklin managed to invent the lightening rod,

the flipper, edit a newspaper, establish a university and found a nation all in one lifetime.' I smiled at my friend's speech; it was an unconscious tribute to himself.

I settled down with a crumpled copy of The Times and had just nodded off when we heard another knock at the door.

'Your turn,' I muttered to my friend, who was still staring into space, no doubt developing a theory. There was a second knock. I was determined to hold my nerve and refused to raise myself from my chair. There were times when I had to remind myself that I was not Holmes' batman, but a doctor of medicine hoodwinked into servitude by my occasionally overbearing friend. There was more than once, I mused, when he had sent me off like a delivery boy with a message to wire or parcel to collect. Mrs Hudson appeared at the door, red faced from the kitchen.

'I can see you're both very busy,' she said, fixing each of us with a familiar look. 'This has just arrived.' Holmes leapt to his feet.

'My apologies, Mrs Hudson,' he said, receiving the envelope between two fingers. 'Your magnificent lunch has put us in somnolent mood.' He collapsed back into his chair, and sliced open the letter with the relish one might gut a fish.

'It is as if you knew this message was coming,' I said, throwing the paper to one side.

'It was by no means a certainty but the odds were certainly in its favour.' I shook my head in wonder.

'Now, Watson,' he said, would you be so good as to record the time?'

'One minute past one o'clock.'

'Thank you.'

Peering over Holmes' shoulder as he scrutinised the note, I took a look myself. Printed in pencil on a piece of torn stationery were three numbers and a name:

334 1859 1700
Best Hen Pen

'This friend of yours a singular sense of humour,' I opined.

133

'What the devil is he up to?'

'Most cryptic,' agreed Holmes, his eyes glistening with interest.

'What about a list of births for 1859. There must be a central registrar,' I suggested.

'A fine thought, Watson,' Holmes returned, 'but my suspicion is that it will be concerted brain work rather than the reference library that will provide the solution to this problem.'

Busying myself with a sheet of foolscap and a pen, I copied down the two numbers. I multiplied them, divided them, added them, subtracted them from each other but found no way to arrive at any kind of sense.

'You are tying yourself in knots, Watson,' remarked Holmes who had moved to his acid stained tabletop and was now preparing an experiment with a quantity of blue powder. 'In my experience, the answer often presents itself when you are least expecting it. It is less a case of hacking at the coal face than waiting in the right place so a diamond might fall into your hands.'

I heard a small cough. 'Mr Holmes, Dr Watson?'

Glancing up from my page, I saw Mrs Hudson once more bearing gifts.

'Not another message!' I exclaimed.

'Not this time. However, if you don't mind, I do have another pudding for you to try. This is my Great Aunt Fenella's transparent pudding.'

'I don't see a thing,' retorted Holmes.

'Mr Holmes,' our landlady returned, 'when I want entertainment, I visit the Alhambra on Ladies' Thursdays.'

'Of course, you do,' smiled Holmes. 'We are very much obliged. Please leave the pudding on the table with Doctor Watson and he will be pleased to deliver his verdict in due course.'

Though not the least bit hungry, through sheer frustration I cut myself a large slice, poured on a generous amount of cream and tucked in. It was splendid.

Holmes fished into his waistcoat pocket then flipped open his watch. 'I say, Watson,' he piped up. 'Would you mind jogging downstairs to answer the door?' I looked up, confused and not a little annoyed. 'I didn't hear a thing,' I replied. At that precise moment, there was a knock. Holmes returned his watch to his pocket.

'Perfectly punctual,' he declared with satisfaction.

Mystified, I once again descended our well-trodden stairs and opened the door to discover a bored looking cabbie holding out a square parcel wrapped in brown paper.

'May I ask who sent you?' I enquired.

'You may ask,' the hansom driver returned in his broad cockney accent, 'but I 'aint at liberty to tell you.'

I returned to our rooms and my friend and I stared at the package.

'Well,' said Holmes, 'we have had a number of singular deliveries of late; I fancy this will not disappoint. Shall I do the honours?' Casting aside several handfuls of packing straw my friend retrieved what appeared to be a pocket watch.

'Why Holmes,' I exclaimed, peering at the time piece. 'It is an exact replica of your own!'

'Not an exact replica,' Holmes corrected. 'Take a closer look.'

'Good lord,' I said. 'How strange.' Around the clock face were no less than twelve iterations of the Roman numeral V.

'A bizarre gift and no mistake,' I opined. 'But what does it mean, Holmes?'

'Naturally a theory is beginning to form,' he began, 'although there are points yet to be clarified. Contrary to my earlier remarks, I believe now is the time to summon our friend, Lestrade.'

Employing the services of one of the Baker Street Irregulars, a scrofulous urchin by the name of Billings, a note of our own was despatched at speed in the direction of Scotland Yard. In the time it took the inspector to arrive, no less than two puddings and another message had been delivered. The note, delivered by a baker's boy and concealed inside a loaf of bread, was a typed invitation, which ran follows:

Step up, Sherlock Holmes, for your unsolved ill brat.
Best Hen Pen

'You do not think Billings is any danger?' I asked in alarm. Holmes stared hard at the note then shook his head. 'No, I believe the boy is perfectly well. This tells another story entirely.'

The inspector trudged up the stairs and nodded warily.
'No more bears I hope,' he began, laconically.
'Not a bear in sight,' confirmed Holmes. 'Now have you eaten yet, Lestrade?' The mealy mouth detective looked momentarily confused, clutching his bowler and peering at the gluttonous delights on the table. 'There's a choice of Crystal Palace or Orange Custard pudding,' my friend explained, 'or perhaps or Batchelor's pudding is more to your taste? I'm quite sure we have a quantity left over.'
'Is this the reason you called?' he asked irritably, 'to invite me to a pudding club?'
'Mrs Hudson's pudding are worth crossing a continent for,' Holmes testified, but in this case, no. We have a beguiling matter which requires your attention: The Problem of the Hourly Message. Holmes showed Lestrade the telegram, the letter, the watch and the loaf.
'Someone is having some fun with you,' he muttered.
'I assure you,' Holmes asserted, 'I have no friends with such a well-developed sense of humour. In fact, I would go as far to say, my only friend is standing here in this room with us.' It was perhaps my imagination, but I fancied that Lestrade took some offence at this.
'And what of this fellow, Best Hen Pen?' Lestrade continued officiously, inspecting the note more closely.
'A pseudonym, surely,' I ventured.
'Perhaps,' reflected Holmes. 'and perhaps not. Let us assume,' Holmes continued, 'that Best Hen Pen is an anagram too. A schoolboy would unravel it in seconds.' Lestrade and I glanced at each other, uncertain either of us could unscramble the cipher had we been granted several lifetimes.
'Doctor, would you care to enlighten us?' asked Holmes.
'Please do the honours, Holmes,' I dodged. He lowered his brows like a disapproving schoolmaster.
'Stephen Ben,' he declared, 'is the name we have to work with.'
'Let me see,' I suggested, 'if he has found his way into our index of biographies. It is possible the man has form in this area.'

'A splendid idea, Watson,' said Holmes smiling despite himself. 'I believe we have an interesting afternoon ahead of us.'

Once again I reached for the huge directory in which Holmes recorded the names of those whose path he had crossed during the course of his investigations. It pages were filled to bursting with the criminal, the insane, the desperate and foolish.

'We have a Stephen Belding,' I noted.

'The Hackney funambulist?' my friend recalled. 'A most dangerous profession as he discovered to his cost. The high wire is the wrong place of work for those who wish to lead a long life.'

'But no Stephen Ben,' I reported, my finger running off the page.

'I thought as much,' my friend concluded.

'Well,' said Lestrade, 'whoever he is, I agree that there is a menacing tone to all this. If it is a question of security, I could station a constable outside your door. Rance is only a street or two away.'

'Thank you, but no,' my friend smiled, pacing towards the window, his hands folded behind his back. 'I am certain that while we are quite safe here, someone else is in jeopardy. Now tell me Lestrade, what did you make of the letter?' The inspector flushed, clearly uncomfortable to be put on the spot like this.

'I have not studied it at any length,' he dismissed.

'Me neither,' smiled Holmes. 'However I have gleamed enough to provide some useful intelligence. Do you see where the page is torn in two? Just below the tear line, there is a minute inverted arc in black print. I have compared this with a piece of stationery in my files, inscribed by the Prime Minister himself no less. The inverted arch is in fact the base of the oblong crest on House of Commons stationery. Gentlemen, it is my belief that this letter originated from the Houses of Parliament.' Lestrade's eyes widened.

'Wait!' uttered Lestrade. 'What about that nit-wit from Finsbury East?'

'Which one?' I put in.

'Stephen Ben, the Member of Parliament.'

'That certainly sounds plausible,' I added.

'I'm afraid,' my friend put in, 'that would leave us the problem of the double n.' We contemplated this in silence. Holmes called us to order. 'Let us consider the clues again. In my opinion, our

137

protagonist has been generous. Suspiciously so, I would say.'

Together we stared at the numbers once more: 334, 1700, 1859 and then the repeated fives on the clock face.
'Are they prime?' I asked, clutching at straws.
'I have no idea!' laughed Holmes. 'Let us take them in stages: 1700 can be matched with the eight on the watch face; it is the equivalent on the 24 hour clock, more commonly used on the continent, specifically Italy, than it is here. That leaves us with the problem of the date. A quick glance at my Encyclopædia Britannica confirmed my suspicion. It is the date that St Stephen's tower was constructed.'
'Big Ben!' I exclaimed.
'Precisely,' my friend confirmed. 'Then everything else falls into place. The same source informed me that there are 334 steps to the belfry.'
'But what,' asked Lestrade, his fingers raking the grey bristles on his chin, 'is the significance of the five?'

Holmes retrieved his hat and coat from the stand then turned to us with grave expression.
'The sign of five I believe is the salient clue. Since noon we have received four messages, each one arriving without fail, on the hour. I am certain that the next message will not be found here but at the Houses of Parliament. Watson, what time do you make it?' I pulled out my watch.
'Thirty five minutes past four o'clock.'
'Then there is not a moment to lose,' he cried. 'To work!'

The three of us bundled out onto the pavement, almost knocking over another street urchin in our haste. He was a scruffy looking pigmy with a shirt so threadbare that it seemed conceivable that it was worn by his grandfather as a boy.
'Watch it, mister!' he called out, then seeing a business opportunity, quickly corrected his manner.
'I do beg your pardon, sirs. Now then,' he added precociously, 'riddle me, riddle me, what is that over the head and under the hat?
'Move along!' I shouted, stepping into road to hail a passing brougham.

'Do as he says,' warned Lestrade or I'll have you arrested for vagrancy. Holmes watched the boy with some amusement and no little fascination.

'Hair,' he said simply, then threw him a coin.

'I could tell,' laughed the boy in delight, flipping the coin into the air and catching it in the same hand, 'you were the one blessed with the brains!'

The afternoon sun broke through the glass, catching our coat buttons and watch chains as we rattled down the Edgeware Road. Lestrade loosened his collar and lowered the window.

'If only the criminal class took themselves down to Margate for the first two weeks of June,' he complained. 'It's too hot for all this. Now a penny for your thoughts, Holmes,' he muttered. 'Do you believe this has anything to do business with Rosebery at the Derby?'

'Everything is connected,' opined Holmes. 'It is merely a case of linking the stars to identify the constellation.'

The skies darkened as we approached Westminster. Like a finger of warning, Pugin's elegant clock tower rose up toward the clouds.

'Naturally,' remarked Holmes, 'there is every chance that this is a trap.'

'And like rabbits,' I put in, 'we are bounding towards the snare.' Lestrade frowned. 'Is there also a possibility you could be mistaken?' My friend raised an eyebrow in indignation. He peered down his long hawk-like nose. 'It is my belief, inspector that we have been summoned to witness a significant and almost certainly unpleasant event. Knowing my natural curiosity, the sender of these singular messages believes that inevitably I will follow the trail here. No doubt some macabre fate awaits.'

Lestrade narrowed his eyes in the bright light. 'I have taken the precaution of detaining the Right Honourable Stephen Benn, MP,' he said. 'Sometimes Holmes, I believe you make the world more complicated than it is. I have also requested that we are met by a number of my constables.'

'As you wish,' said Holmes then returned his gaze to the skyline.

Sure enough, there was a considerable hoopla at the base of the tower. Constables lined the perimeter and a small crowd had gathered, drawn in by rumours of suicide and scandal.'

A bulky sergeant with the cheeks of a hamster and the whiskers of a Cheshire cat approached. 'There's talk of a ladybird at the top of the tower who wants to do herself in,' he informed Lestrade. 'We've sealed off the area.'

'Good,' the inspector returned. 'Keep them well back. What of Benn?'

'I'm afraid he's gone missing, sir.' Lestrade glanced at my friend. 'Admit it, Holmes' he said, with no little satisfaction, 'you didn't anticipate that.' The detective appeared to ignore the comment and peered intently up at the belfry.

'One more thing, sir,' the sergeant added. The entrance is barred and secured with a padlock on the outside'.

'I see. Very good, Devlin.'

As we made our way through the main entrance I pulled Holmes aside.

'Anything I should know?' I asked him.

'I have observed a number of irregularities that are, each in their own way, highly suggestive. For instance did you notice the trail of mud? There is a not a member of either house, or any official, who would dream of traipsing mud through the corridors of power. Then there is the chalk.'

'Chalk?'

'Yes a single piece of chalk has been dropped and ground by the heel of a boot. It has left its own trail alongside the mud.'

'What are we to infer?' I asked. 'A country schoolmaster?'

'A splendid suggestion,' he congratulated. 'Now keep your wits about you, Watson, and as a precaution, have your service revolver at the ready.' My friend strode forward into the Palace of Westminster, his gown whipping behind him as if he was the Prime Minister himself. Holmes and Lestrade inspected the padlock that secured the small door.

'A crowbar will make short work of this,' the inspector said.

'I'm not sure that will be necessary,' my friend said coolly. He twisted the barrels of the combination lock and the padlock snapped open.'

'Remarkable!' I exclaimed.

'Nonsense,' dismissed Holmes. 'Simplicity itself. So far, this has been nothing but a game.' I glanced at the number sequence: 5555.

I peered up the staircase, which spiralled away into the sky.

'You first,' I said, allowing Lestrade to pass ahead. He led the way, followed by Holmes, Devlin and myself bringing up the rear. Each footstep was accompanied by a ghostly echo. But no sooner had Lestrade ascended a couple of steps when Holmes cried out.

'Look there!' he shouted, pointing down. Each step was inscribed with words in chalk.

'Shakespeare,' I said, glancing at the first few steps.

'Correct,' my dear Watson.'

'But whatever does it mean?'

'Patience, Watson!' he cried, moving into the lead. 'Now do exactly as I say.' Stopping on the fourth step he knelt and read the words on the fifth:

'Knowledge is the wing wherewith we fly to heaven'

'Henry IV Part I,' he declared.

'We have no time for this,' hurried Lestrade.

'I beg to differ,' said Holmes. 'Look here.'

Peering closely we saw a thin, almost invisible wire running across the centre of the step, which led to what appeared to be a small explosive charge taped to the side.

'A swift route into heaven,' remarked Holmes, stepping carefully over it. 'Gentlemen,' he added. 'You would do well to avoid every fifth step.' Devlin's eyes grew wide with alarm.

'What else lies in store?' he wondered aloud.

'Plenty, I imagine,' Holmes suggested.

As if in answer, there was clanking echo from somewhere high above us. It sent a cold chill down my spine and instinctively, I gripped the handle of my revolver.

'Dr Watson,' called Holmes, climbing carefully ahead of us, casting his eyes about for signs of further danger. 'It is a somewhat absurd

question given our location, but do you happen to have the time?'
'Nine minutes to the hour,' I returned.
'Then there is no time to be lost. I assume gentleman, you can all count to five?' And with that, he sprinted ahead, skipping over every fifth step. The rest of us followed as quickly as we dared, albeit significantly slower than Holmes.
'Lestrade!' I suddenly shouted. 'Don't move!' He froze, his foot in mid air. The inspector clearly had not paid much attention to arithmetic as a schoolboy.
'Not that one!' We both read the inscription:

'Full fathom five thy father lies'

He nodded his thanks and suitably chastened, continued on his way. Looking up at the spiralling staircase, I saw Holmes' birdlike features staring down at me, as if from an eyrie.
'What is it, Holmes?' I cried, and without thinking, dashed up the remaining steps to join him.
'Remarkable number work, Watson!' congratulated Holmes. 'Or was that mere foolishness with a helping of luck?' I teetered on my current step and glanced back in horror.
'The latter,' I confessed. However a new peril now confronted us.
A solid sheet of metal blocked our path. Across it was drawn a grid containing a series of arrows, variously pointing north, south, east and west. At the centre was a brass door knob protruding from the grid. A slip of paper was attached to this, bearing a question mark.

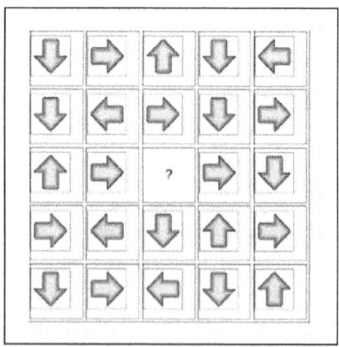

142

Inevitably, the step on which the metal sheet rested bore the legend 'The slings and arrows of outrageous fortune.'

'A fellow after my own heart,' mused Holmes as we gathered round him. 'Clearly we are required to solve this puzzle before proceeding.'

Lestrade narrowed his eyes.

'I don't like these games,' he growled. 'What's to say that solving the puzzle will not result in some new catastrophe?'

'Then I am perfectly open to other suggestions,' said Holmes.

'What would you say, inspector,' suggested Devlin, 'if we laid a charge or two against this door and blew it down?'

'You are clearly a practical man, sergeant,' cautioned Holmes, 'but I would advise against that. Do you see that black power at your feet?'

We glanced down and sure enough a quantity of dark powder spilled from beneath the metal sheet.

'I don't need to tell you that's gunpowder. I suggest there's plenty more of it behind this door. A charge of our own may well be enough to remove the tower from the tourist map.' Holmes rubbed his hands together with obvious glee.

'Another puzzle!' he exclaimed with delight. 'I'd wager our friend here is an acolyte of Mr Babbage and his difference engine. Alas we do not have time to consult such a machine. We will need to rely only on our own wits. Now who can assist me?' He glanced around at us, as if reminding himself of the meagre resources at his disposal.

'Lestrade,' he began, 'with all due respect, I have discounted your help on the basis of your inability to count to five. Now Devlin, do have any form with such brain twisters?'

'I'm afraid not,' he confessed, frowning deeply at the series of arrows.

'Don't be afraid,' consoled Holmes, 'but it is a pity nonetheless.' My eyes raced across the bewildering pattern.

'And you, Watson?' he asked hopefully.

'It's all hokey-cokey to me, Holmes'

'Then I suggest,' he said, 'given the urgency, that we take a guess.' He raised his hand to twist the dial.

'Holmes, no!' I shouted in alarm, but it was too late. The mechanism clicked and the barrier swung aside.

'Good lord!' I cried, realising that we had not combusted. 'The gods are smiling on us today.'

'Watson, you will know by now that I do not rely on the gods to assist me in my work. I knew perfectly well what I was doing. It was merely a question of identifying a simple pattern. You will note how it spirals and repeats.' I stared again at the board but still failed to make any sense out of it.

'Now onwards,' cried Holmes. 'There is not a moment to lose!'

We bounded on until, at last, the belfry hove into view. Breathless, we stood beneath the great iron arches and gazed in awe at the huge, cracked bell and its fearsome hammer that dominated the room. The four quarter bells all hung ominously at each corner, poised to ring. There were still four minutes to the hour. A cold, biting wind blew across us and presently a crow swept through one of the arched portico windows skimmed our hats then disappeared out into the London sky.

'But there's nothing here,' Devlin spluttered, peering around. 'It's a wild goose chase.'

'Don't be so sure,' warned Holmes. 'Look!' Scrawled in chalk on the bell itself were these words:

'You shall hear the surly sullen bell
Give warning to the world that I am fled'

'I have just about had enough,' muttered Lestrade darkly, 'of this English lesson.'

'Congratulations Mr Holmes,' a cold voice rang out. 'You have done better than I expected but still, not quite well enough.' I jumped half out my skin then stared about me.

'Up here, doctor.' Standing a full ten feet above us on an iron beam was the unmistakable figure of Captain Hercules Winter.

'You!' I shouted.

'The very same.' The light glinted from his steel hand; in the other, he held a service revolver which he waved in our direction. Instinctively, I went for my own.

'Keep your hands where I can see them. ' he warned. 'There's a good fellow. Now it would have gone better for you if the government had bought into my scheme. As it is, I have closed the account. Still, I am playing for bigger stakes now. In a few moments

144

you and most of this magnificent tower will be lying in a heap of rubble. Joining you will be the Right Honourable Stephen Benn MP who was kind enough to lend me his stationery and invite me in. Perhaps the people of Finsbury East will be more judicious in their choice of MP next time. I also have another of your friends.'

'Oliver Standbull?' enquired Holmes as if from nowhere.

'Splendid, Mr Holmes!' he congratulated. 'He's another man too clever for his own good.'

'The unsolved ill brat,' my friend added. 'Another of your tedious anagrams, Winter. Clearly you have far too much time on your hands, or should that be hand?'

'Be that as it may,' smarted Winter, 'but he was good enough, or should I say foolish enough, to supply me with the missing play you are all so excited about.'

'Play?' asked Lestrade, with his natural suspicion. 'What play?'

'I shall explain later,' returned Holmes.

'I fancy it will fetch a fine price on the open market,' Winter continued, patting a soft leather satchel slung over his shoulder. 'But this, I fear will be Standbull's final curtain. You, Holmes, I admit, will be a loss. Even I am prepared to admit that one does not encounter a mind such as yours every day. Still, I will sleep easier in my bed knowing you are no longer at my heels.'

'You are a monster,' I growled.

'A businessman,' he corrected. 'Now gentlemen, I fear I must leave you. At the stroke of five, a quantity of dynamite will explode that will bring down this tower. It will make Mr Fawkes' gunpowder plot look positively patriotic. You have your hands full.' With this, he reached up and took hold of a wire with his steel hand, leaned back, then slid clean out of the window.

'Good lord, Holmes!'

'Back down the stairs,' urged Lestrade.

'There's no time for that now,' dismissed Holmes looking as grave as ever I have seen him. He pressed a finger to his lips and peered hard at the words on the bell.

'Of course!' he shouted. 'Winter could not resist giving us a clue. We *have our hands full.* The clock face!'

He raced across the belfry and then stopped. 'But which one?' he asked himself. 'There are four!' He tore down another flight of stairs.

We followed him through a small door and into a narrow corridor. Presently we found ourselves behind one of the brightly lit clock faces, looming massively over us like a huge, circular mosaic of stained glass. We could see the impressions of the hands and the numbers through the translucent panes.

'Not this one!' he shouted and then sprinted on. We arrived in an identical corridor, behind an identical clock face.

'This is it!' he called. Taking hold of the edge of one of the glass panels, he pulled it away leaving nothing but a panel of sky. Gripping the edges of the aperture, he poked his head through and peered upwards.

'Benn is at twelve,' he called, 'Standbull is almost at five!'

'Gentlemen,' Holmes explained briskly. 'It appears Messrs Standbull and Benn have found themselves caught up in an extraordinary imbroglio. I do not recall whether you have a head for heights but in case you don't, I suggest you grow one with all speed.' With this, he clambered out and disappeared from view. Lestrade and I glanced at each other then warily peered out to be greeted by one the most astonishing sights of our lives. The two unfortunate men, Benn and Standbull were trussed to the hands of the clock face like flies on a spider's web. Holmes had somehow managed to get hold of the edge of one of the hands and was working his way, as a sloth might traverse a branch, along the length of one the great metal needles. Upon reaching Benn, my friend drew a knife from his jacket and began to saw through his bonds. Even from my limited vantage point I could see the politician's eyes bulging in panic, alternating their focus between Holmes and the ground one hundred and eighty feet below.

'For God's sake be careful, Holmes!' I cried then clambered out myself to join him. 'One minute to five!' I called, sliding down the short hand and attempting the same trick with Standbull. At this point, I made the fatal mistake of looking down, the streets and grassy areas below spinning giddily beneath me. Soon, I felt bile rising in my throat and my grip growing weak. There was some reassurance then, when I found Devlin directly at my side, offering up a knife of his own with which to free the man.

Just as I reached Standbull, a bell sounded.

'We are too late!' I shouted. The vibrations ran down my arm and rattled through my entire frame. The shock was so great I let go one hand and for a moment dangled horribly. My service revolver slipped from my pocket and plummeted towards the ground. I found I could barely breathe from fear.

'I've got you, doctor!' shouted Devlin, somehow gripping my legs. The chimes continued, but there was no explosion.

'It is merely the quarter bell, Watson,' Holmes called up. 'Still twenty five seconds to avert disaster!'

'We shall never make it, Holmes,' I returned frantically.

'In which case, Watson,' he replied, hauling the terrified Benn along the hour hand, 'your company has been my greatest pleasure.' By some means we found ourselves back at the missing pane of glass and tumbled back into the corridor.

Holmes helped the MP inside, but my friend's face, despite the astonishing exertion and impending catastrophe was strangely serene.

'You are right, my dear Watson,' he said, looking kindly at me, a faint smile on his lips. 'We are too late.' At that moment, Big Ben tolled the hour. It was as if the hammer had struck the side of my head rather than the bell itself. My eyes seemed to come loose from their sockets and I felt sure my skull had splintered in that deafening moment. Then there was silence. The world then came back into focus looking very much as it had a few seconds before.

'We are alive!' I ejaculated.

'Naturally,' said Holmes, his manner changing to his usual brusque efficiency. 'It occurred to me while inspecting the clock face that the excessive weight on the hands might detach the pendulum from the clock mechanism to prevent damage. Thus, the explosive charge, which would be triggered by pendulum, might fail to detonate.' I peered at him dumbfounded.

'And you did not think to tell me?'

'There is no reason, he explained, 'to detain a man dangling from a clock face two hundred feet above London. Now Watson,' he stated, dusting his gloves together, 'there is excellent claret to be had at the Red Lion on Parliament Street. I rather think we deserve a glass.'

147

NINE

The Chase

'I want answers and plenty of them.'

Lestrade paced the floor of his spartan office at Scotland Yard like an irritable schoolmaster. Holmes and I perched on uncomfortable wooden chairs alongside The Right Honourable Stephen Benn MP and the brooding figure of Oliver Standbull.

'Am I under arrest?' demanded Benn. 'You understand, I assume,' he added, 'what is meant Parliamentary Privilege?'

'Perfectly,' growled Lestrade. 'But I suggest that you still have a certain amount of explaining to do. Benn was a beefy, smooth faced, supercilious fellow of sixty with a crest of white hair which crashed like a breaking wave across his forehead. He had recovered sufficiently from his ordeal to regain his pompous air and his chin was once again raised in a look of permanent defiance. His steely gaze fell on Lestrade.

'If you have no plans to detain me,' he asserted, 'then you will excuse me. My constituents require my attention.'

'Please remain where you are, Mr Benn,' said Lestrade icily. 'Before you take your leave, perhaps you can begin by explaining why you admitted Captain Winter to the Palace of Westminster?'

'I am under no such obligation,' the MP replied, 'but I will reply for the simple reason that I have nothing to hide. He is one of my constituents. He requested a visit and I was happy to oblige. He was perfectly within his rights and it was within my power to acquiesce. Now if you don't mind, I would like to report the fact that I am still alive to my wife.'

'Did you know he was a wanted man?'

'I did not.'

'You mean to tell me that you saw none of the newspaper reports about the steel trooper?'

'I did not.'

'Well, as a Member of Parliament,' continued Lestrade, tenaciously, 'you strike me as a surprisingly ill-informed fellow.'

'I take an interest in affairs of state,' he declared, 'not reports aspiring to science fiction.'

'And you accepted no payment or favour of any kind to admit him?'

'I did not.'

'Well, Mr Benn,' sighed Lestrade. 'You are proving something of a closed book.'

'And you sir,' he pronounced, 'have confirmed my worst suspicions about Scotland Yard. From the moment I stepped inside this building I have been treated as a suspect instead of a victim. I'm afraid I take a very dim view of your operation and I believe the Prime Minister shares my view.'

'Oh does he, indeed?' asked Holmes.

'Yes, I believe he does. Good day gentlemen.' He rose to his feet, straightened his tie then bustled out of the room.

'Now as for you, Holmes,' began Lestrade. My friend was bent forward on his chair, folded into his customary figure of eight, looking distractedly out of the window.

'What was that?' he asked distractedly, twirling a pencil between his fingers.

'The play,' the Inspector stated simply. 'Does anyone want to tell me anything about the play?'

There was the clatter of a typewriter from the next room. Footsteps could be heard in the corridor. They passed the door then died away.

'Well don't all speak at once,' said Lestrade crossly. I cleared my throat.

'I don't suppose,' I began, 'that's there is any chance of a cup of tea?' Lestrade collapsed wearily into his chair.

'What about you, Mr Standbull?'

'You have a propinquity, Inspector,' baited Standbull, 'to ask the most obvious questions. It perhaps goes without saying that the last few days have been rather trying. Perhaps you are already aware, my tutor Professor Spenning and I were accosted just off the Mile End Road some days ago.'

'We are. But what were you doing there?'

'We had heard that a bookshop on the Limpet Road was selling a rare, early edition of Coleridge's critical essays on Shakespeare. We were on our way to purchase the volume when we were assaulted by two men. I was bundled into a four wheeler and I feared the worst for Spenning. I heard terrible cries before I passed out.'

'No doubt,' muttered Lestrade, looking accusingly at Holmes, 'your assailants were seeking this mysterious play.'

'Well that's just it,' confessed Standbull. 'As Mr Holmes knows, the play had vanished at this point. I explained as much to my interrogators.' He pointed to a pair of shining black eyes. 'Needless to say, they did not believe me.'

'Quite.'

'And what light can you shed on all this, Holmes?'

'Almost none,' my friend confessed with studied insouciance. 'I admit we have not been entirely forthcoming about this matter. But then it was a private case. It now appears that several matters are becoming conflated.'

'Then for pity's sake, Holmes,' begged Lestrade, 'tell me what you know.'

With a certain lassitude, Holmes furnished the inspector with the bones of the case; how we rescued Spenning from the Serpentine, the trip to Oxford, omitting only Somerville and the episode in the graveyard.

'Quite frankly, Lestrade,' he concluded, 'I am not yet convinced that the play actually exists, or, if it does, that it is genuine. I myself have only seen one page, which is of indeterminate quality. However I cannot deny that the possibility of its existence interests me exceedingly. I did not bring it to your attention because I had determined nothing of substance or illegality. At present, the play is little more than a pipe dream.'

Lestrade moved to the window and stroked his grey bristles.

'Then let us put this whimsical matter to one side. Captain Hercules Winter is now the most wanted man in London. How he managed to survive his escape down the wire is beyond me. Quite frankly, Holmes, I need your help bringing him in.' He turned to the young academic.

'Standbull, do you believe that Winter was one of your captors?'

'It is impossible to say,' he said. 'I was kept utterly in the dark throughout my imprisonment. My mask was only removed by Dr Watson while I was tied to the hand of the clock.'

'You have had a difficult time of it, Standbull, I admit' conceded

150

Lestrade. 'Now I am prepared to let you return to your studies, but insist that an armed guard is placed outside your college room. I trust you have no objection to this arrangement?'

'Not at all,' the young man returned. 'Although you forget I now have no tutor.'

'Yes of course,' the inspector added. 'Now I suggest you go on your way. We will be in touch regarding arrangements.'

'Dear me, Lestrade,' my friend interjected. 'Do you think that's entirely wise? I am not certain that Mr Standbull has fully explained himself.' The young man's face darkened at this provocation.

'Come, now Holmes,' the inspector muttered. 'This man has been subjected to the most repellent treatment; his face tells its own story.'

'It certainly does,' my friend agreed.

'Then for pity's sake, let us leave the matter alone.' Holmes rose to his feet and imposed the full force of his personality.

'Mr Standbull,' he said, bearing down on the student. 'I note that the large sapphire you are wearing on your right index finger is still in place. I observed it the first time we met in Oxford. It is a singular decoration for a man of modest background would you not agree? It seems all the more incredible that it is still in your possession despite your abduction. This must be a particularly chivalrous band of ruffians.' Standbull did not say a word, merely concentrating his stare on the opposite wall. Furthermore, Lestrade,' Holmes continued, 'you will note how there are no blemishes on his face beyond the pair of black eyes and no other injury is apparent. Each blow has been administered in a clinical fashion in exactly the same place. Perhaps the most incriminating feature is the tattoo on his left shoulder. I would be willing to bet my hat that if Mr Standbull is good enough to lower his shirt, you will find the name Romeo tattooed there. Gentlemen, before us is a member of a criminal fraternity and an accomplice of Captain Hercules Winter.'

'What do you have to say to these accusations?' asked Lestrade.

'Poppycock!' muttered Standbull. 'I do not have to defend myself and will not dignify these accusations with an answer.'

'I will be the judge of that,' the inspector warned.

'Very well,' said Standbull. 'I will humour you if that is your wish. I do indeed wear a ring and always have. It is an heirloom from my aunt and has been in our family for three generations. You have seen for yourself the extraordinary nature of Winter and his men. These are not common thieves; they inhabit a bizarre universe of automatons and international conspiracy. We are not speaking of a gang of opportunistic hoodlums looking for beer money. They have their own honour codes and systems. The black eyes I assure you feel one hundred percent genuine. Until this moment, I was unaware there was a right and wrong way to receive them. And as for the tattoo, even if it were true, it is so incredible that a Shakespeare scholar has the name of Shakespearian character tattooed on his person?'

The inspector shifted his head from one to one side, as is weighing up the evidence himself. 'Sounds plausible enough, Holmes.'
'Lestrade,' he warned. 'We find ourselves confronted with a particularly brilliant and devious mind, adroit at manipulation and misdirection.'
'We've all had a long day, Holmes,' Lestrade sighed, 'yourself included. You may feel you are possessed of superhuman powers, but you are flesh and blood like the rest of us. We all need our beds.'
'Then one more thing,' said Holmes in a level manner.
'How does Mr Standbull explain the letter from Winter hidden inside his sock?' At this, the academic stared directly at Holmes, then bolted for the door, flung it open and vanished from view. We each exchanged a moment's glance.
'After him!' shouted Lestrade.

We scrambled down the corridor, past flattened policemen lying dazed where they had been shoved to the ground. We heard shouts from the ground floor and a single shot rang out.
'Don't shoot,' ordered Lestrade, 'we need him alive.' We skittered down the steps, slipping on the marble, Holmes' long legs giving him a natural advantage. I felt my old war wound ache with the exertion, the spot where the rough shot had pierced the skin burning as if I had been shot a second time with that accursed Jezail musket. After the excitement in Westminster, I wondered whether this was a chase too far.

Once in the street we were caught in the tide of pedestrians.

'Out of the way, there,' the inspector called and ran out into the road. Holmes, on the other hand, was standing rigidly still. Immediately I knew he was conducting one of his methodical scans, moving his head in tiny, mechanical increments. Presently he shot out an arm. 'Over there,' he cried, gesticulating in the direction of a crowd waiting to board an omnibus. As cunning as Moriarty himself, Standbull had attempted to conceal himself in the hubbub, his collar pulled up to his ears. Barely checking for the traffic we charged after him as he slipped behind the great black conveyance emblazed across its length with a garish advertisement for Lipton's Teas.

'He's vanished!' shouted Lestrade, as the omnibus moved off.

'Nonsense,' my friend returned, casting about. He crossed the road peered hard into a shop window, concentrating his mind then sprinted back.

'Impossible!' I cried.

'Of course it isn't,' scolded Holmes. He had three options. 'Either run, enter a building or...'

'Or what?' I cried.

'Or board the omnibus from the other side!' Sure enough, as the bus rounded the corner we caught a glimpse of Standbull standing on the crowded top deck, his hat pulled down over his ears.

'Follow me, Watson,' shouted Holmes, his stick pointing in his direction of travel. 'The bus cannot be moving at more than eight miles an hour. A rugby player of your talents should have no difficulty keeping up. The game is afoot!' My heart sank at the prospect.

The three of us gave chase, running at full pelt as the vehicle turned into Northumberland Avenue, where it joined a throng of traffic.

'Aint that Sherlock Holmes?' I overheard one man remark to another as we rounded the corner.

'Someone's got his dander up,' his mate replied. In a moment, I felt the hot breath of a horse and, from the corner of my eye, saw a hansom thunder towards us. I stepped back at the critical moment, the horse swerving to avoid us, the driver roaring his displeasure. Lestrade was not so lucky. The wheel rode directly over his right shoe. I heard him yell out in pain and he dropped to the ground, clutching his foot.

'Leave him, Watson,' Holmes instructed. 'There's no time.'

Abandoning Lestrade, along with my Hippocratic Oath, I flung myself into the traffic and managed somehow to avoid being flattened by the numerous broughams, four wheelers and other pedestrians criss-crossing the highway.

'Pray, what took you, Watson?' my friend enquired as I arrived sweating and pale faced on the other side of the road. It was a quirk of my friend's personality that in the midst of the most urgent crisis he still found time to impress his superiority. 'Now if, like me, you are finding your feet beginning to tire, then I feel it is time to catch the bus.'

We sprinted on until, with a heart-stopping bound my friend sprang for the handrail at the back of the omnibus and pulled himself aboard. Putting on a burst of speed I made the same leap only to find myself an inch or two short. Just as I was about to be hurled into the path of another speeding hansom I felt my friend's vice like grip tighten around my forearm. For an alarming moment I found myself airborne, both legs trailing horizontally in mid air behind the vehicle.

'Another close shave, Watson,' Holmes remarked, hauling me to safety. Pushing our way through the mass of bodies, we fought our way to the steps and climbed to the upper deck. Standbull, who, no doubt, had witnessed our antics, now had nowhere to go.

'Trapped like a bird in a cage,' I opined.

'No so fast, Watson,' my friend cautioned. 'This bird, like most others, has wings.'

We advanced inch by inch along the deck, our eyes fixed on Standbull, who was pressed against the far end glowering beneath the brim of his stolen bowler. It suddenly occurred to me that I had left my service revolver where it fell below St Stephen's Tower. I hoped my friend had his Webley somewhere closer to hand.

'Give it up, Standbull,' said Holmes in low, commanding tone. 'Give yourself up now and it will go better for you.' It was then I saw Standbull betray the merest smile.

'Help!' he suddenly shouted. 'For God's sake, someone help me! These men intend to murder me.' The passengers, hitherto buried in their newspapers looked up and stared at Holmes. One man, with a flat cap, an even flatter nose and cauliflowers ears stepped forward. 'What do you want with this geezer?' he demanded.

'Stand back,' my friend ordered. 'My name is Sherlock Holmes.' 'And I'm Alibaba,' he returned and gave my friend a firm shove in the chest. As the crowd broke into a heated debate as to my friend's identity, Standbull took the opportunity to move to the right hand side of the bus. Holmes pressed forward, only to find the man's hand once more on his chest.

'I assure you,' warned Holmes. 'There is rarely advantage for those who obstruct my work.'

'Leave him be!' called another man in defence of my friend. 'I've seen his face in The Illustrated London News.' Another omnibus, I noticed was coming towards us on the opposite side of the road. 'If that's not Sherlock Holmes,' he continued, 'I'll eat my hat.' Just as these words left his lips, Standbull jumped. I could scarcely believe my eyes. Holmes reacted in an instant.

'Watson, with me!' Before I could even think, I was once again flying through the air, a full fifteen feet above the ground, before coming crashing down into the crowd on the top deck of the second omnibus.

For a moment, Standbull, Holmes and I all stared at each other, perhaps barely able to believe that we had survived. But now the young academic had the advantage; he was at the head of the stairs which spiralled back down to the street level. Meanwhile, my friend and I were forced to barge our way through the commuters all the way from the back of the bus. I tipped my hat and apologised as best I could as I trod on a succession of toes, ripped through a dozen newspapers and spilled a basket of oranges that tumbled down the steps.

Wrestling himself free of the conductor, Standbull threw himself off the bus and into the traffic. Holmes made a dive for him, getting a hand to his shirt, but the man pulled free. When I caught up with my friend, he was still holding the starched collar in his hand. We saw the dark suited figure weaving deftly through the crowd, escaping into the distance.

'He's heading for the river!' shouted Holmes.

'For the bookish type, he's certainly got pace,' I gasped, catching my breath. 'He must have his Oxford blue.' We dashed after him, sprinting down the centre of the street to avoid the crowds and by the time we reached Embankment had managed to gain on him a little. There we came across a policeman conversing with a nut vendor.

'Constable!' commanded Holmes, 'I have a promotion opportunity for you!'

The three of us gave chase along the riverbank towards Cleopatra's Needle, the yachts, steamers and barges drifting lugubriously on the dark, forbidding waters to our right. Holmes was out in front, his long, lanky legs helping him gain ground on the younger, shorter man. The constable and I brought up the rear, the policeman holding his Custodian helmet in place, blasting on his whistle as he ran.

'Is that quite necessary, constable?' I asked him, our elbows jostling together. 'If he hasn't stopped by now, then I doubt that will persuade him.'

'Who is he anyway?'

'A Shakespearean scholar,' I panted. 'It requires time to explain.'

'No doubt, sir,' he returned, quite baffled.

While we were still a good distance from Waterloo Bridge, I suddenly saw Standbull draw to a halt.

'You were saying?' puffed the constable in triumph. He gave another blast on the whistle.

'Stay right where you are, sir!' he instructed.

No sooner had he uttered this command than Standbull calmly climbed over the stone balustrade, lowered himself down and disappeared from view. We ran to the barrier and peered over. The young man was slithering across the silt and mud of the river bank, discarding his jacket and shirt and kicking off his boots as he went.

'I don't believe it,' I cried. 'He's going to swim for it!'

Sure enough, we saw Standbull slip into the filthy waters and begin striking out for the opposite shore.

'Lunacy!' I cried. 'He will be swept away by the tide.'

'I've fished enough bodies out of the Thames,' remarked the constable, 'to know his chances are nought.'

'Wait!' I shouted. 'Where's Holmes?' My friend too had momentarily vanished, only to re-emerge a few moments later from behind a tree in his undergarments, his hat still upon his head and his pipe still clenched between his teeth.

'Holmes, no!' I urged, once again breaking into a sprint, 'It's madness.' But it was too late. By the time I reached the spot my friend was already in the water pursuing Standbull with a strong, steady breaststroke, a thin column of smoke rising from his pipe. The constable, who had finally caught up, peered out at the pair now drifting slowly but perceptively upriver. 'Even if they can keep their heads above water' he remarked, 'they'll end up in Windsor at this rate.'

I stared breathlessly at the two swimmers and soon others joined us, one or two even cheering them on.

'What's the benjo?' demanded a man holding up a barrow laden with bottles of ginger beer. 'A contest is it?' Seeing the crowds swelling and sensing a commercial opportunity, he opened up for business and was soon doing a brisk trade in refreshments.

'Roll up, roll up!' he bellowed. 'Sherlock 'Olmes swims the Thames. Come and get your official souvenir peppermint water here!'

'Alright, alright,' said the constable, waving his hands, 'move along now.' But soon the crowd was too dense to easily disperse. I despaired, but it appeared we had underestimated the swimmers. Both were making headway and had now reached the centre of the river, like two otters chasing the same fish. A small steamer chugged its way between the pair, its pilot almost tumbling into the water in surprise as he spotted them swim by.

'Quickly,' I instructed, collecting Holmes' clothes into a bundle. 'Let's get ourselves across Waterloo Bridge and see if we can head them off.'

'Let's just hope,' sighed the constable, 'that this won't be their Waterloo…'

Once up on the bridge, my new friend deployed his whistle again, this time to commandeer a passing hansom.

157

'Who's paying the fare?' complained the cabbie.

'Her Majesty the Queen,' returned the constable. 'Send the bill to Scotland Yard.'

Soon we were flying like a raven across the water, watching the crowds swell on both sides of the Thames.

'If he gets there before we do,' I said, 'Standbull will disappear directly into that crowd and that will be the end of it.'

'Did you hear that?' roared the constable to the driver. 'Make a name for yourself!' The driver flashed his whip and we flew on. Turning sharply off the bridge, our coach tipped momentarily onto a single wheel. We were now thundering westwards, adjacent to the river.

'Keep going!' I yelled to our cabbie seeing that the mob on the south bank had misjudged the landing point, which looked now as though it might be as far down as Westminster Bridge. The constable leaned out of the window. 'Holmes is gaining on him!' he commentated. 'The other fellow looks like he's shot his bolt.' Standbull was low in the water, his face pale with the cold and exertion.

Suddenly there was a thunder-crack. I was lying on my back in the road and for a moment I believed we had been struck by lightning. Pieces of wood and steel were falling out of the sky landing about our ears, littering the road all about us. I heard a strangulated cry, then a groan and when I opened my eyes, the cabbie was lying bloodied in the road, a shard of wood a foot long embedded in his thigh. The hansom seemed to have vaporised. The mare reared up on her hind legs and then bolted away, dragging little more than her harness and a piece of shorn off timber behind her. Who or what had caused this cataclysm? My questions appeared to receive their answer. A huge black carriage pulled by a pair of stallions loomed over us and two figures leapt out. There was a gunshot and to my left I detected a jerking motion. Instinctively, I threw myself under a bench. There was a spark and bullet ricocheted off the metal, inches from my face.

From this meagre shelter, I attempted to piece things together. This carriage, clearly armoured and reinforced by some ingenious means, had collided deliberately with our cab, utterly destroying it in the process. Through bleary eyes, I saw a tall, elderly man in a battered suit and hat with a cadaverous face striding down to the water's edge. This time I had no difficulty recognising him as the one eyed crone from Baker Street, the Cyclops in a top hat. At his side was a young woman, no older than thirty, no doubt the infamous Elsie Pinner. Both wielded revolvers. In a moment they had returned from the river, hauling Standbull between them; he was dripping and limp, barely able to take a step for himself. Firing another shot towards me, and two more directed into the water, they threw Standbull aboard their carriage, clambered in themselves and were away.

'What a remarkable mess you've made, Watson' observed Holmes. My friend stood over me, his cheeks ruddy and his eyes glistening like gem stones. With his shirt clinging to his skeletal frame, his hair smeared back and a strip of aquatic vegetation draped over his left shoulder he not so much resembled a consulting detective as Davy Jones himself. His pipe, I noted was still alight. He observed the maelstrom of blood, bodies and wreckage around him.

'There's not much we can do for the poor constable,' he said. 'But I believe our cabbie here will live. You must steel yourself. Dust yourself down and follow me. I do hope I haven't swum across the River Thames for no advantage.'

The black carriage had only travelled a hundred yards further, obstructed by a brougham and a beer wagon that together had managed to bar its passage. The villain's driver had pulled his blunderbuss and had already discharged a shot into the beer wagon, causing a keg to explode. The tradesmen dived for cover beneath a frothing shower of ale.

'This is our chance!' Holmes declared. Drawing on inexplicable reserves of strength, he set off at a pace. Dazed, I collected my bowler and stumbled after him.

Like so many times before, Holmes proceeded directly into danger. For a man possessed of such careful thought processes, he could often have an irrational disregard for his own safety. And yet he would never acknowledge courage among his qualities. 'It is a merely a question of risk,' he once explained. 'If a situation demands that I place my life on the line, then I merely consider the significance of the outcome. If I believe it to be of sufficient worth, I proceed. In truth, I value pleasure and mental stimulation more than I value life. I value my life only in so much as it is the necessary vessel to permit the other two states to exist.'

The driver had now negotiated a path between the wagons and the black carriage began to pull away. Holmes meanwhile was busying himself with a rope, tethering a long barge to the shore. His intentions at this stage were quite opaque. I caught up with him just as he had finished this exercise, gripping the loose end of the rope in his hand.

'Watson,' he said, looking directly at me. 'If fortune goes against us, then at least you will have an exhilarating adventure for your readers.' With this, he turned and sprinted the remaining distance to the departing carriage. Incredulous, I watched him not only catch up, but dive beneath its great chassis. Five second later and he was despatched from under the wheels, tumbling head over heels through the dirt and dust of the river bank. I ran to him, horrified by a gash that has opened on his forehead.

'Holmes,' I shouted, 'that was nothing short of suicidal.' To my amazement, he broke into a smile.

'I think you will find it was just short of suicidal. Now count to five.' As I knelt in the road, I looked back and saw the slackened line gradually pulling taut. It was at this moment that I registered Holmes' stupendous plan. Heading east, the carriage had gained an unstoppable momentum, scattering everything in its path, sending the crowd that had gathered running for their lives.

'Now,' said Holmes calmly.

At this moment we heard a sickening crack: the sound of the back axle being rent clean from the carriage, followed by another even louder one as the vehicle flipped into the air and came crashing down again. The driver was thrown clear, for a moment spread eagled against the sky, his crop still in his hand. The rear wheels remained attached to their axle then bounced across the road, demolishing a flower seller's stall before flipping over the barrier and into the Thames.

160

'They're still going!' I cried. Sure enough the horses, clearly spooked out of their wits continued to gallop, dragging the stricken carriage behind them, scattering pieces of its frame in every direction.

We sprinted after the carriage, dodging pieces of flying debris.
'Surely Holmes,' I shouted, watching it pull ahead again, 'it won't hold together.' There was no telling even whether its occupants were still alive.
'It's stronger than I thought,' he admitted. It was only at this point I realised Holmes was still in bare feet. His soles were red with blood and compounded by his various other wounds I became gravely concerned for my friend's condition.
'Give it up, Holmes!' I cried. 'You have done all you can.' He said nothing, but I knew he was done. His efforts had been superhuman. We slowed to a jog and then dropped to our haunches, thoroughly winded, our bodies wracked with exhaustion. We watched as the carriage spun away and the disappeared around the bend of the river.
'We could have done no more,' I panted.

Presently a crowd gathered around us and there were immediately offers of handkerchiefs, water, fruit and even shoes. A policeman came running up and began to address us. We stared at him in a daze, unable to comprehend his meaning. At that moment, there was an explosion. A tongue of yellow flame shot up into the air, followed by a plume of thick black smoke. There were shrieks from the crowd and I stared up in disbelief. Holmes however, looked perfectly placid.
'The carriage!' I spluttered, 'but where did they get to?'
'I believe,' my friend declared, 'that their journey ended at the former site of Shakespeare's Globe.'

We did not see much of the next day. After Holmes and I had been scraped from the streets of Southwark and a perfunctory statement made to Lestrade, we returned to Baker Street to lick our wounds. Mrs Hudson ferried up bowls of hot water, several feet of bandages and untold quantities of brandy while I tended my friend's injuries.

He protested in the strongest possible terms at any sort of fuss and at first resisted all attempts to administer this aid. More than once, the door to his bedroom was closed politely, but firmly in our faces.

No bodies were found in the wreckage. It was too early to say if their remains were eviscerated in the inferno or whether they had somehow made a miraculous escape. The newspapers, when we finally had the strength to read them, made colourful reading: 'Holmes Foiled in Botched Pursuit;' 'Sherlock Holmes Swims Thames – Pictures;' 'South Bank set Alight in Dramatic Chase – Constable Dead' and 'Constable Murdered in Holmes Chase Debacle.'

'Lestrade will be livid,' remarked Holmes, sitting up in bed, propped against some pillows and scanning the headlines. He sipped his tea, laced with something considerably stronger. 'He's lost a good man, let a criminal slip from under his nose and missed his chance to catch Elsie Pinner, the She-Devil of Drury Lane. His one consolation is that the blame sits squarely on my shoulders.'
'But who is the old man?' I asked, perplexed. 'And what caused the explosion, Holmes?'
'We have witnessed a singular series of events,' he said evasively. 'Now be a good fellow and bring in my Persian slipper. I haven't lit a pipe in an hour and my mental fires are in danger of being extinguished.' This small service performed, I left my friend to his thoughts. I returned to the sitting room and peered into the mirror at my own careworn features. The death of the constable weighed heavily on my mind. I thought of his widow and children. These intersecting problems that had presented themselves these last weeks seemed unfathomable and unsolvable. This confounded business of the lost play was a game no longer.

TEN

The Apothecary

'I say Watson, look lively!'

I glanced up from The Illustrated London News to see Sherlock Holmes with his shirt sleeves rolled to the elbows, revealing his pale, white forearms. I was pleased to observe no recent puncture wounds, suggesting my friend was continuing to refrain from his unspeakable habits.

'What's the business?' I enquired.

'A delivery for Mrs Hudson,' he explained. 'You haven't forgotten it's her birthday?'

'Of course not,' I said, then added: 'Is there cake?'

'If there's cake, you'll have to earn it. Now will you assist?'

'Come along then,' I said, gathering myself up and casting my paper aside.

I clattered down the seventeen steps of 221b Baker Street in the wake of my nimble friend to discover a large wooden packing case wedged in the front doorway.

'We have learned to be wary of such packages,' I mused, eyeing it with suspicion.

'There's nothing to fear, Watson,' assured Holmes. 'I ordered this myself.' Two tradesmen leant their shoulders against the consignment while Holmes and I pulled from the inside the door.

'Gracious, Holmes,' I complained, 'it could hardly be heavier if it was a block of granite.'

'You hold in your hands the future of humanity, the invention of the century; a machine that will transform civilisation.'

'A time machine,' I cried.

'Even better, Watson: a dishwasher!'

Some two weeks had passed since the singular business on the South Bank. In that time, the world seemed to have turned upon its head. Rosebery had been brought down and Salisbury once again found himself at home in number 10 Downing Street. Since it was his third occupation of the house, he must have found it an extraordinarily annoyance to have to rearrange the furniture once again to his liking. Just when Rosebery appeared to have achieved his lifetime's ambition, he was toppled unceremoniously from his seat of power and seemingly cast into the abyss of history. Such is the way of politics.

However, Salisbury had hardly time to replace the pictures on his bedroom wall when he was thrown into a fresh crisis. Around this time, there was a spate of poisonings across the city. Scotland Yard was at a loss, the murderer remained at large and all of London had become hysterical as a result. Drinks were no longer accepted from strangers and drinkers took greater care than usual in their choice of companions. The perpetrator seemed to have little discrimination in his or her victims and no social strata was immune to their attention. High court judges were slipping from their benches, curates keeled from their pulpits and bakers were collapsing into their dough. The toxin, strychnine, was identified as the cause of death and the end it was said, was horrible in the extreme. The victim would be thrown into contortions and ultimately asphyxiate. Half of Scotland Yard was working on the case while the remainder were passing their morning tea to their dogs before tasting it themselves. I do not mind admitting that it had unsettled my own usually steady nerves.

Once the contraption was installed in Mrs Hudson's kitchen, Holmes and I repaired to the sitting room to recover our wits. I poured us a glass each of the excellent Burgundy which had arrived courtesy of the grateful client I sketched in the Adventure of the Painted Hand. Yet I found the wine was not doing its work. I felt vexed at our inaction over this public crisis.

'A Battersea schoolmaster, this time, Holmes,' I reported, jabbing at the newspaper. 'It says here that he stopped on his way home for a glass of sherbert water and was struck down before he reached his front door. What's to be done?' Holmes flopped back in his chair like an emperor at the end of a campaign.
'By now Watson, you should know how this agency operates. It does not solicit; it waits for a commission. We do not go prowling after business. I am a hawk, not a wolf.'

'But we cannot very well sit back and watch,' I protested, 'while Londoners fall like ninepin in the street!'

'Is that so?' challenged Holmes and brought the Burgundy to his lips. I threw the paper across the room and rose impetuously to my feet.

'You may well be possessed of the finest intellect north of the Equator,' I rallied, 'but you do not have an ounce of compassion.' Holmes closed his eyes and frowned lightly, pressing a thumb and forefinger to the bridge of his nose as if suffering from neuralgia.

'Really Watson,' he said, in a weary tone, 'this is quite unnecessary. As I have explained, we are neither vigilantes, nor alternative enforcers of the law. I gain no pleasure from seeing the innocent suffer. In this regard, I am in the same position as a banker, a watchmaker or any other civilised fellow. I feel sympathy of course, but I am not in a position to begin an investigation of my own without instruction from a client. Like you, I do not wish to see another person poisoned at the hands of this madman.' I stared at him with something close to distain.

'The same position?' I shouted, my hackles rising. 'Balderdash! You have immeasurable faculties. Your skills far exceed those the finest Scotland Yard has to offer. Within a day, you would have the measure of the man. Within a week he would be in the dock of a court of law. Within two, he would be swinging from the scaffold. You have it within your gift to save life, whether we receive instructions or not.' I was about to fetch my hat and coat and leave Holmes to stew over my words when Mrs Hudson appeared at the door.

'Are you quite well, doctor?' she enquired. 'You look rather flushed. I do hope you did not overexert yourself man-handling that machine?'

'No, I'm quite well, thank you,' I assured her, glaring at Holmes, still slouching in his throne.

'There is a gentleman caller,' she explained, handing over a card.

'Terence Sullenbard,' I read then took a deep breath. 'Will you give us a moment?'

'If this is another birthday surprise,' she added a trifle embarrassed glancing at us both, 'then it is most unnecessary.' I stared at her, barely comprehending her meaning.

'No I'm afraid, it isn't,' I said, softening a little, 'unless Holmes has arranged something else?' He shook his head. 'It has nothing to do with me. Perhaps it is a gift from Mycroft; a hamper perhaps? Why not show him in?'

We were greeted by a man of thirty with a long, sad face, thin lips, large ears and steady, thoughtful eyes. His manner was refined and his suit was of a good cut but it was faded and heavily darned. A white silk handkerchief peeked from the breast pocket.

'I'm awfully sorry,' he said quietly. 'It feels like I have chosen rather a bad moment.'

'Not at all,' countered Holmes levitating from his chair and stepping across the room. The man had a silky, musical voice that was so pleasing to the ear I felt at once that he must be an actor.

'You are employed as a manservant,' noted Holmes, inspecting our visitor. The man gave a small bow that seemed to confirm my friend's deduction. 'Let me see,' muttered Holmes. He drummed a fingertip against his lips and paced the room, suddenly animated like a child playing charades, sensing he was on the right trail.

'A manservant to a clergyman!' he exclaimed, 'Am I right?'

'Perfectly correct,' the man bowed again.

'Miraculous,' I muttered, once again bewildered by Holmes' powers.

'On the contrary, Watson,' smiled Holmes, 'merely elementary. By the by,' he said, interrupting himself, 'Dr Watson, here is my *aide de camp* in all matters of detection. He is a medical doctor by trade, but a sleuth by inclination.'

'I see,' murmured Sullenbard. 'But for curiosity's sake, would you reveal your reasoning?'

'Deduction,' my friend explained, relighting his pipe, 'is a language that may be learned like any other. Once mastered, the world is easily read. Take for instance your voice and manner. It is as cultivated as any gentleman's and yet, there is black polish beneath your fingernails. No gentleman would ever shine his own shoes, no matter how down on his luck he may find himself. Then there is the beeswax that has transferred itself to your cuffs. No doubt you spent the morning polishing the piano and coffee table. So far, so rudimentary; but what of the reference to the clergy? My results may appear remarkable, but like any trick revealed, the solution often seems laughable. It is your buttons, sir that give you away! The originals have long since fallen from your jacket. You have replaced them yourself from a supply that was purchased for your employer from McGinley's of Donegal, famous manufacturers of attire for the clergy. If you look carefully, you will see the faint letter M printed on each button. It is all there to be read as easily as a child reads words on a page.'

Sullenbard smiled and shook his head. 'Then everything they say about you is true,' he marvelled.

'Not all of it, I hope,' Holmes countered. 'Now just one more thing, you were born in Bedford were you not?' The man's bright little eyes shone in triumph.

'There I must correct you, Mr Holmes,' he said, 'for originally I hail from St Alban's. Not quite a full a perfect scorecard. '

'We are all permitted a small margin of error,' remarked Holmes. 'Now take a seat; light a cigarette if you wish Mr Sullenbard and tell us your business, sparing no detail.'

'For three years,' he began, retrieving a silver cigarette case from his pocket, 'I have been engaged in the service of a vicar in Islington, the Very Reverend Joseph Whistler. Perhaps you recall the name from some corner of your absorbent mind? He is a decent man, neither excessively pious nor neglectful in his duties. When I first entered his employ, he presided over a sizable parish: St Mary's, Islington, no less. He moved in the right circles and was often visited by the bishop of this or that, and even more frequently by his fellow clergy from some of the rich and fashionable parishes that lie about. But last year, he was dealt a devastating blow. I am not entirely clear what the specific matter related to; there was talk of some financial irregularity and also of a disagreement with the bishop on a theological point, but the material outcome was that Whistler was relieved of his duties. For the first month, I barely saw his face, leaving meals outside his door along with wine, tobacco and the daily newspaper. However as my housekeeping resources dwindled and my own salary went unpaid I was forced to speak with him directly about our predicament.'

'Go on,' pressed Holmes.

'It took two weeks to coax him from his room and the transformation he had undergone in the meantime was remarkable. He had grown a full beard and acquired a deathly pallor. His skin had turned a horrible yellow and his eyes had become rheumy.'

'A liver complaint, perhaps,' I muttered.

'More likely a mental breakdown,' contested Holmes, his fingers joined above his lips.

'I suggested, of course,' went on Sullenbard, 'that a doctor be called to assess his condition.'

'Very sensible,' I put in.

'But he would have none of it. I knew that it was his fear of the doctor's bill that deterred him. Instead, he drank a glass of brandy then left the house, explaining that he would be resuming his duties.

I could scarcely conceive how this would be possible given his disgrace. However nevertheless, he succeeded in winning some small and irregular work as a supply clergy, hardly a line that would pay for the upkeep of the fine house and my continued services. I somehow managed to convince myself, in my naivety, that this was the end of his troubles. But he found little employment. He returned from long trips directly to his room with instructions not to be disturbed. It seemed likely that these parishes, witnessing his black moods and unkempt appearance, swiftly made other arrangements.'

Sullenbard blew a plume of blue smoke into the air and held his head to one side as he reflected on his narrative.

'Given his precarious financial position I offered my resignation, but was refused. A matter of foolish pride, no doubt. We did however reach a compromise, where I would only attend to him three and a half days a week, spending Thursday to Sunday with a relative in the country, returning on the Sunday evening.'

'Which part of the country?' Holmes interjected.

'North Weald, in Essex,' he answered calmly. 'My sister, a spinster, lives there with her animals and was pleased for the company.'

'Please go on,' my friend invited, in a more genial tone.

'We continued with this arrangement for a number of weeks. Then came a Friday, three weeks ago, when my sister went away on a short holiday for some sea air. I did not wish to occupy her large house alone having no especial liking for animals and therefore decided to remain in my room in Islington. My quarters were on the uppermost floor of the building, one storey above Whistler. As I

168

rarely saw him and knew he did not like to be disturbed I did not inform him of the change in my plans. That night I retired early, only to be awoken at two o'clock in the morning by the sound of the front door slamming hard, a clatter of irons and loud footsteps on the stairs. Fearing an intruder, I crept out of my room to investigate, concealing myself at the top of the banister.

'The figure I saw was also bearded, wore a flat, black hat and a waxed overcoat, both sodden with rain. His heavy boots were thick with mud. Beside him was a garden fork and shovel that lay where they fell in the porch. I am neither a brave nor a foolish man, Mr Holmes, and I had no wish to confront this demonic figure. And yet, I thought of poor Whistler in his bed, his nerves destroyed and perfectly vulnerable to attack. Returning to my room to arm myself with a poker, I therefore steeled myself and prepared for the worst. Just as I was about to leap upon the devil, he removed his hat.' Sullenbard paused, his skin paler than a moment before.

'Yes,' I pressed, utterly absorbed in his tale. 'What did you see?'

'Doctor, I saw Joseph Whistler.' Holmes and I stared at each other.

'Great Gordon's ghost!' I shouted, 'you really had me going there. What did he have to say for himself?'

'That's just it,' Sullenbard continued. 'It was such a strange spectacle, so unprecedented in my knowledge of his habits that I dared not challenge him. I returned to bed, lying awake struggling to think of a plausible explanation. The next morning I slipped out of the house as quietly as possible so that my employer would have no clue that I had witnessed the episode. I returned on the Sunday evening as normal and exchanged a few words with my employer. He seemed as sullen and laconic as ever. The following week I resolved to lay in wait and sure enough, at about the same hour on the same night, he made his dramatic entrance, once again caked with mud. This time, I remained hidden in my room all the next day and night, until the early hours of Sunday morning. However on this occasion he remained in the house, making frequent trips from his room to the ground floor and back again. Peering through my keyhole, I saw him carrying powders, liquids and containers. I found myself in an awkward position: a prisoner in my own room. I became faint from lack of food and water. It was only when he returned to his room on the Sunday afternoon that I felt emboldened to race downstairs and fake my own return to the house.'

'I see,' my friend said, inspecting his fingernails. 'A singular account.'

'One moment, Mr Holmes,' Sullenbard interjected, 'my narrative has not yet reached its conclusion.'

'Then continue by all means.'

'As luck would have it, the next day Whistler was called away to attend to a nearby parish. In his distracted state, he had forgotten perhaps that I had a skeleton key to every lock in the house, including his own room. This was my chance.'

'You tell a fine tale,' commended Holmes, 'but so far, I can deduce nothing illegal in the reverend's activities. Untoward, or out of character, quite possibly, but do you feel you are in danger of casting yourself in the role of the suspicious, not to say unfaithful servant?'

'I agree, Mr Holmes, that my actions seemed somewhat furtive, not to say brazen, but given the man's errant behaviour, I could hardly be blamed for my curiosity. Assuring myself once again that the coast was clear, I slipped the key into the lock of his bedroom door and let myself in. The room was a veritable laboratory, with jars, test tubes, rubber hoses and Bunsen burners filling every available surface. There was the acrid stench of sulphur and acid. And one more thing; the crucifix which formally hung above his bed was missing, leaving only its impression against the wall. An odd set up for a supply clergyman, don't you think?' He glanced around at my friend's own chemical apparatus piled on the acid stained table top. 'Forgive me, but it was not unlike your own room.'

'And does that,' enquired Holmes, 'put me under some sort of suspicion?'

'Naturally, it does not,' he clarified, 'your reputation insulates you from any such insinuation.' Holmes produced a cynical smile.

'My reputation puts me in on higher moral ground than a vicar of the Church of England? You flatter me, Mr Sullenbard!'

'A disgraced vicar,' Sullenbard corrected. 'I left everything as it was, and finally laid in wait one final time, on this occasion, the Thursday evening. I was not to be disappointed. At around two in the morning, once again I heard the boots harrumphing through the hall.'

'Really, Mr Sullenbard,' said Holmes, losing his patience, 'this is beginning to sound like the fretting of a maiden aunt. He is a fully grown man, free to come and go from his own house as he pleases. Come to your point!'

'Mr Holmes,' he said, sitting forward. 'You will be aware, as well as I that there is a spate of poisonings in London. It is my appalling suspicion that the Reverend Joseph Whistler is the Strychnine Poisoner!' Not for the first time, that day, I was dumbfounded.

'Quite a leap!' declared Holmes.

'But not an unreasonable one.' Sullenbard argued.

'On the contrary,' parried Holmes. 'It is entirely unreasonable, based on nothing but circumstantial evidence. You have discovered that the man has a hobby and that he has been out late at night. These are thin grounds for an arrest.' Sullenbard rose to his feet.

'You must assist!' he cried. Holmes glanced across at me. 'So I am constantly being told.'

'If I summon the police,' said the man, 'and my suspicions prove groundless, I will be sure to lose my position. If I do nothing, then his next victim will leave me with blood on my hands.' Holmes joined his fingers and remained silent, no doubt weighing up the matter in his mind.

'Very well,' concluded Holmes.

At this moment, our interview was interrupted by the most appalling commotion. There was the shriek of a woman's voice, followed by the sound of smashing crockery.

'Mrs Hudson!' I shouted, and leapt to the door.

'You will excuse us,' I heard Holmes apologise. Bounding down the stairs, I heard Holmes' footsteps following close behind.

'We're on our way!' I cried, seizing my umbrella from the stand, ready to tackle the assailant. Imagine my surprise then, to find Mrs Hudson alone in the kitchen, hands pressed to her flushed cheeks, recoiling in horror from the newly installed machine at the other end of the room. It was dancing across the floor as if under an enchanted spell, with the remains of a dinner service rattling around its innards.

'Turn it off!' she implored. 'For goodness sake, doctor, turn it off!'

I flipped a switch, spun a dial then gave the machine a kick. It gurgled, clanked and with a sickening crunching sound, wound finally to a stop.

'Some birthday present!' managed Mrs Hudson, a hand upon her bosom. 'Please dispose of it!'

We revived Mrs Hudson with a cup of tea and some fruit loaf while Holmes instructed one of the Baker Street Irregulars at the front door.

'Clearly they have not yet perfected the technology,' he muttered. 'I have sent a note to the firm who supplied the machine. They will be here presently.'

'Either it goes or I do!' she declared. Holmes turned to Sullenbard. 'Set down your address,' he instructed. 'We will be in a four wheeler across the street from your house tonight at ten o'clock. Our driver will be wearing a red scarf. Join us and together we will wait for Whistler to appear. You have presented some singular facts. Against my better judgement I find myself curious if not yet entirely convinced of foul play. We will discover what business Whistler conducts in the small hours. At this moment my friend held up a finger, closed his eyes and pinched his nose, as if to sneeze.

'A handkerchief,' he cried, 'quickly, Mr Sullenbard!' Instinctively, the man whipped it from his jacket pocket and passed it to Holmes.

'I am most obliged. I will return it freshly laundered at some future date.'

Our brougham pulled up at ten o'clock as arranged and our horse whinnied as the driver, a trusted fellow, slowed him to a canter then a standstill. There was unseasonal chill in the air. The rooftops of Islington glimmered silver in the moonlight; the silhouettes of distant spires and nameless buildings announced themselves in the distance.

'He's late,' I remarked.

'He'll show, just you see,' my friend assured me.

'I'm not sure,' I grumbled, 'what precisely we expect to learn from this adventure.'

'The night has a singular ability to shed light on the most opaque of problems. It is when the essential spirit of any animal is revealed and that applies to the human animal too.' Presently a dark figure emerged from the house and clambered into a carriage just ahead of ours. It set off a clip and we were in danger of losing him when another figure emerged, flew towards us and clambered aboard. Holmes gave the signal and the chase was on.

Silently, save for the clatter of our wheels on the cobbles, we darted through the London streets. This was the hour the bang-pitchers, the coves, the rufflers and prig-nappers emerged from their holes, preparing to ply their trade. We saw them slinking in the shadows, fortifying themselves in readiness for their night's mischief. For my own part, I took a small swig from my hip flask then passed it around the company.

'Don't mind if I do,' said Sullenbard. 'I'm partial to a drop myself,' he confessed. 'Give me half a chance and I'm tight as a boiled owl.' The houses began to appear at greater intervals and great swathes of darkness began to emerge between the yellow lights of tavern windows.

'Dash my wig, Holmes,' I cried. 'He's leaving London! If I knew we were going this far, I would have asked Mrs Hudson to make us a sandwich.' I peered out of the window. The tail light of the vicar's carriage was little more than a dim flicker in the distance. Soon, trees began to close around us.

'We are entering the forest,' remarked Holmes, 'home to all the exiled ghosts of the capital. They say the spirit of Dick Turpin still roams these parts.'

'Well let's hope he does not trouble the living,' I replied. 'My nerves cannot stand it.' Finally, we saw the carriage ahead draw to a stop and keeping our distance we too pulled in.

'On foot from here,' whispered Holmes and we slipped out into the night.

Skulking through the brambles, cursing the thorns that tore at my suit, I saw the spire of a church appear against a moonlit sky. All around, I could hear the twitching and rustling of the midnight forest, the hoots and calls of the predators of the night. Edging closer we could hear the sound of a pick or shovel, chopping at the soil and presently could make out a sign that read: Church of The Holy Innocents. We crouched in the shadows.

'He is digging a grave!' expressed Sullenbard.

'Hardly unusual in a churchyard,' returned Holmes.

'At this hour?' he returned. 'What has he got to hide?'

'If he wished to bury a body,' I muttered, 'then surely he would hide it somewhere deep in the forest.'

'They say the best way to bury a body,' continued Sullenbard, 'is to reopen a newly dug grave.'

'Do they indeed?' asked Holmes. 'Well, we can easily ask the police to dig the grave in the morning and find the identity of the occupant.'

We waited for what seemed like all eternity for Whistler to complete his labours. By the time he had thrown the last shovelful of soil back on the grave both my feet had gone to sleep. I finally understood the terrible boredom of the dead. It was bleak, unsettling night, with an uncanny feeling in the air. At about two of the clock, I became convinced I could see lights in the forest. Whether it was a trick of the moon or not, I felt sure I could see spectral figures walking in procession, each carrying a lantern. I tugged at my friend's coat, gestured to the apparitions but when we looked again they were gone. I took another swig from my flask and wiped my lips with the back of my hand.

Finally, Whistler took up his tools, threw them into the carriage and clambered in himself and went on his way.

'We have seen enough,' said Holmes, brushing soil from his trousers. 'Let us return to London and reacquaint ourselves with our beds.'

'But what of Whistler?' asked Sullenbard. 'Surely you will inform your friends at Scotland Yard?'

'I have no friends at Scotland Yard,' retorted Holmes.

'Lestrade would be pained to hear those words,' the man replied in his silky tones.

'If you are so well acquainted with the inspector,' suggested Holmes. 'why not explain this to him yourself, now your suspicions are confirmed?'

'I cannot!' he squealed excitedly. 'You are aware that if there is an innocent explanation, I will lose my position.' Holmes narrowed his eyes at the man.

'You seem quite averse to any contact with the police,' he observed.

'Is a man not permitted to protect his livelihood?'

174

'Very well,' said Holmes at length. 'I will ask Lestrade to inspect the grave then call in at your house to challenge Whistler. We will meet you at the Café Royal at one to inform you of the outcome.'

I yawned, closed my eyes and in a moment it was morning. Like so many days, the first sound that reached my ears was Holmes' violin. He was picking his way through Mendelssohn's Violin Concerto in E Minor, making several attempts at the dramatic dash up and down the scale early on in the piece. It was akin to watching a man making successive attempts to run up an icy hill, getting half up only to slide back down again. The music and how Holmes interpreted it, said everything about his quick intelligence, his curious, imaginative mind and his tenacious manner. In contract with my friend's exuberance however, I was afflicted by a terrible malaise. I slunk into the sitting room and sank heavily into my chair, barely with the energy to bid my friend a good 'morrow. Holmes dropped his bow to his side.

'One late night too many?' he twinkled.

'The only medicine for me,' I muttered, 'is a pot of tea and the morning paper.'

'Don't be such a lie-by-the-fire, Watson,' he chided. 'You have not forgotten we are meeting Sullenbard at one? But before that, if you don't mind, I need to call in on some old friends. Will you join me?'

Otto and Bartholomew Cadwallader's watch repair shop was quite the smallest commercial premises in all of London. Sandwiched between Weir's, the booksellers, and Skiffington's, the wine merchant on Cleveland Street, it was barely wide enough to contain its tiny sign. In fact it was a miracle of the sign writer's art that he had managed to fit the names of the proprietors on such a diminutive sign at all, their names embossed in a barely legible serif above the door. In fact, to call it a door would be grandiloquent, for in truth it was more of a gap than an entrance, forbidding entry to any customer who had treated himself to an extra rasher of bacon or a second kipper at breakfast. The single, thin rectangular window that accompanied it would not have been out of place in the walls of a medieval castle. But it was through this window that the Cadwallader twins could be seen going about their business, clambering past each

175

other to reach a shelf or performing some act of contortionism to allow them both behind the counter at the same time. With two customers in the shop there was barely sufficient oxygen to sustain life, with three there was a very real danger of death.

Only ten minutes' walk from Baker Street, the brothers enjoyed a well deserved reputation for their meticulous accuracy.

'You didn't mention a problem with your watch, Holmes,' I remarked, staring at the doll's house before us.

'Perhaps,' my friend explained, 'that was because there is nothing at all wrong with it.' I frowned as Holmes supplied this information. 'We are calling on other business.' With a gloved hand, he pushed open the door and turning sideways we inserted ourselves one by one into the shop.

Once inside, away from the clatter of the carriages and the cries of the street sellers, there was a sublime tranquillity, punctuated only by the ticking of a hundred timepieces. They sounded, in imperfect unison, like a chorus of cicadas. As if to adapt by some evolutionary means to their restricted space, the two brothers were quite the leanest men I have ever encountered making even Holmes look well nourished. Having practiced since the womb, they were at perfect ease with each other and did not seem to regard the limited space as any kind of impediment to their work.

Like surgeons, the brothers worked away at the counter operating on the innards of a pair of watches, seemingly oblivious to our presence. Springs, coils and cogs lay in pieces before them and they pecked and prodded at the mechanisms with pins and tweezers. Well into their sixth decade, each wore a pair of moon shaped spectacles, a white goatee and were perfectly bald except for merest wisp that clung like a thin atmosphere around a dying planet.

'My dear sirs!' began Holmes, 'It pains me to interrupt two artists at work.' The man on the left carefully lay down his instrument, peered about him as if trying to trace the source of the voice and removed his spectacles.

'Is that you, Holmes?' he asked.

'The very same.'

'No doubt that fellow with you is the good Dr Watson. How is that watch of yours, doctor, still dropping ten seconds an hour?'

'I'm afraid so,' I confessed.

'I keep telling you to bring it in and let Otto and I have a proper look at it.'

'I can't spare it,' I explained, 'even for a day.'

'Then I shall lend you one to tide you over.'

'Bartholomew,' continued Holmes in hushed tones, 'I am here on delicate business. Would you and Otto have a half hour to assist me in a small matter?'

'Mr Holmes,' smiled the first brother. 'I am all too familiar with your small matters. They invariably involve the fate of nations!'

With difficulty, Otto extricated himself from behind the counter and with a flick of the wrist flipped the sign on the door from open to closed. Meanwhile Bartholomew opened a small hatch in the ceiling and pulled down a set of steps. 'If you would be so good as to follow me,' he invited, 'perhaps we can retire to somewhere more convivial.' With that, he ascended into the roof.

A few moments later we found ourselves in what was quite possibly the world's most compact sitting room. On the face of it, the promise of comfort seemed somewhat misleading. There was no more room upstairs than there was below, but what the brothers lacked in space they made up for in style. Holmes and I were seated on a King George II settee in orange velvet with lion claw legs. The brothers meanwhile, were perched on matching French needlepoint chairs. Each of us sat clutching a tiny, handle-less Royal Stafford coffee cup in pink and green bone china. Perhaps I overstate my knowledge of such antiquities. For the record, I knew nothing of the providence of the furniture or crockery until they were explained to me by the brothers.

'Perhaps, Watson,' began Holmes, 'you were unaware that the Cadwallader brothers had a speciality beyond watch repairs?'

'Indeed I was,' I stated. 'But now it is surely apparent that they are dealers in antiques.'

'A reasonable postulation,' agreed Holmes, 'but quite incorrect. They are in fact the authors of the definitive three volume work: Our

177

Lords and Masters: The British Aristocracy 1066 to 1894.'

'Remarkable!' I uttered.

'Quite so,' my friend continued. 'Their knowledge in this area is comprehensive in every regard, which is what brings us here.'

Holmes returned his coffee cup to the table and addressed the brothers.

'Business is brisk at the moment, is it not?'

'It certainly is,' said Otto with a quizzical look, 'but how were you to know?'

'It is easy enough to surmise,' laughed Holmes. 'You are both wearing new shoes, new ties and this couch is recently upholstered.'

'Perfectly correct,' agreed Otto.

'What's more the Prime Minister's own watch is in your pocket.' He spluttered a mouthful of coffee across the table.

'That is confidential!' he cried.

'Then I suggest that you conceal the Albert,' recommended Holmes. 'Half of London would recognise the buttonhole chain and jade fob in an instant.' Bartholomew, who appeared to be the dominant sibling, chuckled and dabbed patiently at the spilt coffee with a handkerchief.

'Calm yourself Otto,' he said, 'these men can be trusted with a secret. Since you know this much I may as well confess that the mechanism is proving a fiendish puzzle. The escape wheel is not engaging correctly with the anchor and we may need to replace the bezel. I have no idea what the man does with it to wreak such havoc. He must treat it like a cricket ball.' Holmes smiled politely at this shop talk.

'Now,' my friend said briskly, 'to business. What can you tell us about the Barundells?' Bartholomew and Otto exchanged a glance.

'Cornish, originally,' explained the former. He raised his cup to his lips and took a sip. 'They descended from the line of Sir John Barundell, born 1420-ish.'

'1421, I think you'll find,' clarified, Otto, 'died 1473. He was knighted by Edward IV.'

'Astonishing!' I marvelled at this feat of memory.

'It is a remarkable gift,' agreed Bartholomew. 'However he frequently forgets where he has left his spectacles.

178

'In fact I am seeking more recent genealogy,' explained Holmes. 'Is the line still extant?'

'Only just,' said Bartholomew, rising and moving to a cabinet that housed one of the splendid volumes. 'I have a nasty feeling that the curse of the Barundells has struck again.

'If I remember correctly, there is a curious curse that befalls every fifth generation. The Barundells were bishops and sheriffs, generals and admirals, but the first born of every fifth generation was destined to suffer an ignoble fate: bankruptcy, disgrace and ruin were the best they could hope for.' Bartholomew found the entry towards the start of the first volume. 'Humphrey, Thaddeus, Merlin... these are the names of just some of those who suffered the calamity of being born at the wrong time and in the wrong order. Separated by decades, they each ended in the same pitiable way. It was then for their offspring to pick up the pieces. As the fortunes of the Barundells dwindled, their estates eroded by these recurrent disasters, they abandoned their ancient seat in Devon and moved to more modest lodgings a little way from the city of St. Alban's.'

'I say, Holmes,' I put in, entirely gripped by this narrative, 'isn't that where that fellow Sullenbard said he was from?'

'Quite right, Watson,' my friend agreed, tapping his pipe. 'But surely, you realise by now that Mr Sullenbard is in fact one of the great Barundells.' I peered at him open mouthed, then slapped a hand to my forehead. 'Not another infernal anagram, Holmes!'

'I'm afraid so, Watson.'

'I thought there was something odd about him,' I mused. 'Come to think of it, he had an extraordinary manner for a butler.'

'Butler?' Otto repeated, baffled at our discourse.

'I apologise,' said Holmes, 'Where are our manners? Gentlemen, it appears I have taken on one of the Barundells as a client. He calls himself Terence Sullenbard.' Bartholomew ran a finger down a page, then looked gravely at my friend. 'If what you say is true, then you received a visit from Tobias Barundell, the last of the line.'

'Holmes!' I shouted.

'He was too proud to abandon his famous name altogether,' Holmes explained, 'and so merely rearranged it. Let me hazard a guess, he

179

has suffered the famous curse?' Bartholomew nodded. 'He inherited a prosperous farm with a hundred acres from his father, Randolph, who had worked tirelessly to restore the name, reputation and fortune of the family. Randolph was a decorated soldier, serving with great gallantry in the Crimean War. But the son, by all accounts inherited none of his father's qualities. We have recorded here that as a young man, he was proud, conceited and believed himself immune from the family curse. But then events began to prove otherwise. Expelled from Eton for drunkenness and idleness, he passed from one public school to the next until he returned, unrepentant to the family seat. He drove his father, now a widower, to distraction, drinking claret in the bath and sleeping for days on end, unwilling to either enlist or manage the estate. Finally he was given an ultimatum. Choose a profession or face disinheritance. The young Tobias told his father he would take up his duties on the estate, only to pay another man a pittance to carry out this work on his behalf. Believing his son had found his vocation, the father went abroad for an extended stay in Austria. Meanwhile the young Barundell did his level best to squander every penny in the clubs and on the gambling tables of Mayfair. This arrangement continued until the local vicar, a Father Simmons, noting the absence of the young noble from his church and connected to the local rumour mill, wrote to the older Barundell to express his concerns. By the time he returned, it was all too late. The estate was sold and the father died of a broken heart.

'Barundell was apoplectic with rage. He blamed everyone but himself and attempted to have the vicar defrocked. Shortly afterwards, he received a short custodial sentence for his violent and threatening behaviour. Eventually, he disappeared leaving enormous debts.'
'Then he returns as a butler to a vicar,' I mused.
'So it would seem,' said Bartholomew.
'Extraordinary,' I said.
'On the contrary,' contradicted Holmes. 'It was an entirely predictable course of action. It seems perfectly clear,' my friend explained, allowing his long slender fingers to dance along the stem of his pipe, 'that Mr Barundell is exacting some sort of revenge against the church. Unable to gain retribution against this Father

Simmons who ended his deception, he instead engineers a plot against a substitute figure – this poor, Father Whistler. By inveigling his way into his service it is my sincere belief that he went about systematically destroying the man, first by losing him his position and then by framing him as the Strychnine Poisoner. He pulled his watch from his pocket, frowned, then gave the timepiece a tap with his fingernail.

'Let me take a look at that,' offered Otto. 'If I recall correctly, your watch suffers from a little stickiness in the escapement. It is remedied easily enough.'

'Thank you,' muttered Holmes, handing it over, 'but my immediate need is merely to know the time.'

'Half past twelve,' I informed him.

'Then we have a half hour before our rendezvous with Barundell at the Café Royal.' He stood up and with great solemnity shook the brothers' hands. 'Gentlemen he declared, 'you have once again provided invaluable assistance. It is possible you have played a part in halting the progress of one of the great devils of our age. I shall return for my watch and to provide an update on our enquiries this coming Tuesday.'

'Good gracious,' I remarked on the way out, peering at a small, luminous portrait of a girl in a red hat in a field of flowers, 'that looks remarkably like a Renoir.'

'That's because it is,' smiled Otto.

London was flooded with sunlight when we emerged from the shop. We squinted as our eyes readjusted to the glare.

'One thing confuses me, Holmes,' I mused as a hansom pulled up to collect us. 'Given their great success and illustrious list of clients, not to mention their publishing enterprises, why do the Cadwalladers remain in such tiny premises in apparent penury?'

'Ah,' smiled Holmes. 'It is a valid question, and naturally we may only guess at an answer but I suspect it runs as follows. Those who provide the most valuable services are rarely those who are most visible. They can be found by those who need to know but equally can avoid the tedium of attending to the demands of the masses. There is another factor too. Did you observe the doors on either side of the sitting room?'

181

'I confess I did not.'

'Then you failed to grasp the perfection of their arrangement. They have an agreement with the bookseller on one side and the wine merchant on the other, allowing them free access to their goods and services. No doubt a reciprocal arrangement is in place. With access to books and wine and the convivial company that attends those two pleasures, what more could a man want?'

'Stop here, driver!' Holmes called unexpectedly as we approached Marylebone High Street. 'We will be precisely three minutes.' With this, he collecting his cane, pulled open the door and leapt out.

My friend proceeded directly to T.P White's, the pharmacist, a green fronted building with large glass orbs in the windows filled with luminescent coloured liquids.

'Are you sick?' I asked. 'Perhaps you have forgotten that your companion is a medical doctor?'

'Not sick, Watson, no,' he answered, hurrying in and ringing the bell.

We stood before a long counter of polished hardwood. Behind it was space for the staff to go about their business. At their backs, shelf units filled three walls and rose almost to the ceiling. Each of these was lined with hundreds of glass jars containing all manner of potions, powders and remedies. At the centre, perched high on the uppermost shelf was a handsome clock, no doubt provided for the benefit of those waiting for their prescriptions to be dispensed. A severe looking gentleman with a white apron over his suit, iron grey hair and an equally steely expression stood with his hands flat on the counter.

'Strychnine,' demanded Holmes.

'Excuse me?' the pharmacist clarified.

'I require a quantity of strychnine,' Holmes repeated. The chemist narrowed his eyes and inspected Holmes and I with suspicion.

'That is an unusual request,' he said slowly.

'Well, do you have any?' asked Holmes, tapping his cane impatiently against the floor.

'You must be aware of the recent spate of poisonings,' the man replied. 'I would need to take your particulars.'

'Certainly,' my friend snapped. 'My name is Sherlock Holmes and

182

this is my associate, Dr John Watson MD. Now are you willing to help me, or do I need to ask the good doctor here to write me a prescription?' Moments later we were rattling along Blandford Street, Holmes clutching the substance inside a paper bag.

'I do hope you know what you're doing, Holmes,' I cautioned.

By the time we arrived, The Café Royal was teeming with the lunchtime crowd; they reflected themselves so as to appear twice their number in the walls of mirrors. Like a ghost in the night, another waiter whirled past our table.

'I may die of thirst if this keeps up, Holmes,' I grumbled. I signalled to another waiter but was ignored by him too.

'Patience, Watson,' smiled Holmes, selecting a cigarette from a silver case.

The walls and ceilings were trimmed with gold and lavishly decorated with painted panels. All things considered, it was a little too garish for my taste. Through the fog of tobacco smoke, the conspiratorial glow of candlelight and against the backdrop of astonishing opulence, a hundred conversations played out. It was a theatre of the rich, the idle and those who aspired to these conditions. The timpani of glasses, pockets of laughter and low tones of the string quartet provided an atmosphere of convivial exclusivity which denied the existence of the poor, the dull or the commonplace. Into this, walked the elegant figure of Tobias Barundell. We watched him look left and right before allowing himself a smile. This, after all, was his world: a life of surface pleasures and superficial relations. It lasted only as long as there was money for another glass of champagne or plate of oysters.

We both stood to greet Barundell as he approached our table, reluctantly accepting his clammy, limp handshake.

'How marvellous!' he exclaimed, gazing about him, in faux-wonder, the light reflecting brightly in his magpie eyes.

'Holmes and I have yet to order,' I informed him. 'What will you have?'

So naturally at home was he, he seemed to forget his false identity and the persona of the humble butler all but disappeared. He removed his hat and gloves and held them out as if expecting a lackey to whisk them away. He smoothed his hair in an urbane manner then took his seat.

'Is champagne,' he probed, 'too indulgent at this hour?'

'Why not,' agreed Holmes. 'I believe our case is nearing its conclusion. A small celebratory glass is perfectly in order.'

'Splendid!' he cried. Without thinking, Barundell raised his hand and a waiter appeared almost at once. I was convinced the waiter was about to speak when the aristocrat silenced him with look.

'You have a remarkable gift for attracting attention,' remarked Holmes. 'It is almost as if you are a regular here.' Barundell shifted uneasily in his seat.

'Now tell me,' the man said, changing the subject and selecting a cigar from his pocket. 'What was Lestrade's view of the case?'

'He was most interested,' Holmes began. 'He visited the grave as you directed. What he discovered surprised both him and me. For within it was the body of a fellow named Alim, the business partner of Arthur Tickler, a dealer in antiquities. It is too early to say for sure, but it Lestrade's belief that he was poisoned by a dose of strychnine.'

'Then I am sorry for the boy,' returned Barundell swirling the champagne in his glass.

'How did you know he was a youth?' Holmes enquired. Barundell stared at him for a moment.

'I am familiar with their business,' he explained. 'But surely,' he added, 'this only confirms Whistler as the killer in our midst. He was concealing the evidence. The poor, dim-witted fool. His attempt to conceal his crime was amateurish in the extreme.' His eyes gleamed like those of the devil himself. 'Surely he had damned himself now.'

'It is a grim business,' said Holmes with feeling. 'Alim was a bright soul with a quick mind and noble spirit. He was caught up in an iniquitous game and did not deserve his squalid fate.'

'No doubt,' dismissed Barundell. 'But what of the scientific apparatus found at Whistler's house?'

'Once again, Lestrade was most taken by the discovery,' admitted Holmes. 'The vessels were those necessary to prepare the deadly solution from the seeds of the *nux vomica*, the strychnine tree.'

'I knew it!' he cried in triumph, slamming a hand to the table, then draining the contents of his glass. 'Then the man is under arrest?'

'He is in the safe custody of Scotland Yard. However there are a number of unresolved points which deserve attention before a line is drawn beneath this problem and Dr Watson commits it to his library of fanciful adventures.'

'Holmes,' I frowned, 'that is beneath you.'

'I mean it only in terms of the greatest affection.'

At this moment we heard a shriek of alarm from a neighbouring table, the clatter of falling chairs and the shattering of cut crystal. A large barrel-chested man in a morning suit was on his feet, his face the colour of plum, staggering dangerously backwards, convulsing in spasms, his eyes bulging and his hands clutching his throat.

'The poisoner has struck!' cried one hot-headed woman in a crinoline dress, who promptly fainted into her soufflé.

'Watson!' commanded Holmes, 'assist him!' I did not need to be asked, dashing across to the man and seized him by the shoulders. Barundell too, was on his feet. But in an instant, I realised that no poison was at work. With Barundell's assistance, I restrained the fellow, leant him forward then delivered two sharp blows to his upper back. At the second, a whole prawn shot from his lips and landed in the lap of an elderly matron.

The large gentleman turned to me, his eyes still bulging in their sockets, but his cheeks mercifully returning to a more natural hue.

'I am very much obliged,' he gasped, collapsing into his chair, his great chest rising and falling like a stormy sea. His face was strangely familiar, I considered a moment, but could not place him. Adrenaline can do strange things to the mind.

'Bravo, Watson!' cried Holmes as I returned to the table. He was on his feet, beginning a slow hand clap. 'The disaster is averted. Applause rang in my ears. We clinked glasses and all three of us drank deeply.

'What a fandango,' Barundell sighed, raising his eyebrows. He drew lazily on his cigar and sat back with an air of satisfaction. 'You were saying, Mr Holmes, about the unresolved points of the case. To what points do you refer?'

185

'Ah, yes,' returned Holmes. 'I had quite lost my train of thought. I found myself wondering why, for instance there were traces of strychnine on your silk handkerchief?'

'What?' Barundell cried. The cigar fell from his fingers.

'I took the liberty of conducting a simple chemical test on the handkerchief you kindly loaned me at Baker Street. I dissolved the residue in a 0.5cc solution of concentrated sulphuric acid, adding a single crystal of potassium dichromate. If strychnine is present, a vivid blue colour may briefly be seen. I can confirm that my experiment yielded a positive result.

'Are you suggesting,' Barundell foamed, 'that I am the killer?'

'That is my inference,' my friend attested.

'Then this is an outrage,' he said, gathering up his gloves.

'Please sit down, Mr Barundell.' The man froze at the mention of his name.

'I have never heard that name in my life,' he hissed. 'What is more, I have grown tired of this affair. I have done all I can to put the evidence before you, to give you the credit you so clearly crave and to preserve the safety of the public. Perhaps I should go directly to Scotland Yard after all.'

'If you walk through those doors,' stated Holmes, 'it is likely that will be dead in precisely fourteen minutes.' I stared at my friend in horror.

'I have added a quantity of strychnine to one of our drinks. However I have no idea which one.'

'Holmes!' I shouted, peering into my empty glass. 'Have you lost your mind?'

'Never fear, Watson,' he added. 'I have an antidote upon my person: a solution of nitrate of amyl, formulated in precisely the correct volume, which if inhaled over several hours, may prevent death. For the man who has consumed the poison, the painful convulsions are inevitable, but with this remedy, they need not be fatal.' Barundell and I continued to stare at him, aghast.

'Perhaps, continued Holmes, 'you will allow me to outline the facts as I see them. If you agree they are a fair and honest summary and confess to your crimes, I will provide the antidote. Your second option is to take your chances, which no doubt you have calculated are 3/1, and take your leave. The choice is entirely yours.' Barundell rose to his feet, his eyes flaming, but there was an agitation about him too, his natural cowardice preventing his flight.

'Then let me hear your absurd story,' he thundered, returning heavily to his seat, beads of sweat forming on his brow. Holmes related the history of his early years, how he tricked his father and the tale of his own undoing at the hands of the local vicar.

As I listened, I was overcome by a growing paranoia; I felt my pulse racing and my face was damp with perspiration. I loosened my collar and removed my jacket, convinced it was I who had consumed the toxin. I peered woozily at my friend as the facts appeared calmly from his lips. How could he be so reckless as to endanger our lives? I had read of this remedy but it was by no means reliable and great pain was unavoidable. Even in my own distressed state, I could see the same thoughts were rushing through Barundell's mind. The arrogance was gone, replaced by a look of horror.

'Is it not true,' Holmes attested, his voice rising in anger, 'that over the last three months you have waged a campaign of fear against every law-abiding Londoner? Your soul was consumed by bitterness at the loss of your fortune and the death of your father. You made an enemy of all humanity vowing to cause pain and misery, to destroy life; to take it away from the happy, the contented and the innocent. They have what you can never have. You framed your employer, Joseph Whistler, enraged at what that first vicar took from you, doctoring the books to make him appear a thief and a criminal with the result that he lost his position in the church. You drove a kindly, educated man to madness and despair. You feigned sympathy, filling his weakened mind with a lunatic, mediaeval scheme telling him how he could produce precious metals through chemical alchemy. You harried him into spending his last savings on chemical apparatus, which in fact you used for your own demonic purposes. He worked feverishly, but naturally his labours yielded nothing but fool's gold. Desperate for paid work, he took up grave digging. So humiliated was he by the notion that he only worked at night for fear of being seen by his peers.

'You yourself are a member of a criminal fraternity. Beneath your shirt on your left shoulder is tattooed yet another name: The Apothecary. You are a paid assassin for the society. You murdered Alim, and knowing where Whistler was to work that night, having spied on his correspondence, you left the coffin for him to bury in place of the original. Then you invited us to witness this work.'

Barundell stared directly ahead, his eyes manic with fear. His breathing had grown shallow and rapid and his pulse raced. Perhaps both us were poisoned.
'The antidote!' he cried. 'Quickly, give me the antidote. The convulsions are upon me!'
'First, your confession!' demanded Holmes.
'Then I confess!' he screamed. 'The world is accursed and I abhor the existence of its every living creature. I made Whistler my slave and my only regret is that I left him alive. I am the man who has brought a reign of death on London. Even the lions of Scotland Yard fear me!'

Holmes nodded at this and folded his arms.
'There,' he said, all trace of anger, having left him, 'it was not so hard.'
'You have your confession,' Barundell spat, 'albeit a meaningless one. Nobody of significance has witnessed it and the evidence is stacked all in my favour. The strychnine you found on my handkerchief is merely circumstantial. Of course it was my poison; my hands brim with the stuff every day. But who would believe it if they had not heard these words for themselves?'
'I would,' said a familiar voice. A man of medium build with dark hair and rat-like features turned around, a revolver aimed directly at the aristocrat. It was Inspector Lestrade of Scotland Yard. Barundell recoiled in terror.
'Tobias Barundell,' recited Lestrade 'I am arresting you for the murders of twenty-nine men, women and children.' Two constables appeared, towering over the man.
'Take him away,' instructed the inspector.
'But my antidote!' cried Barundell again, now wriggling like a child between the two burly policemen. Holmes smiled thinly.
'You do not require an antidote, because there was no poison.'

188

'But Holmes,' I protested, 'I was with you when it was dispensed.'

'I purchased nothing stronger than an aspirin. It was merely the power of suggestion. I explained myself to the pharmacist while you were at the other end of the shop.' Barundell squealed like a trapped animal at this revelation and they dragged him away, almost certainly to the gallows. I collapsed back in relief.

'But why the pantomime, Holmes?'

'It was essential that your fear was plausible enough to convince Barundell of his own. I could not afford to rely solely on your thespian powers, impressive though no doubt they are.' I shook my head in wonder and disbelief. 'Speaking of acting,' continued Holmes, striking a match and setting his pipe tobacco aglow, 'may I introduce my old friend, Shelton Wallis.' The large fellow who had survived the choking episode stepped forward, proffering a hand.

'My dear man,' he said. 'You were marvellous. But was it necessary to hit me quite so hard?' Holmes seemed enormously amused at this. 'Wallis here was ready to choke on that prawn at my cue. It was a necessary distraction to make it believable that I had spiked the champagne.

'Ingenious,' I murmured.

'You last saw him as Kent in King Lear. Do you recall?'

'Of course!' I cried, recognising the genial features.

'Now Lestrade', said Holmes firmly. 'Please let us be clear that I will accept no credit for this trifling work. Barundell practically delivered himself to justice. But will you see to it that Whistler's slate is wiped clean?' The inspector nodded his assent, casting a final look around the scene of this memorable denouement.

'Your modesty denies the public of the sensation it desires,' he opined. 'After the debacle on the South Bank, it would restore the reputation of Sherlock Holmes.'

'I care nothing for the reputation of Sherlock Holmes,' my friend retorted, 'only his work.'

'So be it,' he said, sighing and draining a glass of water. 'If that is your wish, I will respect it and merely record that the men of Scotland Yard apprehended the man at the Cafe Royal.'

'Modesty,' Holmes declared, 'is the privilege of genius. One day, no doubt, Watson will commit it all to the page. I will leave it to him to apportion the credit and award the laurels where he sees fit. But for now, I must concentrate my mind on the business of this lost Shakespeare play. I will not rest until it is located.'

'It is a fanciful notion,' sighed Lestrade, 'but every man has his whim and if it is within the law, then he has a right to indulge it.'

'Inspector,' said Holmes, rising to his feet and shaking hands. 'With every successful conclusion you grow in stature as a policeman and as a student of deduction. One day your powers of observation will match the fervour of your sense of duty.'

'I will accept that as a backhanded compliment,' Lestrade replied. 'But dash it all, Holmes, why do you insist on making everything so dramatic?'

ELEVEN

The Company of Lucius

Like the English arrows at Agincourt, the rain came down in a torrent. Rivers seemed to flow through the gutters and water washed in great diaphanous sheets from the roofs. It was, I suspected, Sherlock Holmes' favourite kind of weather. It rattled against the glass while the yellow gaslight of Baker Street shone blearily through the windows, spilling into our dimly-lit rooms, casting shadows against the wall. The clock showed a quarter past ten.

Paralysed in his chair, his thumb and forefinger pinching his cranium, Holmes stared at the wall as if attempting through sheer dint of effort to peer through it. On his lap was the page of manuscript he had copied from the play, presumably already committed to memory. I on the other hand, could not bear this sort of languor. It was all very well for a winter's night when the world could be ignored and the fire built up, but this was redolent, summer night.

I paced from one end of our sitting room to the other, gripping an unread novella in my hand. Resting an elbow on the mantelpiece, I swiftly exchanged it for the other, kicked a stray piece of charcoal into the inglenook then returned to my starting position.

'Calm yourself, Watson,' my friend counselled. 'It is as if you are on parade at Netley. Take a drink and settle down. If you cannot allow me to do my brain work in peace then perhaps the Diogenes would provide you with more convivial surroundings.'

'I cannot fathom it!' I cried, throwing down my book. 'We have had distraction after distraction. It is a summer of the bizarre, the chaotic, the random and the grotesque. Nothing is resolved and we are no nearer to locating the play. Holmes, it gives me no pleasure to admit this, but I fear we may have to admit to a failure. There is no shame in it. We were lured into a fantastical scheme. Our client is dead; the play, if it ever existed, is lost.' I put my hands to my hips and dropped my head in weariness and exasperation. When I looked up again, I saw Holmes' face peering back at me, as pale a cadaver, his eyes deadly still.

'Do not stare so,' I cried. 'You unnerve me.'

'Watson, my dear Watson,' he softened at last, snapping out of his trance. 'I have been too harsh with you. While my mind leaps ahead, I do not consider how far behind I leave you or how cold it is in the dark. It is time to let you in. Turn up the lamp and we will talk as friends.'

Holmes reached surreptitiously for his Persian slipper and retrieved from the toe-end that filthy blend of tobacco he so favoured. I found his insistence on concealing it in this way almost charming in its childishness. It would be a strange intruder at 221b Baker Street who would choose to pocket the tobacco, in favour of, say, a diamond tie-pin or ceremonial sword. But my friend was a creature of particular habits and these ticks and eccentricities were what defined him. He filled his pipe, then lay back, holding it languidly above him in the manner of raconteur.

'I had my first inklings,' he began, 'that foul night I followed Somerville and his cronies into Highgate Cemetery. You recall how I managed to follow the group only so far into the place before losing them? It was a singular business. One minute they were no more than ten paces in front of me; the next, their lantern lights were snuffed and they had vanished completely. There was nothing but the sound of the rain. I lingered as long as I could but realised that I would perish from hypothermia if I stayed any longer. You and I were distracted momentarily by the problem of the steel trooper, but it was always my intention to return to the cemetery and examine the spot.

'But how would you know the place again?' Holmes gave one of his thin smiles. 'You remember that red handkerchief tied to a branch?'

'Yes,' I nodded.

'It was my own; a marker so I could find the place in daylight.' He struck a match and lowered the flame into the bowl of his pipe before succeeding in bringing it to life with a succession of furious inhalations. You recall how the following day was fair? I knew that any footprints made in the storm would remain for me to examine at my leisure.'

'And what did you discover?'

'The footprints, no less that twelve sets in fact, led directly to a brick wall that formed a step to the next level of earth. I assumed this meant that the company had gone up and over, but I examined the earth above and there was no trace of them. Adjacent to the spot where the footprints ended we discovered the grave of the late Susan Macbeth.'

'In which we found the equally unfortunate Alberto Borgia.'

'So it appeared.'

'So the footsteps led you to the grave.'

'Indeed,' he said thoughtfully. 'I felt sure that the business of the disembodied hand and the conflab in the cemetery were connected in some way and my suspicions was confirmed. But it was at this juncture that I conceived a new notion.' A dog barked in the street and a four wheeler clattered past our window. The sound of its wheels slowly died away. Holmes gripped the stem of his pipe between his teeth and pressed his fingertips together. 'I had discovered the headquarters of the secret society.' I gazed at my friend, then frowned at this fanciful idea.

'This society?' I repeated. 'It meets in a cemetery?'

'Quite so.'

'A grim spot for a social club. But who are they? And what is their purpose?'

'I am not yet in full possession of the facts. But we are acquainted with several of its members. 'Allow me to give you a list.' He extended his hand, palm upwards, parting his fingers. 'First there is Caliban, whose company we enjoyed at the races. Then there is Winter, Standbull, Barundell and Pinner to name but a few. I do not mind admitting, Watson,' Holmes announced, rising from his chair, 'that this case has seized my attention in a way not even I could have anticipated. The reasons, of course, are logical enough; I have a predisposition for Shakespeare and the notion of a new play has gripped me with its imaginative power. It was predictable that I would become personally involved.'

'It seems perfectly obvious to me that Somerville is behind all this,' I declared. 'It is clear that he is the head of this so-called society.'

'Let us not be hasty, Watson. Our conclusions must be predicated on fact and our actions based on sound interpretation of those facts. The business of speculation belongs to the stock exchange and the race course. Tomorrow is Somerville's deadline. I suggest that we pay him a visit and address the matter head on. Naturally we will take every precaution. Now Watson, if you would be so good as to dampen the bottom of my glass with your excellent Dupeyron Armagnac, let us talk of other things.'

The next morning the rain had cleared. Dark maps lined the pavements and the petrichor of the grass in the London parks imbued the city with a wonderful freshness and vitality. Clattering down Blandford Street, our brougham bore us briskly towards Somerville's offices. As we left, Holmes had been careful to check his Webley Bulldog was in good working order; my own revolver, retrieved and repaired following the singular business at the Houses of Parliament, was close to hand. My friend tapped his cane impatiently against the floor of the carriage; in his hands, I knew from long experience, it could be a more effective weapon even than a pistol.

There is something a little melancholy about a theatre in the morning. Deprived of its fairy lights, its glamour and above all, its audience, its magic is annulled. In the unforgiving sunlight, I reflected, its shabby corners and peeling paintwork were there for all to see. I paid off our cabbie, and my friend and I peered up and down the near deserted street. A playbill hung loose from a wall and its edge flapped in the breeze. A pigeon fluttered noisily from one rooftop to the next. With a certain inevitability, the front pages of yesterday's newspaper curled slowly along the pavement, before finally catching at my ankles.

'Look at that, Holmes,' I remarked grimly, seizing the newssheet. 'Not content with ending the career of the most remarkable man in London, The Marquis of Queensbury continues to crow. What more does the man want?'

'He wants what he cannot have,' my friend replied, 'which is for the past to be rewritten. Still, there is always hope for Oscar,' my friend consoled me. 'They say a caged bird sings all the more sweetly.'

Presently, a door swung open and an actress I immediately recognised as Irene Vanbrugh flashed past us. She was an exquisite creature, with dark, gleaming, fiercely intelligent eyes. To my dismay, she ignored me completely, and instead peered at Holmes' who succeeded in ignoring *her* completely, instead continuing to study the newspaper. We had last seen her in April as Gwendolen in The Important of Being Earnest, just before the producer George Alexander (Somerville's great rival) had been forced to close the play in the wake of Wilde's trial. To give Alexander his due, he had held out as long as he could, even going so far as to remove Wilde's name from the publicity, but to no avail. Unless she had just secured herself another role, Vanbrugh was now just another resting actress. It was then I realised that we were being watched. Somerville's bulky figure filled the window of his second storey office, directly opposite the theatre on Drury Lane, peering down at us. We entered through a handsome pair of mahogany doors and ascended a staircase lined with faded red carpet. The walls were covered with play bills promoting the great productions of the 'seventies and 'eighties yellowing in their frames. I suddenly had a vivid recollection of watching Robert the Devil one night with Mary at my side.

Somerville was standing in the doorway in a green, silk dressing gown, a grave expression on his already careworn face. He held a cane in one hand. In the other, a Romeo y Julietta cigar was smoking between his fat, nicotine stained fingers.
'You have my play?' he asked in a low voice.
'Let us have a mouthful of tea,' requested Holmes, 'and we will share all we know.'
'Very well,' he nodded and gestured vaguely towards a low couch while he went to the door and summoned a maid. I looked quizzically at Holmes who seemed perfectly calm. My friend picked up a programme from the table and flicked through the pages.
'Well well,' he whispered, handing me the sheet. 'Recognise any of the names here?'
'Good Lord,' I exclaimed. 'Elsie Pinner.'
'The very same; and note the name of the producer.'
'Somerville,' I returned.
'Everything is connected, Watson,' Holmes muttered, then busied himself with the preparation of a pipe.

Presently a petite girl with dark hair and porcelain white skin entered, carrying a tray of tea things, at the centre of which was a strange, square porcelain teapot with a serpent for a spout. She laid them down in front of us, unsmilingly, then left the room.

'An unusual Wedgewood,' Holmes remarked to Somerville as he returned to the room. 'I would put it at 1775.'

'1778,' corrected Somerville, evidently impressed, despite himself. 'It is the work of the young John Flaxman. I was unaware you counted ceramics among your interests, Mr Holmes?' This was news to me too.

'I have a memory for such things,' dismissed Holmes. 'Now who will bitch the pot?' I did the honours, filling three cups to the brim with Earl Grey, stirring a quantity of sugar into my own.

'Now,' said Somerville, seating himself in an armchair by the table, noting the programme had been moved, 'to business. I'll repeat my question...'

'There is no need,' said Holmes, calmly, returning his tea cup to the table. 'I have the play here in my hands.' The impresario's eyes lit up as if Holmes had presented him with the Koh-I-Noor itself. My friend and I had our own colourful memories of that particular treasure from the singular Adventure of the Ruby Elephants, of which I have written elsewhere.

'Splendid!' roared Somerville. I stared at my friend, astonished.

'But how?' I asked, flabbergasted.

'It helps to have an insider,' smiled Holmes, pouring himself a little more tea from the serpent's mouth.

My friend reached into his coat and produced a thick sheaf of papers, handing them over to Somerville. 'Naturally, I have had a chance to look it over.'

'And your assessment?'

'It is a remarkably good play,' opined Holmes. 'The world is a richer place for it. The Duke is a fully realised character. The moment he banishes his daughter ranks alongside Leontes casting off his wife and daughter in The Winter's Tale. There are shadows and echoes of so many of Shakespeare's plays here, it feels almost as if they have been bundled into one. To my mind, it is neither here nor there whether the Bard is its author.'

'That is where you and I differ, Holmes,' chortled Somerville, now transformed into bonhomie. His cheeks gleamed red and the sparkle had returned to his eyes. He placed a proprietorial hand on my friend's shoulder. 'Proof that it is Shakespeare's work,' he explained, 'will guarantee astonishing revenues. It will mean hundreds of thousands of pounds, possibly even millions. It will play in every theatre in the world and I will demand a royalty for every performance.' He caught my friend's disapproving look. 'Of course you will have your share too,' he added hastily. 'But if you are feeling high-minded about it and want no part in the business end of things, then think what a service you have done to literature.' He rang a bell and the maid reappeared at the door. 'Clear these tiresome things away, Lydia,' he demanded, 'we've had enough of this cat-lap. Bring us champagne and three of my Venetian champagne flutes: those with the gold rim; I do like to take my champagne over gold. We have much to celebrate.' I could barely contain my anger, but restrained myself until the girl left with the tray.

'Holmes,' I announced, my voice shaking, 'I will not stand for this. Somerville is without a doubt a member of this syndicate. You have transferred the world's most valuable treasure into the hands of a criminal. I sincerely hope there is a rational explanation for this.'

'Watson, my dear, sir,' reasoned Holmes. 'William Somerville is the rightful owner of this play. You heard as well as I the testimony of Arthur Tickler.'

'But the society!' I cried rising to my feet. 'This man is in league with Winter. They are anarchists; murderers; worse even. Have you lost your mind?' The two men stared at me, while the room spun.

'Water,' I heard Holmes, cry. 'Give him water!'

It often baffled me why a man of Holmes' immense abilities lived such a modest existence. Further still, it used to bother me why he kept company that offered such little stimulation. One might suppose that a brilliant mind demands another; and yet this is so rarely the case. Two bright fires cannot burn next to each other without extinguishing each other. They draw all the oxygen from the room. There is a cancelling out. Over the years, I have learned to accept my role as a sounding board, a catalyst, grist to the mill, the grit that produces the pearl. With his astounding mind, lightening repartee, his cool reasoning and masterful manner he could have been London's most dazzling QC, its most outstanding politician, most gifted actor or most feared general. If he woke the next morning and decided on a whim to reinvent himself he would have the pick of a hundred professions. Had he chosen the path of convention, surely he would have risen as a captain of industry or as an orator that might have rivalled Marcus Antonius himself. At the very least, even if he had limited himself to his own sphere and operated on a level with Lestrade at Scotland Yard, undoubtedly he would have had become the best of them all. Yet he rejected the mainstream, denied himself the accolades and rewards of his contemporaries. He shunned the clubs and all but the most private recognition of his achievements.

To me, his finances were largely a mystery. He took on as many cases pro bono as he did for reward. I never saw him work at any financial ledger and it was rarer still to see him raise an invoice. He appeared to work on the basis of quid pro quo, resulting in small items of unique value and interest materialising in our rooms shortly after the successful conclusion of a case. Perhaps only now did Holmes see his opportunity. Would this be the end of his detective work? Would the limitless riches from this newly discovered play now fund the simple life Holmes often spoke of, tending his hives, whispering to his bees on the Sussex Downs?

I felt the sting of brandy on my lips then waited for the room to pull back into focus. I found myself lying, with my tie loosened, on Somerville's couch.
'Welcome back to the land of the living,' my friend rejoined.
'Forgive me,' I began. 'But...'
'But you wouldn't be the first to faint in my presence,' Somerville remarked. 'I confess however, it is more commonly the histrionic actress, angling for a better part or a higher fee.'
'Fear not, Watson,' dismissed Holmes, once again pressing the brandy on me. 'I have not taken leave of my senses, nor renounced the forces of good. It takes more than a few guineas and a glass of champagne to buy the soul of Sherlock Holmes.' I straightened my collar, somewhat embarrassed, then sat up, struggling to recover my train of thought.
'I have satisfied myself, Watson,' he continued, 'that Mr Somerville's motive for acquiring the play is merely greed.'

'I say, Holmes,' frowned Somerville, 'that's a bit strong.'

'You have said as much, yourself.' Still, to my befuddled mind, it did not make a great deal of sense.

'But the meeting in the cemetery?' I put in.

'Naturally, I had my suspicions too,' my friend agreed. 'Word got out that Somerville had obtained a play. There is a certain quantity of loose talk in the world of theatre and no doubt this got back to this society, The Company of Lucius.'

'A fanciful moniker,' I remarked.

'Lucius,' explained Somerville, 'was the name of a member of the company of actors who visited Elsinore in Hamlet. You recall the play within the play designed to prick Claudius' conscience?' I nodded then drained my glass, feeling the brandy's restorative powers.

'It appears,' Holmes elucidated, swirling his champagne and inspecting the viscous residue on the glass, 'that they are a group of men and women unknown to all but the inner most circle of government.'

'Men and women!' I remarked. 'What modern thinking.'

'Yes, a most progressive society,' my friend continued. 'Their aims are difficult to pin down precisely, although they may be loosely categorised as anarchists. However they have one singular trait. Each member goes under the name of a character from Shakespeare's plays.'

'But how do we know all this?' I asked.

'Because before you sits Lear.' I was agog.

'You!' I exclaimed.

'No, not me, Watson,' rubbished Holmes. 'Somerville.'

'Then you *are* a member,' I concluded, utterly perplexed.

'It appears,' my friend picked up, 'that when the society heard the rumours of the play's existence, they approached Somerville with an invitation to join their fraternity. Naturally, they kept the nature of their real activities from him: their plans to unsettle the state; their ideas for the abolition of the monarchy and so forth. They merely spoke of their mutual love of Shakespeare, their global connections, the considerable resources they had at their disposal and flattered him with an invitation to become their Lear, the post recently having been vacated. Naturally their colourful naming system and this role in particular appealed to Mr Somerville's sense of the theatrical.'

'It is,' the producer confessed, 'all true. I also hoped they would make me a substantial offer for the play.'

'Now the night in the rain was his first meeting. At first, they were civil and treated him with great respect. But when it became apparent that Somerville, becoming suspicious, did not wish to share the play, nor even confirm its existence, things took a different tone.'

'But what could they want with the play beyond wealth?'

'Perhaps that is all there is to it,' my friend speculated. 'However I cannot help but feel there is something else.'

'They threatened me with my life, doctor,' he said gravely. 'They gave me an ultimatum to surrender it to them or accept the consequences. With the play vanished, I had lost my bargaining chip. I had few options, except to trust Mr Holmes here to find and retrieve it for me.'

'And when,' I asked, 'does the ultimatum expire?'

'This evening.'

'And what is your intention?' I asked. 'Simply to hand it over to them?'

'Certainly not!' the producer snarled. 'However it would be rash of me not to show my face.'

'We have a plan, Watson,' my friend outlined, holding his glass up to the light. 'Tonight we will all attend the meeting.'

'Preposterous!' I shouted. 'We will be murdered.'

'Perhaps and perhaps not. The society has another singular tradition which may work to our advantage. Every member attends their meetings wearing a mask. We happen to know that two members will not be attending on account of their recent demise. We shall go in their place.'

'But what do we hope to learn?' I asked. 'Why do we not simply summon Lestrade and arrest them on the spot.'

'Too easy,' said, Holmes shaking his head. 'First we must discover why they want the play. There is more to this than meets the eye. Now I have a choice for you, Watson: Rosencrantz or Guildenstern?'

We departed in separate carriages: Holmes and I in one, Somerville in the other (in case we were seen to be in league.) However, to my surprise, we were not heading for Highgate Cemetery at all but north east, leaving London far behind. Dense and foreboding and with a smell of moss and damp, Epping Forest enveloped us in its branches. They tore like hands at the sides and door of our carriage as if trying to claim us. At times, my friend and I appeared to be travelling in total darkness despite the fact that it was approaching mid-summer. Holmes, appearing to read my thoughts, pointing out that the society had doubtless been alerted to the discovery of their last meeting place and had chosen a new venue.

Holmes was an odd sort of travelling companion. He was prone to lapse for long periods into silent reflection, with no consideration for social niceties. At such times, it was impossible to know whether he was simply turning a problem over in his mind or had sunk into a fathomless depression. In any case, it was unwise to disturb him. On other occasions, he would converse with immense animation on a remarkable range of topics. This evening, he was in loquacious mood, holding forth on Scottish architecture, molecular biology, the firing mechanism of the British rifle and the comparably limited English repertoire for the viola. Needless to say, these conversations were somewhat one-sided. As we rattled along the thin track taking us to High Beech and into the very heart of the forest, he returned to the matter in hand.

'Truly, Watson,' he said, clutching the cloak and mask that Somerville had provided from his prop cupboard, 'this case has taken us on a circuitous journey to the truth. However I feel we are approaching the heart of the matter.' Shadows flitted across his face and a flash of moonlight blanched his already pale complexion, giving him the appearance of an eastern European count. 'I feel it is only fair to warn you,' he said, 'that I am putting your life in considerable danger.'

'I was aware of that,' I smiled, 'the moment I agreed to share your lodgings.'

'This time will be different,' he said gravely. 'If we are discovered our options will be limited.'

'And you are quite sure Somerville is not leading us into a trap?'

'One can never be completely sure of anything, Watson,' he murmured, 'but I have weighed the balance of probabilities and have concluded that it is a risk worth taking. Somerville is in a certain degree of danger himself. He will announce this evening that he does not wish to belong to the society. The question is whether they will let him go, and if so, whether he will be permitted to take his play with him. I rather think not.'

Presently, we emerged from the forest and found ourselves crossing open parkland. Ahead of us, we could see the outline of an imposing house on a hill.

'I have been here before, if I am not mistaken,' I remarked to Holmes. 'I picnicked here once as a boy.'

'This,' I fear, he said, donning his cloak, 'will be no picnic.'

We paid off our cab some way from the house, electing to complete the rest of the journey on foot. Holmes and I both donned our disguises – a pair of colourful cloaks and two rather grotesque masks of hapless, smiling, pale faced young men. We heard the sound of the horse's hooves retreating back down the driveway.

'If I believe we are in imminent danger,' said Holmes, 'I will utter the words "God save you, sir!" Stay close by me I will guide you to safety. Are we clear, Watson?'

'Perfectly,' I replied.

Two stone Roman figures stood sentinel as we approached the door, each clutching a goblet and palm leaf. The moonlight seemed to breathe them curiously into life. By the front door a flame burned in a glass lantern, throwing yellow light and flickering shadows across the ground.

'Somerville had a ten minute start on us,' my friend advised, 'so he will be here by now. In fact, I can corroborate that fact by the imprint of his size ten boots in the dirt there. Did you notice the unusually narrow heel he was wearing? It leaves an unmistakable impression.'

'I don't mind admitting that all this is giving me the jitters, Holmes,' I said. 'Hand me a rifle and ask me to lead a column down the Khyber Pass and I'd accept that job every time. But this? Who knows what these people are capable of?'

'We shall soon, discover. Now, courage, my dear Watson! Our time is now! We are a long time off stage.'

The door knocker was of a singular design: a brass rendering of a horse's head, with a magnificent headdress of feathers. It was almost identical in fact, to the knocker we found on Winter's mother's door. 'Roman?' I asked.

'Egyptian, more likely,' said Holmes. 'But no doubt he will carry us nobly into battle. "Once more into the breach, dear friend…"' And with that, he lifted the knocker and brought it down with a thud that seemed to echo across the valley.

Presently a small window opened to our left and a voice called from the darkness.

'"Knock, knock, knock! Who's there, i' th' name of Beezlebub?"'

I stared at Holmes. Surely the game was up already.

'"Here's a farmer,"' my friend answered, '"that hanged himself on the expectation of plenty."'

'Enter, friend,' the man answered, 'but there's no need to be waking the neighbourhood. You will have the buried dead of Waltham Cross knocking next, complaining about the dog racket.' He pulled up the window and was gone.

'But how did you know the response?'

'Somerville,' muttered Holmes. 'He have me a few pointers on the etiquette. But it was perfectly predictable. Surely you recognised the Porter's speech from Macbeth?' We heard a click and the door swung open.

We stepped inside fully expecting to be met by the drunken porter, but there did not seem to be a soul alive in the whole place. The corridor was dimly lit with gas light and we moved briskly towards the centre of the house. We heard a low babble of voices. But just as we approached a corner where a wooden globe was mounted on a tripod, a masked figure suddenly appeared carrying a tray. There was no time and I could not prevent the two of us colliding. Two glasses fell through the air and shattered on the ground around us.

'My fault entirely, sir,' the man said, returning to his feet at once and dusting the crystals from his black jacket. 'Forgive me. I am Stephano, your butler this evening. And you must be Rosencrantz. Or is it Guildenstern? The great shame is that those were your drinks.'

'If you two gentlemen would be good enough to proceed to the main hall,' he advised through his mask (which I can only describe as the face of a wheezing drunk), 'I will return with fresh glasses forthwith.' We nodded our acquiescence and continued along the corridor towards the noise of the crowd. Soon, others began to pass us in the corridor; men and women with masks that recalled various faces from Shakespeare's work. There was a Brutus here, an Ophelia there, even, memorably a Nick Bottom wearing the head of an ass. Disconcertingly, they silently turned their heads to peer at us as they brushed past.

We pressed on through the seraglio. The walls were adorned with elaborately stitched tapestries showing scales, Doric columns and candlesticks. Enormous, ornate chandeliers and candelabras cast their light on us like monstrous gold plated spiders. Finally we emerged in a palatial space with high vaulted ceilings, a black and white tiled floor while great, dark oil paintings hung high up on the wall. The room was full almost to bursting with masked visitors, some with ceremonial swords at their belts, others with palm leaves or open books in their hands. I peered about looking for Somerville, but could not see Lear or any of his daughters anywhere in the throng. Waiters weaved through the mass of bodies offering a greenish liquid as an alternative to the wine and it seemed conceivable that some were 'smothering the parrot,' as they say in bohemian quarters. There was decadence in the air, a charged atmosphere of heady anticipation and it felt as if the whole gathering was on the edge of unfolding into something dangerous and chaotic. At the centre of the hall, I could make out the heads of a pair of dancing clowns, who may or may not have been Trincolo and Gobbo, my knowledge of Shakespeare failing me.

Presently, a woman with a sad, beautiful face stopped, reached out her hand and ran her fingernails through my hair. I froze.
'What news, Guildenstern?' I said nothing, thinking my voice would surely give me away.
'Or is it Rosencrantz? She laughed, slightly tipsy it seemed.
'Have you lost your tongue?' she asked, coquettishly. 'Why, it is I Hermione. Have I offended thee? She ran a finger down my chest.'

I bowed low, then, uncertain of my next move, simply pointed to Holmes.

'Then I was mistaken,' she giggled. 'Why then, Guildenstern, what have you got to say to me?' My friend pressed a finger to his lips, then took her hand and pulled her towards him.

With a manic energy, my friend spun her around, then whisked her away, waltzing her directly into the middle of the throng, displacing the dancing clowns. Taken with the ebullient display, musicians started up from somewhere, dramatic strings bowing and sawing, producing an exotic, rhythmic, intoxicating music. Essaying the most astonishing turns and pirouettes, the guests were evidently swept along by the gusto of Holmes' performance, whooping and hollering their appreciation, clapping in time as my friend whipped the room into a frenzy. I heard the woman shriek with delight as she spiralled away, leaving Holmes' outstretched flattened palm in mid-air facing up, as if compelling her to return by a force of magnetism. And return she did, spinning back towards him. Catching her lightly, he then swung back with superb strength and grace, lifted her into the air, twirling her slowly above our heads while she posed like a goddess.

I felt giddy with fear and exhilaration. We had planned, in my mind at least, to arrive and remain incognito, maintain a low profile and wait to discover what we could. Now we had placed ourselves in the limelight. Despite Holmes' panache and remarkable powers of persuasion, it seemed impossible now that we could escape without being unmasked. I stared at the unfolding spectacle, automatically reaching for a drink from a passing waiter and sank it without even glancing at its contents. The room swam as the alcohol hit my bloodstream, making my head and body pulse with a wild delirium. I wiped the absinthe from my lips with the back of my hand. Without warning, a horn sounded, piercing the air with a single, clear note. The other musicians ceased at once and the guests fell back against the walls.

A tall figure in a flowing, ruby-red, hooded gown entered the room flanked by two others wearing robes of electric blue. The group stood for a moment perfectly still in the flickering light then processed towards the east side of the room where a small podium awaited. Their hands were clasped inside their sleeves like emperors from the Ming Dynasty, their masks hidden from view in the shadow of their hoods. They walked directly past Holmes who remained with his partner at the centre of the room. Arriving at his destination, the man in red stepped up to the dais then with deliberate care lowered his hood. The mask showed an older, bearded face with dazzling eyes that glinted with a myriad of colour, refracting the light.

There was an expectant hush, punctuated by Hermione's stifled giggle as she stood clasping Holmes' arm. Their president lifted his hands, as if in a canonical blessing, then, unexpectedly clapped them together. He clapped again and then again, slowly at first but growing in momentum. The crowd joined in until the room was filled with tumultuous applause. After letting this ring out for a few seconds, he lifted his hands again for silence.

'A bravado performance,' he declared. 'Never once do our friends Rosencrantz and Guildenstern fail us. Their guile and wit are matched only by their courage. What men are these we are blessed with in our venerated Company of Lucius!' Applause broke out again and he bowed low as if in our honour. 'Friends,' he said again, calling us to order, 'we find ourselves together on a momentous night. It is the day we have waited for. Legend has told us there was another play. Not Love Labour's Won, nor Cardenio, nor Double Falsehood, its bastard brother. We have lived with the empty promise of these names for too long. I speak of the play Marlowe mentioned in his secret letters. I speak of The Jeweller of Florence!' There was a silence followed by a huge roar.

'All hail Prospero!' called one of the guards. At once each guest dropped down to one knee; I quickly followed. Around me, the crowd responded as one: 'Let your indulgence set me free.' It had echoes of orthodox religious rites, even witchcraft and my blood ran cold. Holmes, I noticed, was also on his knee, too wise to make any show of defiance.

'Now,' Prospero continued, 'I call brother Lear to us.' Somerville stepped out of a group to Prospero's left. He was wearing green robes and the craggy, sorrowful face of the ancient king. He held out in front of him the leather satchel I recognised from earlier. I was still unable to comprehend why Holmes had permitted this; to allow England's greatest treasure to be handed over to a criminal. I was led to believe that he would refuse to relinquish the play. Yet there had to be some sound reasoning. An appalling thought crossed my mind. Could it be that Holmes, with his fetish for Shakespeare was wrapped up in this too? I shuddered. This would be the end of everything. Prospero accepted the gift and placed a benevolent hand on Lear's cowed head.

'Lear may be the newest member of our company but already he has proved himself most worthy. When we heard he had found the play, we sent messages for him to come to us. Most loyal Lear, he knew that this was not something that could be shared with the masses. To them Shakespeare is an entertainment; to us, he is close to a god: a god of truth, of poetry, of magic and power!' The crowd erupted into another seismic roar.

'Yet friends,' he called above the clamour, 'there is still more. Within this play lies another secret, one only I can unlock.' He slid the quarto from the bag, holding it as gently as a new born baby in his gloved hands. 'It is a treasure that will allow us to fulfil our ambitions: topple the imbecilic men who dare to believe they govern us and unseat the illegitimate, so called royal powers. The end of this age of tyranny is almost upon us!' Predictably, there was more applause. 'Now where is our brother Falstaff? A toast, I say!'

At this command, a rotund fellow fell out of the crowd, a tankard in one hand, the other caressing his expansive stomach. His face was a grotesque parody of the town drunk, tears of laughter rolling down apple cheeks. This of course, was one of Shakespeare's most famous creations – the fatuous Sir John Falstaff, friend of the young Prince Hal in Henry IV. He bowed as low as his girth would allow, barely keeping his balance. His respects paid, he turned to the guests and raised his tankard, spilling a good portion of his ale in the process.

'My lords and ladies,' he bellowed, balancing unsteadily. 'I ask, if you are able, to be upstanding. Why, I see that many of you are already, on account of there being no chairs. So, instead, please charge your glasses, not that you need any encouragement. I am not a man who needs an excuse to propose a toast, but today there is reason enough. The Bard has delivered to us a new work, a superb new example of his genius. Or so I am told. I have not read it. It could be a barrel of tripe for all know. But I suspect not.' There was a generous response from such thin material but his personality lifted it above the pedestrian. He was clearly a much loved member of their crowd. 'But we will put that to one side for now,' he continued. 'Let us hear your appreciation for the father of our feast. To Prospero!'

'To Prospero!' they roared back. All along, I felt there was something curiously familiar about him. I suspected of course he simply reminded me of the last time I had seen Falstaff on stage. But there was something else, too, utterly strange and yet recognisable too. Then I saw his shoes. I had seen them before: a pair of unusually long, slender shoes of highly polished brown leather. Naturally it could be a coincidence, but it suddenly made sense of everything else: an enormous man with such lithe, elegant footwear. Once again my brain swam with confusion. The man I was thinking of was Mycroft Holmes. I felt myself teetering and threw a steadying hand against the wall. I had to communicate this astonishing news to Holmes, but how? He was halfway across the room. Suddenly I remembered our code. He was meant to utter the words to me, yet this was surely the only way. Summoning all my wits, I yelled it out: 'God save you, sir!' There was a hearty cheer, the crowd believing I was merely endorsing Sir John's sentiments. But already I could see the flash in Holmes eyes that the words had had their intended effect. He began to make his way to me.

Holmes wormed his way through the mob and within a minute was at my side, placing a hand on my shoulders.

'The companions are together once more,' a man remarked, slapping my friend's back. 'They are two sides of the same coin.'

'Well said,' complimented Holmes. I pulled him towards me.

'I have made,' I stuttered, 'an astounding discovery.'

'Is that so, my dear Rosencrantz?'

'Mycroft!' I hissed. 'Sir John Falstaff; he is Mycroft!'

'Naturally,' Holmes replied. I peered at him as if he had taken leave of his senses. 'Courage, my friend,' he added squeezing my arm. 'It is not long now.' Mycroft was still in full flow.

'Louder, I say!' Mycroft shouted. 'Burst your lungs for the magnificent, the mercurial, Prospero!'

'Sir John,' responded Prospero as soon as he could be heard above the din. 'You are too kind. But equally, you are too drunk for me to believe a word of it. Now take your leave before I take your tongue.' Mycroft bowed again and slipped back into the crowd. 'So now to business,' said Prospero. 'There is a task that must be performed.'

'There is a contemptible and in many ways ridiculous man,' Prospero began, 'currently presiding over the Home Office. His name is Sir Matthew Ridley. He is a man of no great consequence and is destined to be forgotten by history. However we intend to rescue his name from obscurity. How you may ask? By poisoning him while playing his game of chess.' A murmur broke out across the room; Prospero was warming to his theme. 'I intend to send a warning to this government by despatching the Home Secretary this very week. We have it on excellent authority that he will be dining at Simpson's where he plays his Wednesday evening game of chess. I therefore require a man to challenge him. He will accept the bout and during the game will succumb to a slice of beef laced with strychnine. I have long believed that the cooking at Simpson's has been on the slide. So you will be aware that we have recently lost our Apothecary. We now need another. I ask for a man or woman to step forward and prove him or herself worthy of The Company of Lucius. There is of course, one proviso. You must be able to play chess.' The crowd broke into a noisy confab while this appalling plan was mooted.

There was a show of jostling in the crowd while small groups looked to nominate one of their number, before a small, slightly built man stepped forward. He wore a garish, tightly fitting suit of blue and yellow, his mask depicting a conniving, cunning the dark eyebrows knitted into a villainous frown.

'Iago!' laughed Prospero. 'I might have known; our most loyal and worthy brother. Do you accept this challenge?'

'I do not,' he declared. There was an audible gasp, followed by angry voices.

'Silence!' shouted Prospero. 'Explain yourself. If this is humour, then you have misjudged the room.'

'It is you,' the man returned evenly, 'who has made the misjudgement.' He pulled the mask from his face. It was Lestrade.

'Good God in heaven!' I heard myself cry. My heart throbbed in my chest; a shockwave of adrenalin surged through my body. This was miraculous; sensational. Surely, he would be pulled apart by this murderous mob. At this moment some twenty others removed their masks and pulled revolvers from beneath their cloak.

'Nobody move,' cried Lestrade. 'Each and every one of you is under arrest!'

Pandemonium ensued. The room broke into a riot of bodies pushing for the exits; masks were flung to the floor while shouts and curses filled the air as Lestrade's men lunged for the fleeing guests. Attempting to regain control the inspector fired twice into the air, bringing down a substantial portion of the ceiling. A pair of chandeliers came crashing to the floor, shattering like ice, almost ending the career of London's most competent police inspector. Clouds of dust created a smokescreen for the members, coating each in a white film until it became impossible to tell friend from foe.

Prospero's Pretorian guard had closed in on him and I could just make them out as they fought their way to a side door. I felt someone seize me by the arm and realised it was Holmes pulling me towards the same door. Mycroft was also with us, coughing and spluttering, his mask now discarded as we bundled out of the room.

'I'm not entirely sure,' remarked Holmes, 'that went according to plan.' We emerged in an open yard behind the hall and each of us scooped a lungful of fresh air.

Across the yard we saw the three villains clambering aboard a black carriage; the masks of the two lieutenants had fallen away and a pair of white mares and a cloaked driver were ready to bear them away. Each of the horses I noticed, wore the same elaborate headdress we saw on the door knocker.

'By great Gordon's ghost!' I shouted, recognising the faces in the moonlight. 'It's Pinner and Standbull.'

'Stop or I shoot!' I cried, grasping for my revolver. The cabbie turned in a rather disinterested way, reached into his cloak and produced a fearsome blunderbuss. Before I had a moment to react, there was a flash of yellow light, a colossal explosion and the door behind us splintered into pieces. Holmes. I realised, had already pushed my head to the ground and the gravel pressed painfully into my cheek. Mycroft was in a similarly prone position, his mouth full of stones, his eyes staring vacantly into the middle distance as if in some sort of trance. I could not yet fathom the older Holmes' role in all of this; was it possible that he truly was in cahoots with the gang?

There was a whip crack and the horses sprang into life, whisking the carriage out of the yard and onto the road. We saw the silhouette of a constable holding up his hands then another flash as the ancient musket discharged for a second time. Surviving the first murder attempt, the policeman hurled himself into a hedge only just in time to avoid the second.

'Watson,' Holmes cried, 'Attend to Mycroft. I believe a piece of buckshot may have grazed his femoral artery. I'm going after Prospero.' He bolted through the shadows and disappeared into a stable block emerging moments later astride a black thoroughbred stallion. Like Sam Loates himself aboard Sir Visto, Holmes galloped away into the darkness, leaving Mycroft and I lying dazed under the stars.

Mycroft opened one of his bright, watery grey eyes and employed it to glance around the room.
'Bravo!' I cried, encouraged by this flicker of animation, having sat at his bedside the best part of the night. 'Welcome back, my dear sir.'
His corpulent figure, sunk deep into Sherlock's bed resembled in almost every way a beached whale. Massive and immobile, it seemed inconceivable that he could ever be raised from his cot.
'Could you manage a grape, Mycroft?' I enquired. He peered at the morsel with his single open eye and blinked.
'Do you,' he muttered, 'have anything more substantial?'
'Is that wise?' I asked.
'Yes, I think so,' he said, prising open his other eyelid.

'Then perhaps you have a little cold roast veal?'

'Excellent.'

'You've had a lucky escape,' I advised him. 'As Holmes suggested, you grazed an artery. Half an inch to the right and it would have been a different story.' He rolled his eyes as if tired already of this unwanted excitement.

'I see my brother has returned from his errand,' he muttered.

'How could possibly know?' I enquired.

'You are holding a lost Shakespeare play in your hands.'

'So I am!' I cried. The younger Holmes showed his face at the door.

'Mycroft,' he said, rather formally, 'you've given us quite a scare. I'm not entirely sure the nation could afford to lose you. Watson, I remind you that my brother's mind is the Clapham Junction of all government business. He can hold more in his head than a thousand filing cabinets and what's more he can cross reference them all in a moment. He is a human switching station, indispensable to the business of Whitehall.'

'You appear,' noted Mycroft, 'to have suffered a mishap yourself, Sherlock.' It was true; an angry looking welt was clearly visible on the right side of my friend's face.

'A blow from a riding crop, I perceive,' deduced Mycroft, 'administered by a left handed fellow of six foot or more.'

'He came off worse, I assure you,' said Holmes, folding his arms.

'Now will he live, doctor?'

'I believe so.'

'Splendid. Now let us enjoy a little supper.' Mycroft raised his head in alarm.

'Please do not scrimp on the veal.'

Over a hastily compiled spread of lamb's ears, veal and larded oysters, washed down with very quaffable '92 Bordeaux, Holmes went over the events of the evening. The three of us sat at a makeshift table beside Mycroft's bed, napkins tucked into our collars.

'At considerable risk to himself,' my friend began, a piece of veal speared on his fork, 'my brother broke the habit of a lifetime; an existence defined by inaction. He moved beyond the theoretical and entered the fray. Drawing on thespian powers, dormant since his youth, he spent six months infiltrating this murderous set. He has thwarted many assignations and sabotaged bomb plots. Many deaths were still unpreventable. But he gained their trust and slowly learned their secrets. Tonight that huge effort paid off. Scores of these scabrous villains are now in the custody of Scotland Yard. The play is back in our possession. But Prospero himself has escaped. No man is safe until he is apprehended.' I shook my head at this, scarcely registering the words.

'Do pass the salt, doctor,' remarked Mycroft.

TWELVE

A Visit from Prospero

The sun basted the grey Cornish granite and Portland stone of London's brilliant facades. With equal generosity, it warmed my hands and face as I trod the pavements with an air of satisfaction. As I rounded the corner into Baker Street l took a swig of ginger beer from my flask and considered my morning haul: a jar of pickled tongues (a guilty pleasure that Holmes and I had developed a taste for) a fresh box of Wolf's pencils, the hardest and sharpest available, which I used to scribble the first drafts of my adventures and finally a carton of Russian cigarettes, ruinously expensive and impossible to obtain, which I knew would make my friend's eyes light up with delight.

It was a basket of indulgence, funded largely from the inexplicable popular success of The Memoirs of Sherlock Holmes, which continued to sell by the bucket load from Battersea to Barking. What with these burgeoning royalties, supplemented by the fees from my practice, my income I felt sure was beginning to exceed that of my friend, Sherlock Holmes. It was incumbent on me to treat the hero of these adventures with some carefully chosen luxuries.

As I neared 221b Baker Street, I fancied I could hear the sound of a violin. I glanced up at our window to ascertain whether my friend was practicing his sonatas with the window open but to my surprise it was firmly shut. A small crowd had gathered round our front door and I heard beneath the accomplished bow work, the sound of a shilling here and a penny there striking the pavement. Pushing my way through the hubbub, I finally got a look at the fellow. He was a tramp of the first order; tall, lanky and barefooted, with a pair of striped gas pipes covering his legs: tightly fitting trousers which stopped just short of the ankle. Over a grey shirt, which conceivably in a past life, could once have been white, he wore a purple waistcoat, a dirty green velvet coat draped across his skeletal frame. A crooked black hat and a battered looking fiddle completed this eccentric get-up. I peered at his hollow, yellow cheeks and dark

214

sunken, strangely sorrowful eyes, concluding he was at least a bottle to the wind, on the verge of a failure of the liver and almost certainly half rats.

Just when I was about to break up the crowd and move the man on, I found myself captivated by the strange air. It was a slow, haunting, melody, rising and falling and to my ears at least, was eastern European in origin. I saw that it was having a similarly bewitching effect on the crowd. They were men, women and children of every stripe: butchers' boys astride their bicycles, splendidly attired bankers and women arm in arm. All of them were lost in a reverie at the beguiling sound. Presently, the tramp returned his bow to his side and gave a small bow. The crowd thundered their appreciation, many of them in tears. Finally, I snapped out it.

'Alright, that's enough now,' I said, pushing through. 'It's about time you found yourself another pitch, my friend. I held out a crown and pressed it into his hand. 'Better than the average beano, I'll give you that, but it's all about knowing when to call a day a day.'
'I'm much obliged, sir,' he said, bowing once again. 'I didn't mean to be no nuisance. I'll be getting on my way.'
'Very good,' I said, paying him little heed and retrieving my key. Then I turned. 'What was that melody you were playing just then?'
'That?' he said, flashing me a toothless grin. 'The Willow Song, sir. '
I nodded thoughtfully then entered the house.

It was at five minutes past eleven in the morning when Dr Silas Threadgold stepped elegantly into our rooms. He was a splendid figure of a man, with thick, dark curled hair, parted at the centre, a long, handsome face, Roman nose, strong jaw and a noble brow. Attired in a long, dark tailcoat with burgundy waistcoat and matching cravat, he could have easily been mistaken for nobility. He wore his side whiskers in the old style, almost joining at the chin. His intelligent brown eyes had a stillness, serenity and strength of purpose about them that was unnerving. The only incongruous detail in his otherwise immaculate appearance was an purple welt running down the left side of his face.
'Please remain seated, gentlemen,' he said.

215

'I most certainly will not,' I returned definitely, throwing aside my novel and rising to my feet. 'Who let you in?'

'Calm, my dear Watson,' mollified Holmes, who sat implacably watching the interloper. 'Why not let this gentleman explains himself. We already know that he is a doctor by profession but no longer practices. We also know that he is an amateur astronomer. It is a fascinating resume for a man whose work is now predominantly on the wrong side of the law. He would have been with us on the stroke of eleven if he had not paused to have his shoes shined by young Darren Giddings, who plies his trade on the corner of Baker Street and Marylebone Road.'

'Your remarks are true in every respect,' the man smiled, resting his cane against the bureau and impudently picking up a piece of Holmes' correspondence. 'But for my sake, indulge me by explaining your reasoning.'

'It is laughably obvious,' remarked Holmes. 'The design of your cufflinks with the snake coiled around the staff is based upon the Rod of Asclepius, the Greek God of healing. You wear them as a sentimental reminder of your former profession. You were trained in Edinburgh, I see, almost certainly by Joseph Bell, lecturer and personal surgeon to the Queen while in Balmoral. Many of his students, including yourself followed his example of employing only the uppermost button on your tailcoat and wearing one set of side whiskers slightly longer than the other. The interest in astronomy is just as plain. There is the faint indentation of a circle around your left eye. If I am not mistaken the one inch diameter matches the sight scope of the popular oxidised brass telescope popularised by the company, Secretan of Paris.' I widened my eyes in wonder. 'As for your shoes,' Holmes continued, 'I happen to know the enterprising Giddings who performed this service for you. He brushes in an anticlockwise manner and is currently attempting to pass off a very dark brown polish as black, giving your shoes their curious tone. I know this, because I am an occasional customer of his myself.'

'You do not disappoint, Mr Holmes,' Threadgold remarked. 'But how do you know that my dealings are not entirely lawful?'

'For that there is only my instinct,' my friend stated, his tone colder. 'After a while, you get a sense of those who have willingly put their souls in jeopardy.'

How poetic,' smiled Threadgold. 'Your powers of deduction are exceeded only by your mastery of the English language.'

'Naturally, there is one other incriminating detail; the wound to your face is a day old. It was administered by a right handed man of six foot with a slim build. It is the sort of injury you would sustain if a man was to ride alongside your carriage, board it, deliver a sharp jab to the face and steal a Shakespearean play from your hands.'

'I own you had the better of me,' Threadgold admitted, narrowing his eyes. 'But it was the smallest of setbacks.'

'You cannot stop the world from spinning,' Holmes warned, 'even if you believe you can. Prospero had power only over his island.'

'What else do you know?' he demanded.

'As much as I need to,' said Holmes, 'probably more. If you believe it is your job to control everything then it is my job to know everything.'

'Still,' Threadgold responded, 'I am not here to exchange pleasantries. The game is up, Holmes.'

'How so?' my friend returned.

'Thanks to our mutual friend Mr Somerville,' he explained, 'I have what I want. Granted the play was not in my possession for long, but it was time enough. No doubt you have already deduced that the play contains a secret and if I may say so, it is not buried very deep. But for you, the adventure ends here. I am a student of Dr Watson's work, and I might add, doctor, it is a minor thrill to be standing in the same room as a literary lion such as yourself. But the point is this. I am familiar with the stripe of your fiction; you often reach a point in the tale where you have unmasked the villain, obtained the knowledge you sought and unravelled the logic. You then realise you are powerless to go further. This is the part where Holmes respects the ingenuity of his nemesis, takes up his violin, allows him to catch his boat and sail away.' My friend stared at Threadgold with a deadly stillness. 'If you have any sense about you, Mr Holmes, you will not attempt to follow me. I have two men outside who will shoot you clean through the head if you attempt to leave your lodgings in the next half hour. Consider this a warning. There is nothing you can do to prevent my unstoppable rise.' Threadgold seized his cane, turned and slipped away down the stairs. Holmes remained unmoved in his chair, perfectly sanguine.

'Do we go after him?' I asked, as the door closed.

'No, my dear Watson,' he said, 'as Dr Threadgold inferred, it would suicide.' I looked at him, dismayed.

'He is bluffing, Holmes,' I assured him. 'If there is a secret in the play, then you would have it by now. He is simply making good his escape. He only wishes to rile you; make you believe that he has a mastery over us that does not exist. These are the conceited words of a man who cannot accept he has lost. We have the play, Holmes; the prize is ours.' My friend shook his head and slowly stood, a man thirty years older than the one who had sat down. He lifted himself from his chair as if deprived of all his powers, mental and physical, collected his pipe from the table, retrieved the Persian slipper and drifted ghost-like across the room. He turned weakly to me and smiled. 'I will sit with Mycroft awhile. Please advise Mrs Hudson that I will not require lunch.'

I was numb. Only rarely had I seen my friend compromised like this. During the problem known to the public as The Scandal in Bohemia he confessed that he had been outwitted only four times: thrice by a man and once, unforgettably by a woman. Had he now added a fifth to this tally? Staring blithely at the pages of my book I was barely able to conceive that our adventure was at an end. Never before had such an extraordinary case reached such an unsatisfactory conclusion. We had not resolved the authorship of the play, the scoundrel Winter was still at large and the mastermind had walked away with impunity. Most galling of all, the secret within the play, if indeed there was one at all, remained unlocked. My faith in my friend's supreme powers was momentarily shaken. It was as if the foundations of St Paul's itself had begun to slide. The world seemed suddenly empty. My eyelids felt heavy and a terrible hopelessness filled my heart; had I become so dependent on Holmes' spirit to give life its vigour and meaning? My book slipped from my hand.

Presently, I was awoken by laughter. It was a choking, delirious, helpless kind of outburst that unsettled me, as if one or other of my companions had lost their mind. I stumbled from my chair, pulled open the door to Holmes' room to be met by the most extraordinary sight. The elder of the Holmes brothers was sitting up in bed, shaking uncontrollably, his face ruddy with mirth, clutching his chest as if to contain himself. His brother too had tears in his eyes, his hands pressed together in a childlike glee.

'For God's sake,' I cried, unable to understand the cause of this transformation. 'Whatever has got into you?'

'It was so simple,' my friend declared, between breaths, 'so absurdly simple!' This seemed to set Mycroft off again and for a moment, I believed he might suffocate from the exertion.

'For the love of heaven, Holmes, explain yourself!' They both stared at me together and then burst into another fit of hysterics.

'Watson,' my friend cried, recovering himself slightly, running up to me and clutching my hands in his. 'It's an acrostic!'

Holmes handed me the play open at first act and pointed to the first speech from Flavio, the eponymous Jeweller of Florence.

'Look only at the first letter from each line,' my friend instructed, 'then read down the page.' I stared in disbelief and not a little confusion.

FLAVIO,
If I could find a stone to match her beauty,
An orb as lustrous as the sun itself that
May please her eye as that first dawn
Invited Eve to gaze to heaven in delight,
No longer would I suffer so. I would place it in
The setting of gold, a burnished sky and
Her wonder would be at the wealth of my love
Entreating her to marvel at its faculty.
Nothing so much as perfection will do; no
Ornament will suffice. No, dear Vito, I must
Render unto her a bauble of matchless art
That gleams like the tear of proud Niobe.
Her thankfulness will be equal only to the
Priceless gift of requited love. Let me say this:
If such a stone was found, a star-splinter an
Emperor would covet, then I at last I will be
Released from this purgatory. Leave me a while.

'I am in the north pier,' I read aloud.

'Exactly right,' Holmes confirmed.

'Is there more?'

'Not that we can see.'

'Then as clues go,' I sighed, 'this seems like pretty thin stuff.'

'It is all we have,' my friend responded simply. 'What's more, it is enough. But I am not too proud to confess that it was Mycroft who provided the breakthrough. The elder Holmes, who was still dabbing the tears from his eyes, allowed himself a small bow.

'Sherlock is too modest,' he put in. 'I merely helped him see the problem from a different perspective.' Mycroft reached into a bowl of sugared plums and helped himself to a handful. With his free hand he collected four or five more then held them there as if he was a set of scales. 'I gave him the same advice I dispensed when he was a zealous fifteen year-old early in his career as a logician. "You are over-thinking it, old man," I told him. "You are making yourself as cross as a bear with a sore head."'

'At this moment, Watson,' danced Holmes. 'The scales fell from my eyes. Perhaps it was the word 'cross,' which led me to 'acrostic.' Immediately I saw the phrase before me as clear as day. It was simplicity itself.' Mycroft dropped three or four of the confections into his mouth then chewed with immense satisfaction. He was clearly recovering from his ordeal. He glanced over at his brother and a look of great pride and affection swept across his features.

'But who is in the north pier?' I probed. 'Shakespeare? Surely he is buried in Stratford.'

'So it goes,' my friend agreed.

'Then who else might it be? This Flavio fellow? This Jeweller of Florence? But he is a work of fiction.'

'A perfectly reasonable supposition,' agreed Holmes. 'With the exception of his history plays, that would follow the pattern of Shakespeare's work.' I smoothed my moustache, processing this new and puzzling information. It seemed to me that whenever Holmes attempted to enlighten me it only served to deepen my bemusement.

'One more question,' I posited. 'Since when was there a pier in Florence? It is many miles from the sea.'

'Yes, that flummoxed me too, Watson,' he said, extending a finger, 'for a moment. But once again, logic and a little general knowledge provides the solution. The jewellers and goldsmiths of Florence are concentrated around a single area.'

'The Ponte Vecchio!' I declared.

'Precisely,' my friend confirmed. At the time the play was set, the 1590s, the Medici had banished the butchers from the bridge on account of the appalling smell. Instead they invited an altogether more refined group of artisans to populate the bridge. Knowing this much, a little engineering knowledge furnishes us with the missing information. The portions of the bridge which stand in the water are known as the piers. The north pier, therefore, is the reference to the stone structure on the side of the Arno nearest the great Duomo of Santa Maria del Fiore.'

'Then this secret,' I suggested, 'whatever it is, is hidden beneath the bridge?'

'Within the bridge,' Holmes clarified.

'Threadgold!' I shouted. 'Do you believe he has arrived at the same conclusion?'

'We must assume so,' my friend confirmed gravely.

'Then what are we to do?'

'Beat him to it, my dear Watson! We have precisely nineteen minutes to pack if we are to make the 1.24pm from Victoria to Dover.'

'I say, Holmes!' I exclaimed.

'Contrary to Dr Threadgold's claims, Watson,' Holmes smiled. 'The game is afoot!'

Like men possessed, we flew around our rooms at 221b Baker Street decanting anything that might be of use to two Englishman abroad. Holmes produced an ancient-looking trunk which looked as if it last saw use on the Golden Hind and proceeded to fill it with all manner of paraphernalia. The bottom two inches consisted of a bed of loose pipe tobacco, bundled into evenly sized brown paper parcels. My friend clearly distrusted any brand that was native to Italy. On top of this was a layer of shirts, undergarments, a red striped bathing costume, a pair of pocket watches, a cerise cravat and matching braces, an emerald tie pin, a tin of Siberian snuff and a set of golden bumble bee cufflinks. Then in went his jack knife, a pair of green tinted snow goggles, rose tinted snow goggles, canes (two), a fake beard, flat cap and perhaps most intriguingly a lady's parasol decorated with prints of ruby elephants. While my back was turned I am quite certain that he also managed to conceal his Moroccan leather case, containing a syringe and inevitably, the photograph of Irene Adler.

For my own part, I packed a linen suit, a straw hat, a spare pair of brown leather shoes, a basic medical kit, a map of Europe from 1843 (which unfolded would cover most of Regent's Park) and a quantity of socks. Within ten minutes the trunk was filled to bursting point. Holmes tested the lid and finding that it would not close, peered at me in an accusative manner.

'Well Watson,' he mused, 'something's got to give. We will only find room for my violin if you take something out.'

'Me?' I blurted. 'But Holmes, I have packed only the essentials.'

'The shoes you are wearing were purchased only last week,' he noted. 'You are using your receipt as a bookmark. Am I right? Why then do you believe that these would wear out in the space of seven days requiring you to bring a spare pair?'

'They are merely for insurance.'

'They are an indulgence!' countered Holmes.

'And what of your violin?' I parried.

'It is essential to the mind,' he said, 'as sustenance is to the body. Music is the consolation for the pain of existence.'

'I raised my eyes to heaven then duly removed the shoes. With Holmes perched on the lid of the trunk, I finally managed to secure the padlock over the iron bolt.

Heaving the beastly crate to the door it was clear that one man alone could not transport it. Collecting our coats, a quantity of lire which Holmes produced from some hitherto unknown hiding place and scrawling a note for Mrs Hudson, it appeared that we were ready.

'Watson,' my friend declared with that signature glint in his eye, 'we are about to embark on an adventure that might result in the unearthing of one of the great secrets of the Renaissance. We have only our wits, a quantum of intelligence and a train timetable to assist us. Silas Threadgold is a train and a boat ahead of us and is possessed of the same advantages.'

'Bar one!' I returned. 'He is not in the company of Sherlock Holmes!'

'Nor the faithful Dr Watson,' added Holmes dutifully. 'You are possessed of those essential gifts he has never discovered amongst all his riches – integrity and friendship.'

'Tsk!' I dismissed, waving away the compliment but inwardly touched at this rare display of affection. While Holmes' emotions were nearly always kept in check, I can testify that he was no mere logic machine.

'Good lord, Watson,' Holmes started. 'I almost forgot.' He darted to the shelf and ran a finger along the spines, selecting a red leather bound volume with gold lettering. 'Murray's Handbook for Travellers in Central Italy,' he declared, pressing it into my hand. 'We would be like blind men without it!'

Hailing a brougham, we enlisted the services of the cabbie to help us man-handle the trunk down the staircase. Despite our best efforts, the trunk seized the initiative and ended up making its own way to street level, bumping down all seventeen steps. I narrowly missed being flattened in its path. If Holmes was concerned for the welfare of his violin he did not show it. Out in the street I glanced about nervously, keeping my head low in case Threadgold's cronies were still at large. The coast appeared to be clear and part of me believed it was an empty threat all along. Once safely aboard, we promised our cabbie an extra shilling if he got us to Victoria by ten past the hour then settled back with the copy of guidebook and a head full of daydreams. Despite the inevitable dangers that lay ahead, I could not help but feel a modicum of excitement and anticipation at the prospect of our Italian adventure. For too long Holmes and I had trod the grimy flagstones of the capital and the dark byways of the provinces. Now was the moment for the peach skies and balmy winds of the Mediterranean and to embrace the spirit of the enlightenment.

Holmes busied himself with a scrap of paper, staring at it intently, folding it up then unfolding it again and repeating the manoeuvre. I was about to enquire as to its significance when the carriage veered sharply to the left, the axles groaning under the strain.

'I say, Holmes,' I said, clutching the handrail and frowning at the unfamiliar street name, 'this is a devil of a route to Victoria.'

'I've asked our driver to make a short detour,' he said, glancing up. 'I first need to confirm a theory.' After another half mile or so, we emerged in more familiar territory. Then it dawned on me.

'Isn't this where Tickler has his shop?'

'Correction,' uttered Holmes. 'This is where Tickler once had his shop.' He called for the driver to pull in and we found ourselves directly outside Tickler's premises. Slats of wood were hammered roughly across the alcove and no trace of the shop was left behind.

'But,' I began. 'It is as if it were never here!'

'Precisely,' agreed Holmes then pressed his index finger against his lips in thought. Suddenly he sparked back into life.

'The train!' he cried, 'we must not miss the crossing!'

We hurtled down Marylebone Road, overtaking three hansoms along the way before the cabbie despatched us outside the station just in time to earn his bonus. Holmes accosted a porter and our trunk was transferred onto a trolley. Tickets in hand and with the porter, a portly, red-faced man puffing behind us like a faulty locomotive, we arrived just as the guard was about to fill his cheeks and blow his whistle. He gave us a disapproving look and pointed to his watch.

'There's a reason we print timetables, sir,' he remarked superciliously as the porter and I attempted to hoist the trunk into our carriage without acquiring a hernia. Leaving the staff on the platform muttering darkly, the carriage was soon enveloped in a cloud of white steam. A wheeze became a hiss and then a groan and as the pistons did their work, the whistle blew like the start of the industrial revolution and the train began to pull away.

Soon we were thundering through open countryside, plumes of smoke trailing behind us like the white feathers on a guardsman's helmet.

'So Silas made the 12.55,' Holmes announced, 'and he was not alone.'

'But how do you know?'

'We employed the same porter,' my friend explained. 'I guessed that Threadgold would have bought his silence, so I chose the man looking most pleased with himself, enjoying the prospect of his unexpected earnings. A few shillings more and I persuaded him to break his oath of secrecy. There are four of them: three men and a woman. One of them wore gloves and walked with a curious gait.

'Winter!' I cried.

'Excellent, Watson, and the others?'

'Pinner, Standbull and Threadgold,' I stated.

'A despicable quartet,' opined Holmes, then stretched out his legs and joined his hands across his waistcoat.

THIRTEEN

The Jeweller of Florence

I will now attempt to relay the events that led to the resolution of this singular adventure. Even as I bring my pencil to the paper, I am well aware that these pages will read like those of penny dreadful, yet it is I assure you, a faithful account of our voyage. As an old man, weak of mind and pale of eye, I believe I will look back on the summer of 1895 as some strange dream of my youth. This record, is perhaps, the evidence I will need to remind me that it had its basis in fact.

Our steamer was an ancient vessel, twin funnelled, with a pair of rickety masts in case the engines failed. It did not inspire confidence. The passengers were a motley crew of commercial travellers, pleasure seekers and troubled looking individuals who were escaping debts or other unspecified disasters. Together they were an amorphous mass of top hats, bowlers and bonnets all filled with the anticipation of the traveller. The captain was an inscrutable fellow of fifty with a flamboyant yellow cravat and nicotine stained beard. He inspected us all in person as if weeding out possible mutineers. Holmes and I stayed on deck as the steam billowed above us, the great mechanisms grinding noisily into life. We watched, faintly melancholic as England began to slip away, then peered into the grey-green swell as if searching for our own ghosts or a recently dropped pocket watch.

'Were you aware, Watson,' mused Holmes, 'that a quarter of a million years ago a land bridge connected us to our friends in France?'
'I was not,' I confessed.
'The remains of it lie beneath us.'
'Is that so,' I said, feigning interest. 'In fact, I was unaware that geology was within your sphere of interest.'
'Our ancestors could have walked to Europe in a day with little more to aid them than a staff and a sandwich for lunch.'
'I'm not convinced the sandwich was extant in those days, Holmes.'
'I'm famished,' my friend declared. 'Let's see what we make of Mrs

Hudson's meat pie.' We retired to a cramped cabin and unwrapped the repast, dividing it between us.

Holmes was an excellent sailor. He eyed the disappearing shoreline with the same steely nerve Columbus must once have watched Europe recede into the distance as he set off for the New World. Alas, I was not possessed of his sea legs. The slop and roll of the waves could only remind me of the interminable voyage home from my Afghan adventures when I lay delirious in my bunk nursing my bullet wound, my very life hanging in the balance. Holmes was as charitable as he could be as I made repeated trips to the railings. Land could not come soon enough.

While on one of these business trips to the upper deck I received, in equal measure, the sympathy and distain of my fellow passengers, the kindlier of whom murmured an encouraging word or two or laid a sympathetic hand on my shoulder. The salt stung my eyes, the hectoring gulls and cormorants eyed me with scorn. Finally I began to feel a little better and decided to walk the length of the ship to clear my head. As I neared the stern I noticed a man approaching in a white suit and straw boater, a cane in his hand. His attentions seemed entirely engaged with a small volume he held out far in front of him as if he was long sighted. He did not look up, but clearly detected my presence.
'Lovely day,' he murmured.
'Isn't it,' I returned politely and we crossed without another word. Reaching the railings at the back of the ship I was about to turn when it suddenly occurred to me that I had heard that voice before. But where? I found a bench and peered hard at the silvery lines that were etched on the sea. I considered our recent adventures. There was Mr Hilton Soames of St Luke's College, Oxford whom we encountered during the Adventure of the Three Students. There was a similar timbre to the voice. Yet this fellow sounded a little less refined. I glanced back but the mysterious figure was nowhere to be seen. No doubt it would come to me in time.

I returned to our cabin, where Holmes was enveloped in his customary veil of smoke, his eyes glazed over, and his mind somewhere beyond the English Channel.

'Feeling better?' he smiled, snapping back to into life.

'Very much so,' I responded.

'Excellent. We shall be in Paris by three and there is a fast train to Milan leaving at ten to four. It is imperative we make the connection. From Milan there is an ongoing service to Florence. Threadgold must not increase his lead and he will waste no time pressing home his advantage.'

'Holmes,' I said gravely. 'Do you think it was wise not to inform Lestrade of our intentions?'

'It is quite beyond his jurisdiction.'

'I believe,' I contradicted, 'that the suspected murderer of one of his constables would be of interest to Lestrade if the suspect was residing on the moon.' I decided to change tack. 'What exactly are we expecting to find in Florence?'

'I have formulated a notion,' my friend postulated, 'but cannot yet say for certain. Until further points are clarified, I would rather not articulate my theory. Now I can see that you met a friend on the deck.' I leapt from my chair.

'How could you possibly know?'

'I have seen that look a hundred times,' he said with a thin laugh. 'Your eyes are looking up and to the left as if searching the outer reaches of your mind to match a name to a face or voice.' I smiled and shook my head.

'You are quite correct, of course. It was a fellow of five and half feet, a white suit and straw hat. He was carrying a book and a cane.'

'Perhaps you could describe it to me?'

'It sounds absurd, but the cane appeared to be constructed from the vertebrae of some animal.'

'A singular accessory,' remarked Holmes. 'No doubt it belongs to an individual drawn to the strange and curious. Now tell me about the book.'

'I saw only a few words of the title,' I admitted. 'It was The Duchess of something or other.'

'Suggestive!' exclaimed my friend, with baffling enthusiasm, 'most suggestive!'

Arriving on French soil, we had exchanged the grey, English skies for a canopy of cloudless blue. Flashing our tickets at a surly official, we found our carriage and boarded the train. Holmes and I had secured ourselves a compartment in a comfortable carriage with blue velvet upholstery, red curtains and white head rests.

'How perfectly patriotic,' my friend remarked. 'And yet we may also feel quite at home.' Our valise had been hoisted aboard by two porters who muttered in their native tongue using language I did not recall from my own elementary French lessons. The afternoon heat was becoming oppressive and we gladly accepted the opportunity to purchase a *citroen presse* from a passing vendor, enjoying the novelty of mixing the drinks ourselves.

'I fancy that friend of yours is on the same train,' opined Holmes.

'What makes you so sure?'

'In my experience, coincidences often repeat themselves,' he stated.

We soon left the noise and the grime of the port town behind us and as we picked up speed, our view became increasingly agreeable. The undulating fields and lonely roads of northern France slipped past. Lines of Cyprus trees stood to attention as if waiting to greet the president himself. Ancient farm buildings crumbled into golden fields while on the far horizon we glimpsed the faint outline of a chateau casting its ghostly spell on the landscape.

'We must return another time,' I mused. 'What do you say to a grand tour, Holmes?'

'A fanciful idea given our caseload,' returned my friend. 'More generally speaking, I find beauty in ideas and not the colouration of vegetation.' Day darkened into night and we arrived in Paris as dusk was settling on the city.

After the drab alleyways and grim faces of London, Paris was utterly intoxicating. The women seemed to dance through the streets in their pastel dresses, their parasols like lilies twirling on water. Men sported flamboyant waistcoats and garish blooms in their button holes and it occurred to me that this is what had inspired our captain's remarkable yellow cravat. There was an unmistakable optimism in the air, a gaiety the French describe like to describe as a *joi de vivre*. The walls and windows were decorated with striking posters advertising tobacco, tonic wine, bicycles, tyres and even balloon rides. While some things were strange and new, other sights and sounds were more familiar: the harrowed faces of the poor and the oily, unintelligible call of the newspaper vendor.

'Look there, Holmes,' I called, directing him towards a poster for *Cinematograph Lumiere*. 'It appears Mr Acres has competition in the moving picture business.'

'Alas, Watson,' sighed Holmes, watching me drink in these wonders, 'there is no time to savour such delights. Perhaps our return journey can be conducted at a more leisurely pace. Now, I believe that is our train. Our place is aboard it, not lingering here while the world spins beneath our feet. Fortune favours the swift, as well as the brave.'

We had elected to take the sleeper train and after assuring ourselves that our luggage had followed us, we retired to the dining car for some sustenance.

'I cannot tell you how glad I am, Holmes,' I said, lifting a glass of claret to my lips, 'that we did not decide to sail all the way to Italy. I do not believe I would have survived.'

'There are still many dangers that lie ahead,' warned Holmes. 'Now, Watson, I wonder whether, in fact, there will be three for dinner?' I looked at him quizzically.

'Whatever do you mean?' He nodded towards the door behind me. There stood a rather alarmed looking fellow in a white suit and cane.

'Tickler!' I cried. 'Of course. He turned, but realised it was too late to make an exit.

'My dear gentleman,' he said, switching immediately to the genial character we had met those days ago.

'Won't you join us?' asked Holmes.

'Why ever not,' he smiled, though there was an uneasy look about him 'What an astonishing coincidence.'

'Isn't it just?' remarked Holmes. 'Now, I can recommend the salmon with thyme and oranges.'

'No doubt you heard about Alim,' he ruminated. He lifted a fork from the table and turned it slowly allowing it to catch the light before returning it to its original position. 'He was a businessman of exceptional promise. They broke in at night. I was in Peterborough of all places, at the cathedral. There was a rumour, would you believe, that they possessed a rung of Jacob's ladder. Alim was stock taking. He was always conscientious you see. Either that or he didn't trust me. Of course they overwhelmed him easily. They destroyed the shop; but I could not conceive what they were looking for. Afterall, they already had the play.'

'Perhaps,' suggested Holmes, 'they wanted that tiny shoe around your neck?' Tickler feigned surprise. Instinctively he put a hand to his chest, reached beneath his shirt and revealed the item, entirely constructed from gem stones.

'It is a charming piece, certainly,' he admitted, 'but it cannot be worth a human life.'

'You do not know these people like I do,' muttered Holmes. 'Now you have not yet explained what takes you on precisely the same journey as us?'

'I'm not sure I have to explain' countered Tickler. 'I am man whose business takes me all over the world. I may just as well ask you the same question.'

'Very well,' said Holmes. 'But I suspect we have common interests. Are you aware that Threadgold is a train ahead of us?'

'I do not very well follow you.'

'I fear you are playing games, Mr Tickler.'

He stared at Holmes in an unnerving way. 'The salmon sounds excellent,' he said brightly.

'Splendid,' my friend returned. 'Now perhaps you could elucidate us on the origin of that intriguing cane of yours. Watson first saw you with it on the ferry.'

'Ah,' said Tickler, now on more comfortable ground. 'That is a rare thing indeed. It is constructed from the vertebrae of a shark.'

'Indeed!' Holmes exclaimed.

'Would it surprise you further if I was to mention that it once belonged to Captain James Cook?' I confirmed that it would.

We thundered down through France, the lights of nameless towns and villages blurring past. Holmes and I were taking a final nightcap before turning in, the great dark shape of the Alps dimly visible through the carriage windows.

'Can we trust him, Holmes?'

'Of course we can't,' he responded. 'We will keep our wits about us and trust no one but ourselves.' I nodded and swirled my brandy in its glass. 'The world is a friendless place, Watson, which makes an alliance such as ours all the more valuable. I confess that all the brain-work in the world is no substitute for the companionship of a fellow of steady nerve and good humour. You provide an uncomplicated sort of friendship.'

'I will take that as a compliment,' I said, both touched and inwardly amused at my friend's awkward sentiments, then drained my glass.

I woke to the yellow glow of dawn through the window blinds and the creeping, stifling heat of the Italian summer. In the compartment there was a smell of warm leather, espresso and Holmes' tobacco drifting from his cot as he smoked his first pipe of the day. As I lay for those first few moments after waking, I turned over the sequence of events that had led us here; it felt unimaginable, unreal. There was also something else too; a feeling that was both familiar and exhilarating: the undeniable frisson of an adventure nearing its conclusion. As the syncopated rhythm of the wheels bumped and rattled beneath us, I felt it was destiny itself that was propelling us forward.

There was a sudden jolt and I was thrown from my bunk. The train was rapidly braking; I heard the whine of steel on steel and saw Holmes at the window.

'Goat on the line, Holmes?' I shouted.

'I'm not entirely sure,' he frowned, pulling his head back in and climbing into his jacket. He was otherwise fully clothed and it seemed possible that he had not slept, indulging in one of his famous vigils.

'Wait here, Watson,' he said as the train grinded to a stop. 'If it turns out to be a goat, I shall return with milk for our morning tea.'

I quickly dressed then stepped into the corridor. Other passengers were crowding into the passageway in various states of undress. A man with a Fedora and bushy moustache gestured to the unlit cigarette on his bottom lip and muttered something in Italian. I peered at him, unable to understand, as he shrugged and rolled his eyes until I realised he was asking me for a light. The passengers filed forward into the front section of the train, evidently intent on identifying the cause of the delay. Outside the view was a perfect alpine scene: sweeping hills of grass and in the distance the dramatic peaks of the Alps rose in jagged ranges of black and white. Forest covered the lower reaches and clouds brushed the roofs of remote hilltop villas. Presently, I felt a shunt and the train started up again.

'Most singular,' my friend said, returning to our carriage. 'The driver believed he saw a man on the line waving his arms. However after stopping and investigating, the fellow appeared to have vanished.' Holmes took a sip of water from his canteen and passed it to me. 'How do you read the situation?' I was used to such impromptu tests. 'Either this man has crept aboard,' I began, 'or else he has put something on the train and then made good his escape.' The train was once again picking up speed as the driver attempted to make up the delay.

'Excellent,' said Holmes. 'Now I suggest we conduct a thorough search to determine which of these it is. We are due to arrive in Milan in half an hour, let us hope without mishap.' At that moment, there was a loud bang at the end of the carriage and Holmes and I were thrown to the floor. We appeared to be slowing.

'I believe the mystery has solved itself,' cried Holmes. 'We are no longer part of the train.'

I darted out of our compartment and ran the length of the carriage as it lurched wildly from left to right. It occurred to me that we might overturn at any time.

'We are alone!' I cried, returning to Holmes, steadying myself with a hand against a wooden panel.

'Naturally,' said Holmes coolly, turning a page of the guidebook. 'It appears that someone would prefer us not to arrive in Milan. Well, not alive at least. Now Watson, I suggest we locate the emergency brake.' A hole had been blown clean through the far door and the wind rushed through the carriage. I crawled my way forward, then lying flat, peered down into the gap.

'No brake!' I shouted back. 'It must have been blown off with the coupling.'

'Then we must make a jump for it.'

'At this speed?' I cried. 'Our brains would be dashed. Shall we not wait for it to slow of its own accord?'

'You really believe it will?' my friend enquired.

'Surely,' I argued, 'the driver will stop when he realises he has lost a carriage.'

'Only if he wishes it to smash into his train. Then of course there is the bend.'

'The bend?'

'I took the liberty of studying the route before we set off,' my friend remarked. 'I am compelled to report that there is a bend in the track ahead of us which I fear this carriage will not be able to negotiate.'

Holmes threw up the lid of our trunk and buried his head among our possessions. Finally he emerged with just two items: the photograph or Irene Adler and his beloved violin. I almost laughed.

'How do you expect that to survive?' I asked.

'Courtesy of this,' he remarked, removing my pressed linen suit.

'But Holmes,' I remonstrated, 'it is not a week old!'

'Then I shall treat you to another in Florence,' he promised, knotting my trousers and securing the violin into a bundle. He forced in several socks as additional padding. 'After all,' he added. 'Italian tailoring is the best in the world.' There was a crack and the carriage lurched sharply to the right, almost upsetting.

'Now seems as good a time as any,' remarked Holmes. 'Shall we?'

I kicked open the door and peered out, quickly withdrawing my head again as I was almost decapitated by a protruding rock. A few seconds later, we were in more open terrain, a stretch of thin, yellowing grass directly below us, which sloped down to a river.

'"Once more into the breach, my friend!"' Holmes cried, nodded, then clutching his violin swaddled like a new born babe, leapt into the unknown. I took a breath, then followed suit.

And so it was that my friend and I entered Milan, that great city of the north, not in a first class carriage sipping a glass of grappa and fanning ourselves with a copy of *La Stampa* but on the back of a vegetable cart, nestled amongst a handsome crop of gleaming, purple *melanzane*. While I pressed one of the vegetables to my blackened eye, Holmes played selections of Vivaldi and Rossini to the crowds that gathered as we trundled through the city gates.

'My dear Watson,' remarked Holmes dropping his bow to his side,

'I do believe I'm beginning to enjoy our little excursion. Now if we are to make our connecting train, I suggest we find some swifter means of conveyance.' Our cab swerved into the station just as the Florence train was building up its head of steam. 'We must be spry,' commanded Holmes, and handing over a bundle of lire to our driver, we skipped off the carriage and sprinted across the station concourse.

There was a considerable commotion at the station. Pigeons fluttered from one platform to the next as excitable groups of travellers stamped and argued, their speech augmented with the dramatic body language of the Latin race. Even with my rudimentary grasp of Italian I could tell that the cause of the hullabaloo was the missing carriage. A conductor was remonstrating with an official, no doubt attempting to explain why he had arrived with a shorter train than the one he left with. Unaware that his missing passengers had just dashed past him, we left them to their arguments, flashed our tickets and then clambered aboard the next train.

I cannot say, as I found my seat, that I felt entirely at ease to find myself once again inside a railway carriage. In contrast, Holmes appeared to have put the whole episode behind him. He shook out his newspaper and sat back in thoughtful repose. 'I would give anything,' he said, 'for a glass of ice water and some smokable tobacco. My pipe, alas, was snapped in the fall.'
'Better your pipe than your neck,' I suggested.
'Perfectly true, Watson,' he smiled, but seemed unconsoled by this thought. No doubt understanding a little of our English, a tall, stoutly built fellow with dark, thin, hair combed back, leant over and offered us a Mondiana cigarette. My friend gratefully accepted the charity.
'Gracia,' he said and bowed respectfully.
'Mi chiamo Holmes,' he said, extending a long, thin hand.
'Renaldo,' the man responded.

I lapsed into a reverie, a kind of curious waking dream as the ethereal landscape unfolded. The Tuscan hills rolled back to reveal others behind them, horizons giving way to horizons. Like the faces of curious children, sunflowers seemed to peer up from their fields as we passed. Solitary workers toiled on their thin strips of land, breaking up the dry earth, subsidence farming as their forebears had done for generations before them. We caught glimpses of village squares where old men sat silently together in the shade. Mountains rose into the clouds until, in the golden mists of the afternoon, they became indistinguishable from each other.

Rows of trees lined up like soldiers standing to attention. In the centre of a field grooved with plough lines was an ancient villa in pastel pink. A little distance further on, we saw an Italian flag flying from the ruin of a stone farmhouse. Other trees stood in pairs, like the pricked ears of a rabbit or hare. Sunlight lay across grasslands in strips of yellow and gold, as if King Midas himself had recently walked this way. The bell tower of hill top church was silhouetted against the sky like an unthreaded needle held up to the light.

'Wake up, Watson.'
I blinked to find my friend looking intently at me.
'You dreamt of Shakespeare,' he remarked. I rubbed my eyes and frowned.
'How could you possibly know?' I asked.
'You did a little talking in your sleep,' he returned.
'How embarrassing,' I said, sitting up.
'In fact you improvised marvellously in iambic pentameter.'
'What was the gist?'
'Well,' my friend said, the line that caught my attention was "Know this: I am the Jeweller of Florence."'
'Sakes alive!' I exclaimed. 'I assure you I am not harbouring a secret.'
'I'm sure you're not,' he reassured me. 'But plainly this business is weighing heavily on both our minds.'
It was early evening when our train pulled into Florence. I scanned the red tiled roofs and white washed walls of the city buildings. Sunlight flashed in Holmes eyes as he gazed in wonder.
'The cradle of the Renaissance, Watson,' he declared giddily, jumping to his feet and collecting his violin from the luggage rack. 'It is the seat of the Grand Dukes; the battle ground of Europe; a place of a thousand dreams and a thousand secrets.'
'You're standing on my foot, Holmes.'

'So I am. Now let us not delay. It is possible we are already too late.'
No sooner had we disembarked when a man with olive skin, stubble
and a black beret approached. Holmes waved him away, no doubt
believing him to be a vagrant looking for the price of a glass of wine.
'Senor Holmes?'My friend paused and narrowed his eyes at him.
'Si...' The Italian pressed a note into his hand along with a single
coin then slipped away into the crowd flooding from the train.
'Come back!' I shouted, but the man had vanished. Holmes glanced
at the note then handed it to me without comment:

Let's kill him boldly, but not wrathfully,
Let's carve him as a dish fit for the gods.

'A redundant threat,' dismissed Holmes. 'We are quite aware they
wish us dead, just as Caesar knew his fate.' We were about to go on
our way when a woman in a red shawl with a crooked nose and
headscarf appeared before us.
'Senor Watson?' she croaked. She too had a note to deliver. My
friend seemed greatly amused by this.
'Our correspondence seems to have arrived ahead of us,' he
remarked. 'What news this time?' I unfolded the note and frowned.

You stand there looking at nothing, like the fool who tried to look
into his own mind.

'More Shakespeare I presume,' I remarked. Holmes pressed a finger
to his lips.
'That's no Shakespeare that I know,' he muttered. 'Well, well.'

Presuming we were being watched, we took a circuitous route
around the concourse and finally left by a side entrance. Despite the
lateness of the hour, the heat was still oppressive and I folded my
jacket over my arm, my neck damp with perspiration. Heading down
a side street, my friend paused outside an eccentric looking store
selling all manner of goods from brooms to gramophones.
'Ideal!' he exclaimed and dashed inside. Such was the eclectic nature
of the goods, it was impossible to identify the shop by a single name,
but it was perhaps nearest to an English ironmongers. Holmes was

quick to make his purchases. Three minutes later we left wearing workmen's overalls and baggy cloth hats. Holmes also carried a crowbar and I a lantern.

'It is ten minutes on foot from here to the Ponte Vecchio,' calculated Holmes. 'We shall walk the same streets as Dante, Michelangelo and Da Vinci. Let us hope the gods are smiling and that we have arrived in time.'

The great Duomo reared up before us like the red skullcap of a giant. I marvelled at the stupendous green and white marble work that decorated the walls.

'These Florentines must have had plenty of time on their hands,' I remarked.

'There will be plenty of time for gawping later, Watson.'

We slipped beneath stone arches, flowers blooming from the windows of upper stories and finally emerged in the Piazza della Signoria in the shadow of the Palazzo Vecchio with its mighty tower. We had not so much taken a step when an angry looking official strode towards us. He had jet black hair swept up into a crest, a thin moustache and piercingly dark eyes. He gestured towards a pile of animal droppings, handed us a pair of spades and issued a torrent of Italian in no friendly terms.

'Noi risolvere questo problema,' Holmes assured him, dusting his overalls. My friend made conciliatory gestures and patted the man on the arm. The official shook his head and strode away again.

'You have a splendid grasp of Italian, Holmes,' I said admiringly.

'I managed to pick up a little,' he explained, shovelling the excrement into a bucket, 'while resolving that small matter of the murder in the conclave. Pope Leo XIII was most grateful for the quiet resolution of the case.'

'It is not one you have shared with me,' I said, puzzled.

'It was a distasteful business' he added. 'Perhaps I did not feel inclined to rake over the details. Besides, it is not something that can be shared with your public. The Catholic Church would not tolerate the indiscretion. Perhaps it is best if I say no more.'

'These horses leave curious droppings,' I said, holding my nose.

'I am not convinced,' Holmes pronounced, 'that these belong to a horse.'

We did not go directly to the bridge, instead following the riverbank to a set of stone steps that led down to a small jetty.

'Wait,' said Holmes, suddenly stopping and holding up a finger. 'Did you hear that?' Beneath the noise of the crowds, the birdsong, the clatter of carts and the cries of the nut sellers, I caught a faint melody: exotic yet familiar at the same time. I listened again and it was gone.

'The city is full of music, Holmes,' I muttered.

Up ahead, the Ponte Vecchio reflected itself like a great palace on the water. Torches and lanterns illuminated the windows of the shops and apartments that hung over the Arno. A tiny wooden boat was tethered to a post.

'That will do nicely,' said Holmes. 'If anyone asks our business, Watson, we are inspecting the structure of the bridge.'

'You forget I have little Italian. Perhaps you should do the talking, Holmes?'

'You must play your part too,' my friend explained. 'I suggest that we go ahead to the bridge and conduct a recce, but individually. Two men of our build and description will too easy to spot if we stay together, even with our disguises. Repeat after me, Watson: "Sono un ingegnere". I am an engineer. After that, I suggest you pretend you are French.'

'I may just make a run for it, Holmes.'

My friend went first and I followed two minutes later, running my hand along the stone wall in what I felt to be an expert fashion. A shopkeeper stood in his doorway beneath a sign that read Allegretto; behind him was a glittering cave of gold and gem stones. He eyed me with the utmost suspicion. I smiled and raised my cap.

'Sono un ingegnere!' I called. He shook his head and disappeared inside. It was then that Threadgold strode directly past me, so close that our sleeves brushed together. I gasped, heaved in a lungful of air and kept on walking, not daring to turn until I had taken at least ten more steps. When I did, I saw him enter the shop. It suddenly occurred to me that these premises stood directly above the north pier. I pressed my back against the wall of another goldsmith and hid myself in the shadows. Just when I believed it to be safe to cross, I saw a couple approach and heard English voices. My heart froze when I recognised them.

'If not now then when?' I heard Elsie Pinner say. The couple were standing with their backs to me, not five paces away. Standbull scowled and peered across the river. He fished a small tin box from his jacket and moodily began to construct a cigarette from rolling papers.

'You have never stood up to him,' she added.

'Enough!' he shouted, raising a hand into the air. 'I will decide when and where. Have I not risked everything already?' She glared at him.

'For what?'

'Very well,' he said sullenly. 'When we have what we came for, that is when it will be done. Prospero will not live to enjoy his magic book.'

I dared not breathe. My head swam with thoughts and fears. So it was true: there was no honour among thieves. I knew I must get this information back to Holmes, but first I had to extricate myself. While I was still puzzling over my escape, they went on their way, continuing to conspire in low voices. I worked my way back along the street until once again I was almost at the door of Allegretto's. I knelt and made a pretence of tying my shoelace. Muffled, but identifiable enough, I heard Threadgold's voice from within.

'Ask him if there is another room. Tell him he must show us the other room!' I heard footsteps and quickly made off again, not willing to risk another encounter. I spied Holmes on the other side of the road, his hands folded behind his back peering at the window displays. Just when I was about to cross, I saw Tickler at the end of the bridge his white suit clearly announcing him as a tourist. He was being harassed by a man selling items from a tray. From this, it was obvious that he either did not fear being spotted, or else he was in league with Threadgold.

Nonchalantly, I ambled across the street and communicated my findings to Holmes who proceeded to ignore me entirely. Feeling I had done all I could, I made once again for the north bank. It was akin to walking off stage and I heaved a sigh of relief as I stepped off the bridge, only to be confronted by the imposing figure of Captain Hercules Winter. Surely now, the game was up.

'You there,' he commanded. 'Do you speak English?' I nodded, my head bowed, the peak of my hat keeping my face in shadow.

'Fetch me three bottles of Chianti, a loaf of bread, butter and chicken.' He flung some lire at my feet. 'Do as I say and I will pay you more. Steal my money and I will slit your throat.' I collected the money from the cobbles and went on my way, my heart thumping in my chest. Presently, I found Holmes at my side.

'Well,' he said. 'That was instructive!' We stole away down a side street to confer. 'The actors are assembled, my friend declared, 'and the stage is set. Thanks to your fine bit of detective work we now know that Threadgold believes there is a way into the north pier through the shop directly above it. I am less convinced. Now is the time for us to discover the secret for ourselves. How do you feel, Watson?'

'Ready, Holmes,' I assured him. 'Ready to return to Baker Street.'

'Courage, Watson,' he smiled. 'You have the heart of a lion.'

In the encroaching dark we crept down to the boat and silently pushed off from the shore. We dipped our oars into the dark waters of the Arno and glided back towards the bridge. Hidden by shadows, we soon found ourselves beside one of the great grey feet of the Ponte Vecchio. Reeds and lichen clung to the masonry, the stones stained dark from the damp. Above us were the wooden stilts that prevented the overhanging shops from tumbling into the river. Holmes leant far out of the boat and seized a long rope that was secured to a rusting iron ring. Using this to prevent ourselves from being swept away, we began to probe the pier, a brick at time, for any sign of a hiding place.

'Watson,' my friend hissed. 'Over here.' I followed Holmes' long, white finger to some letters etched faintly into the stone: 'JOF'. It could only mean one thing. Judging by their faded appearance, it seemed conceivable they were scratched there three centuries ago. I placed the crowbar into my friend's extended hand and while he worked at the loose mortar around the stone I did my best to steady the boat. I heard muffled voices above and every knock and whisper it seemed, was amplified a thousand time by the darkness. Presently, I heard a grinding sound as Holmes slid out the stone, inching it to one side.

'What do you, see Holmes!' I whispered.

'He sees a gun pointed at his head.'

The voice belonged to Dr Silas Threadgold, standing in a boat of his own that had appeared from the other side of the bridge. He wore a long overcoat, a pair of pistols and an air of magnificent malevolence. Beside him, Winter was seated, his revolver flashing in the moonlight and trained on my friend. 'It appears, Mr Holmes,' Threadgold continued, 'that you have done our job for us. Now perhaps you would be so good as to hand your discovery over to me.'

'Do you mean this?' asked Holmes, nonchalantly. He held in his palm a glittering statue about the size of a pineapple. It resembled a man in a cloak and hat entirely fashioned it seemed, from diamonds, rubies, sapphires and other gemstones; in his statue's hand was a single large diamond. There was another singular detail: he appeared to be missing a shoe.

'May I present,' my friend said, 'the Jeweller of Florence.'

Each one of us stared in wonder and disbelief. Slowly, Winter dipped an oar into water and brought his boat closer to ours, his gun still aimed at Holmes.

'Give it to me,' Threadgold demanded. The brilliant lights from the bridge glinted from the statue and gleamed in his eyes.

'Then catch it,' said Holmes and hurled it into the air. Winter let out a strangulated cry and I heard his gun tumble to the wooden floor of his boat. At that moment, I felt the statue fall directly into my hands. As a rugby man, my fingers immediately closed around it, holding it fast. From the corner of my eye, I saw Winter lunging towards me, and without thinking, I tossed it back to Holmes. He caught it one handed.

Suddenly I found Winter in my boat, his hand locked around my neck. There was a gunshot and I saw a cloud of dust and smoke as the bullet struck the stone bridge. Threadgold meanwhile fell upon Holmes and for a moment they wrestled at close quarters. Holmes I saw, had adopted his bartitsu stance, one foot behind him, with an arm outstretched in front to maintain his balance. The situation was desperate.

'You want it?' I heard Holmes shout, 'then fetch it.' The statue flew in a perfect arc over our heads and with a small splash, disappeared into the river.

'You fool!' roared Threadgold. Winter released his grip on me and stared in horror at the ripples on the surface. Without a word, he dived into the river.

Holmes took advantage of the distraction, whipped both pistols from Threadgold's belt and threw him flat into the boat, a foot against his throat.

'Bravo, Holmes!' I called, just as a steel hand clasped itself around my ankle. Within a moment, I was plunging deep into the icy, green water, Winter's vice-like grip at my heel. His weight was immense, no doubt because of his considerable iron content. I thrashed, and kicked, attempting to prise open the mechanical hand with my fingers but to no avail. His eyes bulged in terror, knowing perhaps that this was the end for him too. The darkness grew and my chest tightened; then a strange calm came over me. I dimly recalled seeing the faint white disk of the rippling sun and the flash of the jeweller's smile as the statue lay glinting in the silt of the riverbed.

'Can you hear me, Watson?'

'Perfectly well,' I replied, flicking open my eyes. I found myself lying on warm cobblestones peering up as Tickler and Holmes crouched over me. My friend, I noticed was also dripping wet.

'Colder than the Serpentine,' Holmes declared. 'Curious that, isn't it?' I sat up, rubbing the back of my head.

'Our friend Tickler here arrived at a useful moment. He brought his friend the mayor and few others besides. He gestured towards the handsome, raven haired man we had met in the square that afternoon as well as several members of the Carabinieri, moustachioed fellows, smartly attired in their tunics and sashes. Between them, they restrained Threadgold, his arms twisted behind his back.

'I was able to hand over guard duties,' explained Holmes, 'which allowed me just enough time to fish you out.'

243

'But the iron hand ...' I started. Holmes held up the crow bar. 'It had more than one use.'

'And Winter?'

'He lies there still. The last I saw of him he was grasping for the trinket at the bottom of the Arno. I was unable to inform him that it was made of glass. You can buy them for a few shillings a piece on the Portobello Road.' I shook my head in bewilderment.

I recovered my wits sufficiently to stand, and accepted a small drink of water. It was then that we heard cries from the far end of the bridge. The crowds, enjoying la passeggiata, the ritual evening stroll, scattered apart and I glimpsed an open carriage heading towards us at speed. It was the vintage type used by tourists to view the city, more commonly seen at the beginning rather than the end of the century, with ornate lanterns and gold trim. It was immediately apparent that this carriage was flying with dangerous haste and that we were in its direct path. The mayor barked a series of commands and his men dropped to the ground, their revolvers drawn. Holmes pulled me into a doorway. As the vehicle drew closer I recognised the black-clad figure of Standbull, holding the reins and driving the horse on. Beside him was the actress, Elsie Pinner, cloaked in a red gown. Ten feet away, Standbull passed the reins to Pinner and leapt from the carriage, a pistol in one hand, a knife in the other. He fell upon one of the policeman, his knife pressed to his throat. The carriage, skittered to a halt and before a shot could be fired, Standbull had succeeded in bundling both the policeman and the unguarded Threadgold inside.

Holmes wasted no time. He sprinted off the bridge, the rest of us scrambling in his wake. But instead of chasing the carriage, he dived for the bundle containing his violin, tearing it open and seizing his bow. It seemed ridiculous, maddening behaviour. Immediately, he struck up the strange, lilting tune we had heard earlier that evening, playing a few bars. Presently we heard a ferocious, guttural roar. From a side street, stepping directly into the path of the escaping carriage was Bosko and his bear.

The great bear reared up on its hind legs, towering high above the cart, its keeper attempting to restrain it by its chain. Standbull did what he could, but their horse bucked in terror, causing the carriage to swerve and tip, spilling its passengers into the road. Another fearsome growl echoed down the alleyways and the café tables emptied instantly, the diners fleeing into the night.

By gaslight, we could just follow the sequence of events: the policeman rolling clear and running back towards us; Standbull pulling Pinner from the upturned vehicle and the lonely figure of Threadgold standing his ground, a long bladed knife in his hand.
'Don't be a fool!' shouted Holmes.
'Do not provoke him,' shouted Bosko. 'He will tear you apart.' But Threadgold would not listen. Believing himself possessed of supernatural powers, he sprang upon the bear, plunging his knife forward. The bear snarled in anger and fear and with a single swipe of its paw, Threadgold lay dead in the road. A woman bystander stared in horror then let out a scream that seemed to split the night in two. We ran towards the scene, but Standbull moved too swiftly, pulling Pinner by the arm, and together they slipped away into the shadows. The police set off in pursuit, the clatter of their boots dying away into the distance.
'So the lovers escape,' remarked Holmes, watching this astonishing spectacle unfold. He made no attempt to join the chase.
'Whatever do you mean?' I asked.
'And so,' he said in measured tones, 'Romeo and Juliette exit the stage. Perhaps it is better to leave them be.'

'I believe a new set of introductions are in order,' said Holmes, accepting a cigar from the mayor and handing one to me. He gestured towards Tickler. 'To begin, may I present one of the finest actors of this or any other generation. Dr Watson, meet Mr Percy Onions.'
'Onions?' I repeated.
'Indeed,' the man assured me. He bowed then shook my hand.

We adjourned to a bar on the Via Dante, the ghost of the great poet haunting the night. The streets were quiet now and barely a soul was abroad as we made our way inside. The barman sloshed three measures of Sambuca into glasses and we drained them there and then. Clutching a second dose we found ourselves a table in the corner and huddled in the glow of a single candle.

'It only seems fair to my inestimable friend,' said Holmes, 'to reveal all we know.' Tickler nodded his assent.

'Watson, we have travelled a thousand miles to solve the mystery of The Jeweller of Florence. In truth, I had the solution before we left London. But let me lay the evidence before you. The statue was not the only object I discovered in the bridge. There was also this.' My friend reached into his pocket and withdrew a wooden hoop, about the size of my palm.

'A child's toy?' I asked.

'A wooden O' correct Holmes.

'"Can this cockpit,"' Onions recited, clapping a hand to his chest in dramatic style, '"hold the vasty fields of France? Or we may cram within this wooden O the very casques that did affright the air at Agincourt?"'

'Then it is a reference to Shakespeare,' I reasoned, 'surely this tells us the play is real?'

'That is one way to read it. Another is that the O is an initial'.

'Rather oblique, Holmes, don't you think?'

'But look, there is another initial – do you see this minute letter W?' I inspected the hoop and indeed a small black letter was carved into the side.

'O…W,' I repeated.

'Oscar Wilde,' pronounced Holmes, 'the true author of The Jeweller of Florence.' The tumbler dropped from my hand.

'Twelve years ago,' continued Holmes, 'Wilde wrote a play called The Duchess of Padua, originally titled The Duchess of Florence. It has a familiar ring doesn't it? It was written in blank verse, in the style of Shakespeare for an actress who, for reasons of her own, turned it down. Four years ago it was revived in New York, but it sank without a trace. He then wrote a second play in the same manner. But unwilling to risk another failure, he put it to one side. Then, as disaster struck with this business involving Lord Alfred Douglas, and his reputation destroyed, he saw an opportunity. He had the play set down and aged by a master forger to provide the illusion it was three hundred years old. He then put it in the hands of an old acting friend from the business, Mr Onions, with instructions to create an old curiosity shop. Knowing the spell Shakespeare cast on the producer, William Somerville, he knew that if he offered the play from a suitably authentic source, Somerville would fall for the ruse and stage it for the world. It would become one of the great plays and join the immortal canon.'

'But the Medici …' I started. 'The woman in Tickler's shop?'

'The whole business of the Medici and the attack of the Borgia was fabricated, devised and scripted by Wilde itself. A mischievous, as well as artful fellow, he could not resist planting a secret message into the play, which he believed may never be discovered, or it was, not for centuries to come. It was a flawless scheme. And yet the clues were there. Did you not see the fan? The handbag? The playbill, or even the copy of An Ideal Husband that Tickler was reading at his desk?'

'Upon my word, Holmes!'

'But yet, Watson,' my friend said, interrupting himself, raising a finger into the air, 'Wilde did not account for The Company of Lucius. As a society they were unknown to him. When Threadgold, who presided over their reign of terror, received word of this lost play from Standbull, one of their youngest members, corrupted by greed and seduced by their decadent cult, looked upon it as a holy relic. They wasted no time stealing it and discovered the secret within the text. Little did he know that the prize was merely a worthless glass statue and an unusual signature from Wilde. Mr Onion's role was to be Wilde's eyes and ears – to report everything that unfolded, including the discovery of the treasure if it were ever found.

'But where does this leave us?' I asked.

'It leaves us,' said Holmes, 'with a play which conceivably could still have been written by Shakespeare. Of course Wilde will never admit to writing it. I speak only for myself, but I will never breathe a word of this business to a soul. My intention is to take its authorship to my grave.'

'My position exactly,' said Onions.

'Then,' I said, my eyes glistening in wonderment, 'I pledge to do the same.' As you now know, from the book you hold in your hands, this is not a promise I have been able to keep.

'Sugared almond, Watson?'
Lestrade held open a white paper bag as the lights dimmed.
'Don't mind if I do,' I said, dipping in. The curtains swept apart and a young man, in Elizabethan garb stepped onto the stage. He was soon joined by another.
'What pains you, Flavio?' asked the first.

The next two hours passed in a pageant of magic and colour. It was a private performance of a new play for William Somerville's inner circle only. Only those who made their living from the stage; a select group of actors, producers and managers were admitted. There was everything one would expect from Shakespeare: comedy, tragedy; poetry and farce. It was in the mould of those infuriating plays where a foolish error of judgement leads to seemingly calamitous results, only for things to miraculously resolve themselves by the close. It was not, I mused, so dissimilar to the present adventure. But for all its quality, the highlight without question was seeing my own friend, Sherlock Holmes in the title role as The Jeweller of Florence. He was a mercurial, beguiling figure, obsessed with his work, bewitched by the beauty in the world and utterly impossible to pin down. The role, I felt, did not tax my friend too much.

As the curtain fell, Somerville rose to his feet, clapping thunderously, tears in his eyes, leading the ovation. There were three curtain calls. The last was for Holmes alone, standing centre stage, gazing up into the gods. He stood there for the longest time, bathed in light and drinking in the applause. Then Sherlock Holmes took his final bow.

My friend and I strolled in our shirt sleeves back through Regent's Park, the night almost as balmy as Florence itself. Stars were scattered across the heavens and crickets chirruped in the undergrowth.
'There are just one or two small points,' I admitted, 'that I cannot fathom. Perhaps you could elucidate me?'
'By all means,' offered Holmes.

'For one, why did you dress as a tramp and play your violin outside our rooms in Baker Street?'

'Ah, yes,' said Holmes. 'There were in fact two reasons. One was to ingratiate myself with the toothless old man. Only when I spoke to him as one vagrant to another could I inspect him at close quarters and see Threadgold for what he was – a man convinced of his superiority over the world. Such a fellow cannot be familiar with Shakespeare's ideas on hubris.'

'And the other reason?' I probed.

'Simply, Watson, because I had an audience. You are familiar with my weakness for adulation.' I nodded and watched the moon ripple across the lake.

'The man in the grave at Highgate ceremony,' I began. 'If he was no Borgia, then who was he?'

'It was the unfortunate Rosencrantz,' explained Holmes. 'He was clutching the key given to him by Standbull. Threadgold disposed of him when he developed a conscience. No doubt poor Guildenstern was not far away.'

'We could easily have ended the same way,' I mused.

'There was another matter troubling you,' Holmes went on. 'The note at the station in Florence, is it not?'

'Why...' I began. 'How could you know?

'It was a line from Wilde's play, The Duchess of Padua. It was Onion's way of telling me he had arrived.

'But,' I stuttered. 'It was addressed to the fool; it was addressed to me.'

'There is a reason, Watson, why Shakespeare grants the greatest wisdom to those considered the clown of the piece.' A bee spiralled above our heads, dancing in a figure of eight before disappearing into the darkness. 'The bee,' Holmes observed, 'is the perfect work of creation. It is useful, cooperative and steadfast. But above all, Watson, it is cheerful. You are a bee, Watson, something that can never be said of me.' We strode onwards.

'And what of the play, Holmes?'

'I broke my vow,' he confessed. 'As I left the theatre, I revealed the truth to Somerville. "Now I am possessed of this knowledge," he told me, "I will leave the play unperformed until such a time when Mr Wilde's reputation is restored and he claims the work as his own."'

Once again I peered up into the night sky.

'Watson,' Holmes mused. 'Three hundred years have passed since the death of our friend, William Shakespeare. But in that time, man has not changed so much. He still responds to flattery, rises to provocation and succumbs to temptation. Now let us make haste to Baker Street and open that excellent bottle of Claret we have been saving for an occasion such as this. It will not drink itself.'

Also from Christopher James

It is summer 1890 and the game is afoot. When an elephant escapes from the London Zoological Gardens, Holmes and Watson become embroiled in one of their strangest cases yet. Engaged by a jeweller in fear for his life, the trail leads Sherlock to two secret societies, each pursuing the eight ruby elephants said to unlock a vault containing the lost Nizam diamond. Standing in his way are some deadly foes: the Archangels: assassins in top hats and tailcoats, hell bent on the murder of the great detective and the acquisition of the treasures of the realm. The adventure leads the intrepid pair to Lord's Cricket Ground, the Royal Albert Hall, a bizarre series of thefts at the National Gallery, deepest rural Suffolk and ultimately the very heart of the Empire. With high speed chases on Penny Farthings and a cast of eccentric characters, it takes all of Holmes' ingenuity - and a little help from Mycroft - to unravel this elephantine mystery.

Also from MX Publishing

MX Publishing is the world's largest specialist Sherlock Holmes publisher, with over a hundred titles and fifty authors creating the latest in Sherlock Holmes fiction and non-fiction.

From traditional short stories and novels to travel guides and quiz books, MX Publishing cater for all Holmes fans.

The collection includes leading titles such as *Benedict Cumberbatch In Transition* and *The Norwood Author* which won the 2011 Howlett Award (Sherlock Holmes Book of the Year).

MX Publishing also has one of the largest communities of Holmes fans on Facebook with regular contributions from dozens of authors.

www.mxpublishing.com

Also from MX Publishing

Our bestselling short story collections 'Lost Stories of Sherlock Holmes', 'The Outstanding Mysteries of Sherlock Holmes', 'Untold Adventures of Sherlock Holmes' (and the sequel 'Studies in Legacy') and 'Sherlock Holmes in Pursuit'.

Also from MX Publishing

"Phil Growick's, 'The Secret Journal of Dr Watson', is an adventure which takes place in the latter part of Holmes and Watson's lives. They are entrusted by HM Government (although not officially) and the King no less to undertake a rescue mission to save the Romanovs, Russia's Royal family from a grisly end at the hand of the Bolsheviks. There is a wealth of detail in the story but not so much as would detract us from the enjoyment of the story. Espionage, counter-espionage, the ace of spies himself, double-agents, double-crossers...all these flit across the pages in a realistic and exciting way. All the characters are extremely well-drawn and Mr Growick, most importantly, does not falter with a very good ear for Holmesian dialogue indeed. Highly recommended. A five-star effort."

The Baker Street Society

www.mxpublishing.com

Also from MX Publishing

The Missing Authors Series

Sherlock Holmes and The Adventure of The Grinning Cat
Sherlock Holmes and The Nautilus Adventure
Sherlock Holmes and The Round Table Adventure

"Joseph Svec, III is brilliant in entwining two endearing and enduring classics of literature, blending the factual with the fantastical; the playful with the pensive; and the mischievous with the mysterious. We shall, all of us young and old, benefit with a cup of tea, a tranquil afternoon, and a copy of Sherlock Holmes, The Adventure of the Grinning Cat."
Amador County Holmes Hounds Sherlockian Society

www.mxpublishing.com

Also from MX Publishing

The American Literati Series

The Final Page of Baker Street
The Baron of Brede Place
Seventeen Minutes To Baker Street

"The really amazing thing about this book is the author's ability to call up the 'essence' of both the Baker Street 'digs' of Holmes and Watson as well as that of the 'mean streets' of Marlowe's Los Angeles. Although none of the action takes place in either place, Holmes and Watson share a sense of camaraderie and self-confidence in facing threats and problems that also pervades many of the later tales in the Canon. Following their conversations and banter is a return to Edwardian England and its certainties and hope for the future. This is definitely the world before The Great War."
Philip K Jones

www.mxpublishing.com

Also from MX Publishing

The Detective and The Woman Series

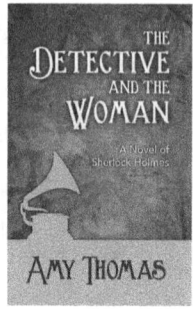 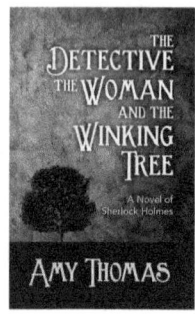 

The Detective and The Woman
The Detective, The Woman and The Winking Tree
The Detective, The Woman and The Silent Hive

"The book is entertaining, puzzling and a lot of fun. I believe the author has hit on the only type of long-term relationship possible for Sherlock Holmes and Irene Adler. The details of the narrative only add force to the romantic defects we expect in both of them and their growth and development are truly marvelous to watch. This is not a love story. Instead, it is a coming-of-age tale starring two of our favorite characters."
Philip K Jones

www.ingramcontent.com/pod-product-compliance
Lightning Source LLC
Chambersburg PA
CBHW071254250626
47159CB00004B/1181